Acclaim for John Casey's

Compass Rose

"Splendid. . . . By the end of the book [readers] may well feel as if they themselves had spent several years living in South County. And many such readers, I predict, will be reluctant to leave." —Troy Jollimore, *Los Angeles Times*

"John Casey luminously celebrates a young woman who is indeed the compass for her fractured family and community. . . . Rose is a literary rarity—the good and tenderhearted character who is also credible. And Casey has written an affecting story of the way it is—messy, difficult and sometimes radiantly splendid." —*The Richmond Times-Dispatch*

"Mr. Casey describes the extreme claustrophobia and menace of small town living well. His Rhode Island hamlet is filled with gossip—that's a given—but also the overlapping, intertwining relationships that exist in these kinds of insular communities. . . . Casey is so adept at presenting character. . . . It would be great to see them crewing the Pequod, searching for that ever-elusive whale. Even Moby Dick couldn't sink the likes of these women." —*Pittsburgh Post-Gazette*

"The enjoyment of this novel is derived from the unobtrusive skill with which Casey charts the entanglements, convergences, repulsions, and compromises of life in a close-knit community. . . . Casey . . . is marvelously adept at conveying the reflections of an intelligent but not intellectual character such as Elsie. . . . The strongest impression left on the reader, however, is how stubbornly the characters remain themselves even as they are inescapably drawn into each others' lives." —*The Boston Globe*

John Casey

Compass Rose

John Casey was born in 1939 in Worcester, Massachusetts, and educated at Harvard College, Harvard Law School, and the University of Iowa. His novel *Spartina* won the National Book Award in 1989. He lives with his wife in Charlottesville, Virginia, where he is a professor of English literature at the University of Virginia.

www.johndcasey.com

Compass Rose

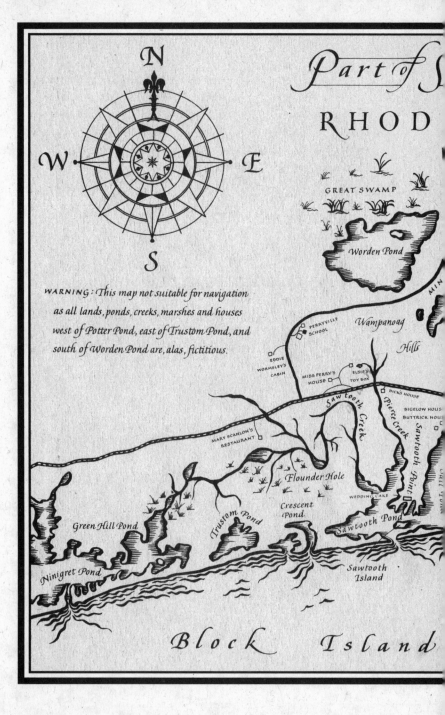

N

W E

S

Part of S

RHOD

GREAT SWAMP

Worden Pond

MIN

WARNING: This map not suitable for navigation
as all lands, ponds, creeks, marshes and houses
west of Potter Pond, east of Trustom Pond, and
south of Worden Pond are, alas, fictitious.

PERRYVILLE
SCHOOL

Wampanoag

Hills

EDDIE
WORMSLEY'S
CABIN

MISS PERRY'S
HOUSE

ELSIE'S
TOY BOX

DICK'S HOUSE

BIGELOW HOUS
BUTTRICK HOUS

MARY SCANLON'S
RESTAURANT

Sawtooth Creek

Pierce Creek

Sawtooth Point

Flounder Hole

GALL POND

*Crescent
Pond*

WEDDING CAKE

Trustom Pond

Sawtooth Pond

Green Hill Pond

Ninigret Pond

*Sawtooth
Island*

Block Island

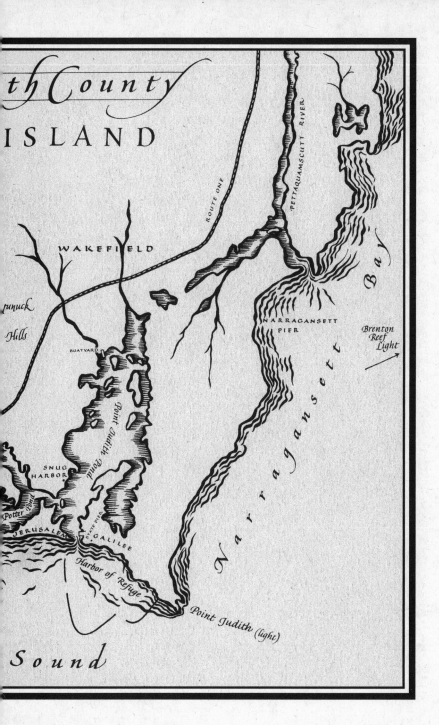

th County
ISLAND

ROUTE ONE

PETTAQUAMSCUTT RIVER

WAKEFIELD

ounuck
Hills

BOATYARD

NARRAGANSETT
PIER

Brenton
Reef
Light

Point Judith Pond

SNUG
HARBOR

Narragansett Bay

Potter Pond

JERUSALEM

STATE PIER

GALILEE

Harbor of Refuge

Point Judith (light)

Sound

Compass Rose

A NOVEL

John Casey

VINTAGE CONTEMPORARIES
Vintage Books
A Division of Random House, Inc.
New York

The Library of Congress cataloged the Knopf edition as follows:
Casey, John.
Compass rose : a novel / by John Casey—1st North American ed.
p. cm.
1. Fishers—Rhode Island—Fiction. 2. Rhode Island—Fiction.
3. Domestic fiction. I. Title.
PS3553.A79334C66 2010
813'.54—dc22 201000520

Vintage ISBN: 978-0-375-70913-5

Author photograph © Erinn Hartman
Book design by Iris Weinstein

www.vintagebooks.com

Printed in the United States of America
10 9 8 7 6 5 4 3 2 1

Part One

chapter one

May sat on the first row of the bleachers, watching the boys warm up. Tom was the second-string catcher, might get in if their team got ahead by a lot. He was good behind the plate—all that practice catching for Charlie in the backyard—but he couldn't hit as well as the first-string catcher. At least Charlie and Tom got to play on a team this year. Before Dick got his boat built he'd kept them busy during the summer doing chores. No games. And while Eddie Wormsley was fixing the house, they'd helped with that. Now there was some pleasure in their lives. Dick still expected them to work at something that brought in some money, but since he was at sea more than half the time, Charlie set his own schedule. He used the work skiff the same way Dick used to—had his tongs, pots, hand lines. Tom at fourteen was an off-the-books boy at the boatyard, but they didn't keep him half as busy as Dick used to. No question about it, the boys were better off. If you just counted material things, so was she. She took some comfort from the boys.

Across the bright green grass she saw Miss Perry walking with her cane. The woman beside her was holding a parasol over Miss Perry's head. May didn't recognize Elsie Buttrick at first because she was wearing a white dress and looked a little plump. May's memory of Elsie was of her in a tailored green uniform or in a swimsuit.

Miss Perry and Elsie moved very slowly. Part of May's mind was piecing together how and why they were here. A more powerful feeling rose through her, making her back and arms rigid. The feeling was nonsense but so strong that she couldn't stop it—she felt that she was the one who'd done something wrong. And everyone was about to see it.

Miss Perry stopped to switch her cane to her other side. Elsie switched the parasol from one hand to the other and moved around Miss Perry. Elsie saw May and opened her free hand—perhaps to show she couldn't help being there. Then she looked down. May was released from her upside-down feeling. She looked to see if Charlie or Tom had noticed Miss Perry. No. She was alone for more of Miss Perry's and Elsie's slow progress. She herself was throwing off thoughts faster than she could gather them back in. She was trying to gather them so that she would leave no part of herself outside her. But there was another: a white dress. Had that woman worn that white dress when she was with Dick? Or was it to pretend she was Miss Perry's nurse?

May's thoughts were like a dog's bristling and barking at something coming toward the front yard where it was chained up short.

She'd caught a glimpse of Elsie Buttrick one summer at a clambake on Sawtooth Island, the local gentry walking around in next to nothing while Dick and the boys were fixing the clambake. May didn't stay. Something she hadn't remembered till now: Dick had said afterward that he thought Charlie had a crush on Elsie Buttrick. That was an idea that was so barbed and tangled that she pulled it inside her and covered it. And sat still.

Miss Perry and Elsie arrived. May got up, shook hands with Miss Perry, nodded toward Elsie. Miss Perry said, "I told Charlie that I doubted that I would be able to go fishing this year, but that I hoped he and Tom would come for lunch. He then very nicely asked me to the baseball game." May concentrated on the slow rise and fall of Miss Perry's voice. Miss Perry's eyes widened as if with surprise behind her eyeglasses. She said, "And here I am." Miss Perry put both hands on the crook of her cane and added, "I'm afraid I dragooned

Elsie into driving me." She put the tip of her cane behind the bench and began to sit down. Elsie got behind her, turned her, and lowered her by her elbows.

May felt calmed by Miss Perry's stately sentences and by the way her presence lessened the Buttrick girl, maybe even contained her. Then May blamed herself for not thinking of Miss Perry's effort in coming out to the game, for not being concerned about how Miss Perry had aged in the last year. May said, "The boys'll be glad you're here. Charlie's going to pitch. We might get to see Tom a little later. Baseball's the first thing they've done on their own, if you see what I mean."

Miss Perry turned to her. "I do indeed. Dick is admirably industrious, but I imagine he may have been demanding in his single-mindedness. Now that he's achieved his own boat, however, one might hope that he will become a bit more like Captain Teixeira. Perhaps not immediately, of course." Miss Perry gave a little cough, perhaps a laugh.

Elsie looked straight ahead during Miss Perry's speech.

Miss Perry said, "I don't intend that remark as a criticism of Dick but simply as a looking forward to spring after a hard winter."

The game began. May hadn't seen a ball game for years— the last one probably a Red Sox game on someone's TV. She was surprised by a terrible tenderness for these teenagers assuming the gestures of grown men: the batter knocking the bat against his spikes and then tapping it on home plate. The infielders crouching, pounding their fists in their mitts. And Charlie on the mound staring intently at the catcher, shaking off a sign with a single shake of his head—the most grown-up gesture she'd ever seen him make.

And the chatter. Their voices had all changed but were still not men's voices. Still thin and sometimes sweet tenors even though they were trying to be menacing or scornful. "No hitter, no hitter, easy out, easy out." "Whaddya say, whaddya say, Charlie boy, right by him, right down the old alley."

High-school boys on a Saturday morning yearning to be

men. In their green hearts, wanting to be like Dick—strong, secretive, hard. She'd seen moving pictures of a crew at sea sorting fish dumped on the deck out of the cod end, using their gloved hands or gaffs to throw the good fish into the hold, using their boots to kick the trash fish off the stern.

These boys, the green field, the summer clouds in the blue sky, poured into her eyes too brightly.

She tried to think of something sensible to say to Miss Perry. Miss Perry was staring intently at Charlie on the pitcher's mound, and May felt a little better.

chapter two

Miss Perry had felt Elsie's restlessness as they drove to the ball field—at first Miss Perry thought it was Elsie's thinking about other things she ought to be doing. Miss Perry had a regular driver on weekdays and hadn't asked a favor of Elsie for months, and Elsie had seemed pleasantly agreeable when Miss Perry asked in a general way if Elsie could spare a few hours of her Saturday morning. But as they walked toward the seats Miss Perry felt Elsie's nerves harden quite suddenly. And then May seemed withdrawn, too, and Miss Perry wondered, could Elsie in the course of her duties as warden have caught Dick when he was up to something with that friend of his, Mr. Wormsley? Or could May resent the way Elsie's brother-in-law had taken over Sawtooth Point and was making into an offensively private domain what had once been perfectly nice fields belonging to Dick's great-uncle Arthur? Which would have been Dick's, had Arthur Pierce not had a run of bad luck . . . But surely May would know—Dick certainly did—that of all that family, Elsie was the one who'd come to care wholeheartedly for the place and the people.

Perhaps this not knowing was simply another effect of age. Miss Perry had once known everything—almost everything—that went on in South County. Of course, she used to see Captain Teixeira more frequently when Everett Hazard was still alive. Among the three of them, they could register incidents from Wickford to Westerly. Now there were a great many details that escaped her. It wasn't just that Everett Hazard was dead; her own attention floated outward—she could think of no other way of putting it—floated outward beyond the things she once knew. It was not an altogether unpleasant sensation. She found herself staring at things, simultaneously puzzled by how particular a leaf was and how unbordered and vague she herself was becoming. On a good day, that is. She had felt that today was to be a good day. She had been very pleased by Charlie's telephone call. He was shy at first but soon warmed. And most pleasant of all, he seemed sure of her affection for him. That was the point of arranging to be here. She had breakfasted well and cleaned her eyeglasses, and there Charlie was in the middle of the baseball field, looking quite splendid.

Baseball was as familiar to her as a shadow play. She knew there were long periods of apparently unproductive pitching and catching and then suddenly a single player might hit the ball and confront another single player of the array of players spread out on the field in an abruptly terrifying instant. She thought this game gave a nervous edge to the otherwise tranquil and consoling line "They also serve who only stand and wait."

She was glad that Charlie had a repetitively active part. For a while she enjoyed watching him throw the baseball again and again, starting with a single elaborately slow step and then a quick whirl. Her mind wandered. The bakery had delivered the cake for Charlie and Tom, but had she put it in

the refrigerator? Ought she have done so? She adjusted her
eyeglasses and found herself admiring the catcher bravely
crouched close behind the bat. She remembered a poem by
Marianne Moore that mentioned the attractive curve of a
catcher's haunches. Indeed. And somehow this was made
more noticeable by the mask that covered his face, reminding her of a gladiator.

The batter swung and the catcher threw off his mask and
ran directly toward her, his face tilted up. When he was
almost at arm's length from her he reached up with both
hands. She heard a distinct *thwock,* but she couldn't see anything but Elsie's white dress. Then she saw Elsie and the
catcher tipping sideways until they were on the ground at her
feet. The catcher raised his glove with the ball in it, apparently to show the umpire, although the gesture also elicited
applause from the audience and cheers from his teammates.
The catcher got to his feet, asked Elsie if she was all right,
then hauled her to her feet with one hand. Elsie smiled at the
boy. Miss Perry was reminded of Elsie's smile as a girl. Never
what anyone would call a sweet child, she would sometimes
be surprised into a brief energetic smile. A charming para-
dox—Elsie's eyes would almost shut, but her face opened. As
it did now. How very nice, how very much like pleasure.

May didn't see the ball, but when the catcher got close to
them the tilt of his body began to scare her. He shuffled
nearer and nearer, then turned his back. May felt the bench
jounce as Elsie got up. Elsie stood in front of Miss Perry with
one hand in the air and the other on the catcher's back. As
he caught the ball he began to fall. May felt the bench move
again as Elsie braced a foot on it and pushed against the boy.
Elsie and he sank sideways and then lay together on the
ground. For an instant May saw Elsie as shameless—clutching him, pressing her hips and breasts against him. Then May
was ashamed.

She saw Charlie standing just beyond Elsie and the catcher. He closed his mouth and his face settled. Elsie was on her feet, smoothing her dress.

The catcher jogged toward the umpire, who was listening stolidly to the coach of the other team. Charlie took a step closer to Elsie. Elsie waved one hand and said, "Fine. We're all fine."

Charlie said, "Ma, maybe you and Miss Perry ought to move back a couple of rows."

May thought there was no end to Elsie Buttrick.

The people in the row behind them made room. May and Elsie stood Miss Perry up, turned her around, and guided her up to the next level.

When Dick got home Charlie would tell him about the ball game, would tell him Elsie Buttrick had saved Miss Perry from being landed on by the catcher. May didn't want to be there to see Dick's careful face.

May was pleased when Miss Perry said, "Really, Elsie. All this fuss?"

Miss Perry thought the game had gone on quite long enough. She thought Charlie himself looked as if pitching was becoming tiresome. He took several deep breaths and threw the ball. There was a sound as sharp as when the catcher caught the ball in front of her, but more resonant. "Blow, bugle, blow— set the wild echoes flying." Tennyson? She looked up and saw the ball suspended against the blue sky. She said "Ah!" as it began to move. She was surprised that she could see it so clearly, that she felt so light and connected to that single speck, as though she herself were flying.

She was startled to find that she was standing, Elsie's arm around her waist. She lost sight of the ball against a cloud, then saw it fall out of the cloud. A faraway player leaned against a fence and watched the ball land. Two little boys beyond the fence began to run toward it. The first time it landed it skipped quite high, as though it might fly again.

Then it bounced gently. Miss Perry was glad to see this—one of the boys caught it and the two of them ran off with it.

She sat down again with Elsie's help. It had been as thrilling as when she'd surprised a stag in her garden and he'd bolted with a snort that froze her in place. Then he leapt over the high stone wall, as if lifted by a wave. How much invisible energy there was in this world—how amazing to feel it press through her still.

She applauded. Elsie touched her arm and asked her if she would like a glass of lemonade. She said, "Not now, Elsie."

May said, "Poor Charlie," and Miss Perry knew—had only temporarily not known—that this splendid moment was unfortunate for Charlie. In fact, after he watched two of the opposing players trot around the bases, there was a gathering around him and a new pitcher replaced him. There was a smattering of applause as he left the field.

May was upset for Charlie but pleased to see him shyly tip his hat to the bleachers of Matunuck fans who cheered him. It was a compensation, May thought—Dick had left a wake of wariness and bad feelings, but now that Charlie got out and around, people warmed to him. Of course, people were nice to her, but that was because she paid her bills now. They were a respectable family. Here she was with Miss Perry, her two sons on the ball team, all in the extra time and space that came of rising just one step in the world.

The midday breeze came up, swirling the dust on the base paths, cooling the crowd's necks and cheeks. On the other side of Miss Perry, Elsie Buttrick sat up and fanned her knees with the hem of her white dress. May couldn't think where to put her. Miss Perry loved her; she loved Miss Perry. She'd been a little heroine. May had managed to put her in a corner of her mind, almost had her sealed up as Dick's last bad craziness. Let her tend to her baby in her house next to Miss Perry's; let her go to the store for food in her Volvo station wagon. Let her know how small she should keep herself, not fanning her knees at Charlie's ball game.

May wondered if she herself could become bigger. What if her mind could hold a larger map so that she saw all the houses and boats and people at a distance? Then she could see Elsie Buttrick's little apologetic wave, her shielding Miss Perry with her body, as acts not poisoned by what she'd done with Dick. There would be a space that was far from the center of May's mind in which Elsie could raise her daughter— May would see the daughter and think of enough different things in the clutter of those lives, different things that would cover the old nakedness.

How did someone get a bigger mind? That sort of a bigger mind? Right now, May's narrow comfort was that Elsie had grown fat.

The game was over. May went to find Charlie and Tom. She saw another mother hug her son, and May was encouraged to put her hand on Charlie's shoulder. She did the same for Tom, who needed some sympathy because he hadn't played.

Tom said, "You know, it wasn't that bad of a pitch. The guy got lucky."

Charlie said, "No. He had it timed. He really clocked it. I've never seen such a long ball. I mean, not in person."

Miss Perry arrived. She said, "I'm glad to hear you say that, Charlie. I confess I was thrilled. I'm afraid I applauded for the wrong team."

"That's okay," Charlie said. "I mean, you don't see that every day."

"Well, it was all perfectly splendid," Miss Perry said. "And you're all coming for lunch, are you not? And your birthday cake."

Tom said, "We'd better clean up some."

Miss Perry blinked behind her thick glasses. "It's a shame your father's at sea, but we'll be a jolly little party. Elsie, dear, you'll stay, won't you?"

Elsie said, "I'm sorry. I'm sorry—I've got to meet my sister."

"I thought she went sailing with Jack. Never mind. It's kind of you to drive me. Now, don't dillydally, boys."

May watched them make their way toward Elsie's car, Miss Perry on Elsie's arm.

"Miss Perry's getting old," Tom said. "And Elsie's kind of plumped up."

May said, "You boys shouldn't say things about—"

Charlie said, "You shouldn't say 'you boys' when it's just Tom. I was going to say Elsie looked pretty good getting up for that foul ball—taking a fall like she did."

"Well, I guess someone's stuck on Elsie," Tom said. "Bet you wish it was you got tangled up with her."

May didn't hear what Charlie said back. She felt another rasp across the same place—no end to Elsie Buttrick. But whether because she'd had an hour or two to grow numb or whether she was grateful for Elsie's lie about having to meet her sister or whether Tom's taunt set her to thinking how relentlessly stupid men were going to be about Elsie Buttrick, May found herself sharing some small part of her distress with Elsie Buttrick. There wasn't anyone May could tell this to.

chapter three

Elsie felt squeezed shut inside. As if her nerves were the roots of a tree that was dug up and put in a small bucket, white roots sprouting wildly but curling back on themselves when they hit the steel sides.

She managed to help Miss Perry across the field. She held the passenger door open while Miss Perry clung to the base of the open window to lower herself onto the seat.

When they got to Miss Perry's house, Elsie felt obliged to help her set out the cucumber sandwiches and a pitcher of lemonade. She got the birthday cake out of the refrigerator and put it on the kitchen counter. Her fingers felt peeled to the quick handling the plates, the tray, the pitcher, the platter that May would be holding in a few minutes.

"Candles," Miss Perry said. "Birthday candles. And the little rosettes to hold them. I put them somewhere. Blue for Charlie and red for Tom. Could you look in the drawer? The one by the sink. I am sorry to be such a . . . It was very hot in the sun."

When she heard Miss Perry's unfinished sentence, Elsie grew alarmed. She got Miss Perry to sit down at the kitchen table and brought her a glass of water. Elsie wrapped some ice cubes in a dish towel. Miss Perry said, "Don't be silly, Elsie," but allowed her to put it on her neck. Miss Perry said, "My father used to soak his pocket handkerchief in witch hazel to cool himself."

Elsie was reassured by this complete Miss-Perry sentence. She found the candles and holders and stuck them in the cake. She considered leaving, decided she shouldn't. She had to push through some shyness to put her hand on Miss Perry's forehead. Miss Perry's brow was warm but not too hot. And not cold and clammy. Elsie put the ice pack on again.

Miss Perry closed her eyes and said, "It was hot in the sun." She opened her eyes and said, "I feel much better." Elsie obediently took her hand away and wondered if she could steady herself with small goodnesses.

She heard May and the boys at the front door. Elsie went to open it. She kept her eyes on her hand on the doorknob and said, "I'm just leaving. Miss Perry was a little bit undone by the heat."

May said, "You boys wait here. I'll go see to her."

"I think she's fine," Elsie said. "But maybe you could call— or Charlie or Tom could call when you leave. I'll be at home."

Charlie said, "Sylvia Teixeira usually comes over with supper. I could stay till she gets here."

Elsie heard the note in Charlie's voice, looked up to see May look hard at Charlie. Elsie left. She wanted a closed door between her and May's thinking of yet another female coming near. If she were May she would peck all calling birds to death.

Elsie got home in plenty of time for Mary Scanlon to get to work. Elsie said, "I won't stick you with a Saturday morning again. Did I leave enough milk?"

"Oh, Rose and I were fine. I think my giving her a bottle's making my tits bigger. And how's Miss Perry?"

"Oh, God. I'll tell you everything in a minute." Mary's breezy talk about her tits jangled, but when she sat down, she felt the comfort of being able to say to Mary, "I'll tell you everything."

chapter four

For all her talk about letting Rose cry, Mary Scanlon was an indulger. While Mary's room was being built, Elsie went to stay at Jack and Sally's cottage on Sawtooth Point. Mary began her job at the Wedding Cake only a hundred yards away. Before she started cooking, Mary spent an hour carrying Rose up and down the point while Elsie took a nap. Elsie would wake up to the sound of Mary's crooning as the pair of them came in the door. Mary had a store of old songs she'd inherited from her father. She also had a taste for the Lucky Strike *Hit Parade* from her earliest childhood. She apparently remembered everything she'd ever heard. Elsie had only the vaguest memory of anything before rock; but then she had more of an ear for a heavy beat than for a tune.

At six or so Mary sent one of the waitresses over with a tray of food and a bottle of dark beer, which Mary said was good for nursing mothers.

At ten Mary would show up again for a few minutes before going back to check the cleanup. She usually brought another dessert for Elsie. Elsie felt like a queen ant, pale, inert, and swollen.

The low point was at eleven. Mary was gone. Rose was sleeping. Elsie couldn't concentrate enough to read. It was too late to exercise. She wasn't as physically tired as Sally said she'd be, but her brain was dull. She could barely remember herself outdoors, moving through the woods and marshes.

Years before when she'd been having supper with Jack and Sally, Jack had asked one of his massive questions: What's the best thing in your life? It was the sort of thing Jack liked to bring up, though not for extended discussion. He preferred quick answers, which he took in with a grunt of approval or disapproval. Jack himself said, "Providing," and grunted with approval. Elsie said, "Adventure. Love and adventure." Jack tipped his head, meaning that was no more than what he expected. Sally said, "Grace." Jack lifted his eyebrows and said, "Yes." Sally beamed. Sally went on to say, "Moments of grace . . . I was listening to Jack Junior—" Jack lifted his hand and said, "Grace was just right. Let's not adorn it." Elsie had actually heard the word *pompous* inside her head. It had swelled from ear to ear, and for an instant she'd been afraid she was going deaf.

Now she heard her own voice saying "Adventure. Love and adventure." What glib twitter.

At the first sound from Rose, Elsie felt her mind blur. Just as well, it wasn't a necessary part of nursing Rose.

Outside, it was high summer. She knew the blackberries were ripe, the spartina tall and thick across the marshes, blue crabs swimming up the salt creeks. By noon the inland air would be hot enough to rise, drawing in a sea breeze. At night the salt ponds flickered with the phosphorescent wakes of fish, the sky with the Perseids. All that was the sort of thing she'd stored up when she was an adolescent tomboy, calming herself by observing the decent progressions of nature. Since then twenty seasons of marsh grasses had grown, withered, and decomposed; twenty years of crab carapaces were now mineral matter in the black mud feeding the field of green.

She felt the comfort of that order, and even in her insulated state, she felt the righteousness of being one of those who knew that order. Dick did, too; this was the innermost justifying of her love. No one knew how mentally alike she and Dick were. Jack had barely kept himself from saying, "You went slumming and we'll make the best of it." Sally's way of putting a bright face on Rose being her niece, her child's cousin, was graver than any big-sister tut-tutting.

And what would Miss Perry think?

Until just now, Elsie had thought it comic that Miss Perry inspired awe. Twenty years ago Elsie had been her pet when Miss Perry taught Latin at the Perryville School. Elsie was aware of the way the other teachers deferred to Miss Perry, but learned only later that she was one of the founders of the school, that she was a venerable relic of the Hazards and Perrys, and that grown men and women still sought her favor as if they were living in a Henry James novel. Elsie had been no more aware than Miss Perry herself that Miss Perry's aegis saved her from a number of punishments. Elsie had thought at first that Miss Perry had singled her out because Miss Perry felt sorry for the hoydenish little sister of the beautiful and virtuous Sally. Then Elsie got A's in Latin and that seemed the reason that Miss Perry urged books on her and took her for long walks in the woods, botanizing and birding. And there'd been Miss Perry pointing to a foxhole and asking her to smell it. "You should know animals and plants by their odor as well as by sight. Do you smell it? My sense of smell is less keen than it used to be. I remember fox musk as somewhat stirring." Elsie looked up. Miss Perry flicked her hand at the hole, urging Elsie to get on with it.

Now, dazed and stationary while nursing Rose, Elsie wondered if she would have loved Miss Perry if she hadn't been Miss Perry's pet, if they'd met when Elsie was older, if she might have thought Miss Perry affected rather than eccentric, patronizing rather than wholehearted in her friendship with Dick, snobbishly dismissive in her treatment of Eddie Wormsley. "What you do on public land, Mr. Wormsley, I cannot control. On my land I do not permit the sort of slaughter you seem to enjoy."

Eddie remembered every word, reproduced Miss Perry's rhythm and tone when he'd told Elsie. He wasn't making fun of Miss Perry, he just couldn't get her out of his head.

Rose sucked, burped, switched sides, sucked, burped, and dozed off. Was there a calming chemical brought on by nursing? After the first tingle of Rose's mouth fastening on with surprising force—it felt like the old practical-joke joy buzzer—there was a deep satisfying tug inside her. Elsie was annoyed by how soft she'd become but was pleased by the flow of milk, at the unurgent pleasure. But, but, but. Maybe when she and Rose began to sleep through the night she'd get her brain back. These days she was lucky if she got three hours in a row. Then a little doze if Rose went right back to sleep. Then the long, bright wasted morning. The blessed relief of Mary Scanlon taking Rose. How could she have even thought a complaint about Mary's singing?

But this time Rose slept for six hours. Suddenly it was dawn. Elsie got out of bed with a livelier body and clearer head. She nursed Rose. She thought Rose looked more alert, too, as if some additional brain cells hooked up in her sleep. Elsie put on shorts and a T-shirt. She said, "Come on, big girl," and carried Rose outside. The Wedding Cake was gray and still. The grass and the loosened tennis nets were heavy with dew. The air was damp but mild. Elsie waded into Sawtooth Pond up to her waist. No wind, but the tide was coming in, ruffling the mouth of the inlet. The sun was just up but veiled in mist. It seemed as if the tide was carrying the gray light all the way from the farthest glimmer, releasing it on the surface of the pond. Her feet settled in the mud. She felt the tide pushing around her legs, Rose moving in her arms.

She said, "Can you see it, Rose? Can you feel all this?"

chapter five

Dick and May and the boys were still staying at Eddie Wormsley's ramshackle cabin while their house was being rebuilt. While Dick was on shore he put some time in helping Eddie and Eddie's new crew. A few days after the ball game May came down to watch. She heard Eddie say, "We're still bracing the studs; we need another half-dozen braces." May was surprised to see he was talking to Dick. And more surprised to see Dick lay down what he was doing and head off to the miter box. Eddie had looked up to Dick since their school days, and Dick had always taken Eddie for granted. Part of it was that for years Eddie scraped by as a handyman for some of the summerhouses and a few of the big houses. Except for Miss Perry's. Eddie had closed the summerhouses, drained the plumbing, fixed the screens, kept an eye on them. For the big houses, Eddie plowed the driveways when it snowed and kept their woodsheds stocked. Beside his cabin he had a shed for his tractor, truck, and snowplow, and an old Quonset hut for a workshop. It was after the hurricane that he'd begun to make some real money. He'd cut up trees that were blocking driveways, fixed damaged houses, cabins, sheds, and wharves. He'd hired a crew and soon enough had a tidy business. No more days off fishing or hunting. He'd even hired Phoebe Fitzgerald to keep his books and answer the phone.

So part of what had happened between Dick and Eddie was Eddie's no longer being the local handyman. When Dick had been at his lowest point—his lowest point financially—he used to say to May, "At least I'm not fixing toilets for summer people." She'd wished his pride wasn't so hard.

Now Eddie was fixing—rebuilding was more like it—the house that Dick had built years before with Eddie's help. Eddie was fitting it in as a favor, that was one thing. May didn't know what the money arrangement was, but she was pretty sure that was a favor, too. But this time it wasn't a couple of guys on their own—it was a construction site with a time to show up and a time to quit. May remembered when Dick and Eddie were building the house—they'd scratch their heads and then Dick would pick up a stick and draw in the dirt. They'd got a bunch of old window frames from the dump and had to jigger each one in. They all went up and down or in and out and were painted neatly, but the house had always looked cobbled together. Now Eddie had blueprints. Dick was helping out. But the bigger difference between then and now was that Dick was walking on eggshells. May let him back into bed, but he had enough sense to know that that wasn't all there was to it.

May stood inside the house and watched Eddie and Dick and the crew flicker back and forth across the space between the studs. At least the back of the house was going to have matching windows.

Eddie's CB crackled. He got into the cab of his truck to talk to Phoebe Fitzgerald. May called to Dick. She took him to their bedroom. She said, "Do you think we could fit a closet—right there where the cedar chest used to set?"

Dick ran his hand through his hair and looked out the window. May felt the bit of effort he made to look back at where she was pointing. He nodded and said, "I could ask Eddie. See what he says."

May said, "A cedar closet. We can put the cedar chest in the boys' room for their sweaters and things. But maybe a cedar closet would fit better in the mudroom."

"We can't change the size of the mudroom."

May waited.

Dick said, "You work it out with Eddie. If he frames it in, I can finish it. Course, he's got to get to his other jobs . . ."

"I've always wanted a cedar closet."

"Okay. You and Eddie . . . I got to get back to work."

He ran his hand through his hair again. Her eyes followed his gold wedding ring. Had he taken it off when he was with Elsie Buttrick? She took a breath and blew it out. She'd asked all the questions she was going to.

A cedar closet. A mudroom addition. A garden shed. A garden shed that would stand where Dick's big wood-frame-and-canvas shed had stood—where Dick had built his boat. It was parts of that shed that the hurricane had blown into the back of the house. Was he through with Elsie Buttrick by the time the hurricane hit?

May knew she had to quit asking for things. She didn't know if she was making sure of Dick or paying him back.

She wished to forgive him. That was still a ways from forgiving him.

Eddie climbed back down from the cab of his truck. Poor old Eddie, yearning for out-of-reach Phoebe Fitzgerald. She had an Irish name, but she went to Miss Perry's Episcopalian church, had gone to a fancy college. What was she going to do with the likes of Eddie Wormsley?

What did Elsie Buttrick do with the likes of Dick?

May wondered how long she'd have to go on pulling thoughts out of her head. It seemed as endless as pulling rocks out of a field.

chapter six

E ddie's putting in some hours," Mary said. "I saw him and his crew working on Dick's house Sunday morning."

Elsie saw Mary suck in a little breath after she mentioned Dick. Mary's fair face was like a screen—the slightest embarrassment sent a blush skimming across it. Elsie said, "Mary, Dick lives just down the road. If you look funny every time his name comes up, people are going to think you're the mother."

Mary laughed. "That'd keep 'em guessing." She laughed again but stopped when they heard a car horn give two beeps. The noise woke Rose. Elsie went in to pick her up. After a minute there were two more beeps and Eddie Wormsley's truck swept through the overhanging branches at the top of the driveway and pulled up behind Mary's tiny pickup.

Eddie said to Mary, "Hey, good! I was hoping you'd be around. I'm just going to take a look, see how you like it."

Elsie was holding Rose, who was crying softly. She cried louder when Eddie waggled a finger in front of her face. Elsie sat down on the front step, unbuttoned her blouse, and began to nurse Rose. Elsie tilted her head back to catch the sun and caught sight of Dick sitting in the cab of Eddie's truck.

Mary led Eddie into the house.

Elsie couldn't do anything but look at Dick's face behind the windshield as Rose's mouth pulled on her. It took him a long time to get out of the truck. When he did, he was as awkward as if he were on the deck of a rolling boat—no, at sea he was tight and nimble. Now he stood uneasily, one hand on the door handle. Elsie felt a puff of heat in her eyes, blurring him. She said, "It's okay. Come see your daughter. Hey, Rose, it's your dad."

Dick said, "I'm sorry. Eddie doesn't know . . . He just all of a sudden remembered he had to look in here."

"It's okay. It's good. Here she is."

Dick knelt and touched the back of Rose's head with his fingertips. Rose didn't stop nursing. Elsie said, "You'll get to see her face when she switches sides."

Mary and Eddie came back. Eddie said, "Oh, I better show you what I changed in the kitchen. Made some more space for your pots and pans." Eddie took off his baseball cap and held the door for Mary.

"See that?" Dick said. "That's Phoebe Fitzgerald's doing. She's working on Eddie, getting him smoothed down for their big-house clients. Look, like I said, I didn't mean to take you by surprise."

"It's okay. Don't worry."

"So. She's healthy and everything?"

"Yes. Perfect." Rose eased up and turned her head. Elsie cradled her and pulled her blouse shut. "She should have a little burp before she gets the other side. You want to hold her?"

Elsie held her breath as Dick's hands took Rose, as Dick's hands touched her. He lifted Rose up to look at her face, then held her to his shoulder and rocked her. Pretty good at it, remembered better than Eddie to go easy.

Rose burped; Dick handed her back. Elsie parted her blouse again and put Rose to her left breast. Elsie looked at Dick's face. She'd wanted him for the certainty of his fierce instincts; she'd put herself in the way of them. Now he was uncertain. Perhaps he was undone by seeing his daughter—perhaps he was undone by the trouble he was in. She wasn't surprised when he moved back, stood up, breathed in and out. He said, "Here we are." He moved his hand in an arc. She knew what he meant—Wakefield to Green Hill, Worden Pond to Sawtooth Point. The bit of South County they lived in. She thought he'd be happier on his boat, out of sight of land.

Mary Scanlon and Eddie came out of the house. Eddie said, "So there you go. So long as you don't get any new ideas. We'd have got Dick's house in shape by now if May didn't get inspirations along the way." Dick looked at his feet and scuffed away the footprints he'd left. "So like they say at weddings, 'Speak now or forever hold your peace.'"

Mary said, "It's grand, Eddie."

Elsie said, "Of course it is. I knew you'd do it just right."

Eddie frowned and said, "I wonder if you could mention to Miss Perry that I've been coming up here to do some work for you. You know how she ordered me off her land."

"She and I share the paved part of the driveway. But I'll mention it."

"As long as you're saying that much, you might remind her that it was a wounded deer. I shot it somewhere else, tracked it here. I was just trying to put it out of its misery."

Dick laughed. "You're really scared of her. That was years back and you're still ducking away."

"Easy for you. You're one of her pals," Eddie said. "Come to think of it, all this time you've been taking her fishing—how come you didn't clear things up for me?"

"Didn't want to spoil the mood, bringing up your bloodthirsty ways."

Mary laughed. Elsie thought Dick shouldn't tease Eddie, the one guy who'd do anything for Dick. And she also thought how in South County a story could last for years.

Eddie said loudly, "Well, what's she doing out there with you? Killing them innocent flounder."

Elsie said "Eddie, Eddie. You'll scare the baby."

Mary Scanlon tousled Eddie's hair as if he were a little boy. "Eddie, we're all for you." She hugged him from behind, a warm cloak. Eddie blushed.

"Hey, Mary," Dick said. "He's got work to do. You're making him go weak at the knees."

A couple of guys and gals, just kidding around. Elsie thought of the years she'd spent trying to be just one of the gang. So she was getting her wish. Here we are.

The men got into Eddie's truck. Eddie made it around the gravel circle without tearing up any grass. The truck eased over the first bump, the tailgate chains clanked, the branches brushed the sides of the bed and then closed behind it. Another clank where her unpaved driveway met the asphalt. Then quiet. If Mary hadn't been there, Elsie would have cried. Instead she said, "Did you ever think of Eddie?"

"Not that way. I'm sort of sorry to say it—he's a nice man." Mary held her hand out to pull Elsie up. "So, Rose," Mary said. "You met your dad."

chapter seven

Elsie put her uniform on again. It was still warm enough to wear the summer-issue shorts and shirt. The shorts were so tight in the waist she cut off the button and resewed it an inch looser. The shirt was tight, too. She unbuttoned the two top buttons. Wouldn't do for facing the public. She put on a sports bra, but while that flattened some things it also squeezed some up and out. She borrowed one of Mary's bras and lengthened the thread on the second button of her shirt. She loosened her web holster belt so that it slanted across the bulge of her lower belly. She blamed herself; she blamed Mary's cooking. She swore she'd eat nothing but fish and salad for the next month.

She volunteered for the longest route, on foot, an unpleasant thrash through bullbriars and low-limbed rhododendron along the Usquepaug and the Queens River. Some exercise, and in all likelihood no people. She tucked a pair of rain pants into her fanny pack for pushing through thorns or poison ivy. For lunch she packed an apple and a carrot. All she deserved.

There was a path into the river, but upstream and downstream, both banks were overgrown. She stuck her hand in the water—too warm for trout? She saw a bird, a dull speck flitting in the tree shade. When it crossed the stream and caught the light it turned electric blue. It wheeled away from her and vanished into the woods. The blue persisted in her. Her eyes were so astonished that her other senses went numb. She wasn't sure if she'd made a noise. An indigo bunting. Not indigo at all—blue, bluer than a jay or a bluebird, absolute blue.

She was alone, blissfully alone, for the first time in months.

She put on her long pants, rebuckled her web belt, and began to pick her way through the bushes, gracelessly at first. After a mile or so she was sweating. Good. Sweat it off. She cut over to the stream and filled the first of her three test tubes. On the far bank there was a stand of cardinal flowers. The blossoms were half hidden by mourning cloaks, some hovering, some attached to the flowers while slowly flapping their wings, velvet black with violet and ivory edging. On the moving surface of the water the reflected red, black, and violet wavered in and out of focus. At first glance it seemed that the colors were being swept away. Then they seemed to be swimming against the current. She looked away to stop feeling giddy. She'd been fooled before—seeing and unseeing. She looked at the butterflies, the real ones, knew what they were up to with the cardinal flowers—their coiled proboscises, grotesquely long fusions of nose and mouth parts, were uncoiling deep into the flowers' cups. She wondered what they felt. Was it just taste, or was there touch? Was that slow flapping just to keep their balance, or was it a sign of pleasure?

A year without sex. More than a year. She hadn't gone that long since she was a schoolgirl. She breezed through her memory of a few fumbling schoolboys, then surprised herself thinking of dresses. Dresses she'd put on to be taken off. Unbuttoned slowly. Unzipped and stepped out of. A few frenzied times hoisted waist-high. Once in Sally's garden. The only red dress at the party. She went into the garden first. He didn't see her until she stepped into a bit of light between the boxwoods. Then back into the dark. A tall man. She clung to him as he sank to his knees, her face in his chest, her right knee jangling the keys in his trousers pocket. He slid his trousers down, her skirt up, the crotch of her underpants sideways. It was close enough to what she'd had in mind. He worked in downtown Providence—she got off by thinking of walking into his office . . .

Then she heard the sound of the party, the blur of voices from the front rooms, the clinking of plates from the kitchen. She heard them suddenly, as if snapping out of a daze on a train.

The knees of his trousers were so obviously grass-stained that he went straight to his car and left. She'd laughed. How far she was now from that hard little self. She could miss it or call it names, it didn't matter. She could call it up for a quick fantasy visit. (Was it odd that she didn't have fantasies— sexual fantasies—about Dick?)

It had been more than a year since she'd gone to one of Jack and Sally's parties. Sally occasionally mentioned that one man or another asked where her sister was. Sally sometimes added, "Did you ever think of him?" Sally meant courtship: mixed doubles, charity balls, theater parties, a first kiss. Elsie had made shorter work of it.

Now here she was back in the woods. She looked under a fallen tree limb and found a black beetle. She tossed it into the stream. It drifted ten feet, then a trout sucked it in.

She ate her carrot and apple, drank half her canteen, and moved upstream.

When she stopped to fill her third test tube, she saw something move. The tip of a fishing rod. It stuck out from behind a pine tree on the far bank. She corked the test tube, put it in her pouch, and circled into the brush. She crept back toward the stream until she saw a man. Not a fly fisherman. An ultralight spinning outfit. He was using live bait, letting it drift. She couldn't tell if it was a bug or a worm. No license pinned to his hat or shirt. He reeled in. He'd lost his bait. He picked a bug from a can and put it on the hook, tossed it upstream, shut the bail.

Not anyone she knew. Middle-aged, nicely faded blue shirt, rolled-up sleeves. Panama hat, beat-up but too classy for this neck of the woods. Sort of like Jack wearing broken-down patent-leather dancing pumps around the house on a Sunday morning.

He got a bite. The rod bowed; he held it high as the fish ran for the bank, almost in front of her. She ducked down. She heard the fish thrash, the drag whine. She pushed a clump of leaves aside so she could peer out. He was playing the fish calmly, not horsing it in. All she had to do was stand up and he'd be flummoxed. She watched. She felt a voyeurish intimacy—his gaze was so intent, his right forearm showing little bands of muscle. The fish ran back upstream. He lifted the rod tip and reeled in. He let it run out some more line. The fish swam in an arc, then another, each one closer to him. He stepped into the stream, lifted the rod high, and grabbed the trout. She thought at first that was a dumb move, good way to scare it into a last wriggle that would free it. But he'd got a finger into the gills. He stepped back on shore, set his rod down, and bent the trout's head back sharply. He held the dead fish at arm's length, his finger still hooked through the gills. She guessed twelve inches, maybe a hair more. He considered it for some time. He wiped his right hand on the seat of his pants and pushed his hat back. She liked his face. She'd always been a sucker for the face of a passably attractive man doing things deftly.

She lay on her side of the stream and watched him gut the fish with a pen knife. He slit open the stomach and squeezed out a dark pulp. He sifted it with his fingertips, plucked out a more or less intact bug. A black beetle? He lobbed it into the stream and watched. A little swirl and it was gone.

He made a small fire on a flat rock. Another violation. He pulled apart the sections of his rod, tucked them into a cloth case. At least he wasn't greedy. He washed the cavity, laid the fish by the fire. He cut a long twig and trimmed it. (Cutting or uprooting live plants . . .) He skewered the fish from anus to mouth and held it over the fire. The tail curled, the skin crisped, the eye turned white. She caught a whiff of wood fire and cooked trout. Still squatting and holding the stick, he moved nearer to the water, groped a bit, and pulled out a half-full bottle of white wine. (No alcoholic beverages inside the park . . . This meal could cost him more than a dinner at Sawtooth Point.) She watched him wiggle the cork loose with one hand and take a swig. He put the open bottle back in the stream, twisting it into the bed. He turned the fish, poked it with his finger. His intentness focused hers, pulled her gaze into a close-up. He sucked his fingers and broke off a piece of tail, then began to nibble at the body.

She was going to let him go. She pictured him licking his fingers, looking up, as she waded across the stream. Brief alarm. And then? Taking in her badge, her holster, her mild hello. Would he help her up out of the stream? Certainly if she held out her hand.

This cameo reappearance of the old Elsie ended. He would eye her badge, her holster, but then . . . The son of a bitch might even laugh at her waddling across the stream on her pale, plump legs.

She watched him suck the last bit of flesh off the bones. He put them on the fire, took another drink from the bottle. He filled a pipe, lit it with a stick from the fire, recorked the bottle, washed his knife, packed everything into his knapsack.

He stood for a long while, looking all around. She began to like him again, liked him for liking what he was looking at.

Maybe in a month. Apples and carrots and riding her bicycle. Or was this the way she would be, cocooned in splashy flesh so that she couldn't even fantasize about a man being startled by her, by her badge and the lighthearted look of her?

The man shouldered his knapsack, tapped his pipe ash into the stream, and ground out the last bit of fire with the sole of his boot. He squatted to splash water on the rock, reminding her that he was serviceably strong in the hip and leg. Were all voyeurs washed back and forth between thrill and loneliness?

She watched him go, heard him for a bit longer crackling through the undergrowth. Then only the stream and her own breathing. She rolled onto her side and tucked her hand between her legs. No—she wouldn't be able to, she wouldn't fit into any of her old fantasies.

She had a moment of self-pity, an emotion she despised. Enough of that. If she wasn't going to arrest anybody or fuck anybody, she could at least do something useful. Go back and test the water samples. And then tell Mary not to bring home any more of her damn desserts.

chapter eight

May was surprised when Phoebe Fitzgerald asked her to have lunch. She couldn't think how to say no. "Oh, good," Phoebe said. "I'll swing by and we'll go to Sawtooth. The food's wonderful, and you'll be doing me a

favor. Part of being a member of the tennis club is I have to
have so many lunches there each month, and Eddie won't go.
Wait—that's not what I mean at all."

May hadn't had a good look at Sawtooth Point since they
put up the yew hedge. "Irish yew," Phoebe said, as if she'd
planted them herself. "And stands of Scotch pine between
the cottages so you don't have to see your neighbors, even in
winter. The big one over there is Jack Aldrich's. Do you know
him? His wife and her sister grew up here. But you must
know all about them."

No end to Elsie Buttrick.

May was just as glad Phoebe went rattling on. "I only met
Jack Aldrich at the interview. He interviews everyone before
they can buy a cottage. He even interviews you just to join the
tennis club. The great big white mansion with the porches is
called the Wedding Cake."

"It always was," May said, "even before it got added on to
and gussied up."

May stuck close to Phoebe when they got out of the car
and went up on the porch. A waiter or maybe the person in
charge said, "Good afternoon, Mrs. Fitzgerald. You'll be two?
Lawn side or ocean side?"

"Lawn, please." She said to May, "I want to see who's playing tennis."

More than half the people around them were dressed in
white tennis clothes. What with the high-gloss paint on the
posts and railings and the tablecloths and napkins, it made
for an awful lot of white. May felt better once she sat down,
not that anyone had looked at her oddly, but she'd felt odd in
her navy blue dress and nylon stockings.

Phoebe leaned forward and said, "You've known Eddie a
long time, haven't you?"

Was that what this was about? "Yes."

"What was his wife like?"

"We didn't see much of her. Then she was gone."

"Was she pretty?"

"Eddie is Dick's best friend. Eddie took us in after the hurricane, carried us for a good while. I'm not one for talking about—"

"Well, yes. Eddie's a very good person. I was just wondering. I mean, I wonder how his son got to be so different."

"Walt's been away for some time now. He just got back."

"Of course, I know how hard it is being a single parent with a problem child. I have a teenage daughter, and she was impossible. She blamed me when our dog died. But then she gives her stepmother a terrible time, too. My ex-husband remarried very quickly—and now she's at boarding school. My daughter, I mean. And maybe that helps. After she called up the vet, she decided it wasn't my fault that Sabu died, and she called me up and we had a good cry together. I'm going to have soup and salad; I've got a game this afternoon. But I recommend the quiche."

May nodded. She was relieved when Phoebe concentrated on penciling in the order and stopped tumbling at her.

May looked at the creek coming out of the woods and into the salt pond. All these people in white with bare, tanned legs sitting on the porch or hopping around on the tennis courts—not a half mile from her house. She'd known there was building going on; she'd seen that over the past year or two. She'd noticed the gatehouse and then the sudden yew hedge transplanted all at once, six feet tall. But it was these people, all one tribe, who made the air different, as if what they breathed on Sawtooth Point was their own air, as new as the tennis courts and houses and brightened-up Wedding Cake. It didn't seem altogether real, as if all these people were dreaming it and she'd somehow walked into their dream.

Now that Phoebe had handed over the order slip, she was eyeing the tennis courts. "I have to play that woman this weekend, the one with the pink headband. We're supposed to wear all white, but I guess . . . So there she is taking a lesson. She's ahead of me on the ladder, but she's not all that good. The pro told me I should be able to move up to the top ten. Jack Aldrich's wife is in the top ten, she and her sister, Elsie Buttrick, but Elsie hasn't been playing this last year. Do you play?"

"No."

"You must be doing something to have such a good figure. I don't know what I'd do without tennis. Thank God they have an indoor court for the winter. And I can go skiing; I still have a share in a ski lodge in Vermont. But I'm afraid Eddie's worried about that."

"I don't see why. His business'll slow down when the weather turns."

"Oh, it's not that. He doesn't make a fuss, but he gets this *look* when I go back to my old haunts. It's not that I have a particular beau. You've probably guessed that Eddie's in love with me."

Different air or not, it sounded wrong to say it flat out. May was afraid Phoebe was going to say more, but Phoebe veered off.

"How long does a person have to live here to really live here? It's been three years and people still say, 'So you're staying on past Labor Day again?' Not these people." Phoebe waved her hand. "Everyday people who live here. It's as if being part of life here is harder than joining Sawtooth. It's as if there are things you have to know but that nobody tells you. I thought I might get to be friends with Miss Perry. I rent my little stone house from her, I go to the same church. I ran into her when she was taking a walk and I said I'd heard she'd sold land to Elsie Buttrick and I said how much I love my little stone house and would she ever consider selling it. She said, 'That really is out of the question. I thought it was well known that I am bequeathing everything to the Perryville School.' I felt put in my place. Very much put in my place."

May said, "Miss Perry's old. You likely took her by surprise."

"I thought it might be because I'm Eddie's office manager. Maybe anyone who has anything to do with Eddie."

"No. She knows Eddie and Dick are friends and she'd do

just about anything for Dick. Of course, she's known Dick since he was a boy."

"Well, there it is again. I'll be a newcomer until I'm old and gray." Phoebe sat back and crossed her legs. She looked at her pretty knee as if she was making sure old and gray were a long ways off. "I'm usually good at fitting in. I like getting to know people and having people get to know me. But around here it's as if everyone already knows what they need to know, and what's the point of talking about it."

"There's some truth in that," May said, "but it doesn't mean they're thinking about you one way or the other." Phoebe let out a breath and slumped a little. May felt as if she held a fluttering bird in her hands. This pretty woman with business sense, with big-city sense, with all kinds of sense, wanted a breath of comfort, a little puff of air to fluff up her feathers. Phoebe was stuck on herself, but at least she was nervous about it. And—what May had held off on account of her own nervousness—Phoebe was trying to make friends with her. Why on earth would someone like Phoebe want that? And yet now that Phoebe wasn't trying to pry out things about Eddie, May didn't mind Phoebe's treating her as an authority on South County. She saw how she could get to like Phoebe's coming toward her so eagerly. Now that Dick and the boys were going their own ways, and her family wasn't scraping by and she wasn't so busy making ends meet, she wouldn't mind getting out more. She would have had a good time at the boys' ball game except that Elsie Buttrick showed up. For a while she'd let herself get penned up in her own house for fear of seeing Elsie Buttrick. Now she was angry at herself for shrinking away.

Today was an accident; she'd let herself get towed along. Not even Phoebe's first choice, but here she was. Not even sure she liked it here, but pleased to take a look at all this.

She said to Phoebe, "If you'd like, next week we can have lunch at my house. I can't tell you much about what's going on around *here* lately, but I know how things used to be."

"Oh, that would be lovely, that would be absolutely lovely."
May thought it didn't take much for Phoebe to brighten up.

After Phoebe dropped her off, May stood still in the middle of
the kitchen. She thought she might as well put on some long
gloves and pull out the poison ivy from around the raspberry
bushes. The boys both got poison ivy worse than most. Come
to think of it, next week she and Phoebe could pick raspber-
ries. She could show Phoebe a thing or two about the salt
marsh, too, show her the bit of salt crystal that the spartina
pushed out, how it could live in salt water that would kill
any other plant. If it was a low tide, she and Phoebe would
get into the creek down near the mouth, find a few quahogs.
It'd be pleasant enough to have someone along for company,
someone who didn't know these things.

But there it was again—Phoebe was more likely to want to
know other things. That easy way she'd talked about Eddie
being in love with her, about her divorce and her bad daughter—she'd be one to want to trade girlish secrets. May didn't
have girlish secrets. She didn't have but one secret. It wasn't
her own, but it kept her locked up. Alone in her kitchen she
said out loud, "Damn him." It floated softly in the air. She
said it louder so it echoed.

She changed into her gardening clothes, put on her
elbow-high dish-washing gloves, and went to tear out the
poison ivy.

chapter nine

E lsie and Mary were working things out pretty well. On work days Elsie got up early, nursed Rose, made her own breakfast, and then opened the door to the stairs to Mary's new bedroom so that Mary could hear Rose. Mary usually didn't have to get up till nine or so. Mary took Rose with her when she drove to Sawtooth Point. She picked up one of the sous chefs or a waitress, and all three of them went to do the shopping, Mary cradling Rose with one arm, pointing, poking, or feeling with her free hand. Rose spent most of the day in a corner of the big kitchen, either in the car seat or in the portable crib. At four or so, Elsie picked Rose up. Sometimes she nursed her in the kitchen, happy to watch Mary and the two sous chefs chopping, stirring, peeking in the ovens. Elsie was a little sad to leave this heat and bustle. When she got home she turned on all the lights, a new bad habit for which she reproached and then forgave herself. It wasn't until after Rose went to sleep that she felt trapped. She dealt with this feeling (sometimes just restlessness, once in a while bleakness) by buying an Exercycle and pedaling hard for forty minutes, hoping for some endorphins to kick in. Another remedy came to her one evening when she remembered Jack saying to a table full of guests that the birth of a child was a five-year jail sentence. Sally had winced and then laughed at him. "I seem to remember you slipping away every morning without a lot of sirens going off."

Laughing at Jack made her feel better. Bigger and better. She put on her gym suit and started pedaling.

She was just beginning to sweat when the phone rang. She

got to it on the third ring, said hello while listening to hear if Rose was waking up. She couldn't hear a voice on the line, said hello again. And again, with an edge in case it was a crank call. Only a breath, but now she knew who it was, had feared this sound and put it out of her mind. At last a word. "Elsie?"

"Yes, it's Elsie. Are you all right?"

A silence. "Elsie. I can't . . ." Silence again.

"Miss Perry? You're at home, right?"

"Yes. It's odd. I'm sorry."

"I'm coming. Did you fall down? Where are you?"

"Elsie. It's very odd."

"I'm coming."

Elsie thought of calling Sally. Jack. Mary. Dick. Captain Teixeira. Nine-one-one.

Miss Perry had called her. She scooped up Rose, put her in the car seat. Down the hill, up to the door. Locked. The key was in the fake rock. She'd told Miss Perry that any robber . . . Never mind, there it was.

Miss Perry was sitting on the bottom step of the stairs, leaning against the newel post. She was still holding the phone. Elsie hung it up. Miss Perry was breathing weakly. Elsie felt her pulse at her throat. It seemed fast but strong. Her face looked pale. It didn't look as if she'd fallen—just slumped against the post. What else? What else? Elsie saw the yellow highlighting she'd used in her EMT textbook but nothing else. No, nine-one-one. They'd put her through. She should know the pulse—she touched the side of Miss Perry's throat again. Twenty, twenty-one. In ten seconds. Times six. Rose began to cry in her car seat. Miss Perry opened her eyes, one of them wider than the other. Elsie said, "It's Elsie. It's all right. I'm just going to call .. .."

A woman's voice answered the phone. Elsie said, "We need an ambulance. We're just down the road from South County Hospital." She gave more directions. A man's voice came on and asked all over again. He said, "Okay, the driveway with the stone columns."

Elsie said, "Right. My car's out front. I'll turn the blinker on."

Rose was crying louder. Elsie went out, pushed the turn signal down, and went back in carrying Rose. She held Rose in one arm and sat down beside Miss Perry. She put an arm behind Miss Perry's neck and cradled her head with her hand. Rose stopped crying but was still fussing. Miss Perry said, *"Non sum qualis . . ."* For an instant Elsie thought she had to either translate or identify. Horace or Virgil? She realized that her mind was gnawing at either/or—either a heart attack or a stroke. Pallor, rapid pulse, breathing—could be either. She looked at Miss Perry's eyes. The left eye was only half open. She leaned forward to look closely at Miss Perry's eyes. Rose fussed louder. Miss Perry said, "What?"

Elsie said, "It's just the baby." Miss Perry rolled her head. Elsie said, "We should stay still."

Miss Perry said, "What baby?"

Elsie said, "It's all right. I'll take care of the baby." But every time Rose made a noise, Miss Perry either rolled her head or raised her right hand. Elsie turned Miss Perry so that Miss Perry lay along the wide bottom step, the back of her head on Elsie's thigh. Elsie pulled up her sweatshirt, opened her nursing bra, and lifted Rose to her nipple. She said, "It's all right. It's going to be quiet now. A doctor's coming."

"Odd," Miss Perry said, but she lay still.

Elsie wasn't sure if she should keep Miss Perry from falling asleep. In her mind's eye she could now read some of the highlighted lines: comfort and reassure. That implied keeping her awake, didn't it? Loosen constricting clothing. Remove all dentures and dental bridges or false teeth. Why? Maybe she was mixing in advice from the epilepsy chapter. Or was there a possibility of a convulsion? Didn't look like it—Miss Perry was breathing fast but evenly.

Elsie was pretty sure Miss Perry didn't have dentures—wouldn't she have noticed?

Rose was sucking steadily, her plump legs light and loose. Elsie moved her so that the bottom of Rose's blanket wouldn't brush the top of Miss Perry's head.

"What happened?" Miss Perry said. "When it turns."

"Turns?"

"Yes."

Elsie thought at first Miss Perry meant dialing, but when she looked at the phone she saw that it was new and had buttons. Dumb—she'd just pushed nine-one-one. Then she thought Miss Perry might be worrying about the key. "You called me, and I came. I found the key. I'll put it back." Miss Perry rolled her head to the right. Elsie noticed her left eye again. Another highlighted fragment: "unilateral weakness . . . mouth drawn to one side." It was hard to tell, since she was looking at Miss Perry's face upside down. Elsie got it then. She said, "Dizzy. You had a dizzy spell."

"Yes."

"It'll be all right. The doctor's coming. It's all right."

Elsie looked out the open door. She couldn't see the blinker itself, but she saw the light flash on the lower leaves of the copper beech. She said, "The leaves are turning. I mean, changing color. The ash, the sycamore by my pond."

"Yes," Miss Perry said. "Trees."

Elsie went on. "Your red oak. All the maples." Rose pulled away, made a face, but then nursed again. Miss Perry lay still but appeared to be listening. Elsie settled into a state of mind that could go on and on, as if she were a pond fed by a slow spring. Rose fell asleep.

When the ambulance pulled up behind her car, she thought of getting up, looked around for a pillow, something to put under Miss Perry's head. No need. The two men moved Miss Perry onto a gurney. One sat beside Elsie and took notes as she recited what she knew. Miss Perry's head was toward the door, only a little higher than Elsie's. Miss Perry turned her face to the right. Elsie added, "Maybe paresis. The left eye and cheek."

Miss Perry said, "Elsie, will you . . . Don't go."

"Yes." Take Rose along? Call Mary? Sally? She'd figure out something. "Yes. I'll stay with you. I'll have to see to the baby."

"Yes. Baby."

chapter ten

J
ack asked Elsie to have supper at the Sawtooth Point cottage. Since it was usually Sally who invited her, Elsie guessed that it wasn't to be a purely social occasion. Jack held off until they finished eating. Elsie nursed Rose and put her to bed in the portable car seat. Sally cleared the table. Jack stood up when Sally and Elsie sat down. He held the back of his chair and said, "I'm wearing lots of hats in all this. Too many hats. I have been Miss Perry's lawyer. My firm drew up her will. I've since become the chairman of the board of directors of the Perryville School, which is the chief beneficiary of that will. I was also to be the executor, and I've had her power of attorney. In case Miss Perry takes a turn for the worse, I don't want to get caught flat-footed in what might appear to be a conflict of interest."

Sally said, "Jack . . ."

"So I've rearranged everything. Elsie is to be executrix."

"Jack," Sally said on a higher note. "I think you're being . . . I thought you were just going to talk it over. Elsie's been through a lot."

"We're all very concerned, but this has to be faced. I'm not insensitive to the emotional situation. As it happens, I'm trying to avoid problems that would compound everyone's distress at a later date. If you'll let me get a little further, you'll see that this plan is to the benefit of all concerned." He pulled two sheets of paper from his inside coat pocket, smoothed out the fold, and laid them on Elsie's place mat. "I've covered the major points here. You don't have to take them all in right now. I've arranged for a capable lawyer to help you. He *was* an associate in my firm, but he's on his own now." He put a hand on Elsie's shoulder. "So really all you'll be doing is taking care of Miss Perry in very much the same way that you'd be doing anyway. I'd like to help more, but in light of this conflict of interest, I have to be Caesar's wife, not just beyond reproach but above suspicion."

Elsie ran her hand through her hair briskly enough to dislodge Jack's hand. He moved to her other side and put his finger on the top of the page. Elsie said, "I can't read this with your hand in the way. If you'll just sit down and give me a minute . . ."

"It's a bit technical; I thought I could clarify some of the legal language."

"I'll read this tonight then, and if I have trouble, I'll call your capable lawyer."

Jack sighed and sat down. "It would be more expedient—"

"Oh, Jack," Sally said. "Just let her skim through it. This is no time for you and Elsie to start one of your . . ." Sally lifted her hands and flicked her fingers apart.

Jack got up again and went to the pantry. He said over his shoulder, "There's brandy or port, if you like."

Sally said, "You know brandy keeps you awake."

"This isn't so hard," Elsie said. "All this about the books Miss Perry gave to Charlie and Tom Pierce. 'Donative intent.' Of course she intended to give them."

Jack reappeared in the doorway. "Well, there you are," Jack said. "The problem is that the rare editions are still in her bookcase. She only actually handed over reader's editions. To avoid tax consequences to the donees, it would be better if the books were out of the house."

"That happens when the boys have their eighteenth birthdays. Charlie will be eighteen next summer."

Jack said, "Of course, we all hope—" Sally held up her hand. Jack stood still for a moment, squinting and wrinkling his forehead, visibly considering. "All right," he said. "I can understand your concern for Elsie's feelings. I happen to think Elsie's made of sterner stuff. I think that she, like me, will find comfort in dealing with the formal necessities of the situation." He turned to Elsie. "But perhaps you're right, perhaps it will be easier talking to a lawyer with whom you have only a professional relationship. All we have to settle is that you accept that you'll be the executrix and have power of attorney. In our last clear conversation, that is what Miss Perry told us she wants. That is the factor I should have put first, rather than my own need to stand clear. Miss Perry considers you the person most capable of understanding her intentions and making sure that they are fulfilled."

"All right."

"It will give her the peace of mind that—"

"I said yes."

Jack bobbed his head several times. As much to shake away the unused bits of his speech, Elsie thought, as to reply to her. "All right, then," Jack said. "So the next thing is for you to get in touch with the lawyer. If you'll look at the third item on my memo, you'll see that the lease on the stone cottage comes up for renewal. You might as well let the lawyer handle that. Do you know the tenant? That woman who works for Eddie Wormsley; I've seen her play tennis here. If she can afford that, she can pay a fair rent. As it stands now, it barely covers the taxes and insurance. Miss Perry is land-poor, and the cash flow may not cover nursing expenses. I have people on the waiting list for a cottage here at Sawtooth who'd be more than happy—"

"I thought you had to steer clear?"

"Oh, Elsie," Sally said. "Jack is just being helpful."

"And all I'm doing is pointing out that using Miss Perry's rental cottage as a waiting room for his Sawtooth enterprise isn't exactly steering clear. I'm just trying to help him be Caesar's wife."

Jack glared at her. "I was merely making a point of comparison. Never mind. Sometimes you have the attention span of a kitten. Pouncing at shoelaces. Take the goddamn paper home. When you get stuck, call the lawyer. And don't be a pain in the ass with him."

"Jack," Sally said. "Sometimes—"

"Sometimes," Elsie said, "he's more bearable when he's cross."

Jack swirled his brandy snifter. "You see," he said to Sally, "if I let her have the last word, she's not so unbearable herself."

Once when Sally was tipsy she'd told Elsie that Jack liked his spats with Elsie. She'd added, "In fact, afterward he can get quite amorous."

That thought, not one to dwell on at the best of times, was enough to start her gathering up Rose's things and then Rose in her car seat.

chapter eleven

Phoebe Fitzgerald called to ask if she could come over. "It won't take a minute. I'm a little bit up in the air about something . . ."

May just had time to make biscuits. When Phoebe came in, May put the teakettle on and got out a jar of her rose-hip jelly. May didn't feel so slow around Phoebe as she had at first.

She'd figured out that Phoebe went through a half-dozen little items while she worked her way to the main thing on her mind. May didn't think Phoebe meant to fool anyone, just that Phoebe wasn't sure how to get where she was going. According to Eddie she wasn't that way with clients—she let them say their say while she nodded and smiled and took notes. Eddie was crazy about her handwriting—he'd unfolded a page to show May. Poor Eddie.

Phoebe asked after the boys, ate a biscuit with a dab of jelly, wondered how rose hips could be so sweet, repeated after May "apple slices and lemon juice," as if that's what she'd come to hear. She asked if May knew any of the pink ladies at the hospital; she'd thought of volunteering but she'd heard that a man had come in carrying his cut-off thumb, held it out in the palm of his hand. She said, "I don't know how I'd be. I'm afraid I might come apart. You know about Miss Perry?"

May nodded. "Apparently Elsie Buttrick found her. One of the pink ladies . . . I was at the hospital asking about volunteering, and she started to tell me about it but a nurse cut her off. She—the pink lady—said that a neighbor . . . Miss Perry only has two neighbors and I'm one of them. Of course, there's Mr. Salviatti, but he's farther away and he's not . . . I've never even met him. Have you?"

"Not so as he'd remember. He had a boat in the yard when Dick worked there." May tried to think of something else about Mr. Salviatti, hoping to steer clear of Elsie Buttrick. "It was a funny color, sort of raspberry. Some people made jokes about it: 'There's Mr. Salviatti in his pink yachtie.' That was back before Mr. Aldrich bought Sawtooth Point. Of course, Mr. Aldrich married into part of it."

"Yes, Sally Aldrich. So it was Sally and Elsie's family who bought it from Dick's grandfather?"

"Great-uncle. Uncle Arthur."

"Didn't he build the Wedding Cake? Why on earth did he sell it?"

"Had to. Ran out of money. He put money into a little factory that made silk stockings just when nylon came along. It was all way before my time. Dick only knew Uncle Arthur as an old man. Dick joined the Coast Guard out of high school, and when he got back, Uncle Arthur was dead."

"But still . . . I mean, Arthur must have been a rather significant figure. The Wedding Cake is very grand."

"Arthur Pierce was a sheep farmer who had a few good years and got ahead of himself. Nothing grand about him, except his notions. Even the Wedding Cake wasn't all that grand. It got added on to later, the wings and porches. Back then this wasn't a place people came to. Not like Newport or Watch Hill. It was farming and fishing. Most of the people who lived here had no idea that the pieces of land they grew up on would ever be worth much. When Uncle Arthur sold Sawtooth Point it was just not-so-good farmland. It's too rocky and salty for potatoes or corn, and raising sheep got so it didn't pay. They used to mow the marsh grass to make salt hay for the sheep. I guess that got too expensive; it took a whole gang of men. Anyway, it's all different now. Those new cottages on Sawtooth Point go for three or four times what a regular house ought to cost."

"Well, you get more than the cottage. There's the tennis club and the yacht club, and there's going to be a spa. That's why people pay so much."

"That's what Uncle Arthur missed out on. People pay better than sheep."

Phoebe laughed. "Oh, May, that's very funny." May hadn't thought to be funny, she just got caught talking, trying to avoid saying anything about Elsie. Phoebe said, "But right now I have a problem with Miss Perry. I don't even think Miss Perry knows about it—I mean, she's still in the hospital. I got a letter from her lawyer. Or rather from a lawyer acting on behalf of Elsie Buttrick, who's somehow managing things for Miss Perry. I've never had an official lease, just a handwritten note. This new thing is a form letter—boilerplate with lessor and lessee and so forth, but the part that's filled in is the rent. It's simply staggering. So I was wondering—you seem to know something about everyone. How well do you know Elsie Buttrick?"

May's face went numb. May felt the same way she had at the baseball game, that she was the one who'd done something wrong.

Phoebe said, "Eddie says she's perfectly nice. That one time when he shot a swan . . ."

May took a breath and said, "Yes, she did Eddie a good turn. And she's close to Miss Perry, so it's natural she'd look after things." Her voice sounded loud and far off.

Phoebe touched her hand. "I think I hear a 'but' in there."

May looked at Phoebe's small hand. Then at Phoebe's pretty, wide-eyed face. Was this what Elsie Buttrick could do? Put her little paw out, tilt her face, and look creamy?

Phoebe leaned back but kept her fingers on May's. "May—honestly. You look so fierce." Phoebe let out a short high note, maybe a laugh, and said, "It's a little bit scary."

May looked at the floor and compressed herself. She couldn't pretend much now. Couldn't make up some cock-and-bull story about . . . anything else.

"Oh, May. Whatever it is, I'm on your side." May jerked her head at that. Phoebe was no fool. She'd said "whatever it is," but she wouldn't stop at "whatever it is" for long. "I feel terrible. I came over with my little problem . . . If it's anything I can help with, just say."

May was tired. She'd meant to turn over a good part of the garden. Now she felt a weight. It wasn't Phoebe's talking. Listening to all that was like watching a hummingbird. It was Elsie up there in her sunny little house with her baby daughter and her friend Mary. And Dick on his boat, and from the little he'd said, as pleased with his crew as with the other parts of his life at sea. And here she was carrying around the secret, carrying it to the ball field, to the grocery store, bringing it home, not able to let it go in her own kitchen. And here was Phoebe looking at her with her big green eyes. May wondered how Phoebe would look at Dick if she knew—would she draw back? Or was she the other sort of woman? One who'd come close enough to see if she could get his attention. One dark look she could wonder about.

Phoebe said, "We can go on to something else. Just tell me I haven't made you mad at me. I'd really be at a loss without our little get-togethers. I mean, right this minute I *am* at a loss. There we were having a lovely talk . . ." Phoebe tucked her chin in but kept looking.

"I'm not mad," May said. "I just thought of something and it got hold of me."

"Well, I certainly know what that's like. Anyway, now that we've gone this far, I'll say one more thing. I absolutely will never tell anybody else anything that we talk about. Never."

May felt stuck to the chair. She knew that if she didn't say anything, Phoebe would go on. It was her own fault. Just let everything knot up inside her and pull her face apart.

Phoebe said, "Oh, May. I have this little problem, and now I've . . . without meaning to in the least. But I'm sort of stuck. If I just get up and leave, it would be heartless. I mean, it wouldn't *be* heartless, it just might seem heartless. But if I don't say anything else, then you'll be left wondering. I mean, you'll be left wondering what I'm wondering. I suppose I could promise I won't even wonder. Maybe if I were like Eddie. Eddie is someone who can just not wonder. You know Eddie built another room up there since Mary Scanlon moved in? Since I was doing the time sheets I asked what kind of a job it was, and he said a bedroom and a bath on the east side and walling in the screen porch on the other side for when the baby needs a room of her own. It was as if it were just another detail, like what kind of windows. Eddie can be amazing that way, he just looks at the job. It's not that he doesn't have an imagination. He can imagine what things will look like, he can say, 'If I fix it that way it'll look funny, but if I do this . . .' It's just that I've never met someone as uncurious about people."

May felt an odd relief, as if Phoebe's chatter were in the future—everybody knew and nobody took much notice anymore—Elsie Buttrick's child just another piece of small change, worn smooth by jingling with all the others—Mr. Salviatti's company's repaving Route 1, the red-crab packing plant's hiring, Captain Teixeira's retiring again . . .

Phoebe said, "So of course I said, 'What baby?' but Eddie started talking about whether Miss Perry would make a fuss about his going past her house. For an instant I thought that Eddie . . . that it was Eddie."

May sat up straight. She didn't say anything right off. Then she wondered just how well Phoebe knew Eddie, for all the time she spent with him. Of course, it could be that Eddie was changing; maybe he'd changed enough so he'd seem more of a risk. Used to be he'd just as soon be alone in the woods, but if you needed something done and didn't mind waiting, he'd get around to it. People would say, "If you need a new dock you can get one at the boatyard, you don't mind paying. Or you can get Eddie. Keeps to himself, but he's handy." Phoebe had said Eddie was "uncurious," as if that was a fault. Maybe where she came from it was. That was of a piece with the way Phoebe dished out praise. No holding back. When Eddie put in a new porch railing at the Teixeiras' store, Captain Teixeira gave it a pat and said, "That's not the first one you've built." Captain Teixeira might speak Portuguese at home, but he knew just what to say to Eddie without any extras.

Right now, whether she meant to or not, Phoebe had got her backed into a corner—all those extras, all that hovering and darting.

May looked her in the face and said, "It's not Eddie."

"Oh," Phoebe said. "How do you know?" She put her hand over her mouth. Phoebe looked away, squinting over the next question. It didn't take her long. She said, "So if Mary Scanlon is moving in, it's to help out."

"That's right."

Phoebe said, "If it's Elsie's baby, then who . . ."

May watched Phoebe take it in. She was relieved Phoebe didn't say anything. Then May felt a greater relief. She was in the kitchen, her kitchen. She felt it was her house for the first time since it got fixed. She said, "I'm going out to the garden." She looked at Phoebe's shoes. "You can put on Tom's boots if you want to come along. They're by the back door."

When Phoebe got the boots on she fluffed her skirt. She looked like she was looking around for a mirror. May handed her a basket and said, "You know how to tell a ripe tomato?" Phoebe raised her eyebrows. "Give it a turn and see if it falls into your hand."

Phoebe admired the vegetable garden, the new garden shed. May said, "The shed's in the same place Dick built *Spartina*. His shed was bigger, big posts and beams so he could use a chain hoist. Covered it all with canvas. When the hurricane hit, the canvas didn't tear off. It caught the wind like a sail. Carried the beams right into the house. You saw what that was like. Dick kicked himself about it later. At the time he was running around, getting his boat out to sea."

Phoebe said, "I always wondered—why out to sea?"

"He thought he could get her out past the storm. But even if he didn't, she stood a better chance at sea than in the harbor. Half the boats smashed into each other. One got picked up and rolled onto Route One. He had some idea about how it'd be, so he fueled her up and took off."

"What did he say to you?" Phoebe said. "I mean, did he ask you?"

May laughed. She said, "No more about that than the other thing he got up to."

Phoebe's eyebrows climbed up her forehead. Phoebe opened and closed her mouth. She finally said, "I'm sorry, I guess that was another joke. It's good that you can put things at a distance . . ."

May pointed across Route 1. "If it wasn't for those trees we could see Elsie Buttrick's house." She pointed to the creek. "If you throw a stick in there, it'll float right by her sister's house. Dick didn't get his baby on some hula-hula girl in the South Seas. It was right over there. Pretty soon I'll be in the supermarket and I'll run into Elsie Buttrick with her baby in her grocery cart and I can either fall over in a faint or I can say, 'Well, look at that. She's got Dick's eyes.' So I don't see where there's much distance."

Phoebe blinked and her eyes teared up some. Phoebe's bit of weepiness was probably nothing more than crying at the movies. May didn't doubt she did a good deal of that. Let her take it whatever way suited her. May was breathing easier. She'd wrestled with forgiving Dick until she didn't know what it meant. And there was no talking to Dick—he was walking on eggshells. She sometimes liked him that way; other times it made her feel the two of them were drifting around inside a gray day that wouldn't turn into anything but kept her on edge waiting for something.

Phoebe started picking tomatoes. She made slow work of it—each time she stooped she smoothed her skirt over her rear end and held it against the backs of her knees. Then she twisted the tomatoes so delicately that even some of the ripe ones didn't fall. When she did pick one she laid it in the basket as if she was making a flower arrangement. Then stood up, moved the basket, stooped, smoothed her skirt.

May said, "You don't need to be so dainty. Here." May knelt beside her and picked three in short order.

"I'm sure it's going to be all right," Phoebe said. "I mean, here you are with everything he could want. You're so good and beautiful in a real way." She held her hands out wide. "I mean, it's as if all this is a part of you."

May felt the side of her mouth twitch down.

Phoebe said, "I know, I know. I should just think those things."

May picked two tomatoes and another two. She said, "That's more than enough. You'd better take some home with you."

"I'm going back to the office," Phoebe said. "I'm probably late; I am late. They'll be all right in the car?"

Phoebe left in a flurry, shuffling to the back door with a pair of tomatoes in each hand, shaking off Tom's boots, trotting out the front door in her high heels, waving out the car window.

May stood on the porch, a little let down. At first she thought it was because she'd been talking too much. Then she thought, what if Dick was to find out? No, that made her cross, not sad. Dick was out to sea, where he didn't answer to anybody but himself. No reason why she shouldn't do what she pleased in her own place. Then she had a suspicion that Phoebe had got round her, had got the better of her. No to that, too. Phoebe was clever enough behind all that giddiness, but she didn't think Phoebe meant her any harm. Phoebe was lonely, was aching to find a friend.

So what did it mean that Phoebe picked her?

chapter twelve

Elsie reread the instructions for hooking up the answering machine, one of the many small items on her list. In fact, they were all small, Lilliputians wrapping their tiny ropes around her just when she wished to do something big. She'd imagined that Miss Perry—Miss Perry's situation—would require largeness of spirit, a beaming of will and encouragement. Instead she felt like an IBM typewriter ball tapping out one minuscule letter after another. The day nurse had immediately taken command of Miss Perry's bedroom. On this first day she'd popped out four times to suggest things Elsie could do. All perfectly sensible. All elaborations of doctor's orders. An electric heater, at least until Elsie got the plumber to bleed the radiators. A hot-water bottle. A tray with legs for meals in bed. As soon as Elsie arrived with one thing the woman would meet her in the front hall wanting another. And now this answering machine with instructions that seemed to be translated from Japanese.

The day nurse came down the stairs and said, "Lydia's asking for you. Don't stay long. Oh, we need baby aspirin. And I couldn't find coffee. There's tea, but I prefer coffee."

"Baby aspirin?"

"Yes. Adult-strength would irritate her stomach, but we need a small dose as an anticlotting agent."

"Okay. Baby aspirin. While I'm out, why don't you see what you can do with this answering machine . . . It'd be a big help. I'll put coffee on my list. Oh, by the way, it's Miss Perry. We all say Miss Perry. Only Captain Teixeira . . . but he's her oldest friend." The nurse lifted a hand. Elsie said, "I'll bring my coffeemaker, and we'll have a chance to chat about everything tomorrow. Oh. We're having meals brought over from Sawtooth Point, whatever's the special. Once the answering machine is hooked up, just turn the ringer off and it won't bother you anymore. And let me know if there's anything you can't eat. You're okay with seafood? No problems with clams, lobster, squid?"

"I haven't ever had squid."

"Okay. No squid. After I see Miss Perry, I've got to run, but I'll be back to meet the night nurse. Do you know her?"

"No. I don't know who—"

"One of the Tran girls. She's an angel. If you have any trouble with the answering machine, she's very handy. They're all very bright. The young ones all have perfect English."

As she went up the stairs Elsie thought she'd just done a Jack. Not the stony-faced wait-'em-out Jack but the nipping-at-your-heels border-collie Jack. Couldn't be helped; the woman was driving her nuts.

She trotted up quickly, a last little display of border collie. She slowed in the dark hallway. She'd never been in this part of the house. She stopped short in front of the half-open door. To go into Miss Perry's bedroom seemed a terrible intimacy.

She knocked. Miss Perry's voice floated to her, a single unsteady note. She went in. The light from the windows silvered the large lenses of Miss Perry's glasses. In her long white nightgown and bed jacket, she looked like a snowy owl.

"Elsie."

The sound of her name went through her. It had the odd effect of erasing her. It was a relief. It brought her to Miss Perry as a very simple organism.

"Elsie. Sit here." Miss Perry moved her hand across the bed. Elsie sat. At this angle she could see Miss Perry's eyes, one opened wider than the other. "I want to talk." She waved her right hand back and forth without lifting it from the bedspread. She looked at her hand and said, "That means I'm laughing." The right side of her mouth smiled.

"Yes," Elsie said. "What are you laughing at?"

Miss Perry crooked her forefinger and slowly raised it. At last it reached the top of her head and tapped once. Then her hand seemed to dribble down back to the bed. She said, "Think."

"All right. I'm thinking. You said my name . . . You know Captain Teixeira?"

Miss Perry shook her head. "Things." She looked out the window. "Tree."

"Yes. Tree."

She waved her right hand. Not a laugh. "Things you know. I know. More words for trees."

"Oh. Ash. That tree is an ash."

"Yes. Ash. Say a tree I don't see."

"Beech. The copper beech in front." Miss Perry nodded. "All right. Sycamore. By my pond. It always looks like it's peeling," Miss Perry added. "And there's the white oak beside it." Miss Perry moved her hand, this time a laugh. Elsie said, "What's funny?"

"*Quercus alba*." Miss Perry touched her head again and said, "Odd. I know Latin. I don't know *beside*."

Elsie was afraid she was going to cry. She squinted and squeezed her nose as if stopping a sneeze. She said, "Beside." She held out one hand, put the other out. "This hand is beside that hand."

"Odd," Miss Perry said. She closed her eyes. She lay back and waved her hand at her hip.

Elsie said, "Do you want to lie down?"

"Yes." Elsie reached under the covers to slide her down. As Elsie touched her, Miss Perry's eyes opened. She said, "I remember. When it was odd, I called the telephone. I called *you*."

"Yes. Let me take your glasses off."

Miss Perry's eyes were blurry for a moment, then grew distinct. "You came. I said . . . Did I say thank you?"

"I'm sure you did."

"You talked. You said trees. The same trees."

"That's right."

"I remember the men came. The . . . car. Not a car. What is it?"

"Ambulance. We'll talk tomorrow. You'll remember it all tomorrow."

"And the baby."

Elsie said, "Yes, that's right," as if Miss Perry were a child trying to put off bedtime by saying to the grown-up reaching for the light switch, "I remember . . ."—what she saw at the beach, what she ate that day that was good for her, the end of a fairy tale.

chapter thirteen

Elsie was to meet Mr. Bienvenue at Miss Perry's house at eight in the evening. She sent the night nurse, Nancy Tran, to babysit Rose. Elsie set out the memoranda, appointment books, and letters on Miss Perry's desk. She laid a fire in the fireplace. She was still in her uniform, thought of going back to change, thought Mr. Bienvenue might arrive. She decided to go up to tell Miss Perry what was going on; Miss Perry would wonder when she heard a man's voice.

Miss Perry was speaking more clearly now, and the doctor was pleased at how much she'd improved in a month. Miss Perry still had difficulty with prepositions. She had a theory that her grasp of prepositions would improve as she began to move around.

Elsie said, "A lawyer's coming over this evening."

"Is it Jack? I should very much like to see Jack."

"No. It's someone Jack recommended. We're just going to go over some papers."

Miss Perry said, "I see," but after a moment she said, "What does 'over' mean?"

"Oh. Sorry. Go over, look over. *Over* is like on. You remember *on.*"

"'Look on my works, ye mighty, and despair.' But you said, 'Over.' 'A lawyer is coming *over.*'"

"I should have just said a lawyer is coming."

"Very well. A lawyer is coming. Am I to meet with him?"

"No. He and I are just going to put a few things in order. I thought I'd tell you so you won't worry when the doorbell rings."

"All this fuss." Miss Perry suddenly glared at Elsie. "It is tiresome. Now please go change your clothes. What will he think when you open the door? He'll think you're the cleaning woman. Your clothes are covered with something, I don't know what."

"It's just bark. I brought wood in for the fire."

"The fire is not . . . You look slubben . . . slubbenly." Miss Perry closed her eyes and clenched her fist. She beat her forearm on her hip, not hard but over and over. She stopped and opened her eyes. "Slovenly."

It was the feebleness that evaporated Elsie's spurt of anger. She said, "All right. I'll take care of everything."

Elsie got to the bottom of the stairs and sat down. She felt dumb. What did she know that could change anything? How had she ever thought she knew what was going on? How had she imagined that anyone could do anything but mumble a few words about what little they knew? Jack's lawyer's words, the doctor's what-we-know-about-the-brain words, her own wonders-of-nature chirps. They all might as well be Miss Perry exhaling stale poems and Latin prepositions and then a burst of bad temper. Every living thing had a few bubbles of one kind or another going in and out one kind of hole or another. When the in and out was over, it was back to matter. She saw it—particulate matter fluttering down through darker and darker water toward the seabed. A stupor spread through her, weighing down her arms, her chest, her head. She reached across her chest and put her fingers in the grooves of the newel post. They fit smoothly. She rested her cheek on the back of her hand, smelled her skin. She ran her fingertips up and down the grooves until another thought came to her. Not cheerier but on a smaller scale. Dick had told her she was spoiled, called her house "the toybox"—of course, that had been part of his pleasure as well as his irritation. He should see her now. He should get down on his damn knees and think of her taking care of his baby, taking care of his friend and protector Miss Perry . . .

The truth was . . . The truth was she'd be doing everything

she was doing anyway. She'd wanted a baby. She'd loved Miss Perry since her first Latin class. She wasn't bossed into this by Dick. She wasn't bossed into this by Jack. Maybe this paper-work she was about to do with some bozo protégé of Jack's— that was something Jack owed her for.

When she opened the door to Johnny Bienvenue she didn't get a good look at him. He was wearing an overcoat and scarf, and a hat with a brim. He pulled off his glove to shake hands, then turned toward the coatrack. She started off toward the library before he was through hanging up his things, and she was lighting the fire when he followed her in. She said, "I hope you don't mind the uniform. I haven't had a minute to change since I got off."

"You're a Natural Resources officer, right? Jack calls you the warden of the Great Swamp, but that's not the official . . ." He stopped, probably because she was staring at him so intently. The Queens River. He was the man who'd caught the trout, made the fire, and drunk the wine—the man she didn't arrest. She tucked her hair back and blushed. And then, thinking that she'd thought of him from time to time, when she pedaled her Exercycle or when she fit back into her uniform, she blushed again. "Yes. I mean, no. Warden of the Great Swamp is what the guys at work say. Kind of a joke." And then more coolly— after all, she'd seen him, he hadn't seen her—"But I get around other places. The salt marshes. The Queens River."

But he'd put on reading glasses and started to look over the papers on the desk. He said, "Jack says Miss Perry is recov-ering. Do you think she'll be able to manage her affairs on her own?" When Elsie didn't answer right away, he looked up. He said, "I know. It's hard to say. Does she strike you as knowing what's going on?"

"Yes."

"Does she understand numbers?"

"I don't know. We talk, but numbers haven't come up."

"On this list of books here—gifts to Charles and Thomas Pierce—where do these figures come from?"

"I found the receipts. The first figure is what Miss Perry paid for each book. I called a rare-book dealer and he gave me a rough idea of what they're worth now—that's the second figure. The dates I got from her appointment books—Charlie and Tom's birthdays."

"But I understand these books are still here."

"Yes." Elsie pointed to the glass-paned bookcase. "She gave them reader's copies. She always said the same thing—it was sort of a joke after a while. 'If you don't scribble in this book or tear the paper I'll give you a new one when you're grown up.' What's in the bookcase are first editions of the same books. Some of them are worth two or three thousand. But Jack told me there's no problem if the gifts are under ten thousand in any one year."

"That's right. But the donor—Miss Perry—said, '*If* you don't scribble in them.' An outright gift has to be unconditional. This wouldn't be a problem if the total was under ten thousand. But each boy's collection is worth . . ." He scribbled on a notepad. "Roughly twenty-five thousand."

"It was a joke! Maybe when she started saying it, when Charlie was six or seven, maybe she meant it then. I was there for their birthday—not this year but before—and Miss Perry laughed and the boys laughed. The reason she was giving books this way was that if she'd said to the boys' father that she was going to pay for them to go to college, he'd have said no. He's very . . ." Elsie saw them, saw the day, Miss Perry catching a flounder, reciting a bit of Beatrix Potter. Dick and the boys, not May, May was fixing the cake, Miss Perry and Dick and the boys in the skiff. The late-afternoon light on the water, the summer-green spartina. A year later, the boys' next birthday, they were at Charlie's baseball game, Miss Perry innocently attentive, May rigid with pain.

Elsie sat down, closed her eyes. She saw May. She saw May looking at her. She felt May. She felt a space in herself fill up with cold astonishment. And then a sense of desolation—as if she were May looking at her house after the hurricane, the broken corner posts, the roof sagging, the wall gaping open, the things inside strange, hers but not hers.

"Are you okay?"

Elsie said, "Just a minute."

"We can do this another time."

"No. Let's go on."

Elsie looked at one of Miss Perry's appointment books, found the dates of Charlie's and Tom's birthday party. "There. Look at that one. 'Gave Charlie Pierce *Sailing Alone Around the World* by Joshua Slocum. First edition, mint. Gave Tom Pierce *Two Years Before the Mast* by Richard Henry Dana. First edition, good condition.'"

Then she started crying. It was a sudden burst, her body bent forward, her face jerking in her hands, the appointment book at her feet.

When she half recovered and was wiping her cheeks with her fingertips, she heard herself say, "I've never cried. I mean, I've never cried in uniform." That was a bit of babble that normally would have made her laugh. At least she stopped crying. She said, "Oh, God. You must think I'm . . ."

"No, no. I can guess it's been . . ." He bent down to pick up the appointment book from the floor. His hair was cut short or the half-curls would have been ringlets. He pulled a small packet of Kleenex from his briefcase. He puzzled over how to open the cellophane. He had thick fingers, a heavy, broad face. A general width—when he finally broke the wrapping and pinched out an edge of Kleenex, she felt as if she was being tended to by a bear.

He said, "I guess you've felt a lot of strain. Jack said you're like a daughter to Miss Perry. So look. I can take the appointment books and the Everett Hazard folder, xerox them. We don't have to wrap everything up right now."

Elsie didn't want him to go. She wanted him to sit by the fire and pay attention to her. She said, "Let me just look in upstairs. You're going . . . where? Woonsocket? And that reminds me. Phoebe Fitzgerald wants to talk to you."

"Oh, yeah. The tenant."

"I could make you a cup of coffee. For your drive. You can smoke your pipe if you'd like." He looked surprised but said, "I'm only going to Providence. But sure. A cup of coffee'd be nice. Black."

When she came back he was looking at the books in the boys' bookcases. She put his coffee on the table between the two armchairs facing the fireplace. She sat down in one of them, tucking her legs under her, a kittenish pose she hadn't struck for a long time. He sat in the other armchair, planted his feet. "So tell me something about Miss Perry," he said. "But first tell me how you know I smoke a pipe. Some sort of Sherlock Holmes thing? Or was it something Jack told you? Probably not Jack. He doesn't notice details. At least not about men."

"Oh?" Elsie was surprised by this bit of spin on his serve but was pleased to bat it back. "Of course, that's true of men in general."

"I don't think so. But let's not get into one of those men-in-general talks. The pipe . . ."

"I'll tell you a little bit about Miss Perry. We'll get back to the pipe." He stretched out his legs. So this wasn't going to be one of her old daredevil encounters, nothing like her fantasy of wading across the Queens River, having him at her mercy.

She told him school stories, about being Miss Perry's prize student in Latin and natural history. A glimpse of herself as a tomboy. "My sister was the great beauty, so I took to the woods." He raised his eyebrows but didn't make a courtly objection. "I would have been just sullenly thrashing around, but Miss Perry took an interest. Just asked a question or two at first. Then asked me to take her to where I'd seen something extraordinary. The first thing was a lady's slipper. On the way she pointed out other things. One time she slit open a little swelling on a twig and inside there was a nymph."

"Oh, sure, nymph. Like a maggot or a grub. Good bait for trout."

"So you're a trout fisherman."

"When I was a kid, Grandpère used to take me. Now it's rare." The *r*s in *grandpère* were trilled French-Canadian rather than lightly gargled French-French.

"Did you grow up speaking French?"

"Some. My father's family's from Trois Rivières. They speak Quebecois. You hear it about half the time in Woonsocket—*au coin*. When the governor gives a speech up there in our corner, I do the introduction in French and English."

She said, "So what are you doing here? This little job . . ."

"I'm a lawyer. And I owe Jack. He tell you I worked for him? I'm not the kind of guy Jack usually hires for his firm. I didn't make partner, but I learned a lot in five years. Now I run my own shop—an office in Woonsocket and one in Providence. Run-of-the-mill cases, but I'm seeing more people."

"So, being a governor's aide—how does that fit in?"

"I'm not ruling out doing something in politics."

"'I'm not ruling out'—that usually means someone's dead set on it. I hope you don't imagine Miss Perry's a moneybags who'll bankroll your campaign."

He smiled. "You look a lot like your sister, but you talk a whole lot different."

Elsie felt both flattered and stopped. He sat there smiling pleasantly. She wondered if he was really so at ease. She wasn't used to being the one who wondered. She wondered if he was at ease because there she was in her uniform, a state employee, and he was a big cheese. She said, "So, if you get stopped for speeding, you let the cop know you work for the governor? Is there some little something on your license plate?" She held up her hand and said, "Never mind. I don't know why . . ." She gave up the idea of playing her little trump card—trout, fire, wine. She felt her edge grow dull. She'd relied on that edge for years. When she was at Sally and Jack's she was the daring gadfly. In the woods she had her badge. And although she'd worked at being just-folks, one of the guys, she had to admit she'd never quite given up the privileges of class. She'd denounced them when she saw them in someone else, most usually in Jack. She sometimes thought that her life had leached them out of her. She sometimes thought that the whole idea of class was fading, the radioactive emissions were weaker and weaker. Nothing like the Boston or Newport of a hundred or fifty years ago. But deep inside her, sometimes hidden even from herself, there was a trace. One of the chief privileges was the assurance of being the final judge of all other claims of worth—money, power, beauty, fame, intellect, or even good works. She'd used it—it wasn't just her sassy talk or body that set men off. Her college English prof had imagined he was fucking Daisy Buchanan. The striving lawyers at Jack and Sally's parties, not quite as literate, still sensed an allure of risk. When they were through she might turn on them, remind them that sex was pleasant enough but now that she was herself again she could see they weren't quite the thing.

And now—as if her bursting into tears in front of this bearish man was as physically intimate as fucking—she'd felt the old urge to put him in his place. And she'd started—"I hope you don't imagine Miss Perry's a moneybags . . ." The breezy way she mentioned money, the poke at his ambition from her position above ambition, the backward tilt of her head as if she'd finally bothered to pay attention. (One of the minor privileges—no one was really there—of course there were always people around, but no one was really there until you decided to notice.)

She didn't have it in her anymore. She hadn't debated it, hadn't examined her conscience. In fact, she'd been about to make another entrance in that role. Performance canceled.

She hadn't crossed the Queens River because she'd looked like the Pillsbury Doughboy. With all her Exercycling and her fish-and-vegetables diet she was on better terms with her body—she didn't mind that her feet were a half size bigger, her hip bones a bit wider, and of course her breasts bigger.

He was staring into the fire. Without looking up he said,

"No, it's okay. I ask myself that. I'm as suspicious of my ambition as I am of anybody else's. I won't give you the speech about caring what happens to people. But is there a part that wants the applause? The deference? The special treatment?" He shrugged. "I can't say there isn't some of that. But so long as it stays in the corner . . . The part of myself I question more is curiosity. I applied to Jack's firm out of curiosity. What would I see in there? What would I see *from* there?"

"And what did you see?"

"At first work was work. But after a while I saw they didn't want to change much. They work hard, but it's to keep things in order. They're less corrupt than some of the state politicians because they aren't desperate. Why should they be? They're sailing along in a big ship. You know Jack. Half of what he says is like he's the captain of a big ship."

"Why didn't you make partner? Did Jack tell you?"

"Yes. When I worked for one partner or another I was competent at research and writing briefs. The firm's main income is from two sources—there are corporate clients like Ciba-Geigy or Electric Boat, and there are some rich families. I wasn't good at attracting clients of either kind. In fact, one of the few clients I took on was some guy in an accident. The insurance company got him to sign a release for peanuts. There were more things wrong with him that they wouldn't pay for. I won the case, on the grounds that the boilerplate form doesn't represent an agreement between two parties in equal bargaining positions. The firm doesn't represent that particular insurance company, so there wasn't a conflict of interest, but the precedent has been a thorn in the paw for all the insurance companies, and some of them *are* clients of the firm. When I did it again I guess they thought 'plaintiff's attorney,' the polite way of saying ambulance chaser. Of course, that's a story that makes me a good guy. David beating Goliath. There were other times when I did an okay job when I should have done a very good job. I have no grievance. And when I was on my way out, Jack suggested to the governor that I could be useful."

"But Jack's Republican. A right-wing Republican."

"Jack knows lots of people. A law firm can't be attached to one party or the other. Jack's views are no secret, but he manages to keep on speaking terms with whoever's in. Sure, he can be . . . overemphatic."

"That's delicate."

"Okay. He can put his foot in his mouth, but that's when he's on his own time. When he's at work, he focuses. But there's another thing. He likes to know what's going on—not for work, just stories. He knows odd things about every corner of the state."

"That's because he thinks it's his."

He looked up. Out of amusement at first but then a slower satisfaction. She guessed he didn't spend much time talking like this, certainly not a lot of time talking to women. He looked like someone surprised by a small pleasure, like a woman stroking the sleeve of a silk blouse.

When he finished his coffee and gathered up the folders, she walked him to the door. As he put his overcoat on she had an impulse to touch his back. She resisted it—he had enough to think about. He shrugged to settle the collar, turned around, and said, "You're okay, are you?"

"Oh, yes. That was just . . . I'm fine."

"So I'll be in touch." He tipped his head at his briefcase. He put his hand in his overcoat pocket. She read the lift of his face.

"Your pipe," she said. "Maybe next time. I'm afraid I have to let you go now."

After he left she suddenly didn't know what to make of it. Had she embarrassed herself? Or had she had the pleasure of pleasing? She'd certainly gone into female display—in fact, several variations of it. She puffed her cheeks and popped a breath out. Now all she was was tired.

She slogged up her driveway, checked on Rose, paid Nancy Tran, and waited up for Mary, the comfort of telling Mary.

When Elsie was done, Mary said, "Aw, go on. You're awful hard on yourself. By tomorrow Miss Perry will be all apologies. And so what if you busted out crying in front of the lawyer?" Mary laughed. "Were you still sniffling when you said, 'I've never cried in uniform'? I'll bet that charmed the socks off him."

chapter fourteen

Phoebe was now taking her lunch hour with May once or twice a week. May liked this arrangement, especially now that Phoebe worked her way through her own complaints more quickly and cheerfully. There was Eddie's roughneck son, Walt, but the bright side was that Eddie was beginning to notice Walt's erratic comings and goings. There was that awful rent increase, but Phoebe was making more money. "Eddie and I are really a very good team. You remember you asked me about that strange glow you've been seeing over at Sawtooth? It's an inflatable cover for a lighted tennis court. Jack Aldrich put it up because the tennis players wanted it, but then he saw it at night and he said it looked like a giant sea slug. So he called Eddie, and Eddie and I went over there to meet with Jack and Mr. Salviatti.

"Somehow it came up that Mr. Salviatti has relatives in Westerly, and I said, 'Oh, where they make those beautiful statues.' I happened to have seen an exhibit at RISD. I gushed about them. Especially the angel statues, and it turns out they were loaned by guess who. He invited me to come see them again—they're in his garden. So that got us off on the right foot. And then Eddie was good with Jack. The problem with the inflatable thing is that it's a great success. It's booked every night. Now that it's fall a lot of people can only play after work, and Jack doesn't want to shut it down while we build something that's not so ugly. He's making an awful lot of money. As I well know, and I only play twice a week. Anyway, Eddie walked around the outside and said he could put up a building *around* it. Something that would look like a traditional barn. Mr. Salviatti thought that was fine. Jack, who had *asked* us to come, was the naysayer at first. He said a barn would get too hot during the summer and it would cost a fortune to air-condition. At least he could deflate the inflatable thing and have an extra outdoor court. Eddie said that the lights would bother the cottage owners. A barn would keep the light inside. As for the heat, we could put two ventilation towers on it, same as a barn. He said, 'That way the sea breeze'll suck the hot air right out the top. No sense in paying for something that nature'll do for free.' So then we went inside and there was Elsie Buttrick all by herself batting back balls—there's this machine that shoots them out. Jack called out, 'Ahoy, there, Elsie! Can't find anyone to play with?' She ignored him, hit another ball, but then the machine was out of balls so she came over, probably to say hello to Eddie; she's very fond of Eddie. But Jack said, 'I hear you and Johnny Bienvenue hit it off.' As if we weren't there or as if we don't matter, as if Eddie and I don't know . . . Then Jack said, 'I knew you'd get along. Diamond in the rough. I'm thinking of making him a member. He said he doesn't play tennis, so I gave him a three-month guest card, told him he should learn, get his game up to a weekend level. It'd be nice if you took him under your wing. Fun for both of you.' Elsie looked very uncomfortable. My guess is that it wasn't just from Jack's bossing her around. I have a sixth sense, and I think she already has her eye on this fellow as a new beau. I thought that might ease your mind."

No. It didn't ease her mind. No, she shouldn't have told Phoebe if Phoebe was going to make it her business. And no to Elsie. Elsie should know to keep to herself, not go pranc-

ing around as if she was free as air, as if she could flit back
to Sawtooth Point as if nothing had happened. Elsie was the
mother of Dick's daughter; that baby was Charlie and Tom's
sister. If there wasn't a baby, she and Elsie could have been
ghosts to each other, but there was no pretending away flesh
and blood.

"Oh, May," Phoebe said. "I honestly thought . . . But okay.
Let's forget that part. The part that's good is there Eddie and I
were with two of the men who pretty much run things, and
Eddie fit right in. I mean, he was himself but the best part of
himself. He really does love to think of ways to fix things. At
first I thought it just might be little things, but he turned to
Mr. Salviatti and asked what was under the tennis court—
all that about gravel and frost and soil compression. Just a
friendly chat about what most people don't stop to consider. I
was really proud of Eddie. And when Jack said, 'Can you get
it done before winter?' Eddie said, 'Depends on two things.
The weather's one. The other's what Phoebe can work out
with her schedule. She's the manager.' After all the snubs
I've had—and it's not just Miss Perry; Jack Aldrich looks at
my legs but can't be bothered to remember my name—I felt
validated."

Phoebe had distracted her for a moment. May was glad
for Eddie, and she tried to hold on to that bit of cheer, but
when Phoebe swung round at the end to toot her own horn,
May went into the dark again. Elsie, Phoebe—they were like
water, water running into everything, wherever there was a
crack or a weak spot, they puddled up and then streamed on
through. And then no again. If she felt helpless, it was her
own fault. If she ducked away whenever she heard Elsie's
name, it was her own fault. No sense in blaming Phoebe for
bringing the news about Elsie Buttrick. There might be no
end to Elsie Buttrick, but there was no way of knowing about
that unless she got out and took Elsie's measure. Let Elsie
know that she and her daughter didn't live in some other
world. Elsie might get herself up in her uniform, she might

have the run of Miss Perry's house, she might play tennis in that bubble at Sawtooth, but she got her daughter out of this family right here.

May said, "That's good for you and Eddie. You got your work cut out for you, though. There's usually a good-sized gale about now."

"Oh, I know," Phoebe said. "I love summer, I love winter. It's fall that depresses me."

May kept from saying "You can't pick and choose." She herself liked fall, the hard November fall—the first bite of cold, the trees bare, the spartina in the salt marsh blown into a tangled cover for the part of life that was meant to winter over.

chapter fifteen

Elsie let Miss Peebles go, kept Sylvia Teixeira on for a couple of hours in the afternoon and Nancy Tran to spend the night.

Miss Perry could now use the telephone and even the answering machine. She and Elsie took short walks around the garden and then longer ones up and down the driveway, Miss Perry's arm in Elsie's, *"Bras dessous, bras dessus,"* as Miss Perry suddenly remembered.

Miss Perry was now quite fluent. If she got stuck on a word, she flowed around it. One day she asked, "Is there another . . . another sending our army to fight?"

"War," Elsie said. "No. Not now."

And then one day as they were walking, Miss Perry said, "Yes. Shall we go up to your house? I feel quite fit today."

"I'm afraid it's a mess."

"We don't have to go in." Miss Perry stopped and freed Elsie. "I am sorry I called you a ragamuffin. These days I can't say why I say some things. Senseless. The parts of me that ought to keep silent make bubbles that burst. And the things I want to say all too often elude me." Miss Perry took Elsie's arm again and started up Elsie's driveway. "What is odd at my age is to feel oneself as unaccountably changeable as an adolescent. I was reading a simple little poem from *A Child's Garden of Verses*. 'The Lamplighter'—'O Leerie, I'll go round at night and light the lamps with you!'—and I began to weep. I read those to Charlie and Tom Pierce when they were little. It may have been that. When I was a child we had an Irish maid of whom I was fond. Possibly that, too." Miss Perry stopped to readjust her arm in Elsie's. "On the other hand, some things strike me as funny in a new and peculiar way. At first my snappishness and weeping and laughing made me feel as if I was not myself. Now I suppose I am myself but that my boundaries have shifted, perhaps for the better, in the long run for the better. Though not intellectually." Miss Perry's shoulder moved. Elsie wasn't sure if it was a sigh or a very soft laugh. "Quite the reverse. I fear this will be too grand a comparison, but I have been reconsidering the last days of Rome. The emperors are transient and weak, the senate fearful, the people dwindling. The Huns have come and gone, the walls have been breached and will be soon again. If one's point of view remains Roman, it is indeed bleak. But there is a great deal going on in Pannonia, Gaul, Iberia, North Africa, even the British Isles. Amazing voyages of tribes, some admirable chieftains. Gibbon is helpful here in his way, but I imagine there is much more than marches and countermarches. Gibbon leaps from battle to battle, pausing only for a plague or a scandal at the Byzantine court. But there are decades and decades of unrecorded life, which I am now imagining as full of the enterprises of unlettered but resourceful people."

Elsie was astounded.

Miss Perry said, "Did I say that clearly? I may have mud-dled—"

"No, no, I understand. Rome is your . . . Rome was your center, your mind. And now your feelings are moving on their own like the barbarians. And you're changing your mind about the barbarians. Maybe there was more to them . . ." Miss Perry stood still. She looked at Elsie, her eyes enormous behind the lenses. Elsie said, "I think you're speaking better than the ninety percent the doctor thought."

Miss Perry shook her head. "I must confess I rehearsed that speech. I said it aloud when I was alone."

It was only a few more steps to her house. Elsie felt warmed and confident. She said, "Shall we go in? We can have tea."

After Elsie opened the door she took Miss Perry's hand. There was a step down into the main room. She settled Miss Perry on the sofa in full view of the playpen, the baby bottle on the table, the swing set with a padded safety seat. Elsie watched Miss Perry look from one thing to another. She paused at the Exercycle. Elsie said, "Oh. That's mine." And then in a rush, as though to another mother, "If Rose is still awake when I want to exercise, I put her in the swing seat and wind it up—it has a spring mechanism that rocks her. And she seems to like the sound of the Exercycle."

Miss Perry said, "Rose. And where is Rose now?"

"She's with Mary Scanlon. I usually pick her up about now."

"But Rose is your child?"

"Yes. I've been meaning to tell you, but it was . . . difficult to know when. I didn't know . . . I didn't want to add another perplexity, but at the same time I thought—and then I knew you remembered." Elsie took a breath and said, "But mainly I was afraid of what you would think of me."

Miss Perry sat still. After a while she said, "I'm being quite slow. But I think I would be slow even if I was not . . . already slow. I am supposing . . . your last remark leads me to sup-pose that you are not married."

Elsie said, "No. Not married."

"How very difficult. And I'm afraid I have made your life even more difficult. That is the first thing that occurs to me. But you are worried about what I will think of you." Miss Perry closed her eyes, breathed, opened them. She said, "I never thought you would do as you were told. I knew that much long ago. I admired your spirit. My only worry then was that you would involve other people in your adventures, other people who did not have your resilience. You and I are coming back to me as we were then, and I'm afraid I can't avoid a schoolmistress sigh. But perhaps the father is as resiliently free as you, and perhaps your daughter will be as well." Miss Perry rested for several breaths. "Now," she said. "Now we are friends. There is no justice between friends, as Aristotle has it, which is to say there is no judgment because each one wishes the best for the other."

Elsie heard this as high-minded iciness. Miss Perry pulling Aristotle out of her hat to remind herself of duty. Elsie had had a spurt of hope—for what? Unqualified forgiveness and sympathy?

When she was alone with Rose she didn't swing back and forth between anxiety and hope, shame and defiance. She said, "I'll drive you back. I've got to go get Rose."

They rolled down the hill in silence. Elsie helped Miss Perry out of the car, through the door, and toward the stairs. Miss Perry stopped and said, "I believe I'll go to the library. Nancy Tran will be here later, will she not?"

"Yes. I'll stop by again, too."

"It's much nicer here now that Miss Peebles is gone. I get on very well. I don't want to be an extra burden."

"No, don't worry. Of course, now that you know all about Rose, I could bring her with me sometimes."

Miss Perry said, "I'm afraid I don't very much like babies."

Elsie laughed. Then went numb, as if she'd been slapped. When she drove off she couldn't remember if she'd turned and left or helped Miss Perry into the library.

chapter sixteen

It snowed around the clock. The snow drifted up to the bottom panes of the northeast-corner windows. Dick brought *Spartina* in just ahead of the worst of the blizzard. He took the Tran boy to the hospital with what he was pretty sure was a broken arm, then he went back to the boat. Tony Teixeira unloaded the catch with the help of some of the crew from *Bom Sonho*. Captain Teixeira (Tony's great-uncle) had brought her in earlier but still had his crew stripping her for some refitting.

Dick told all this to May when he came home. Then he said, "Looks like I'll be underfoot for a while."

May was a little surprised at his soft tone. She said, "How'd he break his arm?"

"Fell. I didn't see it. First thing I noticed was him trying to do something with one hand. Tugging at a pot, then holding on to a stay, then tugging again. We were bouncing around some. I got him below. Still stuff to do on deck. By the time I got a chance to look at him his arm was swollen. It was time to head home, anyway." He stretched his legs out. "I feel bad for the kid."

"I'm sure it wasn't your fault."

"I didn't say I felt guilty. Just bad for him. He's a good kid. I should have started him on a full share earlier. He and Tony get along."

Dick was sounding drowsy now, talking into his chest. She hoped he wouldn't nod off before supper. He didn't take naps well, woke up cross. She said, "You want a cup of coffee? The boys'll be back soon."

"No, thanks. Maybe a little fresh air. It's awful warm in here. Let's go for a walk."

"In all this snow?"

"Yeah. Put your boots on. Just down to where we can see the salt marsh."

May didn't feel like it, but she didn't want this mood of his to change. The wind had died. The snow was falling steadily, but if she looked through it she could make out the snow-covered hummocks, the black creek bank with fringes of ice at its foot. The creek itself was still running, swallowing the falling snow.

Dick stopped and stared. May moved closer to him. He put his arm around her and said, "Not cold, are you?" He looked for a while longer and then started back. He said, "Old Captain Teixeira just keeps going. Says he's retiring but still goes out. Not every time. I don't know what he does all day when he doesn't. His daughters run the bakery and the rest of them run the fish store. I guess he keeps busy looking in on his family. Oh. He asked after Charlie and Tom and you. I was kind of at a loss, I couldn't remember all his kids' names. Had to say something like, 'All your family doing okay?' I asked Tony how he remembers all the Teixeira kids, and Tony said, 'I'm used to a big family—all you got is two.'"

May said, "Three." Dick hunched his shoulders and walked back to the house. For a moment May wished she hadn't opened her mouth. Then she ran after him. She caught up to him by the back door. She said, "So it's against the law to say anything? Is that it?"

Dick nodded at the door. "I think the boys are back."

"And when are they going to find out?"

"Not now."

"You think everybody's life stops when you go to sea? Mine doesn't. I don't disappear. Elsie doesn't disappear. Your daughter doesn't disappear. Elsie and Rose don't just stay put up in that little house. And it's not so little now that Eddie's added a room. And how come? So Mary Scanlon can live there and help Elsie take care of Rose. You go out in your boat and it's you say and your crew does. You come back and you make your list of things to fix on the boat. Maybe you better start another list."

"What makes you think I don't think about all that? Because I do think about it. It's not something to just toss around."

"I imagine you and Elsie Buttrick talked—"

"You through?"

"Oh, go ahead and clench up. But I'm not going to be the one tiptoeing around pretending nobody knows. Fact is, I've got a mind to go up there and see this child of yours."

"I'm going in." Dick put his hand on the doorknob but turned around. "I may go check on the boat. Take the boys. Let 'em see what puts supper on the table."

He went in. May thought of ways to hurt him. She thought of ways to hurt herself. She pushed both away.

"What puts supper on the table"—he said that. But before that he'd put his arm around her. He'd been talking about old Captain Teixeira; he'd been drifting into thinking about how he'd be when he got old. Old and what? Settled? Happy? And she'd said three. Then blistered him when he walked away. Did she want to be the one who got angry? Was that the choice? Angry or sad? Something else was going on in her. Those things she'd said—she couldn't remember them all, but just saying them had opened up a new part of her. Dick had a whole stretch of sea to roam around in—she only had her way of looking at things, and she hadn't gone very far from where she started, just stayed at home. Imagining her life becoming bigger made her dizzy. But at the same time she felt less at the mercy of unhappiness.

She stopped worrying about what to say to Dick when he got back. She would make supper, he'd come in, he'd say something or he wouldn't. Didn't matter if he groused or acted sheepish. She'd just see how *she* felt.

chapter seventeen

Phoebe telephoned early the next morning. Dick was still asleep. Charlie and Tom were outside throwing snowballs at each other across the backyard. Phoebe said she was going up to see Mr. Salviatti's statues, and would May like to come along? May said yes and laughed.

Phoebe said, "Well, you're in a good mood."

"Good timing's more like it. The boys are on vacation and Dick's back. I'd just as soon let them look after themselves for a bit."

When they got in Phoebe's car, Phoebe said, "I may be flattering myself, but it occurred to me . . . Maybe it's all non-sense, but I did have some let us say 'awkward' moments in Italy. Of course that was years ago. Anyway, when I asked if I could bring a friend, Mr. Salviatti said, 'Certainly, certainly,' perfectly nicely."

"Oh," May said. "You thought he might get fresh?"

"He is an old charmer—not *that* old. Oh, I fibbed a little bit and said you'd been to see the RISD show."

"What?"

"Oh, I know. It just came out in a rush, and I don't think he was paying attention." Phoebe reached into the backseat and handed May a folder. "I saved the catalog."

"I'm not much good at pretending."

"You can take a look and . . . I'm sorry, it was just this little bit that popped out. It's not as if he's going to . . . I mean, we'll go into the garden and then we'll see them and if we talk about anything, we'll talk about that."

They stopped at a large gate. May was impressed that

Phoebe immediately knew what to do. She herself hadn't noticed a little brass grille in the middle of one of the pillars. Phoebe got out and said something into it. May saw the puffs of Phoebe's breath. The gate swung open all by itself.

Mr. Salviatti came out to meet them. Standing at the top of the steps, he opened his arms. "Mrs. Fitzgerald, Mrs. Pierce—welcome." He came down and shook their hands. "If you don't mind, we'll go right to the garden. Then we can have a cup of coffee and get warm. Good—you've got the right kind of boots. All this snow. But it gives a different look to the angels."

May thought his garden was beautiful. It was big—the size of a football field. Walled in. There were apple and pear trees in squares, their black limbs dusted with snow. Along the paths there was green—rhododendron, arborvitae, and dwarf juniper. There were things that looked like haystacks along the north wall. Mr. Salviatti came up beside her. "My fig trees. They would die in this weather, so we cut them back and make overcoats for them. Out of straw."

Phoebe had gone straight to one of the angels. She gave a little cry. "Oh, I'm so glad it snowed! They're so gorgeous in the snow."

Mr. Salviatti went to her. May followed in his footprints. She found the angel a little frightening. She had to look up to it even though it was kneeling on one knee. It? She? There was a sort of gown, but the chin, nose, and cheeks were large and definite. The outstretched hand was broad and had knuckles like a man's. The wings had bits of snow caught in the carved feathers, which made them look more like scales. The two angels in the corner of the garden were smaller and much sadder. They faced each other, heads bowed, their hands— smaller and prettier—pressed together in prayer. May felt she was being asked to believe in something Catholic.

Phoebe examined the smaller angels—walked around them, touched the hands. She said something, and her breath drifted past the mouth of an angel so that it appeared for an instant that the angel had breathed. There was something wrong, May thought, in making real-life pictures of things that were meant to be invisible. It was as if horror movies and religion got mixed up.

She was glad Phoebe was finding plenty to say. She didn't know what she herself would talk about when they went in. Mr. Salviatti walked back to her. "Mrs. Pierce, you may not remember, but we met once, a long time ago."

"Yes."

"I miss your husband at the boatyard. I'm glad he's doing well for himself, of course, but the boatyard isn't the same." Mr. Salviatti rubbed his hands together. "And the angels— are they in the right place? Or should we put them in the middle?"

"Oh, not in the middle. I like your garden. It's like Miss Perry's but bigger. And more out in the open. I can imagine what that north wall looks like when the fig trees leaf out. But to tell the truth, that big angel is sort of frightening. Maybe that's just me—I wouldn't want to think about death when I'm gardening."

"Ah. Of course. You're right—the statues were meant to be in a cemetery. But the hand—the way the hand is reaching out—what is it saying?"

May thought she'd already said too much. She looked at Mr. Salviatti. He lifted his arm so it was doing the same thing as the angel's. She said, "I guess it's saying that it's time. It's all over."

"Ah. Yes. That would be if the hand is lifted over a living person. But I think of it as over a grave, and it means rest. Don't be frightened, just rest." He smiled. "Not so bad, then. Am I changing your mind at all?"

"Maybe. Maybe a little."

"I'll tell you another thing. It's technically more difficult to make a statue with the arms away from the body like that. So when I look at it I think of the man working on it. When you saw the exhibit you saw the name of who made it." May thought she should tell him Phoebe had—what?—been confused. But Mr. Salviatti went on. "Ugo Serra. But it didn't say that's my uncle. My mother's brother. When I was a boy, I saw him work. So I like it when someone like you sees it fresh. And I like it that you think it's frightening. Don't let me talk you out of it."

Phoebe joined them, and Mr. Salviatti asked them to come inside and get warm.

The view from the main room was wide and long. When she was down in the harbor and looked out to sea, Block Island was on the horizon—from up here it was well this side of it. There was the sound, then the island, and then a good stretch of ocean before it glimmered into the gray sky. Closer in, she saw the tip of Sawtooth Point, the roof of the Wedding Cake. Still closer but to the east there was the end of Rocky Bound Pond and then the tall trees that hid Miss Perry's house. And then the rise where Elsie Buttrick had her house. May felt a satisfaction—this was the view she wished for, the map she'd used to comfort herself. The houses and the people were hedged in by trees that in their slow growth outdid whatever else went on, absorbed the breaths of all the creatures who ran around wanting one thing and another.

The same maid who'd taken their coats brought in a tray with two coffee pots and crinkly pastries. May wondered where Mrs. Salviatti was.

"Come have some coffee," Mr. Salviatti said to May. He pointed to the bigger pot. "This is American, the other is Italian."

Phoebe said, "I love Italian coffee."

May joined them but picked a seat so she could still look out the plate-glass window. When she sat down, the far wall of the garden cut off the end of the pond, the near wall the first rows of fruit trees. She said, "If your angel is putting out her hand to say rest, it'd be nice if you put her so she's looking out to sea."

Phoebe said, "Oh, May," as if to say, "What's got into you?"

"Ah. So she'd be telling the sea to be calm," Mr. Salviatti said. "That's good. I'll think about that. My older daughter wants me to move it somewhere else. She knows I'm thinking of having it over my grave, and she says she doesn't want to think about that every day. My younger daughter, she's not around enough to have an opinion."

"Is she at college?" Phoebe said.

"She was. Off and on. You know how that goes—finding herself. You have kids, you love them—" Mr. Salviatti lifted his hand and let it fall. "You love them and then they go away."

"You have two daughters . . . ," Phoebe said.

"That's it—just the two."

May said, "A pigeon's clutch."

Mr. Salviatti laughed. "I'll bet you got that from Mary Scanlon. That's an Irish saying. She's got a million. And songs. Every time I go to Sawtooth, I look in on the kitchen—she's got three pans on the stove, one in the oven, two other cooks she's keeping in line, and when she's not talking over her shoulder at them, she's singing. One time I went in and she was holding a baby in one arm, stirring soup with the other, always singing. So it's crazy in there, but good cooks are a little bit crazy, like artists. I told Jack—you know Jack Aldrich—I told him just leave her alone."

May felt as if she was picked up by a wave. No weight to her, her feet and hands somewhere far away, her body suspended, her eyes open but telling her nothing about up or down.

She didn't think she said anything, but perhaps she made a sound. Phoebe and Mr. Salviatti looked at her. She put her cup and saucer on the table, pressed her feet to the floor. She decided to go see Elsie and the baby.

chapter eighteen

Mary Scanlon's little pickup had four-wheel drive. When Mary went to work, Elsie was left with her old Volvo, which wasn't any good in snow. She called Miss Perry's house and talked to Nancy Tran. Everything was fine. Time for a day off. Just Rose and her.

She bundled Rose up and went to the new shed. In the jumble of outdoor toys Sally had dropped off there was a plastic sled—just a bowl, really. She put Rose in it and pulled it to the back of the house. She held on to the rope and lowered the sled to the edge of the pond. She walked onto the ice. Thick enough. She pulled the sled halfway up the slope, set Rose in her lap, and slid down. They picked up some speed as they went over the bank and ended up in the middle of the pond, slowly turning.

"What do you think, Rose? Fun?"

Rose made noises. She hadn't said a recognizable word yet, but she'd begun to make noises that seemed to have the rhythm of conversation.

"So we'll do it again. From the top. Or shall we just lie here?" Elsie spun them around with her feet, and Rose laughed. Elsie acknowledged laughing but not Mary's reports of singing or saying words. Elsie was the skeptic and was annoyed at Mary for making her the skeptic. Mary, in addition to singing to Rose, talked baby talk to her. When Mary was around, Elsie found herself speaking in formal complete sentences to Rose. Now that she and Rose were alone, she just opened her mouth and wrapped Rose in whatever came out. "She says she doesn't like babies. What was that about? Was it just an aftershock?"

Elsie spun them around again. Rose said, "Ah," and then higher, "Ah, ah."

Elsie said, "Okay. I give in. We'll call that singing." Elsie gave another push with her feet. As they spun to face the house, Elsie saw May walk past the station wagon. May disappeared on the other side of the house. Elsie lay still. When she heard May knock on the door, her feet skittered on the snow and the ice, moving the sled a yard or two. More knocking. Elsie turned Rose toward her. She had to twist herself onto her knees to get up. She had no idea; she had a storm of ideas. May reappeared. She might have walked back down the driveway without seeing them. Elsie waved.

May turned her head and stopped. Then she walked down to the pond. Elsie stood still. May came across the ice, taking small shuffling steps that left a channel in the snow. Elsie had forgotten that May was taller than she. Most of the times Elsie thought of May, May was an invisible presence that came up through her and filled her. This May, in her wool overcoat with a scarf over her head, emptied her.

May took off a glove and moved the side of Rose's hood. She stared at Rose's face. Rose lifted a hand. Elsie took off Rose's mittens, May touched Rose's palm, and Rose held on to May's finger. May bent her head, and it seemed natural to Elsie to lift Rose higher. Perhaps because Rose felt herself being lifted, she turned and raised her arms. May picked her up and began to rock her gently with a little sway of her hips. Rose put her fingers in her mouth and drooled. May made a little noise, as near to a laugh as Rose's noise had been. May wiped the drool away with her fingers and dried them on her coat without taking her eyes off Rose.

"You're a good baby," May said. "You're a pretty girl."

Elsie said, "It may be time for her bottle. Would you like to come in?"

May handed Rose back to Elsie and said, "I don't believe I can just now."

"Perhaps another time."

May looked up at Elsie's house, then back at Rose. "Perhaps." Elsie shifted Rose to her shoulder and dropped Rose's mitten. May picked it up. She said, "That's hand-knit."

"Yes. Mary Scanlon knits." May put the mitten on Rose's hand. Elsie said, "Mary takes care of Rose most mornings. Here and then at Sawtooth. I'm here after five. Unless I'm with Miss Perry."

"Yes," May said. "Miss Perry."

Elsie couldn't tell if May was weighing good deeds against bad or if she was still wondering what it would be like to go into the house. Elsie had no idea what details May might have asked Dick to tell, what pictures came to May's mind. Now it was just as well they were outside, bundled up in winter coats.

May said, "I think Dick should see her. I think he should see her over at our house."

Elsie took a step back. Then she pretended she was looking for the sled. She bent down and picked up the rope. May said, "Here. You'll need both hands going up the hill." May took the rope and led the way, walking in the footprints she'd made. She stopped halfway up and looked at the attached greenhouse.

Elsie said, "I usually have some greens, but this year . . ."

May didn't say anything. When they reached the driveway, Elsie said, "Did you leave your car down by Miss Perry's?"

"I walked. It's not that far." May leaned the sled against the side of the house. "You haven't said anything." May sounded mild but deliberate. "You haven't said anything about what I said."

"I thought . . . I would have thought . . ." Elsie felt herself flustering. She took a breath and said, "I thought it would be better if we kept apart."

May put her glove on and folded her hands. "That'd be fine. If it was just about you and Dick." Elsie felt herself out of time with May's steady matter-of-factness. She wondered if May knew what it felt like to listen to these long pauses and short sentences. And then she thought that was the way Dick talked.

"You could keep Rose to yourself," May said. "Or . . . Dick could come over here. Least that way Rose would know her father. But then Dick might end up thinking he's got two families. If Rose comes over to see us, then she's the one with two families."

Elsie made a noise. It sounded like the yip of a dog having a dream. Rose stiffened. May nodded once, as if Elsie had said something conversational. May said, "Charlie and Tom don't know. They will. It's getting to be not much of a secret. I expect they'll be hard on Dick for a while. Course not so hard as if they heard it somewhere else."

Elsie hadn't thought—or hadn't let herself think—about Charlie and Tom, about Charlie and Tom judging her. She shrank from it. Then she tightened. She felt herself grow sharper. Had May been busy figuring out more ways to make her feel bad?

She looked at May. May was pulling the ends of her scarf tighter, her eyes on the ground. Whatever energy had brought her up the hill was spent. Elsie didn't dare imagine the pain and anger May had felt, but she imagined May now. She imagined that May's short, practical sentences weren't an attack—they were May's trying to shift the weight she carried, not that it would be lighter but that there would be some relief if she could carry it differently.

If Charlie and Tom learned about Rose, they would sympathize with May, and that would be part of May's relief. Hard on Dick. That might be part of the relief, too. Then Elsie wondered how much further along May imagined all this. Did May see herself and her sons sitting around with Dick as he dandled Rose on his knee? Or did May imagine Rose in her own arms? Did she imagine herself growing fond of Rose? And Rose fond of her? And what about when Rose was six or seven? Summer boating with all the Pierces and Elsie—and

Mary Scanlon and Miss Perry, too? Jolly flounder fishing, a birthday party?

Elsie looked at the black and white of the trees and snow around them, the hard, low sky. She said, "Just how do you see these visits working?"

May looked up. "Bit by bit. I could get a car seat for Rose. Pick her up one day when Dick's home. The boys back in school."

"I'm afraid Rose would be afraid."

May considered this, nodded. "Maybe you or Mary Scanlon. She's used to Mary, I guess. One of you could come along till she's used to us." May shivered and wrapped her arms across her chest. She said, "Dick was good with babies. When the boys were babies. He's been a good father. Strict about work, but when they do a good job, he says so."

"Work . . . I don't think I've looked that far into Rose's future. I'm just trying to fit in next month's doctor's appointment."

May said, "Dick's helping with all that—still making a regular contribution?" She said it mildly.

"Oh, I didn't mean . . . Yes, he is."

May nodded. She said, "I expect you'll want to think it over. It's time for me to get back, anyway."

"I wish I could give you a ride. It's awful cold. I'm just afraid I couldn't get back up the driveway."

"I'll warm up once I start walking." May took a few steps and turned around. "Eddie could do your driveway. I know he's got a couple of his boys out plowing. Or is he still shy about coming onto Miss Perry's property?"

"No. I mean yes, he can come up the driveway. You're right, I should call him."

"If he's out, you can talk to Phoebe Fitzgerald. She's over at their office now. She gets on a CB and talks to him in his truck. No sense in your being stuck."

Elsie watched her until she got past the first turn. It was the last part of the conversation—about Eddie—that lingered. What did it mean that May could just talk to her about the driveway, calm and neighborly? She took Rose inside. Rose began to fuss. Elsie touched her cheeks. They were very cold, probably hurt as they warmed up.

"I know, Rose, I know. It'll get better in a minute."

She heard her voice, saw her fingers unzipping Rose's snowsuit. She slid Rose's arms out of the sleeves, her feet out of the quilted booties and legs. She put Rose into the swing, but Rose fussed. Elsie picked her back up and walked her around the room. When she stopped moving, Rose fussed again. "What's the story, Rose?" If she'd had a hand free, she would have smacked her forehead. "Oh, yeah. Bottle."

They settled on the sofa while Rose sucked on her bottle. Elsie thought she should call Eddie. She should turn on a light. She should stand up and do something or she would sink. She couldn't bring herself to the phone. The afternoon was nothing but heavy emptiness. It had taken her ten breaths to get to her feet when it was time to feed Rose. Once Rose was asleep, Elsie went to bed half undressed. Whatever there was to be done, whatever she felt, whatever facts there were—all equal. Nothing connected, anything connected.

chapter nineteen

Elsie woke up to a clanking and scraping. She went out in her bathrobe and boots. Eddie was plowing the driveway. It turned out Mary had called him. He was sorry to be making a racket this early, but he had to get over to Sawtooth, couldn't fit the driveway in once he got going with his crew—cold as it was, he had to keep the boys moving.

Eddie's good cheer would have weighed her down last evening. She'd barely been able to get Rose in her crib. Now she was hungry and cold but ready to do one thing at a time. She got Rose into the crib in Mary's room without waking either of them. When she got to the Great Swamp office nobody wanted to go outdoors, so she volunteered to take a tour. She drove back home and got her touring skis.

She parked on the south side of Worden Pond, saw two ice-fishing huts near the north shore, almost a mile away. Halfway across, she wasn't having fun. When the wind gusted it almost stopped her, sent cold air up the skirt of her jacket.

The fishermen had pulled their huts onto the ice with an all-terrain vehicle. The tracks came from the eastern shore, not from the Great Swamp Reservation, and they had their fishing licenses pinned on their hats. Elsie smelled whiskey, figured they were lacing their coffee. Nice old navy retirees, called her "Miss." Not likely to freeze—they were as round as barrels in their orange snowmobile suits. She recognized one of them when he pulled back his hood to sip from his thermos. "Hello, chief. You the designated driver?" Her face was too stiff from cold to smile, so she added, "Hope you catch a mess of fish."

She headed for shore toward the only high ground in the swamp, a drumlin just big enough to break the wind.

In a cove some wintering-over Canada geese and a couple of ducks had kept a small pool of water free of ice. She wondered again—was it instinct or did they figure out that paddling around kept the water from freezing? Did they take turns? When they flew in their vee, they took turns being the lead goose. They took turns at sentry duty when they were feeding—there was always one with his neck stretched up, swiveling like a periscope, while the others waddled around, beaks to the ground.

She got off the ice and shuffled along the lee side of the drumlin. She wasn't getting much glide. If she came back in the tracks she made, she'd sail along. Fun later on.

She saw rabbit tracks, the paw prints close together on the wind-packed snow. Walking, pausing—nibbling the bush tops? Then the prints were suddenly farther apart, the forepaws overtaken by the hind feet pushing off together. The prints swerved left, then right. Then a hole in the snow. No more tracks. On either side of the shallow hole there were faint ridges—the marks of wing tips. A streak of blood on the broken crust. Owl? Hawk? Night? Day? She looked up the hill. A lot of scrub but some taller trees. An owl or hawk could perch up there, have a good view of the open ground—come down fast.

She touched the blood. It was frozen into beads—but that could have happened in less than an hour. The wind wasn't fierce on this side of the hill, but it was still sweeping the loose powder along the crust, would have filled in the tracks if the kill had been last night. Most likely a hawk, though she'd seen owls hunt by day. One fall afternoon—her first year on the job—a great horned owl had followed her, hovering only twenty feet above her head. It had frightened her at first. With its wings at full spread and its face looking down, she saw it against the sky as flat as a painting; only the slightest movements kept it aloft. It didn't come any closer, and she wondered more calmly what it was doing, began to admire its ease, even had a moment of fairy-tale giddiness—perhaps wild animals sensed her kindred spirit.

The owl had suddenly swooped into the knee-high grass a stone's throw ahead of her. When it lumbered up into the air she saw it had a mouse in its talons. After a moment she realized that her walking through the grass had been stirring up whatever was hiding there—any creature that would have been better off staying still. The owl had been using her as its spaniel. So much for her as Saint Francis.

Then she'd wondered how the owl worked this out. Perhaps one time it had seen a fox or a stray dog trot across a field and noticed the scampering away of a field mouse, chipmunk, or rabbit, or the slithering of a garter snake. The owl had seen her disturbance long before she saw the owl.

After that she stopped thinking of herself as an unobserved observer. Any patch of ground was web upon web of awareness. Even if she was crouched in the bushes with her binoculars, invisible to other humans, she was giving off body heat sensed by ticks, odors that attracted deer flies. Even the littlest flash of color attracted something—a butterfly once landed on her cheek, perhaps mistaking her bright eyes and dark nostrils for what? Something in the iris family?

So she was sensed as well as sensing—but for a while she'd kept on thinking of herself as a central-exchange operator and a slow-but-sure decoder of everything. Then, as she read and thought about a hawk's eyesight, a dog's nose, a bat's sonar (which certain moths could feel and then save themselves by folding their wings and plummeting), a goose's migration (possibly navigated by the earth's magnetic fields—the jury was still out on that)—she gave up.

She'd spent some time in anger and frustration at what she wouldn't ever know. Then some time in a shriven state for having presumed too much. A little comeback—she knew more than most people. But even if true, so what? And at last an easier attitude. It wasn't her job to know everything but to know enough to let some other people know enough to wonder. Be fierce enough to keep out the vandals. Encourage the teachable—"Be not afraid, the isle is full of noises, / Sounds and sweet airs, that give delight and hurt not." At least if you're higher on the food chain than a rabbit.

She worked back from the crumpled snow along the trail of zigzag leaps, of creeping and nibbling. Then back to the edge of the woods. The undergrowth was too thick to go through on her skis, but she followed the trail with her eye. A crisscrossing of rabbit tracks in there. Had the senior rabbits claimed the rights to the nearby food and forced junior out into the field? Were rabbits less cooperative than geese? Or was junior just a silly rabbit?

She'd ask Eddie. He knew more about animals, at least edible animals, than her colleagues. She missed running into

Eddie out in the woods. She wondered—was Phoebe Fitzgerald ruining his life or was he happy making his fortune? How odd it had been to see Eddie and Phoebe walk in on her, along with Jack and Mr. Salviatti. And then Jack almost leering about her and Johnny Bienvenue. So everyone got to wonder about odd couples. Eddie surprised her. She'd known him as capable in the woods, almost tongue-tied with most people and thrown into a complete tailspin by Miss Perry, or even the mention of her name. But he'd spoken up to Jack and Mr. Salviatti with assurance, almost in asides, as he looked over the building problem. Phoebe had turned this way and that, and every male but Eddie had taken it in—the willowy sway, the pleated skirt brushing her pretty calves, the wide eyes and slightly parted lips. This would have amused Elsie if she hadn't noticed a flick of Phoebe's eyes toward her, a snapshot assessment of Elsie bundled up in sweatpants.

And yet here she was on a cold winter's day hoping that Phoebe was preening for Eddie and that Eddie was taking a step forward. Now that she was out of the wind, she was full of goodwill. No question about it, when she was moving around out here she was nicer than she was anywhere else. Unless, of course, she ran into an offender against her territory. Part of it was fresh air, sunlight, maybe endorphins. But most of all it was her eyesight ranging out, going from wide focus to narrow when her eyes lit on a detail that led to another. Another part was more elusive. Once in a great while she was released from figuring things out, from knowing or not knowing, and she felt herself displaced by a wordless humming alertness beyond well-being.

Not today. Today was okay. Low end of well-being. Too cold for more.

She set off again, a few long strides in her own tracks, then had to break trail. She was grateful for this snowfall, not just for the pleasure of ski touring but for the benefit of other animals. A foot or so beneath the snow, voles were having a fine time in their grass-lined passages and rooms, insulated from the cold wind, hidden from foxes and feral cats. Their only alarm would be as they felt the vibrations of her skis across the top of their world.

By noon she reached the railroad embankment, which served as a windbreak for her when she turned northeast. No need to patrol the Great Swamp Fight site, somebody on duty there. Even from inside the building they could keep an eye on things.

At the northeast corner of the reservation there was a rise of open ground. It fell away more steeply to the east, enough shelter from the wind for a deer yard. The low ground was bordered by the Chipuxet River—shelter, water, enough vegetation by the stream for browsing. Elsie was of two minds about deer—admirable runners and astounding leapers, but now that there weren't any natural predators, there were too many deer munching on young trees. She wouldn't mind more guys like Eddie—like Eddie used to be—stalking the herd with his homemade crossbow. What she didn't like were the guys spraying buckshot or slugs that could go through a car door, too wired with buck fever to wait for a sure kill and too ignorant or lazy to track a wounded deer. The only time she'd fired her own pistol had been to put down a cripple. She'd hauled the deer out and brought it to Eddie. He dug a trench with his backhoe and buried it. Explained that unless the deer was killed quick the meat was more than likely spoiled. "Adrenaline or something. You know how when you almost have a car accident your mouth tastes funny? Like zinc. A wounded deer tastes like that. If a deer doesn't know what hit him—if it's just lights out—then you get some sweet meat. Course you got to hoist him on the spot, gut him, and drain the blood." He'd said "him," but she knew he took a doe as often as a buck. Fine with her. Even a few surviving bucks could service the does. To reduce the herd you had to kill does.

Elsie slogged up the hill, the wind at her back. She crossed to a fringe of brush and picked her way to the edge of the eastern slope. She saw trampled snow in the dell, then fluffs of vapor farther back in the scrub, and then some movement.

She'd noticed on her own—and Eddie had confirmed—that the way deer spotted a human was primarily by the movement of arms and legs. They also seemed to see something alarming in a face. Maybe just the eyes. Most wild things were alert to eyes—butterflies and fish often displayed large eyelike patterns on their wings or flanks, just enough of a fake to make a predator hesitate. Was that bite-sized prey or the head of something big and dangerous?

Elsie pulled her wool cap over her eyes, stretched tight so that she could see through it. She pushed off downhill, then tucked her arms and poles behind her and squatted. She'd done this a couple of times before, got to within twenty feet of a deer before it bolted.

She was sliding fairly slowly, the powder snow pushing up around her ankles. Two or three deer lifted their heads. With their large sideways eyes they could see in a greater arc than a human—they could even see a bit behind them—but they had little depth perception unless they focused both eyes to the front.

When she'd first skied up to a deer herd, she'd pretended it was field research. Logged it in: deer, close observation of. Now she was having fun.

Halfway down the slope she heard a shot. She saw deer start to run, a stream of brown dotted with white tails. She heard another shot. Through the knit of her hat she saw with eerie clarity a white streak across the bark of a tree just ahead of her. She tossed herself sideways, slid on her hip and hand. She had to gasp a breath before she could shout. No idea what she said. Maybe just "Hey!" She pulled her hat up off her face. Another breath. She yelled, "Don't shoot!" She didn't lift her head. She was still uphill from where the shots came from. Somewhere off to her right. She pulled herself toward a tree trunk with her hands. The straps of the poles rode up her forearms, tugging her sleeves up. Her mouth tasted like zinc—Eddie was right about that. Her web belt had twisted so her holster was in the middle of her back. Her skis were anchored in the snow.

She wriggled backward so she could reach the bindings, head down, ass in the air. She was pushed onto her side as if someone had kicked her. Her right buttock stung, then hurt like hell. She pulled herself to the tree trunk. Was she behind it? Where was the gun? She tried to yell. It came out a bleat. She took a breath and yelled, "No!" She took off her gloves, reached back where it hurt. The seat of her pants was shredded. Her hand was wet. She looked at it. A smear of blood. Goddamn fool shot her. Shot her in the ass. Okay, she wasn't dying. But the dumb son of a bitch could have killed her. Still out there with his gun. She held her breath so she could hear. Nothing. Had he heard her yell? She felt her ass again. Touched her holster. She pulled out her revolver, fired a shot into the air.

A man's voice shouted. "Don't shoot! Don't shoot!"

She yelled, "Don't *you* shoot!"

Now that she heard where he was, she pulled herself to her knees. She peered around the tree trunk. Whoever it was was lying in the snow, waving an orange glove. She holstered her revolver. Even that bit of twisting hurt. Trying to ski hurt. She put her weight on her left ski and poled herself toward the man. The more it hurt the angrier she got. The anger didn't make it hurt less but helped her keep moving.

She stopped five feet away from him. She said, "You shot me." The man lifted his head. He put his hand on his shotgun. Probably just trying to get to his feet. She didn't care. She put her ski tip on his wrist. She said, "Don't touch your gun." She moved her ski. "Just get up."

"All right, all right. Jesus."

Her hat was leaking melted snow down her face. She took it off.

He said, "You're a girl."

"It gets better," she said. "I'm a Natural Resources officer.

That's game warden to you." She opened her jacket to show the badge on her shirt.

"I didn't mean to . . . I saw deer."

"Deer season's over. I'm taking you in." Where was this B-movie dialogue coming from?

He said, "Are you hurt? Where'd you get hit? Maybe you should get to a hospital."

She picked up his shotgun. Pump-action. She ejected two rounds. Double-aught buckshot. When she picked them out of the snow she felt woozy. She rubbed snow on her face. She said, "You got a car? Where's it at?" He pointed back along the trail of his boot prints. She said, "Any more shells? Turn your pockets inside out." He held out a handful of shells. "Drop them." He hesitated. She said, "Now." She put her hand on her holster.

"Jesus, lady. I'm peaceful. I'm going peaceful."

She gave him his empty shotgun and pointed with her ski pole.

It was slow going. Even stepping in his boot prints, he was slogging. She was barely keeping up. When they reached his pickup she told him to put the gun in the bed. She put her skis in, and one pole. She used the other pole to limp to the passenger door. The door was locked. She felt dizzy again, leaned her forehead on the window.

The next thing she knew she was blinking at the sky. She lifted her head. She wondered why she had a ski pole in her hand. *Oh, yeah.*

The truck was gone. She lay flat again until she felt how cold she was.

chapter twenty

Elsie limped to the hardtop in the tracks of the guy's pickup. She was wet from the snow she'd lain in and melted. No cars for a long time. Then a pickup. Relief. Then fear that it was the guy coming back. She checked her holster. But maybe he'd gone for help. What color was his pickup? She couldn't remember, she was useless, she hadn't even asked for the guy's ID. And the son of a bitch stole her skis.

It wasn't the guy. This pickup had an ATV strapped down in the bed. It was the retired navy CPO and his two buddies, shoulder to shoulder in the cab. She asked if he would drive her to her car. He asked what happened. "I got shot in the hip."

"Then we'll go to the hospital. You guys ride in the bed. First we help her in."

When they got to South County Hospital he draped her arm around his shoulder and walked her to the front desk. He said, "Gunshot wound. Where do I put her?" He waved away a wheelchair. "She can't sit down; look where she's hit, for God's sake. And get her warm."

The front-desk nurse looked cross. Elsie said, "Hey, he's been great."

He said, "I'll phone Natural Resources. Your boss'll be wondering. I'll give him my number so you can let me know how it goes."

"Thanks, chief."

The nurse took her ski pole and helped her to an examination room. Elsie felt light-headed but this time with an odd lilt of cheerfulness. She said, "He's retired navy, used to giving orders. Something to be said for those old guys with their big solid bellies. Shall I take my pants off?"

"Wait for the doctor. Just lay down on your front. It'll just be a minute."

"Wait," Elsie said. "Could you call my sister? Ask her to pick up Rose. Don't say I've been shot. Just a little accident. Rose gets frantic about now and Mary gets too busy. Wait. I know I'm babbling. Okay. My sister Sally. Sally Aldrich. I'll write her number on your clipboard." The nurse looked cross again. Elsie said, "I'm sorry. Okay. There is one other thing. Please ask Sally not to tell Jack."

"Jack Aldrich?"

"Yes," Elsie said. "He's the one not to tell. Sally's the one to tell."

"I'll call Mrs. Aldrich for you."

"Thank you, thank you. Jack gets into everything."

"We see something of Mr. Aldrich here," the nurse said, sounding much more sympathetic. "He's on our hospital board."

The doctor came in with a different nurse, who helped Elsie get her wet clothes off. "Not the pants," the doctor said. "I'll cut the pants. Looks like there's some shreds in the wounds." He began to cut her pants away, saying to himself, "Uh-huh. Uh-huh. Okay." He ran warm water onto her buttocks. It felt good for a second, then stung. She winced. "Saline solution," he said. "Clean things up so I can see." He gave her a shot. There was a series of wheelings here and there, perhaps another shot, or was he just poking? She heard the doctor talking to the nurse or to himself. She heard him say, ". . . subcutaneous adipose tissue," and she heard herself say, "That's fat. Are you saying I have a fat ass?" She laughed to show there were no hard feelings.

She heard a chime. She asked what it was. He said, "I'm dropping the pellets into a bowl. You're doing great. Not long now."

She asked or perhaps thought to ask where the navy chief was. She *did* ask, because the nurse shushed her. She waited for a long time and then asked if Sally had picked Rose up. "Yes," the nurse said. "Everything's fine."

The doctor said, "Just one more. Can you lie real still for one more? I can numb you a bit more if you like."

"It's funny," Elsie said. "It hurts, but the pain is sort of off to the side." She pointed. "Maybe over there."

"Good. Now put your hand back where it was, take a deep breath, and relax, and we'll just . . ."

The pain came out of the corner and shot from her ass to her right foot, from her ass to her skull.

"Squeeze her hand," the doctor said. "I've almost got it."

Elsie said, "Oh, fuck!" The nurse said, "Ow!" The doctor said, "There!" He said, "Listen," and Elsie heard the last pellet chime and then roll into the others. The nurse massaged her own hand.

"Sorry," the doctor said. "That last one was in there pretty far. Sort of shrink-wrapped. How do you feel now?"

"I'd like some more of that first stuff, whatever it was that put me on cloud nine. But first I want to be sure Sally's taking care of my daughter. And how soon can I go home?"

"We'll keep you overnight. I want to keep an eye on you, just a precaution." He said to the nurse, "Could you go see about a bed?"

When the nurse came back, she said, "Mr. Aldrich has arranged for a private room. He says to tell you he gave Mary Scanlon the night off and that she's taken Rose home."

The front-desk nurse came in. She said, "I'm sorry. I called your sister. When I said you were here at the hospital she gave a shriek and then Mr. Aldrich got on the phone."

Elsie sighed and said, "Oh, God." Then she said, "Just don't tell him where I got shot or he'll make dumb jokes for the next ten years."

The doctor said, "When he calls again, you can say the hip. Lacerations and contusions to the hip. She's resting comfortably, but we're still in a sterile field here. Visitors in the morning. Assure him nothing grave, best of care and so forth. Oh—aware of and grateful for his interest."

"Thank you," Elsie said. "I think I'm ready for bed. What about another shot of cloud nine?"

"We'll see. Your pulse is still too low. That's why I didn't put you under."

"My resting pulse is forty-eight. Because I exercise. Okay . . . I *was* a little fuzzy, but I'm all the way back now. I'm not in shock, I'm in pain. My right butt feels like a hamburger in a hot frying pan. It feels like it's been jumped on by someone wearing track spikes."

"You don't want to get too vivid. It'll just make you—"

"Right. So give me a little something to make me less vivid."

chapter twenty-one

May let Charlie take her Dodge Dart to Wakefield so he and Tom could buy some things, go to an afternoon movie. She put off Phoebe, who wanted to have lunch. She wasn't sure what to do about Dick. He'd said he was going to look in on the Tran boy, then maybe do a thing or two on the boat. Part of her wanted him to show up, find her and Mary Scanlon and Rose. Another part was afraid he'd get angry, and she wasn't sure she had the energy to rise to that, or that her sense of right, strong enough when she'd gone to see Elsie, would hold up.

Mary Scanlon had made it sound easy. "Sure. I'm free when we stop serving lunch. I can let this crew out of my sight for an hour. It'll be a breath of fresh air. For Rose, too.

Better put your good china out of reach; she's crawling and clambering to beat the band."

May had felt a note of pleasure. Rose crawling and clambering—what else? Was she learning to stand up? May remembered holding Charlie's hands, Tom's hands, helping them take a step, admiring the swell of their small, perfect calf muscles.

When Mary Scanlon's pickup pulled into the driveway, May went out to meet them, watched with interest the elaborate unbuckling from the baby seat. "Is that the best kind?"

"I'm sure it is," Mary said. "It's a hand-me-down from his nibs." May must have looked blank. "Jack Aldrich himself, the squireen of Sawtooth Point," Mary said as she lifted Rose and set her on her hip. Mary tilted her face toward Rose. "I'm not speaking ill of your uncle Jack, mind."

Rose looked at Mary's face. May could swear Rose understood every word. She didn't dare to ask to hold her yet, but she offered her hand and smiled at her. Rose touched her hand and studied her.

May said, "I forgot to ask what she likes to eat."

"She had her lunch, but she wouldn't say no to a snack. Elsie's strict about sweets, maybe a bit of toast . . ."

"I've made biscuits. And there's jelly. There's very little sugar in my jelly." May led the way in, fluttered around the kitchen. She knew she'd do better to calm down. She thought the way Mary pulled Rose out of her snowsuit was too rough-and-tumble, but Rose plainly liked Mary's touch. May split a biscuit open. Still too hot for a baby. She got the paper bag in which she'd hidden the teddy bear she'd bought. She was pleased she remembered that plastic bags were dangerous. "Can she get it out by herself?"

"Oh, yes, she's a great explorer of bags. Aren't you, Rose? Just hold it out to her. Rosie, look. She understands if you say 'It's for you.'"

May was tongue-tied. She finally managed to say "Rose." Rose looked up at the sound of her name but sat still in the middle of the floor. May knelt and held the bag out. Rose stared at May's face, and May wished herself pure of any harm she'd ever wished on Elsie. She leaned forward, elbows on the floor, until the bag was at Rose's feet.

Rose touched the bag and looked at Mary. "Aw, go on, Rosie. Don't be such a tease." Mary's voice sounded like a roar to May, but Rose smiled.

"It's for you," May said. "For you." Rose picked it up and put the top edge of the bag in her mouth. She chewed on it without taking her eyes off May's face. May felt dizzy. It was all more than she'd bargained for. She was relieved when Mary laughed.

As if Mary's laugh set her off, Rose grabbed the bag with both hands and swung it up and down, thumping it on the ground. Mary laughed again and said, "A good thing you didn't give her a teacup." The top began to tear, and Rose saw the teddy bear. She pulled at it, got it half out, and looked sideways at May, a sly smile that took May by surprise. It was devilish and pleased and, it seemed to May, meant that Rose knew that May was part of her pleasure. Rose got hold of the bear's ear. May put a finger on the bottom of the bag and the bear popped out. Rose found the face and began poking at an eye.

May was exhausted.

She got back in her chair, and it was a minute before she remembered her manners and offered Mary a cup of tea.

"If it's no trouble," Mary said. "I think we've got a quiet moment while Rose tortures her new bear. And I have to say I'm glad you didn't get her a squeaky toy. Eddie, God love him, got her a rubber duck that quacks, sounds just like the real thing, I'm expecting mallards to be flying into the house any minute."

Mary kept on talking blithely while May made tea, but when May set the teapot down, Mary took her by the wrist, looked her in the eye, and said, "I see you're taken with our Rose, and I'm glad. I can imagine . . . But this way is for the best—if Rose grows up knowing you, it'll give her just that much more."

May was startled, then embarrassed. It was false credit. She didn't dare explain—she wanted Rose with an ache that had nothing to do with doing the right thing. She wanted Rose to want to be in her house, to like the smell of her kitchen, to hold her arms out to be picked up.

She heard stomping and scraping on the front porch. She hadn't heard a car. Dick came in, said, "I smell biscuits." He didn't seem surprised to see Mary, but he stopped short when he looked down at Rose. He looked at the far corner of the kitchen, his mouth set, his head nodding. Certainly not agreeing with anything, more likely moving with his pulse. He turned around and started for the front door.

It was Mary who was quick on her feet. She darted around Rose and got to Dick in the front hallway. She said, "Oh, no, you don't!" and wrapped her arms around him, half tackling him, half hugging him.

He snarled and pushed at her arm. May was terrified they'd struggle their way back into the kitchen. She got down on her hands and knees beside Rose. But Mary laughed and said, "Oh, Dick, for God's sake—it's nothing to be afraid of. We all love you, you great lummox." She kissed the side of his head. "Though I'm sure I don't know why." Dick stood still. Mary kept an arm around his shoulder—May hadn't ever taken in how really big Mary was—and kept on talking. "So you want Rose to grow up thinking Eddie's her father? She's about to start saying Da-da—it's any minute now. So come on, there's nothing happening here that wasn't bound to happen sooner or later. And don't start up with May. I'm the one brought Rose over; you can't expect me to keep her by myself the whole day without a moment of relief."

Rose sat looking up at Mary, holding the teddy bear to her chest with one arm. May thought how easily attentive Rose looked, as if Mary was singing. And it was a kind of crooning, a kind of coaxing that hadn't ever been heard in this house. It was as if the snowstorm had blown in any number of things May wasn't used to—Mr. Salviatti's angels came to mind, mixing up religion and pleasure—and here was Mary Scanlon, another RC, come to think of it, all in one breath scolding and coaxing, strong-arming him and now hugging him front-on, one hand stroking the back of his head, as if she was about to kiss him on the mouth.

And what if she did?

Mary and Dick stepped around May and Rose, and Mary sat down and poured herself a cup of tea. Dick sat in May's chair. Rose looked at them for a second. May was sure that Rose thought to herself, Those two aren't going to be fun for a while. Rose held the teddy bear out toward May. May put the bag over its head. Rose furrowed her eyebrows. May pulled the bag off. Rose looked only slightly amused.

May went through all the foolishness she could remember—peekaboo, itsy-bitsy spider, this little piggy—at first through Rose's socks and then, pulling one sock off, on Rose's bare toes. She couldn't resist kissing Rose's foot, which smelled like carrots with a bit of earth still on them. Rose found her toes of interest, too, and she and May examined each one as if they were leafing through a book together.

And then Mary was on her feet, bustling Rose into her snowsuit, scooping her up off the floor, holding her face up to May's to be kissed, then up to Dick's, and Mary was out the door.

May sat down at the kitchen table. Dick got up. He put two biscuits on a plate, poured himself a glass of milk, and ate standing up at the sink. He washed his plate and glass and said, "I don't want you going behind my back like that."

May didn't say the first thing that came into her head. After a bit she said, "All right, now you know. I want Rose to visit here."

"Suppose the boys had come in."

"I sent them off to Wakefield to the picture show."

"So you're pulling the strings."

"I don't want Rose to grow up not knowing us."

"I've gone to see her."

"I said 'us.' And when it comes time to let the boys know, it won't be so hard on you if they see that I've come around."

Dick jerked his head and stiffened. Then he sat down and stared at the floor between his feet.

May was tempted to push him down further. She could still say, "Who went behind whose back?" She also felt sorry for him—just not enough to say something that would make him feel better. She thought of Mary Scanlon, jollying him out of his snarls. Hugging him, teasing him, kissing him. Let him get squeezed by jolly Mary Scanlon if that's what it took to get Rose over here.

chapter twenty-two

Johnny Bienvenue called to say he'd like to talk to Elsie about a couple of things.

"Okay. Shall I come to Providence? Or are you in Woonsocket?"

"I've got to go to Sawtooth, so I can save you the trip. Are you back at work or still on leave?"

Elsie thought Jack must have been talking. "No. Another couple of days off."

"So you're okay?"

"Pretty much. If you want to come during the day, I'll be at home." She was about to ask why they couldn't just talk on the phone. She kept her mouth shut . . . why miss another chance to get a glimpse?

He came the next afternoon. She said he could smoke his pipe—Rose was still with Mary. "So what are we talking about?"

"First off, in a while I won't be able to help you represent Miss Perry's interests. I can do it for the next several months, but then I'll be running for public office."

"Well, good. That's what you've wanted. Your visit to Sawtooth have anything to do with that?"

"Jack wants to have a talk. See if I'd like to have dinner next week with some of his Sawtooth pals."

"He gets into everything. Oh. Is it on account of Jack you know about my accident?"

"This is the hard part. I have independent knowledge. In Woonsocket a lot of people come to me with their problems. A lawyer came to me, said he needed some advice. He chose not to say who his client is. I had no idea this would involve you. It turns out his client is the guy who shot you."

"So who is he?"

"I don't know."

"But this lawyer friend of yours knows. You could find out."

"This lawyer of my acquaintance. At this stage, I can't."

"What's going on here? How does this lawyer of your acquaintance know who I am? How does he know you know me?"

"Your first question—there's only one female officer who patrols the Great Swamp and who's on sick leave. Second question—he doesn't know I know you. He just knows your name."

"So why doesn't the lawyer come see me?"

"The client is very cautious, so the lawyer is very cautious. The client is both fearful and wanting to make amends. Up in our corner—*au coin*—there's a feeling that really bad things happen to people who get tangled up with anything official. So the client wants to make things right directly—pay your medical bills, something for pain and suffering."

"And get off scot-free?"

"After he pays."

"This is like a bribe. This is like hush money."

Johnny looked down. He didn't say anything for a while. He looked up and said, "I can see how you see it. I can also see how he may be seeing it."

"What are you doing this for? How do you get involved?"

"Like I said, people come to me. They know I know people—"

"You're like a French-Canadian godfather."

"Not in the sense—"

"You're asking me to lay off this guy . . . this *gumba* of yours."

"Look, you've been hurt. The guy appears to be willing to come forward—at least part of the way. I don't know why exactly he doesn't want a public reckoning. He may have a rational reason, I don't know. Or he may have an irrational fear. So tell me what you would like to see happen."

"I won't take his money. I'm paid to do my job, and my job is to do something about guys like him. He is a dangerous idiot. I want his hunting license and his gun. I want him banned from possessing a firearm."

Johnny said, "Let me think. I'll go light my pipe outside. It makes a lot of smoke at the beginning. It's not so cold today. No wind." He went out the front door.

She was surprised to see him making his way down to the pond. He tapped on the ice with a stick, shuffled out a few steps. He looked at the trees, the bullbriars at the far side. He looked all around. When he saw her at the window he waved, then beckoned for her to come down.

When she stepped off the bank onto the ice, he held her hand. He said, "I'm sorry. I forgot it might be hard for you."

"I can walk perfectly well. I'll try tennis next week. You want to know how bad it is? The extent of my injuries?"

"I'm not representing this man. I'm only asking."

"I'll be fine. But I'm not the point."

"Okay. You want this man punished not for wounding you but because he broke the rules. He did something wrong in your woods. I'm impressed by your strictness." He looked at the trees again. "I honest to God had no idea it would be you. But here we are." He shrugged. "So are you saying you want a criminal case?"

"Well, maybe not the whole mess, his lawyers dragging it on and on, probably trying to make me look like a liar."

"That might be the only way to ban him from possessing a firearm—to convict him of a felony. Proving criminal intent . . . that's a reach. His lawyer says he called a rescue squad from a pay phone. He wouldn't say that unless there's a record. So leaving the scene of an accident is maybe not in play. But taking away his hunting license could be an administrative matter . . ." He let out a long breath that turned white in the cold.

She said, "You're not smoking your pipe."

"I changed my mind. I like the taste of the air, the air over a frozen pond. I played a lot of hockey on ponds."

She said, "I've been in an administrative hearing. It was just like a trial. Lawyers digging up every detail. They pulled up a memo that said I was overzealous. And this time . . . could they make the doctor testify? Make him talk about my subcutaneous adipose tissue? Make him show the X-ray? It's mostly bones, but it probably has a milky outline of my rear end. No, wait—all those pellets would show up. It'd be a connect-the-dots picture of my bare ass."

Johnny's head popped up an inch or two. He squeezed his mouth shut. He said, "I don't think . . ." He stopped. He said, "I'm sorry. I don't know where we are. I guess you're asking about the admissibility of medical records."

"You think it's funny."

"No."

"I saw you trying not to laugh."

"Okay. Just for a second there I thought of a kid with a big orange crayon and a Howard Johnson place mat with a connect-the-dots puzzle."

"There. I knew it."

"But then I thought of how it must've hurt and I lost what

we were talking about. I was getting angry at this guy for hurting you."

Elsie said, "Oh," and her hand flew to her collarbone.

She thought, There are people out there who can meet someone and not think of possibilities. She wasn't one of them.

Johnny said, "You're smart and you've got a lot of imagination, but I want to be sure you know what you're doing. You'd be giving up a lot of damages, not just medical bills and pain and suffering, there's punitive damages . . ."

"I have medical insurance with my job. I've told you what I want."

"Okay. Here's what I can say to the guy's lawyer—she doesn't want money, and that's a damn good deal. All she wants is for this guy to come to me and promise to give up hunting."

"You? He'll promise *you*?"

"Yes, me. His lawyer says the guy is one of us. It'll turn out I know the guy, probably some of his family, his friends, his priest. If he breaks his promise he might or might not feel guilty, but he'll be shamed. And his lawyer'll be shamed, and I'll be shamed. Shame is a group thing. When a group mistrusts the outside, they have to trust the inside."

"So you *are* like a godfather."

"Oh come on," Johnny said. "This isn't some Hollywood movie. I'm more like a switchboard operator. If I made a nickel out of this, it wouldn't work. You think about it, see if you think it gets you what you want. What I'll think about is how to tell the lawyer and the guy about you. How come you gave up the money part. I guess I'll say nature is like a religion with you; the Great Swamp preserve is like your church. So you're like a really strict nun."

Elsie laughed.

He said, "The reason you laugh is you didn't get taught by nuns. I say 'nun,' it'll make him think about when he was in fourth grade and got caught doing something bad. Sister Margaret Mary with a ruler."

"Is that right? Is that what 'nun' makes you think of?"

"Yeah, sometimes." He looked at her so intently she wondered if he was going to kiss her. He said, "It's funny. What you know and what you don't know."

She took a step back. "When you say 'you,' do you mean people in general? Or do you mean me, the ignorant girl who hasn't had the benefit of Catholic schooling?"

"I just meant—"

"I guess I missed out on those thrilling punishments at the hands of Sister Margaret Mary Dominatrix."

"You know, you're right about one thing—you're probably better off not going in front of a judge and jury. At least, not in Rhode Island." Before she thought of anything to say to that, he said, "Okay. Let's not . . . Probably my fault. Look—first time we met you gave me a few jabs, but there you were taking care of Miss Perry, and when we talked about her giving her books away, you cried. And just now I wasn't sure—you got in a couple more jabs. But when you said, 'I'll be fine. I'm not the point,' I got it. I admire how you care for Miss Perry and the way you're a purist about your job. So think about what you want me to do, and let me know."

"Do it."

"You're sure?"

"Yes."

"Okay. I'll get you what you want."

"Maybe one more thing. How about you bring me his trigger finger? The first two knuckles."

Johnny squinted. "How come you got to get in a shock? Does it make you nervous when someone says they admire you?"

The last question stopped her. It was a relief to be stopped. Miss Perry stopped her. Sometimes Mary Scanlon stopped her. Dick used to stop her. She said out loud, "One of these days I'll get around to stopping myself."

Johnny looked abashed. He probably took what she said for an apology. They both started to say something, then held back so that all that came out were their puffs of breath that turned white and floated away.

She said, "You go first."

"I shouldn't have—"

"No. It's okay."

"You got a right to be angry."

"I think I was trying to be funny."

"Ah."

She hoped he wouldn't say anything else, and was pleased that he didn't, pleased that he held out his hand for the big step onto the bank, held on to help her up the slope, and let go at the top.

After he left she worried that she'd made his awkward situation more awkward, worried about his getting involved with Jack. She supposed that that's what it took to run for office . . . to have to go to people like Jack with your hat in your hand. She'd ignored politics because she thought that politicians were putting on an act, and not a very interesting one. She didn't think much of lawyers, either, but here she was worrying about someone who was both, worried at first that he might be too much of a backroom guy, now worried that he might be too decent for the likes of Jack.

It surprised her that she was worrying about Johnny Bienvenue. She was naturally pleased that an interesting man had shown up, and happy that she'd poked at him and he'd poked back and that he'd then startled her with plain, fierce sympathy. But she was also surprised that it somehow all felt slow. Because there was something to settle? Because she was still a little gimpy?

She reached into Rose's playpen to pick up a bottle. A twinge. A while before she'd be ready for their tennis lesson. No rush. Enough that she could look forward to his attention, to his attentive curiosity about her. And she looked forward to her attentive curiosity about him. The sort of considered courtship Sally had given up wishing for her.

chapter twenty-three

Tom had always been the cutup of the family. After Christmas dinner he said, "So where is everybody?"

It startled May. She hadn't noticed they'd all been quiet.

Tom said, "Okay, Dad's looking out the window at the weather. No surprise there. Charlie's daydreaming about his girlfriend. So where are you, Mom?"

She might have just waved Tom off, but he'd got everyone's attention. She tried to think of something other than Rose. She said, "I was just thinking how peaceful it is for a change."

Tom tilted his head back, about to say more, but Dick turned toward him and said, "Don't be a smart-ass with your mother." He said it mildly. May'd been afraid Dick was going to start up with Tom. She was relieved, then touched. She squinted and said, "Oh, Tom didn't mean anything."

Dick and Charlie both looked at her, Dick from far away, the table's length like a stretch of water between them.

Charlie said, "That's right." May saw him trying to come up with a smart remark. "He'd like to mean something . . ."

Before Tom could cut back in, May said, "We should have asked Eddie to eat with us."

"I figured he'd be doing something with Phoebe," Dick said.

"No. She's gone skiing with her daughter. But maybe Walt's with him."

"Walt," Dick said, and shook his head. "Phoebe. Poor Eddie. A motorcycle bum for a son and a la-di-da girlfriend. He can't tell if he's coming or going."

"Phoebe's been good about his business," May said.

"The better things go for his business, the more Phoebe and Walt have to fight over. It's not like Walt's decided to settle down. The only reason he shows up when he does is to keep his hand in. He knows Eddie's soft on the idea of Wormsley and Son. And Phoebe's chewing on the other side of him."

"Scylla and Charybdis," Charlie said. Dick looked at him. May was startled that the boys were paying such close attention. Charlie said, "It's from the Bulfinch's mythology Miss Perry read to us."

"So that's where that's from. Captain Teixeira said it one day and I couldn't place where I'd heard it."

Tom said, "Bet you don't know which is the rock and which is the whirlpool."

May was afraid Tom was asking Dick, but Charlie said, "Scylla's the rock."

"That's just 'cause I said 'rock' first. Bet you don't know where the word *tantalize* comes from."

Charlie said, "Sure I do," but Dick said, "Wait. I remember that one. Hold on a second." May couldn't think of the last time Dick had played with the boys like this. "It's in there somewhere," Dick said. "In that same book."

"Tantalus," Charlie said. "He did something, I can't remember what, and the gods got mad and put him up to his neck in a pool of water, but when he bent over to get a drink, the water went down, so he was always thirsty and always an inch from drinking."

"There you go," Dick said. "Like Eddie with Phoebe."

Charlie and Tom laughed. May said, "Dick—"

"They're not kids anymore."

"It's not that," May said. "Phoebe's getting to be a friend of mine."

"All right," Dick said. "But leastways you can see the boys paid attention to Miss Perry's books." He leaned back in his chair. "I'm glad you boys had that. I'm not saying you'd have turned out like Walt Wormsley without it, but I guess part of how you turned out so good is on account of Miss Perry."

May was stunned. She was so stunned she didn't notice for a bit that Charlie and Tom were stunned, too. Dick had sometimes looked over a piece of work that Charlie or Tom had done and said it was good—a sheet bend or an eye splice, or how they'd gutted a mess of flounder. Nothing as big as this. May was glad for the boys. She was so glad that she snipped off a bud of suspicion that Dick was setting things right with them against the day they'd learn about Rose.

Dick didn't seem to notice. He was staring at the corner of the table. "Wormsley and Son won't work out. But neither will Pierce and Sons. Different reason. There's not an Atlantic fishery has a future you can count on. Not cod, not scallops, not lobster. The government gave away half of Georges Bank to Canada just to get some oil pipeline, so there goes the cod and pollack. They're overfished, anyway. Red crab is an oddity. Nobody knows much about them. If the red-crab plant loses the Boston market, then Captain Teixeira and I are out of luck. I won't grouse about it, least not if I get another few years. But what about you boys?" Charlie and Tom shifted in their chairs. Dick heard either the creak of the wood or the change in their breathing. He looked at them, and May saw he was still far off, as if this was how his mind worked when he was lying in his bunk aboard *Spartina*. Dick said, "I don't know any more than you. You're going somewhere I don't know much about. We know some college-educated people. There's Miss Perry, of course. And there's Jack Aldrich. There's the guy who started the packing plant. Some folks with sailboats, that whole crowd. Walt Wormsley went to URI and so far as Eddie can tell he learned to drink beer, chase girls, and ride his motorcycle. It's not like the Coast Guard, where there's rules about everything down to how you put your socks in your footlocker. You'll be on your own. What's more, you'll be on your own with a little money in the bank. When I was your age, I felt things squeezing in. The only place I didn't feel squeezed was on the water. I joined the Coast Guard like a dumb cluck—thought I'd put the uniform on and they'd give me a boat. Being dumb is one thing, going on being dumb is dumber."

Tom laughed. Charlie was too wide-eyed to laugh. Dick didn't appear to hear Tom's laugh. Dick said, "I somehow had the idea it was wrong to ask questions. I thought it was better to keep what you knew and didn't know to yourself. I knew a couple of things I'd picked up here and there. I watched what was going on. But I didn't want anyone finding out what was going on inside me. I thought if you ask about things someone'll get inside you. Keeping myself clammed up like I did was dumb. All I'd've had to do was ask. I wasted a lot of time." Dick closed his hands tightly, then opened them. "So when you go over there to your college, you learn to ask."

Charlie said, "So how did you get to know all the stuff you know?"

"Too slow. And that was just the nuts and bolts. I didn't begin to figure out what other people are like until . . ." Dick turned away. May's head lifted, and she thought, Elsie. Dick said, "I get along with my crew. Course that could be 'cause they're good at getting along with me."

May tried to keep on being glad for the boys that Dick was talking to them, but she felt bleak. If he was keeping away from Elsie, it wasn't on account of the comforts of home. His comfort was at sea. He'd told Tom, "Don't be a smart-ass with your mother," and she'd gobbled up that crumb. Then there was Charlie, all admiring, saying, "So how did you get to know all the stuff you know?" She could bring it all down in a second.

It was terrible to be that close to wickedness.

chapter twenty-four

Elsie woke up with all the symptoms—the languor from hip bone to hip bone, fractions of scenes as jumpy as movie previews. Some were of her own movements, her hands reaching out. Others of him (not necessarily but probably Johnny Bienvenue), medium close-ups of him turning toward her, touching her hip, her shoulder, or, more shyly, her elbow. Various dresses, various places. Some calculations of when and where. Then further reveries—the stammering of undressing, the fluency of skin.

As she brushed her teeth she saw one funny part. The poor guy still asleep in Woonsocket without a clue that he was being considered for the role. As she fed Rose, she cooled. She carried Rose up to Mary's room and put her in bed with groggy but welcoming Mary, and she started thinking again: she wouldn't call him. See how energetic he was about calling her.

She spent the morning at her desk, in a better mood than if she'd just been filling out reports. She alternated official paperwork with thinking of possible babysitters, wondering if Jack and Sally would give a party—Sally wouldn't mind if she asked that Johnny be included. Elsie saw herself in her red dress, her blue dress, a blouse and skirt—deflecting any old suitors in favor of Johnny in his not-off-the-rack but rumpled brown suit. Or would it be simpler to arrange a tennis lesson, not in her sweat suit. But even on the indoor court it wasn't warm enough for a tennis dress. Maybe one of her bicycling outfits, the red spandex uni-suit. If she still wasn't thin enough for the uni-suit, meet him at the court in a dress, let him think about that. Come out of the changing room in tights and a sweatshirt.

By lunchtime she felt clogged with fantasy.

At the end of the day she felt herself stir again when she pulled the seat belt across her lap.

When she picked Rose up at Sawtooth, she asked Mary if anyone had called during the morning.

"Anyone?" Mary said. "Look, he left his number yesterday. Don't be coy. Or if you're going to be coy, don't be all jittery about it. And that reminds me—Rose needs a bigger playpen; she crawls back and forth in this one like a caged animal. Maybe one of those expandable baby corrals. I saw one in Wakefield—it's like an old-fashioned elevator gate—not the door but the lattice thing that the operator folded to one side and said, 'Fourth floor, ladies' lingerie.' Except the baby corral is a circle and it's made of wood and—"

"Fine."

Mary stiffened and stared at her. "Ah, well," she said, "perhaps it's a detail the staff should take care of without bothering the upper echelon."

Elsie took a step back. Even so, she had to look up. She hadn't realized how this irritated her. She said, "Don't pull that shit."

"Oh? And just what—"

"Your poor-little-me, I'm-just-the-scullery-maid-to-the-gentry shit. Look. I work. You work. Just because Jack patted your ass—"

"This is nothing to do with Jack, it's you and your flouncing around. Any calls for me? No? Then I'm off. Something about Rose? Don't bother me."

"I said it was fine about whatever that thing is. It's fine. It's your babbling on about elevators and women's lingerie that's boring."

Mary stood still for a second, then walked away. Elsie picked Rose up out of the playpen. Rose squirmed and reached back for her teddy bear. Elsie fumbled with the knob on the door. One of the kitchen staff opened it and held it for her. Had he enjoyed the show? No—he looked sheepish and scared. Not a good night to be working for Mary. Fine.

It wasn't until Elsie finished strapping Rose in that she stopped being too mad to think. Now she felt the first cold aftermath. She should have stopped at "Don't pull that shit." "Babbling" and "boring" would linger with Mary. She looked at Rose, who was far too quiet, sucking her thumb and clutching her teddy bear. Her head was tucked to one side, as if she'd understood everything and was having her own dark thoughts.

"Aw, come on, Rose. I love you. Mary loves you. You're the darling of the whole kitchen. I can't even get a date."

When she got to her house Dick's pickup was idling in the turnaround. He shut off the motor, got out, and came over to her car. He had an envelope in his hand.

She said, "Let me get Rose inside. Come on in."

When they got to the front door, Dick said, "You want me to get the door or hold the baby?"

She handed Rose to him. "She knows her name," Elsie said.

Dick walked around the room with Rose, jiggling her. Rose held her arms out to Elsie. Elsie said, "She's not in a good mood right now. I'll get her a bottle. You can put her down. She likes it if you get on the floor with her."

Dick handed the envelope to Elsie and sat on the bare floor.

"What's this?" Elsie said. "She likes it better if you lie flat."

She read the note. "Dear Elsie, I want to talk about Mary bringing Rose over to the house. Is this your idea? Dick."

Elsie put the bottle in a saucepan of hot water. She said, "May and I talked about it. Mary said she might do it this week. Did May talk to you?"

"I just walked in and there was May and Rose and Mary."

"I didn't know—Mary didn't . . . I just saw Mary, but I guess other things came up."

"So who's in charge? I figured you're the one in charge."

Rose crawled across the floor to Elsie and pulled on her pants leg. Elsie said, "She's not used to a man's voice. You'll have to talk softly."

Dick lay down on his back and put his hand over his face. She picked Rose up and gave the bottle a couple of shakes.

"Jesus, Elsie," he said into his wrist.

"Still too loud."

He lifted his hand and whispered, "Jesus, Elsie. Now I've got every female in South County telling me what to do."

Elsie laughed. Dick turned his head and stared up at her. She gave Rose the bottle and walked over to Dick. She turned Rose around, held her under the armpits, and lowered her feet onto Dick's chest, jouncing her up and down. Rose got into it, taking little prancing steps, making her little laughing noises.

"Put your hand on your face again," Elsie said. "She likes peekaboo."

But when Elsie sat Rose on Dick's chest she crawled off and began to suck on her bottle. Elsie knelt. She leaned over and kissed Dick. She lifted her head and said, "Oh, God," and kissed him again. She pressed into him. He rolled away.

She felt a cold shock. It stopped her from scrabbling after him.

He lay on his side, his back to her. He gave a groan that made her feel a little better. She got to her feet and sat in a chair. She said, "I guess you're right." He lay still. Rose looked at him. With the nipple in her teeth and the bottle dangling, she crawled closer to him. Dick sighed and started to get up. Elsie said, "Careful. Rose is right beside you." Dick rolled onto his back. Rose studied him and then dropped her bottle onto his stomach. Dick picked it up and slowly handed it back to her. Rose sat up and started sucking again, holding her bottle with both hands and watching Dick.

Elsie felt a tenderness that dizzied her and numbed her. She was afraid it would make her cry if she didn't do something. She said, "That's right, Rose. At least one of us knows how to behave."

Dick seemed to ignore her. He put his hands over his face, opened them, and said, "Peekaboo." Rose swayed a little but didn't take her bottle out of her mouth. Dick said, "That's good, Rose. You're no pushover." He looked at Elsie. "I don't know. I'm sorry. It's not that I . . . It'd be too much."

Elsie knew him. The way she knew him was even more powerful than the pang of tenderness that had just touched her. She forgot herself, and as if she were floating in the air around him, she absorbed what he felt—his pleasure when she kissed him, his alarm, his regaining his balance. And, from what seemed a horizon in him, there came the reason he feared losing his balance—the turbulence he would have to weather when Charlie and Tom found out. And another distant glimmer that was puzzling until it touched what she herself felt when she was alone in the Great Swamp knowing more than she could name. He, too, sometimes knew more than he could name. He depended on coming into grace when he went to sea. He was careful about being in a state to receive it. There had been a time when he thought her sense of things was attuned to his. Of course, he'd been at odds with almost everything and everybody then, so fiercely desperate that she'd been the only person to want him as fierce as he was.

She came back to herself. She leaned against the arm of the chair. She wasn't as saddened as she'd been afraid she'd be. What the hell, no worse off than other days.

She said, "I guess you're right."

Rose crawled closer to him and swung her bottle onto his stomach. This time he didn't pick it up. He moved his hand toward it and then stopped. Rose stared. Dick touched the bottle and then pulled his hand away. Rose put one hand on his stomach and with the other pushed the bottle onto his chest. He ran his fingers over it as if his hand were a mouse. Rose climbed onto him and grabbed the bottle. She sat on his chest and started drinking. He pulled his knees up to give her a backrest and held her hips. He said, "Charlie used to do that. Except you had to watch out for when he'd throw it. Catch you in the face if you weren't looking."

"All coming back to you, is it? A dad all over again." Every time she opened her mouth she sounded either glib or lame.

The phone rang. It was Johnny Bienvenue. It took him a while to get around to saying, "Any chance of some tennis?"

"I'll have to see. I want to, but I'm in the middle of something right now. Can I call you back?"

When she hung up, Dick was sitting in her chair jouncing Rose on his knees. "'Trot, trot, to Boston, trot, trot, to Lynn,' Look out, Rose, you're going to fall . . . IN!" Rose laughed as Dick swooped her down and caught her. No question about it, a real laugh.

Elsie said, "That was Miss Perry's lawyer."

When Dick got to the front door he handed Rose to her. "It's good the way you're looking after Miss Perry. You're putting me to shame. Charlie is, too. He's been going over there pretty often."

Elsie's eyes flicked open so fast there was a pop of light. She blinked and looked at his face. "I'm glad you came by." She touched his cheek. "And don't worry. Everyone'll get to know Rose, and then Rose will just be Rose. Don't worry. Go see Miss Perry. Go out in your boat. It'll be all right."

When he got to his truck she said, "Be sure to call first. Before you go see Miss Perry."

She closed the door. "You're a minx, Rose. I saw you. He made you laugh, you little minx, and now you're too excited to eat your supper."

chapter twenty-five

Elsie had learned very early how to separate things—one day from another, one place from another. Herself at one time and place from herself at another time and place.

When she had Rose inside her she didn't have any reason or any wish to move in space or time. Now that Rose could tell the difference between herself and her mother, and, although it wasn't quite the same process, now that Elsie could tell the difference between herself and Rose, Elsie's skills at compartmentalizing reemerged. Not the simple difference between her in her green uniform on this side of the bay and herself in her red dress on the other. The new array of possibilities would be more complicated and less clearly marked. One new variable was her house: from being hers alone, whether as toybox or the place she'd seduced Dick, it changed into a nursery, a more serious kitchen, a place where Mary Scanlon sprawled on the sofa, offering comfort or annoyance, a place that instead of being empty when she left was full of Mary with Rose.

So her old gray Volvo station wagon was where she kissed Johnny Bienvenue. While they were playing tennis it snowed again. The Volvo was a mound of new snow. The Wedding Cake was dark except for a faint glow from a chandelier in the front hall. Elsie locked the door to the tennis court and turned off the outside light. Johnny opened the passenger door. He said, "If you've got a scraper I'll get your windshield."

"Get in for a second. It's like being in an igloo."

He said, "When were you in an igloo?"

"I built one once. A school project. The boys tried to build a big one and it caved in. Mine was just a little den. Perfectly comfortable—snow is a good insulator. The thing you have to watch out for is your body heat melting the snow"— she didn't mention letting one of the boys in—"melting the snow under you. I made a mattress out of the tips of hemlock branches."

"Didn't the twigs stick into you?"

"No—the ends all droop the same way. That's why hemlocks look so mournful. I was so warm I had to unzip my sleeping bag halfway and sleep naked."

"You still do stuff like that?"

"Winter camping? Not lately. If there's snow, I try to get out on skis during the day. And try not to get shot by some nut from *au coin*."

"I am sorry. But he has sworn—"

"I'm teasing you. And thank you for bringing back my skis. But look. See how peaceful it is in here. Snow all over the car. Snow over everything. I don't understand why people get depressed in winter. Snow makes me feel more alive." She leaned back and put her hand on the sleeve of his overcoat. She wondered how shy he was, how inexperienced at noticing encouragement. Or maybe he thought he was too old to neck in a parked car. Wait—if she had Miss Perry's power of attorney and he was Miss Perry's lawyer, did that make him her lawyer, too? Was that a problem? She knew that psychiatrists and doctors got into trouble . . . The teacher-student problem hadn't stopped her old college prof. But she'd acted freely, she'd known what she was doing, and she couldn't imagine putting a different face on it. It wasn't a point of honor, it was a matter of not being pathetic. Did Johnny think she'd go crying to the Bar Association? Haunt his political career? Tell Jack?

All this busy wondering made her take her hand off his arm.

She said, "You're not getting cold, are you?"

"No. You're right, it's peaceful. I like snow, too."

"And trout."

"What?"

She got onto her knees and faced him. She said, "I saw you last fall. On the Queens River. You caught a trout and cooked it."

He lifted his head. She leaned closer to his ear. "I could have run you in. You used live bait, you built a fire, you even brought a bottle of wine."

"And where were you?"

"Across the stream."

"So why didn't you—"

"You were enjoying yourself. You looked around and you liked the water and the trees. I thought, There's a perfectly nice man taking a day off. Why not let him have his one trout in peace?" She moved her mouth even closer to his ear and whispered, "So your secret's safe with me."

He laughed. He whispered, "I think it's okay to talk. I don't think anyone can hear us."

She touched his cheek, turned his head, and kissed him.

She was more aware of her mouth than when she'd kissed Dick. Kissing Dick had been irresistible impulse; kissing Johnny was art, not so much showing off as exploring the form, the discipline, of a restricted medium. For one thing, the gear shift between them; for another, their winter clothes. These restrictions made her singularly aware of her lips and his. He had full, wide lips, and she was enjoying pressing softly, brushing sideways, finding the corner of his mouth, moving back to the center.

She sat back on her heels and took her left glove off. It dropped in his lap. She touched his hair, his forehead, his cheek. She couldn't tell if that was what he liked or if his sigh was for her fingers on his mouth. She moved her hand to his other ear and traced around the rim, then inside the ridges. A jagged breath—good—not everyone liked that.

She was enjoying her deliberateness, the effect of her

deliberateness on him, so it surprised her that a piece of her mind lagged behind and spun out a line of thought: her life— maybe everybody's life—crystallized around the *things* in it as much as around people. Her own life around her house, her car, her badge, her revolver, her bicycle, her skis (yes, her toys) . . . Miss Perry's around her house and garden and books . . . Mary Scanlon's around her stockpots and griddles and her songs (songs, things—why not?) . . . Dick's around his boat . . . Jack's around Sawtooth Point . . . (men seemed more limited, or perhaps more focused). So many parts of all their lives—thoughts, emotions, skills—were thing and self, self and thing.

She had thoughts and emotions about Johnny, but at the moment her skill was certainly part of the thickening of the air between them.

She was seducing herself as well. She was feeling deeper and heavier jolts. She kissed him on the mouth and, distracted by the heat of his hand on her knee, slid her tongue between his lips.

It was almost dark inside her gray Volvo. What light there was came from who knew where—Wakefield? Narragansett? It bounced off the clouds, then into the field of snow, and then seeped through the frost on the car windows. Inside, there was a dark glow in which their bodies were visible only because they were even darker. It was in her mind that she knew how to find the buttons of his overcoat. And it must be in his mind that he knew how to find the lever that tipped his seat backward. Buttons, a lever—how human and modern to register these things as stages of the courtship ritual. Nothing like a male fiddler crab waving his one outsized claw, fireflies blinking, herons bobbing and bowing . . . The middle button of his suit coat, the belt buckle, top button of his pants, zipper. Carefully unzipping.

He cleared his throat. Did that mean they should have the conversation now? She said, "Just a minute," and found the opening in his boxer shorts—a raccoon at night fishing with her delicate paws. When she slowly filled her mouth she imagined his eyes widening. His fingertips combed her hair, brushed her scalp. When his hand began to tremble, she lifted her head and climbed between the seats into the back. She'd folded the backseats flat to make room for her skis. She shoved them aside and put her tennis racket on top of them. "It's all right," she said.

He began to move, rustling and jostling that seemed to have no relation to his shifting darkness against the dim windshield.

"I mean, we don't have to worry."

He moved sideways. He was trying to slide over the back of his seat.

She said, "Wait. I'll put that down. No, wait. You'll have to put your seat back up." He opened his door and the overhead light came on, which made the pulling and pushing of the seat backs easier but did away with the spell of her igloo, of the subtleties of touch and sound.

He shut the door, managed his way between the front seats. He had the good sense to lie still. After a while he put his arm around her shoulders and said, *"Nous voici."*

She had enough French to translate: here we are. It took her a moment to think of why this plain phrase should stop her. It was what Dick had said when he'd appeared in her driveway and Mary had gone inside with Eddie, and Rose was nursing, and Dick had moved his hand in an arc and said, "Here we are." Maybe he'd said it just to say something, but it had landed on her then. And now.

Johnny said, "Are you a little tired? After all that tennis? It's okay."

From chill to anger. She wasn't ready to go home. She turned her anger on amiable, inadvertent Johnny Bienvenue. She wouldn't mind a little fierceness. She sat up and pulled a boot off. She threw it into the front seat. Then the other. What else? For an instant she forgot what she was wearing. The wool dress she looked good in. She'd admired herself in the locker room, come out swinging her gym bag so he'd look at her.

She hoisted her hips and pulled off her tights and underpants, then smoothed her dress back over her legs. "Tell me what I'm wearing," she said. "See if you've been paying attention."

"A goose-down jacket."

She took it off. She said, "That's too easy. Now what?"

"A blue dress. Wool . . . Dark blue. And blue stockings."

"Wool is right. Blue is right. The rest is wrong. Too bad." She turned around and pushed her bare foot against his arm. She slid it along his sleeve until it reached his hand.

She thought of his legs as he stooped beside the stream, of his forearms as he played the trout, of his thick, dark hair as he bent to pick up the papers in Miss Perry's library. She thought of herself thinking about him. Fantasy? Even though he was right here? Was that the discipline? It wouldn't work if she thought of him as a nice, solid, comfortable man. What if he'd got the guy off? What if he'd said he'd see to it that she got in trouble? She liked the thought of him as a bit mean.

She leaned forward and moved his hand onto her calf before this fantasy dissolved. It was flimsy stuff but carried just enough charge to draw a sound from her throat when he touched her leg. She came back into her skin. Part of her was lethargy, part urgency; her mind slowed, her nerves quickened. A current of pleasure spiraled up her ahead of his touch, subsided, then gathered again as he peeled her wool dress up to her ribs. She felt his weight. She smelled the wet wool of his overcoat where snow had melted on the shoulder, and that became part of the jumble of winter clothes and bare skin of which she was now the center.

chapter twenty-six

The snowstorm made it a slow night in the kitchen at Sawtooth Point. The few cottage owners who came in ate early. Mary got home and offered to drive Sylvia Teixeira, but Sylvia said she was just going down the hill to Miss Perry's.

"I thought Elsie'd be back by now," Mary said. "I'm sorry to keep you late on a school night."

"No problem. Oh—I hope it's okay—Charlie Pierce came by to help me with math."

"As long as Rose got to sleep." Mary looked Sylvia over. "So Charlie's good at math, is he?"

"Oh, yeah. Math and biology. All that left-brain stuff."

"Is that right? I thought he might have a touch of the poet. All those books of Miss Perry's." Mary wondered at herself, trying to sneak a peek into Sylvia's love life.

"Well, sure. I didn't mean he doesn't read, you know, other stuff."

Mary looked at the snow on the greenhouse roof and said, "It's coming down some. It wouldn't take a minute to drive you."

Sylvia said, "I mean, he's really sweet." Mary heard the breathlessness she'd been listening for. She held up the car keys. Sylvia said, "Oh. No, I'll be fine. I've got boots."

Mary said, "It's not too much for you—taking care of Miss Perry on top of going to school?"

"I'm mostly there just so someone's there. It beats going home. Someone always has something for me to do at home. This way I'm doing something Uncle Ruy wants me to do."

"Captain Teixeira is your . . . What? Great-uncle?"

"Yeah. But he's the head of the whole family. For instance, my cousin Tony asked him if it was okay to work on Captain Pierce's boat. And if I want to go to college, I'll have to have a talk with him. I mean, he's nice and everything, but still. Like he has this idea that everyone should spend a year in Portugal. Three of my cousins did that. I'm hoping that on account of my helping out with Miss Perry, I can maybe get out of it. At least till I'm out of college."

"You want to go to URI? Is that where most of the kids in your class are going?"

"Yes."

Mary stopped herself from saying, "And Charlie Pierce." She didn't really want yet another piece of someone else's life. She saw Sylvia out the door. She looked in on Rose. Sound asleep, one arm hooked around the new teddy bear. Would she still be around to quiz Rose about her love life? Both yes and no terrified her. She loved Rose. She loved Elsie, even though Elsie burned her up twice a week. She felt for the first time the dulling effect of the choices she'd made. Each one was okay by itself. She'd been as much a sister to Elsie as Elsie's real sister, so why not move in and help out? And she'd been exhausted running her own restaurant, so why not get into something that didn't weigh on her every hour of the day? Because she was becoming the background. She'd been tired the year after her father died. But now that year was up, she was back on her feet, she had some money in the bank, and she was still living on scraps from other people's meals. Even little Sylvia Teixeira's.

She climbed on Elsie's Exercycle, got off and raised the seat, got on and pedaled. After two minutes she wondered what could possess someone to do this night after night. She remembered watching TV in her father's hospital room, an interview with a boxer at training camp. The reporter held the mike up near the boxer while he was skipping rope and asked what he thought about during the boring parts of getting in shape. Without missing a beat—in fact, keeping time with the whir and tick of the jump rope—the boxer said, "A million and change, a million and change."

So what did Elsie think about? A longer life? Getting good at games? Men?

And what was she herself doing on this ridiculous machine but trying on another bit of Elsie's life? As if the machine were magic, a way to conjure health, adventure, romance: a way to spin a counterspell to the routine of child care and work.

Be fair, be fair—Elsie wasn't on a joyride. She was good with Rose, had run to help Miss Perry with Rose on her hip, and then managed Miss Perry's household . . . which was how she'd caught the eye of Johnny Bienvenue.

Mary pedaled slower. The Exercycle was minor witchcraft compared to the way she herself was being transformed into doting Aunt Mary, plumping into middle age, no longer bothering to pluck the gray from her long, red hair, happy to have Elsie bring Rose to her bed weekday mornings, to feel Rose nuzzle into her. Of course she loved that time—Rose and her under the covers. Rose making humming noises while Mary sang. And she loved the way Rose was with her all day. Rose was sociably happy to be held for a bit by this one or that one of the kitchen staff, but she called for Mary if she was wet or hungry, had begun to say something that sounded like Mary, Mayee, Mawee, something distinct from the "Mama" she cried out to Elsie when Elsie showed up at the kitchen door.

She wouldn't give up a minute of it. She wanted to teach Rose to sing, to tie her shoes, to read, to tell jokes, to stand on a footstool by the stove, taste the soup, and say, "It needs a pinch more salt." She would give in to time seeping through her if Rose would walk along the beach with her or shuck corn with her on the kitchen porch, and someone walking by—May or Dick or Elsie's sister, Sally—would hear Rose make a snappy comeback or sing a bit of song and say, or just be keen enough to think, "There's a good deal of Mary in Rose."

Mary stopped pedaling. What if Elsie got married?

And what brought that to mind? A test thrown up to measure her—a little race between good and bad. She was pretty sure she'd thought first of what would be good for Rose and Elsie, second of how she herself would be shunted into an outer orbit. Pluto, Neptune, Uranus—whichever was coldest and farthest. Once she started examining her conscience she wondered if her eagerness to bring Rose over to visit May and Dick was a way to keep herself near the center of Rose's life.

And what if it was? It was still the right thing to do. May deserved whatever comfort she chose; Dick deserved some difficulty. And that brought her back to herself, to how she was busting into every life but her own.

Elsie came in laughing. She stomped snow off her boots, dropped her bag and tennis racket, slid out of her goose-down jacket and let it fall. She said, "I haven't done that in years." She glided across the room and sprawled on the sofa.

Mary got off the Exercycle and hung up the goose-down jacket. She swept up the snow by the coatrack and threw it out the front door. She said, "Where's your car?"

"I left it at the bottom of the hill. I'll call Eddie tomorrow." One arm lay across her eyes; the other trailed across her stomach. One foot was on the floor. Her knee swung out a little, then back against the sofa cushion. She said again, "I'll call Eddie," her voice floating out lazily.

Of course. Eddie to plow the driveway, Sylvia to spend the night at Miss Perry's, Mary to mind Rose, Elsie to purr on the sofa.

Mary squeezed her lips together. She would rather her hair turn completely gray than let herself turn cold and spiteful. She could live with her warm-blooded sins—anger, lust, gluttony—but not this hiss of envy.

Mary thought of her old days on her own, the Sunday-morning brunches she'd prepared after closing on Saturday night. How had she had the energy? Red-crab bisque, brioches stuffed with veal kidneys, smoked trout, oatcakes with lemon curd. Soups and stews were all the better for being in the pot a day or two, and the cold dishes had only to be laid out—it was the oatcakes and brioches that made for an early Sunday-morning flurry. But she'd loved it. She'd felt whole, more than whole—abundant.

Once in a while this boyfriend or that stayed after closing on Saturday; once in a great while one of them actually helped. She'd give them a spoonful to taste, stir the lemon curd in the double boiler, roll out dough on the marble counter. They all thought she was sexy in her kitchen.

When the lids were back on the pots, the raw oatcakes stashed in the fridge, the trout sprinkled with dill and covered with wax paper, she'd collapse into a chair, drink a cold beer, let her hair down. She'd sometimes put the long cushions from the window seat in front of the fireplace and spend the night, wake up with the winter sun, take a bath standing in a metal gardening tub, sponging off the smell of dill or cinnamon or sex. She liked sex, just hadn't had a lot of luck finding companionship, a sense of humor, and satisfying sex all in one person. Two out of three wasn't enough to set up house. She'd only had passing glimpses of men who set off full fantasies of lovemaking, conversation, and breakfast. She sometimes thought she could have been happy with the short, bald musician—one of a trio she'd taken pity on when they'd showed up just as she was closing on a snowy night. The last she'd heard from them was a postcard from all three—they were playing in Vancouver.

And here she was with Elsie. Elsie, who thought a big meal was sabotage, who thought singing was so much noise, and who now lay swooning on the sofa.

Mary made an effort. When she was ten she'd got an English bicycle for Christmas, a bigger present than the baseball mitt and football her brothers got. They stared at her bicycle, slouching and sour-faced. Her father said, "Never mind all that. We're off to Mass, and I want to see the two of you on your knees praying for the decency to rejoice in your sister's good fortune."

The phrase became a family joke. She couldn't remember how long it took to fade, maybe as long as it took her to outgrow the bicycle. She did remember that being the object of envy was painful. This sensation lingered in a fragment of memory that detached itself from time but drifted back across her clear remembering, the way a floater drifted across her eye.

She got back on the Exercycle. She gripped the handlebars and began to pedal slowly. ". . . On your knees praying for the decency to rejoice in your sister's good fortune." Elsie lolling on the sofa, her lips a little puffy—not exactly the good fortune the old man had in mind that Christmas morning. But if you gave him enough time he'd get the joke, even if it was on him. At least he'd got that one. But what about this one? What's my favorite daughter got up to now? (That was an even older joke: "Ah, here she is—my favorite daughter." "But Dad, you've only got one." "Is that right? Just the one?") And here she is pedaling a bicycle that's going nowhere, minding a baby that's none of her own, wishing away a pang of envy, and hearing his voice, hearing now the shy love in it.

She began to cry. Just tears and a sniffle at first, then a sob she couldn't help. Elsie took her arm from over her eyes. "Mary?" Elsie sat up and came over, tried to hug her but bumped into the end of the handlebar, came to the side and had to fend off Mary's knee with both hands as it cycled up.

"Jesus," Mary said, and took a breath. She was still crying as she started to laugh. "This thing is a menace."

"Mary," Elsie said. Mary could see Elsie was also caught in between—wasn't sure if she should laugh yet.

"It's okay," Mary said. "I was just remembering some stuff. Look out now—I'm getting off this thing before it kills us both."

Elsie took a step back, reached forward to take Mary's hand. Elsie said, "I'm sorry I was late. I'm sorry for . . . whatever it is."

"I'll tell you in a bit. What with pedaling and crying, I'm ready for a beer. So. You and Johnny hit it off?"

There. Halfway there.

Mary went to the fridge and held up two bottles of beer. Elsie nodded. They sat on the sofa. Elsie said, "In my station wagon," and laughed the way she had when she'd come in.

Mary heard Elsie laugh, heard herself laugh, felt the beer go down her throat, heard Elsie go on talking, but she herself wasn't all the way back from where she'd been. She'd always been proud of her memory; she remembered songs, stories, conversations; she was the one her brothers called late at night to remember things for them. When her memory jogged along the regular paths, it was a pleasant little outing. Now she was wary. Time might be less ordering than she'd thought. The tenses—I am, I was, I will be; I love, I loved, I will love—lost their certainty when she was engulfed in memory that pulled her . . . Where? Why was the North Pole up, the South Pole down? She could get dizzy thinking about the earth in space, and once the earth turned or fell over onto its beam ends, all the other pretty pictures, the solar systems, the—What next? The galaxy?—she got the spins.

It was only luck, a little puff of memory that brought back the favorite-daughter joke. Brought back from where? There might be no end of moments that weren't in the calendar of Christmases, birthdays, school years—that hadn't snagged on another memory but sifted into the time that was beyond the gravity of her memory. Time flowed into everyone and then out again, more of it unremembered than remembered. She thought of time growing fainter and fainter as it lost what gave it life—what people heard or saw or touched or smelled or tasted—and then going back to being nothing.

Elsie was laughing again. "In the middle of it—not the middle middle but the middle of the beginning—I suddenly got mad. Have you ever . . . ? When you were a little bit angry? It reminds me of how you put lemon juice on figs or that fancy Italian vinegar on strawberries and they taste sweeter. Is that like homeopathy? You put in a little bad thing to make the whole thing better?"

"No," Mary said. "Not homeopathy. I don't know about homeopathy. The acid breaks down the fibers, and the fruit gets juicier."

Elsie laughed.

Mary made an even bigger effort but only got as far as saying again, "So you and Johnny hit it off."

Elsie turned so her back was against the arm of the sofa, tucked her knees to her chest, and took a swig of beer. "What was nice in another way, in a completely other way, was that afterward we both burst out laughing. We must have thought the same thing—here we are, like a couple of teenagers. The windows steamed up, clothes all tangled. A couple of teenagers."

"Like Sylvia Teixeira . . ."

Elsie looked up. "Oh, God, Sylvia. Was she okay about staying late? I told her nine o'clock. Have you been back awhile?"

Mary pressed her lips together and took a second. Mary said, "She was fine. I got back early. Rose was asleep. Sylvia walked down to Miss Perry's. Everything's fine." Elsie closed her eyes and rested her head on her knees.

Mary said, "When do babies start remembering? I mean, remember for life. When Rose is four she won't remember what's going on now, but she'll remember from then on, right? I'm picking four because that's when I remember stuff from, it might have been three, but maybe it could happen even earlier with Rose—she's smart for a baby."

Elsie lifted her head and looked hard at Mary. Mary heard the tone of what she'd just said as if it was on a tape recorder—her voice higher than normal and breathlessly needy. If she was tending bar she wouldn't give that woman another drink. Mary said, "Never mind all that." She sounded like her father, though he never used the phrase to cancel anything he himself said, just to get everyone else to pipe down.

Maybe it was that bit of wry remembering, maybe it was that Elsie finally concentrated on her, or maybe it was that Elsie said, "Oh, Rose knows who we are." There. Elsie said "we." Mary resurfaced into the present. Elsie said, "She's like a baby duck or a goose; we're imprinted on her. You can read Konrad Lorenz about that. His geese hatched and he was the first thing they saw, so they followed him around as if he were their mother."

Trust Elsie to give a nature lecture. But Elsie's effort met her halfway, as good an effort as Mary herself had made, good enough to call it a night.

She and Elsie were in orbit around Rose. The two of them might be aligned or opposed, they might spin their days and nights at different intervals, but round and round they'd go . . . Until when? Until Rose grew up? Never mind time. Time wasn't the only thing that mattered. Rose would be in their memory, and they would be in Rose's. Elsie had said "we"; she'd said, "Rose knows who we are." Never mind the geese. Never mind Elsie's night out. The three of them would move together, making a force field of shared memory that would catch more of time than if each of them was alone.

This vision held for a moment, then slid away. Mary felt she'd performed a mental act that obtained grace as surely as she'd once believed in grace through prayer. She felt the ghost of all those novenas and rosaries and composition-of-place meditations ("Feel the crown of thorns on our Savior's brow; feel the weight of the Cross"). And if it was all that that brought her to the same near swoon she used to feel when she'd been lifted up from her aching knees and clasped hands, and the smell of her wet wool scarf—if that piety came back to her in the here and now of how she loved Rose—what of it?

It was hers—she remembered what she remembered without worrying about blasphemy or sacrilege. And all the other old tunes of her life, when Rose grew old enough to sing them, would snag the new parts of their life, keep them on earth, keep them from flying unremembered into space.

Elsie had nodded off. Mary woke her up enough so that she could sleepwalk to bed. Mary reached under the quilt and pulled Elsie's boots off, left her in her wool dress. It looked comfortable enough. She turned Elsie's alarm on, checked the woodstove, and went up to her room, looking forward to breakfast, to Rose, to the day when she and Rose would be sitting at the table by the window having a long breakfast together.

Part Two

chapter twenty-seven

Miss Perry's recovery from her stroke had been, according to the doctor, remarkable for someone her age. He had given her passing marks in motor and language skills. Elsie thought the recovery was remarkable in a different way. It wasn't that Miss Perry wasn't Miss Perry, but that—as Elsie struggled to describe it to the doctor—the colors of her moods were more intense. The doctor nodded and then said, "You've been a great comfort to her," and Elsie understood that they weren't going to have a discussion, certainly not one that might become metaphysical.

Sylvia Teixeira, although now a student at the University of Rhode Island, still came in the morning and again at suppertime. It was Mary Scanlon who told Elsie that that's how Sylvia put off having to go to Portugal for a year. Elsie dropped in on Miss Perry after work before going to pick Rose up at Sawtooth and, later, day care.

When Rose started going to kindergarten, Elsie said to Miss Perry, "My daughter isn't a baby anymore."

Miss Perry understood at once. She said, "You may bring the child with you, and we shall see. Do you remember what ages Charlie and Tom were when I found them agreeable companions?"

Elsie said she didn't.

"I do remember they knew how to s-swim," Miss Perry said. She stuttered slightly on some sibilants. "The first time we all went out in Dick Pierce's skiff, I asked, perhaps over-cautiously, if the little boys knew how to swim. Dick no more than nodded, and without a word they took off their shirts, jumped in, and dog-paddled to the far bank and back. Dick held out a length of rope, they both took hold, and Dick swung them up over the gunwales. He held them in the air for a moment, their little brown legs dangling, both of them grinning. Dick smiled one of his shy, proud smiles, and I was quite enchanted. It wasn't simply the display of s-strength, though the boys together may well have made up a hundredweight, but rather the sensation of being the single audience for their larking about. A fortunate consequence was that the boys were released from feeling that I was an inhibiting presence." Miss Perry paused. Elsie thought she might have lost her train of thought, but Miss Perry was simply composing her next sentence. "When I fear from time to time that I have not done enough with my years, I find that my consolation is not so much in the active parts of my life—although teaching, particularly teaching you, certainly required a good deal of activity—but rather in moments like that in Dick's skiff, when affection and pleasure simply rose up around us. You have a more vigorous nature than I ever had, and on the whole I admire it, but I hope that after a few more hectic years, when your daughter is grown and I am dead, you will let yourself become a more reflective tutelary spirit. One of the things that contributed to the flowering of New England was that the powerful families almost all had a poor cousin, either actual or figurative, who acted as their conscience. You have devoted a good deal of your energy to defending the natural world. But there is s-something else for which I can't find a name. I can say only that Captain Teixeira, Everett Hazard, and Dick Pierce are more essential to South County than Jack Aldrich. I am fond of Jack, but he has skewed ordinary life by isolating his part of the community in private luxury. It is disconcerting that someone I don't much care for, I mean Phoebe Fitzgerald, has taken a wider interest in everyday life than Jack has. When I am in a disparaging mood, I see her as a schoolgirl trying desperately to be popular. When I am in a more sympathetic mood, I grudgingly admire her darting about as the self-appointed town crier." Miss Perry opened her eyes wide, as if staring at what she'd said. "Oh, I see I'm lingering in the disparaging mood. Let us pass on. What I am attempting to say to you is that you can be a better form of what I have tried to be. If I had to say in a single phrase what my life has been, it is this—a love affair with this small piece of rock-strewn woods and ponds, and the people who truly live in it. It has been perhaps too passive a love but keenly felt. The general confession in the *Book of Common Prayer* will have to stand for the rest. 'We have left undone those things which we ought to have done; and we have done those things which we ought not to have done.' I have been s-snobbish about Phoebe Fitzgerald, mean-spirited about Eddie Wormsley, too timid and reclusive to accept Captain Teixeira's invitations to his family parties. And, of course, I have taken your affection for granted." Miss Perry sat back in her armchair, rested her head on the antimacassar, and closed her eyes. Miss Perry's rehearsed speeches made Elsie rigid with the effort it cost them both. She hoped Miss Perry hadn't fallen asleep. She didn't like waking her up, but she couldn't leave her asleep in a chair until Sylvia Teixeira came.

After a few moments Miss Perry opened her eyes. "Rose," she said. "It *is* Rose. Does Rose know how to swim?"

Elsie said, "Yes."

Miss Perry said, "I remember Charlie and Tom jumping in. Were you there that day?"

"No, but you described it very clearly."

"Ah," Miss Perry said. She smiled her lopsided smile. "I had a cousin who in his old age began to repeat himself. He would list all the mountains in New England that he'd climbed. I learned to say, 'Yes, Chocorua—I remember how vividly you described it. I feel as if I've climbed it myself.' Would you please help me upstairs? Actual conversations are more tiring than the conversations I have in my dreams."

chapter twenty-eight

The parts of Elsie's life that she saw as her own history and geography seemed to her so much the same for such a long time that she couldn't tell the years apart. Rose growing. Miss Perry reviving, declining, reviving. Elsie quarreled with Jack about different subjects, but it was the same quarrel. She was still undone when she would unexpectedly run into Dick. One time was so sharp that it kept jumping out of sequence—it came back to her as if it had just happened, leapfrogging what was in fact a longer and longer span of time. She was down by the docks; *Spartina* was in port. Dick was splicing two cables, weaving two starbursts of metal strands into a slowly lengthening joint, a bit thicker than either cable but neatly uniform and hard. Elsie watched the splice grow, watched Dick's forearms and hands with the kind of absorption she usually felt only when watching something wild. It was when she turned away that she felt desire—not a sexual desire but a desire to sense again his inmost savor. It was such a sharp desire she felt hollowed out by it, as if by fear.

Another intensity that had an eccentric orbit in her memory—she couldn't tell if it happened before or after she saw Dick working on the cable splice—was the red squirrel. She was sitting in the undergrowth on the edge of a clearing. She heard the chiming note of a red squirrel, so different from the chatter of a gray squirrel. She tried to imitate the sound, first by whistling, then by humming very high. She came closest when she half clucked, half whistled inward. The red squirrel appeared halfway down a maple tree. It was small even for a red squirrel, probably young. She called again. It looked around, came down to the ground, apparently didn't see her. She called again and it hopped twice, two small arcs toward her. It turned its head, twitched its ears, hopped again. It was within six feet of her boots when she felt the air move. There was a blur and then a perfect stillness. A hawk folded its wings. The red squirrel was turned on its side, motionless in the talons. The hawk turned its head and looked into Elsie's eyes. She was held absolutely still as the hawk's stare moved through her. Then the hawk was gone.

By the time she got to her feet what had happened in front of her eyes was in fragments. She tried to reassemble it then, and many times later. She never got it whole. It didn't matter.

Sometimes she felt guilt, sometimes not. She could place it in a season only because she'd gone over to the maple tree and seen where the red squirrel had gnawed a bare patch on which some maple sap had crystallized. So probably March. She couldn't remember if she'd been cold. She figured it was most likely a broad-winged hawk, but that was only a guess— larger hawks would have had trouble stooping into such a small clearing. She was a terrible witness—no details about wingspan or plumage—she couldn't even say whether the talons had pierced the squirrel or clutched it. What she did have was an instant of intimacy that was both ferocious and serene.

As she had with Dick.

A milder exchange with Johnny Bienvenue, not one that plummeted so vividly through her, turned out in retrospect to be the start of a gradual rearrangement of her life. It was one of the rare occasions when they were in her bed. Rose was spending the night at May's house, and Mary was at Sawtooth. Elsie was completely relaxed, happy to lie there, waiting until Johnny got up to make them tea. He rolled onto his side, kissed her shoulder, and sat up. He said, "Have you ever thought of having another child?"

She was in the middle of a yawn. On the exhale she said,

comfortably, "God, no. It's taking everything I have to raise this one."

Johnny kept moving, stood up, and said, "You want something to eat?"

"Just tea."

It was a few days before she replayed the question and answer in her head. She drew a sharp breath, partly at how obtuse she'd been, partly in sympathy for Johnny. But in the end the only thing she felt bad about was the truth coming out on a languorous postcoital yawn.

They kept seeing each other, usually every other week. She did two things consciously. She asked him more questions about his work, and she got him to be the one to start their lovemaking. He'd been pleasantly surprised in the beginning and even after several years, that she would be the one. His experience wasn't nearly as varied as hers, and he'd been surprised to find that a woman could have been thinking about him that way. During what she was pretty sure was the slow uncoupling of their love life, she didn't want him to think he'd been—she picked a lawyer's word he'd taught her—fungible. A fungible partner, fungible body, fungible pleasure.

She found herself wondering whether she'd prepared him for the marriage he was bound to have—in fact, needed for his career—or if the habit of secret trysts might have spoiled him for it.

In the long run, she was glad that the truth about her not wanting another child had come out, because it precluded her having to say anything further—for example, that the idea of being a politician's wife set off an attack of claustrophobia in her.

All of this was a diffuse and intermittent part of her life. In fact, the drifting apart, which she'd thought would take a few months, went on for more than a year.

Mary Scanlon, Elsie's only confidante about Johnny, said, "The pair of you are making more farewell appearances than Nellie Melba."

Elsie said, "Nellie Melba?"

"An old opera singer. You can substitute Cher."

What Elsie didn't tell Mary was that it was precisely because these were farewell performances that they were (a) so sentimentally as well as erotically charged that it would be a shame not to have another, or (b) not quite the right note to end on, so it would still be a shame.

There was some artifice on Elsie's part. She often said, "Let's just have a nice lunch and take a walk." Sometimes it was just that, but it was pretty much up to Elsie. She genuinely liked talking with him about his problem cases, whether they presented perplexities of law or politics, but she also knew she had the geisha-like ability to convert his pleasure at being listened to into physical desire. One time she squeezed his wide paw of a hand and said, "Wait. Sorry. My brain just reached overload." She laughed. She looked at him two seconds longer than called for. She turned her head and lowered her eyes. She waited while the air between them grew thicker. She put her fingertips to her forehead and, mixing the words with a soft breath, said, "Do you have to get back to work right away?"

She told herself that it wasn't so much artifice as method acting. She wasn't just indicating a feeling, she was experiencing the feeling, or at least using a remembered feeling to set off a present feeling. Because she saw Johnny infrequently, it took her a long time to see that she was splitting him into two people: One, a guy she really liked, who liked her, who in his turn listened to her, understood and sympathized with her, but, compared to her, was wholehearted and innocent. Two, a smart, powerful man whom she could seduce as if he were someone from her red-dress days, with that extra whiff of pleasure she got from turning an upstanding citizen into a bad boy.

One Sunday before Johnny showed up for a picnic, she saw in the style section of the *Providence Journal* that he was one of Rhode Island's ten most eligible bachelors. She felt a succession of pangs—what? How dare they? He should be ashamed. She read it to be sure her name wasn't there. When he showed up she said, "Seen the paper yet?"

"No."

A bright Sunday morning, Mary doing brunch at Sawtooth, Rose helping May in her garden. She drove them to near where she'd seen him catch the trout. She walked in toward the stream. When he saw where she was taking him, he laughed. She set the picnic basket down and spread a blanket. She took out the Sunday *ProJo* and began to read it, lying on her stomach.

She said, "Slow news day," and offered him the first section.

He said, "It's our day off." He sat down beside her. "I'm going to be away for a while; I have to go to a conference. Do you happen to know if New Orleans is on the other side of the Mississippi? I've never been across the Mississippi. In fact, I've never—"

She rattled the paper and said, "You're on the same page as a basketball player and a TV weatherman. And someone designing a yacht for the America's Cup. Did you go to church today? It says you went to Our Lady of Mercy in Woonsocket, where you were an altar boy. I didn't know you were an altar boy."

After he read the piece, he said, "Oh, shit." After a moment he said, "Maybe it'll die down while I'm away."

"Oh, no," she said. "Ex–hockey player, ex–altar boy at Our Lady of Mercy. Cute picture. When you start looking for the perfect wife this'll be a big help. You probably shouldn't marry a French-Canadian, you've got that covered, but there's Italian and Irish and Portuguese. Maybe not Portuguese, I can't think of any Portuguese political families. Of course, Captain Teixeira does have a lot of very pretty nieces and grand-nieces. But he's not political. Italian or Irish makes more sense. Mr. Salviatti has two daughters; one of them's attractive. Rhode Island has had some very patrician Wasp senators—Pell and Chafee—but then you'd lose the Catholic vote. Unless you could get a beautiful Wasp to convert. Now, that would be a feather in your cap."

"You about through? You're not that funny."

"I'm not being funny. This is serious. And why was I thinking inside the box? Rhode Island is pretty closed in, but a nice Kennedy cousin from Massachusetts . . ." Elsie felt herself slipping from teasing into a more reckless urge. She wasn't sure what she wanted to provoke. Perhaps that he'd say he thought of her but that she was impossible—unwed mother, non-Catholic, and likely to say anything that came into her head.

She said, "I may have spoiled you. You may have developed a taste for bad girls. Suppose you end up with a politically alert Sunday-school teacher who's willing to be your broodmare but honest to God thinks sex is just for procreation. Never crossed her mind to undo your belt with her teeth. Of course, speaking of Kennedys, you might have an arrangement on the side. But these days they end up blabbing. Used to be a mistress kept her lip buttoned. So here's what we hope for . . . political family, Italian soccer mom, you have three kids, she stands by your side the whole campaign, gives great talks to women's groups, Red Cross volunteers. But she has a secret dark side, an inner bad girl. That only you know. That only you know how to set off. Like if she hides in the bushes and watches you catch a trout." Elsie's mouth opened with surprise at what she'd just said. And just as unexpectedly as she'd said "catch a trout" she said, "You fuckhead eligible bachelor!" She tore the page in half. Her mouth opened again. "You fucking altar-boy attorney general! Go make some baby altar boys with your dumb altar-girl wife." She got up and walked into the stream. She sat down. The current piled up on her back as if she were a rock. It spilled over her shoulders.

He waded out to her, stood her up, and walked her back to dry ground. As she was wringing out her clothes she felt how neutral her nakedness was. Good old naked Elsie. She went about the business of spreading her clothes on branches.

He said, "I could build a fire."

"No. We'd have to arrest each other."

He laughed. She wrapped herself in the blanket. He said, "You don't really want me, not for a life." She didn't say anything. "And you're right. You're a wonderful woman, but most of my life would bore you or make you angry." He picked her pants off the branch and wrung them out more thoroughly. Then her shirt. He sat down by the picnic basket. He lit his pipe. He took off his shoes and socks, wrung out the socks. He squeezed some water out of the cuffs of his pants, then rolled them up to his knees.

She said, "They won't dry like that."

"I am not seeking the remedy of dryness. I am merely reducing the sensation of wetness."

She liked his making fun of his lawyerishness. She'd telephoned him at his office one afternoon, heard rustling and crackling. "What're you doing?"

"I am eating steamed shrimp seriatim."

She'd been charmed then. Now she dried her hair with a corner of the blanket and wondered if she was going to fuck him for one puff of charm.

Or because her own tantrum had stirred her up.

Or because it had been two—no, three—weeks.

Or because she was Nellie Melba.

Her nakedness was of more interest to both of them now that she was wrapped in the blanket.

chapter twenty-nine

One day Elsie was cutting Miss Perry's toenails. Miss Perry began to cry. Elsie had never seen Miss Perry cry. Elsie felt the hunch of Miss Perry's shoulder as the motion ran down her body and made her foot jump. Elsie looked up and saw Miss Perry's face squeeze tight. Then Miss Perry held still and a tear came out from under one lens of her eyeglasses.

Elsie didn't know what to do. She lowered her eyes. She dropped the clippers and held Miss Perry's bare foot in both hands. She laid her forehead on the top of Miss Perry's foot.

Miss Perry cleared her throat and said, "What on earth are you doing? I am not an Oriental potentate." Elsie picked up the clippers and finished cutting the last two toenails. She gathered up the clippings and put Miss Perry's slipper back on.

Later in the day Miss Perry said, "I have known two or three men who became more courteous, even sweet, after they had their strokes. While I admired their transformations, at the same time I had the unkind thought that they had a lifetime of bad temper for which to atone."

Elsie was setting the table for supper. She laid a fork down and straightened it with her fingertips. She said, "Are you saying that you, conversely, have a lifetime of sweetness that you intend to make up for?"

Miss Perry laughed. She stopped when her rib hurt. "Elsie, dear, I was making my way toward an apology, but you have trumped me."

chapter thirty

May's life was immeasurably richer once she became one of the three crucial women in Rose's life. May couldn't bring herself to have another conversation with Elsie, but she'd always liked Mary Scanlon. She felt grateful for the part Mary had played in handling Dick—bullying him with hugs that were part strong-arm tactic, part bosomy squeezes. That first time Mary had done it, Dick had given in to a combination of Mary's physical strength and her flood of argument. True, she'd added some hugs and kisses then, and May had counted them small payment for having baby Rose in her own kitchen.

As Rose grew to middling size, she would run from Mary's pickup into May's arms. If Dick was at home, Mary hugged Dick and jollied Rose along. "And here's your father, Rose, home from the sea." If Rose needed more jollying, Mary would add, "Not every girl has a handsome sailor for her da," and hug him. "He's a bit shy now, Rose, but he's dying to see you."

If any other woman were to cling to Dick like that . . . If May had come on Mary alone with Dick carrying on like that . . . When May was alone and thought of Mary Scanlon's long arms and flying red hair whirling around Dick, May had to cut the thought off. Sometimes. Other times they wrapped their arms around each other and floated toward a vanishing point in May's mind. And then it was gone. Easy as that.

For a while Rose called Dick "da." She said to May, "Have you been on my da's boat? All the way out to sea? When I'm bigger, can I go on da's boat?"

May thought Rose's saying "da" was a good idea. She

wondered if Mary had chosen it as a smart compromise between Rose's saying "dad" or saying "Dick." Perhaps it was just part of Mary's Irishness, or perhaps Mary's way of putting another mark on Rose. It didn't matter—it kept things in place.

When Tom found out, he was in college at URI, still popping into the house when it suited him. The first time he actually saw Rose he'd sat and watched May and Rose make tea for the teddy bear and two dolls. When Mary Scanlon came to take Rose away, Mary didn't bat an eye. She gave Tom a hug and said, "Give Tom a kiss, Rose, and then we're off. Good Lord, Tom, are you raising a beard? Never mind, Rose, there's a nice bit of cheek right there." Rose hid her face in Mary's skirt, then turned around.

Tom held out his hand and said, "Can you shake hands, Rose? I'm Tom." Rose stood on one foot and held out her hand. Mary laughed. May held her breath.

After Mary and Rose left, May sat down. She said, "Your father told me he told you."

"How old is she now? Six? He took his time. And he didn't say much. He sure didn't say you got down on the floor and played dolls with her."

May said, "Don't poke fun."

"I'm not. I'm just . . . I'm just catching up; I'm just taking it in. So you're doing okay, then." He hit his palm on his forehead. "Well, duh." He looked at her. "I'm sorry. I'm goofing around. I think it's great, the way you're . . . doing it this way."

May wished she had Mary Scanlon's quick hugs and kisses in her. She said, "You were good. The way you asked her to shake hands."

Charlie was another matter.

After Dick told him, he didn't speak to his father for years. He graduated from URI and then from the URI graduate school of oceanography. He stayed on as a research fellow and spent a lot of time at sea on the R.V. *Trident.* May missed him terribly. He only phoned home if he knew Dick was at sea. When Charlie was in port he would ask May to lunch over in Saunderstown, a dozen miles away.

It pained May that Charlie seemed to have become as grim and stubborn as Dick—as Dick had been when he was building *Spartina*. It pained her that her family had flown apart. Every so often she blamed herself. If she hadn't taken to Rose the way she had . . .

May's life had been Dick and the two boys. Now it was Rose, with Mary Scanlon as a bonus, and Phoebe. It was for Rose and Mary and Phoebe that May made her garden bigger after Rose became old enough to help. Mary accepted some fresh corn and squash as a gift, and then asked if she could buy a basket for Sawtooth, whatever was ripe any given week. Mary said, "There's one or two who eat there who can tell the difference."

Phoebe liked the way the garden looked. She said, "Someone should paint a picture. Call it *Abbondanza*." Phoebe had taken to throwing in an Italian word or two, about the time she started referring to Mr. Salviatti as Piero. May didn't think much about it—Phoebe called Mr. Aldrich Jack— until Phoebe brought her a dozen figs. "Piero sent these. He remembers you admiring his fig trees in winter."

May said, "Well, be sure to thank him next time you see him. I didn't think he comes down off his hill all that often. But I guess he looks in at Sawtooth."

"I see him at his house," Phoebe said. "In a way, it's you who gave him the idea. You said that you thought one of his angels, the big one, should be looking out to sea. So he asked us up to see if our company could build a base for it down by the town dock. And then he thought he might commission a new one. We went to Westerly to look at the work one of the younger sculptors is doing. It's all still in the planning stages, but he said, right in front of all those men, would I consider posing as the model? Of course, I laughed. I play a lot of tennis but I'm not a young girl. And then I had to blush. He made me stand on a block of stone, and they all talked in Italian. So just for now the sculptor is coming up to make a few sketches at Piero's house. Oh, May, you look horrified. Really, it's just . . . I mean, I'm not posing nude."

That possibility hadn't occurred to May. May wasn't sure what it was that bothered her. It wasn't just that she suspected that Phoebe had liked standing up on a block of stone while a bunch of men looked at her and talked Italian. And it wasn't Phoebe pretending to be a Catholic angel. Not just that, either.

May said, "Mr. Salviatti means to put this up by the town dock?"

"Yes. He wants to do something for the community, something that shows he cares for the fishermen. We'll call it *The Angel of the Harbor of Refuge*. Of course, all the people taking the ferry to Block Island will see it, too, and Piero likes the idea that a larger public will see what sort of art Westerly does."

May remembered when the Perryville School started. Some of the people wanted to call it Miss Perry's School or Miss Perry's Academy. Miss Perry said no. She'd told Dick there was no helping the fact that the village of Perryville was named for a distant relative who'd been a hero of the War of 1812. She herself felt constrained by the old New England rhyme, "Fools' names and fools' faces / Often appear in public places." May imagined the unveiling of the angel. There would be Phoebe's statue in the middle of a crowd of lobstermen, fishermen, and dockworkers. The real Phoebe in one of her fluttery dresses next to rich old Mr. Salviatti. May couldn't think how to explain just how jagged a joke it could turn into. May said, "Maybe you should talk to Captain Teixeira. He's been around forever. He's practically the chief of the town dock. And he'd know something about angels, him being Catholic."

"Funny you should mention him. I said to Piero it would make more sense to ask Sylvia Teixeira to be the model. She's very pretty in a Portuguese sort of way. Maybe a little too sexy for an angel." Phoebe popped her eyes open. "Weren't she and Tom . . . ?"

"No," May said. "That was Charlie."

"Really? I seem to remember seeing Tom and Sylvia walking up to Miss Perry's."

"Tom? When was that?"

"Right after Sylvia graduated from URI. Just before she went to Portugal—she finally did have to go, after all—but this was when she was still helping Miss Perry. I remember when she came back, the Teixeiras had a family party for her down on the town dock and she seemed to have a new beau, someone much older this time. But you're right, we should talk with Captain Teixeira."

For a moment May thought that Phoebe had mistaken Charlie for Tom. May had been picturing Miss Perry's front steps and a boy and a girl, blurred by Phoebe's saying "I seem to remember . . ." But when Phoebe said, "a new beau, someone older this time," it was like turning the focusing knob on a pair of binoculars, and May saw clearly. Not the Teixeiras' party on the town dock but Tom and that pretty Portuguese girl.

Tom wouldn't have . . . not if Charlie was still . . . But then Charlie held on to things, took a long time before he gave up. Tom thought each day was new. It's what let him take to Rose without tying himself in a knot about where she came from. Charlie put out to sea. What would ever bring him back?

Phoebe didn't seem to notice that May pulled back some. "Boats," Phoebe said. "There's something to do with boats I wanted to tell you. It'll come to me. Did you hear about the smugglers? That's not it, but it does have a boat. They were bringing in bales of marijuana and they stacked them in a hayfield and stacked real hay bales on top. But a bird-watcher who was up before dawn saw them in her nightscope. I love it—the little old lady in tennis shoes. Oh. I remember. The smugglers used a Zodiac to come in from the mother ship. It was near the oceanography school, so they probably thought people would think their Zodiac had something to do with the *Trident.* Anyway, I met the captain of the *Trident,* and he's just crazy about Charlie. He said a lot of the researchers he takes out aren't very handy with small boats. What he actually said was, 'Some of them are piss-to-windward sailors.' It took me a minute to figure it out. Have you ever heard that?"

"Yes. Often enough. What'd he say about Charlie?"

"He said Charlie's the only scientist he trusts to handle the boat. One time the motor in the other Zodiac stopped working, and it was getting pushed onto some rocks, and Charlie drove his Zodiac right in next to them and towed the other boat. I'm not sure I understood everything the captain said, but apparently it was hard to do, what with the rocks and big waves. So Charlie's a bit of a hero, like his father."

Phoebe looked pleased. May shook her head. She'd been worrying about Charlie keeping away on account of his pain and anger at Dick, and Phoebe had added the possibility that Charlie was mad at Tom as well. May'd been thinking of Charlie as more or less safe on the *Trident,* but now there he was tearing around in a small boat. He might have done the right thing, but he was most likely driven to it just to get even with his father. Men. Men wanting more . . . Now she had another man out at sea to worry about, thanks to Phoebe's chirping.

It helped to blame Phoebe. Vain, flibbertigibbet Phoebe. May tried to be fair. Phoebe wanted to be her friend, came in to brighten the day, had no idea how she'd made it darker. All right, then—poor, fluttering Phoebe.

But what *was* she up to with Mr. Salviatti? Didn't people ever get done with all that?

chapter thirty-one

Mary had become the person everyone told things to. Or had she always been that person? Come to think of it, yes, God help her. Rose told her about May and Tom, and how her uncle Jack fussed over her but then ignored her if a pretty woman came along. Eddie, God love him, was always a beat or two behind the rest of the band, at least when it came to that sort of tune. May hadn't so much told Mary about Phoebe's visits to Mr. Salviatti's as *asked*, wanting to be reassured that her friend Phoebe wasn't a bad person. May hoped that Mary could offer, from what everyone seemed to think was Mary's large store of worldliness, an assessment of possibilities ranging from completely innocent to dangerously but not wickedly flirtatious.

As May questioned her, Mary had two trains of thought. The first was about May herself. Mary had always liked May, thought she was long-suffering—God knows Dick was a hard man to put up with, even to himself—but also that May had something in her that matched Dick's fierceness, that he could live with. But listening to May worry about Phoebe, Mary heard a tone that made her wonder if May wasn't so much thinking of sexual urges with disapproval as thinking them not worth all that fuss.

Lord knows it could come to that.

The second train of thought was that Mary wondered just what Phoebe *was* doing up there in Mr. Salviatti's grand house and walled garden all set about with Italian statues and fig trees. She'd pooh-poohed it to May by saying that Mr. Salviatti was a mysterious figure and that Phoebe was just the kind of person who couldn't leave a mystery alone. Not so much actual mystery, which was much less his doing than the fact that he'd spent too much money setting himself up on his hill, above most of the county but not to the taste of the gentry. But they all still talked, and what Phoebe probably found irresistible was being one up on all the talk. And then, looking at Phoebe from Mr. Salviatti's perspective, why wouldn't an older man look forward to Phoebe's pretty face and figure? Wasn't there always a man or two lingering by the tennis court whenever Phoebe was playing? Just to take in the way she bent over to pick up a ball, not scooping it up with the edge of her racket but giving the ball a little pat to start it bouncing. "She knows how to add an ornament," Mary said. "And what's going on up there on the hill is most likely just ornamental."

May narrowed her eyes and tightened her lips. Mary couldn't tell if May was satisfied. Then May sighed and changed the subject. To Rose, of course. The subject of Rose softened May's face, and the softening made her surprisingly beautiful, though not, Mary thought, in a way a man would notice.

chapter thirty-two

A pulling boat. Sixteen feet length overall, with a four-foot beam, narrow and fast. A bit tender. Two sets of oars. Dick said to Rose, "It's not just because you never know. You can set her up to have two rowing stations. The middle thwart slides aft like so . . . and then you put the pegs in and she's still trim with two rowers. Or you can row from the bow and take a passenger in the stern sheets."

The hull was all curves—the gunwales flaring from the stem to the middle rowing station, then tucking back in to the wineglass transom.

Dick said, "You learn to row, then I'll add a little lug rig. She's got a pretty long skeg under her stern, but there's a well for a daggerboard. But first you learn to row."

On either side of the bow there was a compass rose and, in red lettering, "Rose."

"And this here's something Eddie made." Dick held up a long canvas tube inflated to a sausage shape. "You could use that as a life preserver, but it's mainly a beach roller, so you don't scratch her bottom if you haul her up." Dick lifted the lid of the stern seat. "In here you got a little toolbox with some extra screws and such. A water bottle. A waterproof chart. A storm whistle—you can hear it a mile away. You know SOS, right? And here's a little binnacle—"

"Dick," Mary said. "Not everything at once."

"Just one more thing. You see there's a place for an oarlock in the stern. In a real narrow creek you can scull her along with one oar. You waggle it back and forth. It takes some practice, but it's a handy thing to know. The basic principle is—"

Elsie and May laughed. Dick frowned. Rose said, "It's really neat."

"*She*, not *it*," Dick said. "You row her an hour a day, four, five times a week, you'll be as trim as she is."

Mary followed Rose as she stomped off.

May and Elsie both said, "Oh, Dick."

Dick said, "Well, God damn it—she's awful touchy." Then he drooped. He opened his hands and looked at them. He looked at the boat and said, "I might as well take an ax to her."

"Forget the boat for now," May said. She gave him a shove. "Go see your daughter." Dick left. May sat on a log and put her face in her hands.

Elsie looked at the boat, at the reflection in the creek,

motionless at high tide. The boat sat lightly. A beautiful boat. A patient gift undone by one slip of the tongue. Elsie said, "I don't know which of them I feel more sorry for."

May said sharply, "You don't?"

Elsie could no more unsay her words than Dick could. She knew she owed it to May to turn around. May stood up. Elsie had feared what May would look like, but May looked purely reflective. May said, "I don't guess you do."

After a bit May said, "We'd better haul her up. No telling when they'll be back." May stooped and got hold of the stern. Elsie got the bow. When May nodded they lifted her and carried her to a set of slings. She lolled onto her beam end on account of the skeg but lay steady. She looked awkward showing her white belly. May kept on up the path. Elsie lifted the stern and moved the sling forward so that the boat sat upright. May came back. Elsie said, "I just thought . . ."

May took hold of Elsie's wrists. She looked straight into Elsie's eyes. She said, "I'm not sure what I've lost on account of you. I suppose Dick might have gone off altogether. For a while I blamed Charlie's staying away on you, but it's not just you. All that's as it happened. But Rose . . . Dick asked me once. He said, 'Don't you think it's unnatural how you care so much for Rose?'"

There was a silence. Elsie took a breath and asked, "What did you say?"

"What do you think I said?" May held Elsie's wrists together.

Elsie said, "You probably didn't have to say anything." Elsie lowered her eyes. "You love Rose."

"That's right. It's no harm to Dick, it's no harm to you. I love Rose as much as I love Charlie and Tom. As much as if I gave birth to her." Elsie's arms jumped. May loosened her grip but didn't let go. "Don't worry. I'm not asking anything more. I'm not out for anything. You and Dick got her, and you bore her, and when I got through feeling terrible, I felt empty. I wished you would go away. Then I asked for Rose to come to my house. I didn't know and I don't guess you knew how it would turn out. I don't feel empty now. I get along with Dick. I can see you. It used to be the sight of you stung me. But right now I can see you and talk to you and touch you. I heard you get worried and tender for Dick just now. It doesn't matter so much now. On account of Rose. She grew up around me." May let go of Elsie's wrists.

"Yes," Elsie said. "And Rose loves you, too."

But May had drawn back. May said, "And now we're all going to watch Rose grow up and go away. Charlie and Tom are like Dick and me. Charlie may go to sea, Tom may go here and there, but they won't settle anywhere but around here. You and your sister are different. You're both good mothers, but you raise children so they can go anywhere. It's not just money. It's not books, either. Charlie and Tom have books. So what is it? When I drop Rose off to see Mary Scanlon, Rose goes up the front steps, says hello to the people on the porch. I don't know how I know, but all of them sitting at those tables—they could go anywhere. It's true what I'm saying, isn't it? Rose is one of them."

Elsie said, "I don't want Rose to go away any more than you do."

"Maybe you don't. But you're not saying I'm wrong."

Elsie couldn't argue that she herself had given up all that. Not with May. She said, "Rose just turned fourteen today. She's not going anywhere for years. Rose loves it here." Elsie couldn't bear another minute of May's looking at her. Elsie said again, "Rose loves you."

May said, "Let's go see if Dick's pulled himself out of that hole he dug."

chapter thirty-three

Rose said to Elsie that if Elsie didn't stop being cross all the time, Mary might go away.

Elsie said, "Mary and I have a solid friendship—a complete adult friendship—something I hope you'll have when you grow up. Because you're sure as hell a long way from it now."

"Like you're a grown-up. You still fuck your boyfriend in the backseat of a car."

Elsie didn't slap her. Elsie wanted to do something more painful and long-lasting. She said, "I can't wait till you're going to the Perryville School. And not just because you'll be out of my hair. Mainly because I can't wait to see you try being a spoiled brat over there and some of them will be smarter than you and better than you in so many ways, and you can be sure of this, too: some of them will be just as poisonous as you."

Rose laughed. "You can't afford to send me to Perryville."

"You're going as a scholarship kid. It used to be that some of the other kids thought that was cool, but nowadays that'll be just one more thing for them to needle you with."

"You mean along with me being a bastard."

"That's right. A poor pudgy bastard who isn't good at games and hasn't ever been to Europe."

"I'll go live with May."

"May and Dick are with me on this. And your aunt Sally and uncle Jack."

"I'll ask Captain Teixeira to adopt me and send me to Portugal."

"That'd work."

Rose walked out.

Rose was calmer the next day, still hostile but her hostility was patchy, maybe clearing. At supper she ate salad and a few bites of fish and string beans. When Elsie offered her an oatmeal cookie she said, "What? You want the thin, rich girls to laugh at me?"

Elsie said, "I was mad. I'm sorry."

"And you're sort of a liar."

"Yes, you're not a pudge."

"Not that. I talked to Aunt Sally and Uncle Jack, and Perryville isn't like what you said. Uncle Jack said it's got all kinds of kids. He's on the board of governors, and he knows stuff you don't. He said trips to Europe and being rich don't count as much as character and . . . other stuff."

"I guess by 'other stuff' you mean he said not to forget you're Jack Aldrich's niece."

"Not just that. He said you and Aunt Sally going there counts, and so does our being friends with Miss Perry. Uncle Jack said she's giving the school her house and everything. I mean, when she dies."

Elsie stared at Rose. Rose took a step back.

"What?" Rose said. "I'm just saying what Uncle Jack said."

"No," Elsie said. She wasn't sure what she meant by it. She couldn't name what Rose had done.

"What?" Rose said again, turning one way and then the other as if looking for help.

Yesterday Rose had fought her to a standstill. Now Elsie could crush her, whether she called Rose the names that began to occur to her or whether she stared at her in silence.

"All right," Rose said. "I talked about Miss Perry dying and she's like your religion." Elsie held still, was relieved by this note of rebellion. Rose took a breath and let it out. She was close to tears. She said, "You love her more than me."

"No," Elsie said. She touched Rose's shoulder, and they stumbled into each other. We're drunks, Elsie thought. We're drunk on fighting.

chapter thirty-four

For a while Elsie thought there wasn't much left of Miss Perry. Miss Perry's day started late and ended early, and most of it was subdued. Then one day she watched Miss Perry make her way to the bathroom with small steps. Miss Perry paused at the door, one hand splayed across the grooves in the doorjamb. Out of nowhere—not from anything in Miss Perry's face, which was turned from her, not from any sympathy for Miss Perry's effort—in fact the feeling came during the moment Miss Perry paused, it came into her and rose in her all at once: This is Miss Perry, whom I love now.

Everything was easier after that. Gathering up the skirt of Miss Perry's nightgown, holding Miss Perry's upper arms to lower her onto the toilet seat after making sure that Miss Perry had closed her fingers around the bundled hem. Even the conversation with her boss when he furrowed his brow over Elsie's application for "compassionate leave" and said, "I don't see how . . ." Elsie saw that he was bracing himself. She'd flared up enough over the years. She put her hand on his desk as though she was putting it on his hand. She said, "I know. I know it doesn't quite fit." She spoke to him in a voice she hadn't ever heard from herself. "Just so you'll know, and then maybe something will occur to us—I love my daughter, and I love Miss Perry. I know it's a funny sort of family tree . . ."

When she was through, he swung away from her in his swivel chair. "Let me think about it. If it were just up to me . . . I can see how you feel, I really do. But look, for right now you've got a lot of sick leave."

She said, "Yes, but I'm not sick."

She told all this to Sally, not as a problem but just to let Sally know her state of mind. But Sally told Jack, and Jack called her up. "Oh, for God's sake, Elsie, I'll take care of it. You've got enough to do."

"Jack, you don't understand. I don't want some backdoor deal. I can't explain—"

"I do understand. You always think I don't understand when in fact I have a perfectly clear understanding. Miss Perry needs you, she has no one else, and now some little time-server behind a sheet-metal desk . . . That's who doesn't understand." Jack was getting so loud that Elsie held the phone away from her ear.

"Fiat justitia, ruat caelum."

There was no talking to Jack when he got to Latin. Elsie said, "Could you put Sally on?"

But Sally's line was that Jack was more upset about Miss Perry than he let anyone see, and why not let him feel better by letting him do something? She'd be sure he didn't do anything that hurt anyone's feelings. "I know he sounds furious, but he's really very temperate when he's actually *doing* something."

Elsie let it go.

She apologized to her boss when he handed her the approved leave request. "I really didn't ask anyone to poke in; I tried to head it off."

"No, it's okay," he said. "I'm off the hook. They worked it out up in Providence, CCed me on a memo in legalese. You know, 'Immediate family may be considered to include another relationship if in the judgment of the office of the attorney general . . .' and so forth and so on. So I'm okay, you're okay. Sorry. I didn't mean . . . I just meant okay as far as this goes. I'm sorry for your trouble."

Elsie was about to say, "No trouble," but she recognized the phrase from a Mary Scanlon story. "I'm sorry for your trouble" was the canonical Irish condolence at a wake.

She became calmer and more careful, not by an act of will but by the continued emanation of that moment in Miss Perry's bedroom. It was strongest when she was in Miss Perry's house, but it had also worked just now to make her softer with her boss.

chapter thirty-five

When Rose climbed onto Mary's bed, Mary was having a musical dream or had just had a musical dream. The notes were all over the room, the room in her dream, the room she was in, the bed she was in, the bed that listed toward Rose. The notes faded in the sunlight that was blinking in her face.

Rose laughed. Mary tried to hum and made a sound that made Rose laugh again. Mary cleared her throat and half opened her eyes. Green leaves were stirring outside the window, not in time with the song.

It wasn't that she woke up not knowing *where* she was—there was no wall or window off by ninety degrees waiting for wakefulness to swing it into place like a compass needle. It was that she didn't know *when*. She was fogbound in time, among wisps of songs she'd sung to Rose. The one that was fading in the light might have been one of them. Now she heard a bar or two from Rose's baby days—"Where Is Thumbkin?"; "Hush, Little Baby, Don't You Cry"—but then a Cole Porter medley—"You're the Top," "Let's Do It, Let's

Fall in Love"—that was too racy for baby Rose. Then, passing through in a single breath, a complete stanza of a sailor's hornpipe.

> *And when we get to the Black Wall docks*
> *Them pretty young girls come down in flocks,*
> *And one to another you can hear 'em say,*
> *"Here comes Jack with his twelve months' pay."*

When was that? Toddler Rose? Tomboy Rose? Plump, moody Rose? It would be moody Rose who liked Cole Porter, who liked Gershwin's difficult intervals because she had an ear and Elsie didn't. Was it in a dream that Rose sang "Stardust" so it broke your heart?

This was making it harder for Mary, her own songs mixing with Rose's. But then something simpler—Rose surprising Mary by clinking out a tune on her toy xylophone, "You Are My Sunshine," from beginning to end. Surely that was memory, the way Mary heard it now, heard it melt into "Red River Valley," heard herself singing and Rose joining in.

> *. . . do not hasten to bid me adieu,*
> *Just remember the Red River Valley*
> *And the cowboy who loved you so true.*

Herself singing the Welsh lullaby "Sleep my child and do not waken, all through the night," and little genius Rose breaking into "Men of Harlech." And quite right. It was nearly the same tune quickened into a marching song. It was tomboy Rose who liked a good march—she speeded up Mary's "Goodnight, My Someone" into "Seventy-six Trombones." She wouldn't be one to sit still for moonlight and roses. But then hadn't she made all the Teixeira women, and some of the men, weep when she sang "Ave Maria" at Sylvia's wedding? Had that really happened? Each note pure, the phrasing as easy and sweet as a brook curling over a rock.

Was that the music in her dream? Was her dream one of those dreams that trailed on into waking, letting the dreamer undream gently, measure by measure? Mary didn't want to turn her head. She'd turn her head and find a little girl who hadn't learned the songs Mary had sung to her, who hadn't taken on Mary's ear or voice or even that bit of meat on her bones.

She turned her head. Rose put her hand on Mary's shoulder and sang "Lazy Mary, will you get up, will you get up, will you get up? Lazy Mary, will you get up, will you get up this morning?" Mary felt the weight of Rose's hand, looked up at Rose's arm, bare to the shoulder of her summer dress, an arm as round and full as her own. The dress was Elsie's.

"Mom called," Rose said. "Miss Perry wants johnnycakes."

The sunlight from the window covered the wall behind Rose with leaf shadows. Mary said, "What time is it?"

"It's nine. I called Sawtooth and they've got the brunch thing covered. Mom says she's sorry but Miss Perry hasn't been eating and she just woke up and said johnnycakes."

Now Mary was truly waking up and it was as good a place to start as any, someone wanting something for breakfast. And did Miss Perry like her johnnycakes plump and soft or thin and lacy at the edges?

Then Mary was awake to the pattern of the day ticking back into place from the day before: Elsie caring for Miss Perry as she had for years but this time more haggard and dazed by a stronger tug of grief. And there would be Dick, Captain Teixeira, Jack and Sally . . . Dick and Captain Teixeira standing by with silent, tight faces—they had sent their boats out without them, not uncommon for Captain Teixeira, a first for Dick. Elsie had turned snappish. Snappish with Jack, of course, but with Sally and Rose, too. Never mind—she'd be good with the old woman.

Thinking about Miss Perry's johnnycakes or even thinking about these people who moved in the same bit of earth as she did, the strip between the hills and the salt water, was no more than a tilt of her head, a shallow breath, away from dreaming.

She touched Rose's hand, her arm, her shoulder. "Come on," Rose said. "You know how Mom is these days."

Mary thought it might be time to leave this house. This wasn't baby Rose or tomboy Rose or even plump, moody Rose. Rose was wearing Elsie's dress. If Mary stayed she'd be in between Rose and Elsie. The more Mary loved Rose and Rose loved Mary, the harder it would be. Elsie and Rose were locked in their growing apart—it had to happen for a while at least, and the ease and comfort Mary could give to Rose couldn't be given in this house.

Even what she said in the mildest way made it worse, even though she waited to say it privately to one or the other— "You know, I think Rose'll figure that out on her own" or "If I were you, Rose, I'd . . ." They wanted their fights to hurt. The pair of them wanted to reach complete fury at the same time and exhaustion at the same time and their dark wordless recognition of each other at the same time.

She'd leave them to it. Not yet, not quite yet. Not while Elsie was sitting by Miss Perry's bed. But she had to go. She'd go and wait for them on the other side of Rose's stormy adolescence.

Rose stood up and pulled on Mary's hand. Rose was growing out of her plumpness; her bones were giving her a lift out of girlhood.

Rose said, "Come on. I'll leave the door open and you call down the stairs—you know all the stuff we need."

Rose was out the door, swinging through it with one hand on the jamb, then down the stairs in three steps. The room was full of Rose's voice and will, an Elsie-like swirl of energy that cleared out the last scattered notes of song.

ary got herself out of bed. Rose had laid everything out—the canister of cornmeal, the butter, the salt, the griddle that stretched across two burners.

She said to Rose, "I suppose you'll want some, too."

"Nope. I'm on a diet."

"Breakfast is no time to diet. By noon you'll be off somewhere eating junk."

"Do you know how many calories there are in just one tablespoon of maple syrup?"

"Never mind the calories. You're growing like a weed."

"You've been saying that for years, and I'm still fat."

"You're nothing of the sort."

"Then how come Mom's always after me to exercise?"

"Because she's an exercise fanatic."

"And you're a cooking fanatic. Between you and Mom, I feel like a tennis ball. Eat. Go jog. Eat. Go jog."

"Forget I said anything."

But Rose was on a tear. "But it's even worse when you and Mom are on the same side. Mom says, 'Take Latin,' and you chime in, 'Oh, I've always been glad I had a little Latin!'—like food has Latin names the way plants do. And—"

"You're on a diet, fine. But don't you go sneering at the work I do."

Rose acted out "Huh?" as if she was playing charades, palms up, fingers spread, face twisted. Then she said, "You know what you are, you're a thin-skinned rhinoceros. You trample around telling everyone what to do, but if anyone says the tiniest little thing, I mean, like so tiny a normal person wouldn't even notice, and you get all huffy and like, 'I'm wounded, oh my God, call nine-one-one.'" Rose fell onto the sofa clutching her heart. She lifted her head. "Call the rhinoceros-abuse hotline."

Mary was still pissed off but about to laugh anyway when Elsie came in. Elsie said to Rose, "What are you doing lying down? You were supposed to bring the johnnycakes." She took in the unlit stove. "You haven't even started yet?"

Rose poked her head up over the back of the sofa and looked at Mary, raising one eyebrow (as she'd recently learned to do). Mary was glad she held back a sharp answer when Elsie sat down and held her face in her hands. Rose said, "First I had to call Sawtooth to tell them Mary—"

Mary waved a hand at Rose. "Not just now, Rose." She lit the burners, tossed the pats of butter on the griddle, and began to mix the johnnycake batter, keeping an eye on Elsie. She waved at Rose to come over to the stove. She put her arm around her and whispered in her ear, "Your mother—"

Rose pulled away and said, "I *know*."

"Listen to me," Mary said, pulling her back. "She's doing things and doing things, but there's not a thing she can do. She knows Miss Perry is dying, but she hasn't—"

"Accepted it. I know that."

"You do and you don't."

"And besides, if Miss Perry's asking for johnnycakes . . ."

"The day before my father died he asked for steamer clams and blueberry muffins. There's a lot you don't know. When you were about to be born, your mother wanted to know exactly when, and of course no one could say. No one knows exactly when someone's going to be born, and no one knows when someone's going to die. And it's a good thing it's a mystery, because a mystery wears you out and slows you down to where you're not able to think—otherwise, no one could bear to be that close to someone they love who's that close to eternity."

As Mary had been pouring this into Rose's ear, Rose had relaxed and even leaned into her. And now Rose put her arm around Mary's waist and squeezed and said, "Sometimes you are so *corny.*"

Mary went rigid.

Rose moved away. Mary couldn't bear to look at her. If it had been anyone else, Mary would have slapped her across the face with the wooden spoon.

Rose said, "Oh, God, you're going ballistic again. I didn't mean it's a bad thing."

Mary said in a voice that carried across the room, "Elsie— does Miss Perry like her johnnycakes thin and lacy at the edges or plump?"

Elsie raised her head and said, "Thin."

Rose said, "Come on, Mary."

"Don't talk to me."

"All right, it may have sounded—"

"Get away from me."

"Fine. I'm going to May's."

After Rose shut the front door behind her, Elsie looked up again. Mary said, "You go on back to Miss Perry. I'll bring the johnnycakes along in a minute or two."

Mary wrapped the platter of johnnycakes in a linen napkin and put it in a Sawtooth delivery box that had ended up in her truck. After she dropped it off, she drove to Sawtooth. She saw Rose walking on the shoulder of Route 1, headed home. Rose waved at her to stop. Mary rolled down the window. Rose said, "May told me I couldn't stay there until I apologized. So I'm sorry."

"That might be good enough for May. Not for me. Make of that what you want. I have work to do."

chapter thirty-seven

When Miss Perry woke up from her nap, her voice was crusty. It reminded Elsie of granular snow. Miss Perry said, "I believe I saw s-something of what comes after. The afterlife. They were waiting. No one I know. They were waiting for my brain vapors. They didn't say 'brain vapors,' but they thought brain vapors. Odd. I didn't like it."

"A dream;" Elsie said. "A bad dream."

"Please don't interrupt. The dogs were coming in and going out. I have never kept a dog. My father kept several. Let them out, let them in. I thought, I am old dogs. They murmured approvingly—the ones who were waiting. It was alarming. I did not wish to lose grammar. I did not wish to become dogs. I told you. I told you that later."

Miss Perry closed her eyes. Elsie thought she'd fallen asleep again, but then she saw that Miss Perry's fingers were tugging at the edge of the coverlet. Elsie reached for them, felt the awful distance of Miss Perry's fingers from Miss Perry's effort to be. Elsie willed herself to touch them. She willed her hand to touch Miss Perry's, as if it were happening at some other time. Their hands were framed in too sharp a focus. She took a breath to blur herself. If she was to be of any use, she should do simple things simply.

chapter thirty-eight

The youngest of the Tran girls was on during the day. She was also the chattiest. She stopped Elsie in the upstairs hall one day and said, "How should I spell my name? My parents spell it L-I, but in American it could be L-E-E or L-E-A, which means 'field,' or L-E-I-G-H."

Elsie said, "Why not stick with L-I? It's very pretty—if you choose L-E-I-G-H, some people will pronounce it 'lay.' If you spell it L-E-A they might say 'lee-ah' or 'lay-ah.' When I see 'L-E-E,' I say it longer than 'Li.' When I see 'Li,' I hear a short, bright sound—a little ring to it."

Li laughed. "You explain things like Miss Perry." Then she looked down. "I'm sorry, I shouldn't laugh."

"Hey—it's just us. When it's just us, we can take it easy every so often." Elsie was surprised at her own mildness. At home she'd been either biting someone's head off or enforcing silence by being heavily silent herself. Now she felt clear and nimble, just another of the Tran girls, moving weightlessly.

This mildness served Elsie well for the few days that Miss Perry lay still. Miss Perry didn't recognize Elsie, didn't suck on the plastic straw that Elsie put in her mouth. During the afternoon of the third day Miss Perry became restless, tried to put her hand on her face. Elsie thought it might be because of the flickering of sunlight. The leaves outside the window were stirring in the light air. Elsie got up and pulled the curtain. It bunched on the curtain rod. As she reached up to smooth it she heard Miss Perry's breath catch. It caught twice, hesitated, was gone.

Elsie lost the next minute or minutes. It was only when Li

came in that she knew she must have called out. When Li bent over and put her ear to Miss Perry's lips, Elsie remembered that she herself had bent over and listened, but it seemed to have happened a long time before.

Elsie called Mary Scanlon first. Mary made a long sympathetic noise and then told Elsie to open a window in Miss Perry's room. Elsie didn't ask why. She called the doctor, who said he'd come right over. Elsie said, "No hurry," and was embarrassed. The blood came back to her cheeks.

While she was on the phone Li had made the bed neater. Miss Perry's arms were on top of the covers by her sides, and her eyes were closed. Li said, "Do you want to be alone?"

Elsie said, "No." Then, "Yes."

Li had pulled the curtain back and opened the window. Elsie said, "Wait. Is that a Catholic thing—opening the window?"

Li blushed and said, "No. It's just an old superstition." Elsie nodded. She sat down, closed her eyes, and floated. Her chin sank a little, but her head kept on nodding as if bobbing in a current. She was blank and that was all right, let whatever was happening happen, she'd stay out of the way.

When the doctor came, the sun was much lower and she was mute. The doctor looked at Li, and Li gathered Elsie up with an arm around her shoulders. Li took her down the stairs. Elsie stopped on the last broad stair, where she'd nursed Rose on one side and held Miss Perry on the other. Mary Scanlon came in the front door.

Elsie said, "What happens now?"

"It's all right," Mary said. "They'll take care of things upstairs. You've done everything. Hasn't she, Li? Right up to the last." Mary drove Elsie home in her little truck, continuing to murmur a white noise of common comfort.

chapter thirty-nine

Jack took over. Mary blamed herself since she'd been the one to call him to say that Miss Perry was dead, and she'd gone on to say that Elsie could use some help. Jack installed a secretary at Miss Perry's house to answer the phone, he called the local newspapers and the *Providence Journal,* he called the Episcopal priest. All that was okay. But he called again to say he'd decided to have the reception at Sawtooth. Mary said, "That's generous of you." Jack cleared his throat in a way that Mary thought meant he'd bill the estate. He changed the subject. He said, "I've got an idea for the music. A couple of hymns that we'll all sing; I've been looking through the hymnal. But then I also thought we should have a little Latin for Miss Perry. And it would make the RCs feel at home. There's Mr. Salviatti and all those Teixeiras and the Tran girls. They're not Buddhists, are they? The *Agnus Dei* from the Verdi Requiem. It's a duet for soprano and mezzo-soprano. Didn't Rose sing at the Teixeira girl's wedding?" Jack didn't pause after either question. "So there we are," he said. "You and Rose. The organist is on board, and the padre says you can rehearse in the church. After the service the timing might be a little tight for you to get back to the kitchen, but the rest of the staff'll be there."

He said good-bye before Mary could say any of the things that occurred to her. When Elsie got back—she'd gone for yet another long walk in the woods—Mary told her, thought she was telling it the way she usually told stories about preposterous Jack. Mary added, "I think I know what's going on. He's having a grand dream about his own funeral."

But Elsie seized on the phrase "might be a little tight for you to get back to the kitchen." She repeated it twice and then said, "That thick son of a bitch." When Elsie picked up the phone, Mary said, "Don't," but she saw that Elsie had gone into a zone of rage, a rage she'd been storing up, and why not let her fire it off at Jack?

But Elsie apparently got Sally on the phone. She said, "Tell him to call me. Have him call me before he does anything else." Then she listened for a long time. She finally said, "Don't tell me not to get upset. And don't tell me that he's trying to spare me. This is more like some gala promotional event for Sawtooth."

Elsie hung up. Mary waited while Elsie banged around the room. Mary was amazed at Elsie, at how fast she'd turned into an angry little ball. For a day or two she'd been a cloud, her comings and goings so soft Mary had to look to see if Elsie was in or out. Now Mary was wary of Elsie's filling the room. Mary said, "It's more his tone than anything else, isn't it? I mean, I'm happy to do whatever has to be done in the way of cooking. There is going to be a crowd when you come to think of it. If you want to put your hand to things, it wouldn't be a bad idea. For one thing, it'd be better if you picked the pallbearers."

Elsie sat down. "Pallbearers. I guess that's right. How many does it take?"

"Six, I think."

"All men? Do they have to be men?"

"I don't know as there's a rule. I've only ever seen men. The casket weighs enough so they have to put some muscle into it."

"I'm not sure Captain Teixeira's up to it."

"It depends on who else."

"I suppose Dick and Charlie and Tom."

"They'd make up for Captain Teixeira."

"I suppose I should ask Jack. He's a cousin of some kind. How many is that?"

"Five."

"I could do it myself." Elsie lifted her head. "But then there I'd be in front of half of South County alongside Dick."

Mary said, "I don't know as how people would make much of that. But you may be right that now's not the time to be trying something different. Why not one of the Tran boys? Or old Mr. Tran himself? Miss Perry took more of an interest in the girls, but Mr. Tran could stand for all of them."

Elsie nodded. Then she cried a bit, not hard. She sniffed and dabbed her cheeks with her cuff. She said, "You're right. I should get busy. You're right. You are . . ." She made fists with her hands and pressed them hard against each other. "A wonderful friend."

Mary almost laughed at the effort it took Elsie to get that out. Then she thought, How am I going to tell her I'm leaving?

chapter forty

May had just got off the phone with Elsie when it rang again. May was thinking of how to get in touch with Charlie on the R.V. *Trident*, of whether he could get back for the funeral, so at first she was pleased to hear a woman's voice say that she was going to give Charlie a ride home. A ride was a help, since May's car was in the shop. May wondered if Elsie could have radioed the ship to tell Charlie about Miss Perry, but then the woman said, "Charlie's all right, I'm sure he's going to be fine."

May said, "What? What happened? Where is he?"

"Oh. I thought the captain . . . This is the first you've heard? Charlie's in Boston. They're running one more test right now, just to make sure. He's got a broken collarbone and maybe a mild concussion. They're pretty sure everything's fine, but you know how they are. They took X-rays and now another MRI or maybe a CAT scan, and they're waiting for a specialist. She's on her way. But that's just an extra precaution. It may sound like . . . I thought you knew and were waiting to hear that it's pretty much okay, which it pretty much is. He's complaining about having to stay on that flat board they strap you on."

May hadn't pictured anything clearly until the word *strap.* "Oh my God."

"No, no, that's good. It's good that that's what he's complaining about. If it was worse he wouldn't be complaining. They're just keeping him immobilized as a precaution. I'm sure he's going to be fine. I'll call again as soon as—"

"Wait. Don't go. I don't know what happened."

"Charlie took us to an island, me and one of the other researchers, and he, the researcher, was climbing a little way up a cliff to look at a bird's nest and he got stuck. So Charlie started up to help him. I told Charlie I'd go—I'm a mountain climber—but he went. The researcher somehow broke off a piece of rock and it knocked Charlie into the water. There was a little bit of a sea running and he got swept out, but I dove in and got him to shore, and I got the other guy down and set off a flare and they sent another boat from the *Trident.* After a while a helicopter came and took Charlie and me to Portland and then Boston. We're at Mass General now."

May was pressing the phone to her ear so hard it began to hurt. She sat down. She said, "Can I talk to a doctor?"

The woman said, "I'll try to get one, but it might take a while, so I'll call you back. Okay? So bye for now."

May felt her body wrapped with what this woman said: Boston, going to be fine, precaution, pretty much okay. Who was this woman? What did she know? May made an effort to block the pictures. Nothing would be true until she touched Charlie. She swept the kitchen floor, concentrating on her hands on the broom handle. She blocked the board and straps, the boat, the sea, but she couldn't block what it was like to fall.

The weightless falling came up from her chest into her head.

She should call the boatyard; someone there could call out to Dick, he'd row in from the mooring. She pictured that, his stamping his boots outside the office before he went in to pick up the phone.

Wait. What if the doctor called while she was calling Dick? She swept the little pile of dirt into the dustpan. She'd got used to waiting for Dick; waiting for Dick wasn't like this. She put clean sheets on Charlie's bed.

Nobody called—not a doctor, not the woman.

When Dick came home for supper, May told him. He stood still. He asked her a question she couldn't answer. He asked another. When she said, "All I know is what that woman told me. She said she'd get a doctor to call."

Dick nodded, said, "I'm going," and was out the door. May heard the motor and then the tires crunching on the gravel.

She was stunned. She was so stunned her deepest feeling didn't rise to the surface. She thought that maybe it was her job to stay by the phone.

May put away the food without eating. She trusted the woman less and less. She was sure she wouldn't be able to sleep. When she went to get a book she saw the books Miss Perry had given the boys and she turned away. She put her hand on the phone three or four times and finally called Phoebe Fitzgerald. Phoebe began to talk about how sad she was about Miss Perry and how sorry she was for May, for May and Dick and the boys, for so many people. May said, "I can't stay on the phone long. I'm waiting for a doctor to call." And then she had to say Charlie had had an accident.

Phoebe said, "Does Dick know?"

"Yes. He's gone to Boston."

"I'm coming over," Phoebe said. "I'll be right there."

So Phoebe was there when the woman finally called. The woman said, "Things may take a little longer. They're not explaining exactly why. I told one doctor I'm an EMT, but he didn't seem to . . . And I haven't seen the specialist, but they did say she's here, so maybe I'll get to talk to her."

"Who are you?" May said.

"Deirdre O'Malley."

May repeated the name out loud, then said, "Are you one of the scientists or one of the crew?"

"Sort of a researcher."

May wrote the name down, had to ask how to spell Deirdre. She didn't want to talk to Deirdre, but she didn't want to hang up. She said, "Charlie's father is on his way. He'll get there in another hour or so. He'll likely be the only person wearing big rubber boots. Could you ask him to call home? I forgot to remind him he's supposed to be a pallbearer tomorrow."

The woman either coughed or laughed. May was about to hang up when Phoebe took the phone. Phoebe said, "Deirdre O'Malley? Did you used to be an instructor for Women in the Wilderness? We called you Didi? I can't believe it! Oh—you may not remember me—I'm Phoebe Fitzgerald. It was a long time ago, I'd just got divorced . . . No, she was the other one, sort of plump. I remember, I remember every minute."

After Phoebe hung up, she said, "Well, that is just surreal."

May wished Phoebe could stop being Phoebe, just for a while. She put the kettle on and asked Phoebe if she'd like a cup of tea. Then she thought that if she couldn't sleep and couldn't read she might as well let Phoebe talk. It would be like waiting in a doctor's office, turning the pages of a glossy magazine, watching your fingertips turn page after page of things that didn't matter.

"Well, that is just amazing," Phoebe said, and May watched Phoebe's pretty mouth and hands. "I remember Didi O'Malley; I remember her because she was so young but we had to listen to her every word or we wouldn't survive. It was actually called that: Women in the Wilderness, a survival program. We made tea from pine needles; we made fire by the bow-drill method. Didi would disappear at night—just leave us, ten women alone in the dark. No blankets, just a pile of leaves you made a nest with. Didi told us later it was a metaphor for how to deal with anything—you just start taking care of little things and pretty soon you're feeling better about everything. I don't mean to say that we weren't glad to get out of the woods. And glad to see the last of Deirdre O'Malley. The first night someone said, 'So where do we sleep?' and she said, 'Remember that squirrel's nest we saw? Think about it.' And the woman said, 'You mean we should climb a tree?' And Didi just raised one eyebrow in this totally exasperating way."

May let Phoebe go on. Sometimes May took in the details—Phoebe picked up a wooden spoon to illustrate the bow-drill method of making a fire. But mostly she let Phoebe's voice drift over her, a haze that soothed her, but then her neck twitched or her knee jumped and she snapped into wide-awake waiting again.

Dick called. He said, "They don't know." May waited. Dick said, "I talked to two of them. I asked when they would know. The woman doctor said she needs a better picture."

"Did you see him?"

"No."

"Did they say if he's in pain?"

There was a pause. May was afraid Dick hadn't asked. Dick finally said, "They said they're holding off on the painkillers until they know more. If it was just his broken collarbone they could give him some, but with a head injury they want to hold off."

May held on to the phone with both hands. She said, "Did you ask . . . ?" and then started over. "Did they say he—"

Dick said, "He's not going to die."

He said this fiercely, and May felt all of Dick at once, his years of *doing* things pressing through him. No use. No use for her. She set him aside and hoped her own hope for Charlie.

She said, "I don't expect you'll be back for Miss Perry's funeral. I'd better call Elsie and let her know." And then in the same tone, as if it was another practical detail, she said, "You should have taken me with you. Call when they know something more. I'll be awake."

She hung up the phone. She felt so dragged down she didn't hear what Phoebe was saying to her. Phoebe took her hand to get her attention. Phoebe said, "May, listen. I'll drive you." May stared at her, trying to attach her to what was going on. Then, as if to prove she was the real Phoebe, Phoebe said, "I have an old beau who's a doctor at Mass General. He's been there for ages, so if we need any help . . ." May nodded. Phoebe said, "I'll just call Eddie while you change." May was ready to be bustled along but was puzzled. She stood still. Phoebe said, "Oh, you know—something cheerful for Charlie but serious for the doctors. I know—that dress you wear when we go to Sawtooth for lunch."

Never mind if she's putting a ribbon on it, she's taking me to Boston.

chapter forty-one

Tom called Elsie early in the morning to say Dick and Charlie couldn't be pallbearers. "Charlie's in the hospital. Mom's sorry she didn't call last night, but she was—"

"What is it?" Elsie said. "Is he going to be all right?"

"They seem to think so. He's got a hematoma, which is a clot, and it's in his head, but it's small, and the neurologist says she thinks it'll just go away, so they're not going to start cutting. I was set to go there, but Mom says to go to the funeral first, so I guess she's not so worried as she was. Anyways, that's where Charlie and Dad are."

"Where? At South County?"

"No. Boston. Mass General. The *Trident*'s been down east. Charlie fell off a cliff trying to help some damn bird-watcher. So that's where Charlie and Dad are, but I'll be on hand for you. Have you thought of asking Eddie? Eddie and Walt both, you want strong backs. Hold on—I just remembered about Miss Perry and Eddie—"

"Don't worry, I'll think of someone."

"You want me to tell Rose about Charlie? No, I'd better wait till after the funeral in case she's nervous about her singing. Say, have you ever wondered where she got that voice? Dad can't carry a tune in a bucket. And Rose tells me you're not much of a songbird."

"Have you ever wondered where you got your talking so much? Not from your mom and dad."

Tom laughed. "Okay, you got me. But I got to say one more thing. One time Dad said to Charlie and me that we wouldn't have turned out so good if it wasn't for Miss Perry. And there's you and Miss Perry. I'm thinking about you and her. You're both good people around here."

She said, "Thank you, Tom."

She called Johnny Bienvenue and asked him to be a pallbearer. She decided she'd be the sixth pallbearer. If people thought that was funny, to hell with them.

What she hadn't counted on was that she'd be undone, so undone she was afraid that she'd be too weak.

Jack had wanted to give a eulogy. She'd said that Miss Perry didn't need one. He could be the second lay reader, after Tory Hazard. It was Tory Hazard's reading that undid Elsie. Tory didn't break down, but she was on the verge. It wasn't only that—Elsie had a spell of dizziness that made her grab the edge of the pew. It was a vertigo of time rather than space. Tory Hazard had been Miss Perry's pet before Elsie; she brought old time and new time into one perspective, a perspective that was both long and horribly foreshortened. Elsie looked at Tory's fingers curled around the sides of the lectern, felt her own fingers straining to hold herself in place. Elsie knew Tory only by name and an old story or two. Tory was now much older than in her story, her thin, pretty face beginning to loosen. But it wasn't Tory's name or story or face—it was her hands on the lectern, more immediately intelligible to Elsie than the words of the reading, that reminded Elsie of Miss Perry's dream in which death was the loss of grammar, the last sinew of her consciousness that had held her back from nothingness.

Tory finished reading. There was a rustling—people shifting in their pews, picking up their programs, breathing, clearing their throats—a stir of wind across dry reeds.

It was Jack who brought Elsie back to the world with his handsome gray suit and black armband. Elsie considered that armband an affectation—too European, too mourning-chic. Jack adjusted his reading glasses and scanned the congregation over the rims. What? Was he checking the guest list? The seating arrangements? After a prickle of resentment, which, she had to admit, steadied her, she gave way by degrees. Jack read very well; the cadences of the King James Bible were right up his alley. "I will lift up mine eyes unto the hills, from whence cometh my help." His voice, which could be annoyingly enveloping at close range, carried easily, was suited to this dignified, well-decorated church. She thought he might have gone too far when, at the end of his reading, he stared heavenward. What was this? Was he lifting his eyes unto the hills? It turned out he was cuing Mary and Rose in the choir loft.

Elsie could hear that they were in time, an octave apart but perfectly linked, and she could understand the words. "Agnus Dei qui tollis peccata mundi . . ." At first it was just Rose and Mary, then the choir, then Rose and Mary lifting above the choir. When they finished, Sally, seated on her right, breathed into her ear, "Oh my God, I had no idea. I mean, that was as good as a record." Elsie touched her hand and pointed her chin at the minister, who was starting again. When he turned, stood at one end of the casket, and looked at Elsie, she hesitated. He held out his hand. Jack and Captain Teixeira stood. Captain Teixeira took charge, nodding to Tom and Mr. Tran. Johnny Bienvenue was standing in front of her, taking her hand. She didn't get up. She was sure something was wrong. For a second she was afraid she was wearing her red dress. She looked at Johnny's hand, saw his navy blue sleeve, her hand, her navy blue sleeve.

Captain Teixeira arranged the six of them sensibly—Tom and Jack at the front end, Elsie and Johnny at the back end, and Mr. Tran and himself in the middle. Tom and Johnny, the two strongest, were at opposite corners. At Captain Teixeira's nod they picked up the casket. It weighed more than she'd expected, but the effort concentrated her attention. She saw nothing but Captain Teixeira's broad back, felt nothing but the weight. A burn flared in her arm and shoulder, and then fixed itself a notch below pain after she moved closer and put more of her back into it. The weight wasn't Miss Perry, it was a mass of oak and bronze that had less to do with Miss Perry than did Captain Teixeira's back. He was very old, but his back and shoulders filled the black broadcloth of his suit coat, and Elsie felt less scattered as she fitted her steps to his.

After they slid the casket into the hearse, Elsie floated toward him as if she were a ghost floating through a wall. She pressed against his back, and when he turned she clung to him. He put his arms around her and held her until she was still. He said, "Lydia." It took her a second to recognize Miss Perry's name. She'd seen it on envelopes, on documents, on the stern of Captain Teixeira's second boat, the *Lydia P.* "Lydia loved you so much, you did so much, you are as good as the best daughter." His voice croaked in her ear, rattling into her brain, for the moment blessedly empty of any modest denial or polite answer or, for that matter, any sense that anyone was watching.

She let go of him when she thought she was about to kiss him. She stood up straight and put her hands on his chest. "You. You're Miss Perry's best friend." They were standing between the back of the hearse and the front of the church, the people flowing around them. Had she been about to kiss him? On his mouth?

And then she was in Captain Teixeira's three-bench van along with a part of his family—Sylvia and her husband, and Dick's sternman, Tony. Captain Teixeira got out and pulled Rose in. He called to Mary Scanlon, but she called back, "I've got to go to Sawtooth. See you there!"

Tony was at the wheel. Captain Teixeira told him to turn his lights on. Then he said, "Wait. We should bring Tory Hazard with us. Sylvia, go get Tory. She's right there at the top of the steps. Tony, if you turn the lights on, you have to run the motor. Rose, you sing beautifully, as good as Mary. One of these days I'm going to teach you a fado. Maybe Sylvia better teach you, I don't sing so good. I lost my whistle. Tony, let the priest's car go ahead. Then let Jack go, that's the only family car. That's nice, his armband. Lydia liked traditional things."

Sylvia and Tory arrived, and Captain Teixeira made room for Tory beside him on the middle seat. He put his arm around Tory and said, "You okay?" He turned to Elsie. "I've known Tory since she was a little girl. And her father—"

Tory put a hand on his knee and said, "Ruy, please. I'm sorry. It's just . . ."

Captain Teixeira shrank a bit, took a breath, and said, "You know Elsie, right? And her daughter, Rose? Rose sang the soprano part. Mary Scanlon was the alto."

"Mezzo," Rose said. "It's an octave lower than my part, and it could be an alto but it's a mezzo-soprano. There's other places she has to sing higher."

"You little smarty pants," Sylvia said. "I used to change your diapers."

"Okay, Tony," Captain Teixeira said. "Right behind that car." He looked out the back window. "That's Eddie Wormsley's pickup; he could've cleaned it up some."

Elsie looked. "It's okay. He's driving Tom Pierce."

"Now you mention it, where's Dick? He was around yesterday. I know Charlie's at sea."

"Dick's in Boston. Charlie had an accident, and he's in the hospital there."

Elsie felt Rose lean forward even before she heard Rose's voice. "Mo-om! Why didn't you tell me? Jesus, Mom."

In between Elsie and Tory, Captain Teixeira turned, squeezing Elsie one way, Tory the other. He said, "Don't talk to your mother like that." He said this matter-of-factly. He stayed turned. After a long pause he added, "You've got a beautiful voice and you're a beautiful girl, so be a good girl. Now your mother's going to tell us about Charlie."

As Elsie began to tell what she knew, she felt she was dropping stones in a still pool, sending ripples to every side—to Tony, who was Dick's right-hand man; to Sylvia, who'd been in love with Charlie; to Rose . . . Tom was the brother Rose saw more of, joked with, but she'd cried out for Charlie, even if she turned her alarm into blame.

Captain Teixeira said, "Oh, *meu Deus*! That's a terrible thing for Dick and May."

"That's all I know," Elsie said. "And Rose—Tom thought he'd better wait to tell you till after you sang. So . . ." Elsie heard herself speaking to a van full of people who knew her place in this story. It had seeped drop by drop into common knowledge, so completely that Tory Hazard was the only one who had to furrow her brow.

Captain Teixeira said, "Tony, only the hearse goes through the gate. You pull in beside that black car. Okay. We'll take a minute before we get out so we can each have a good thought for Charlie to get better."

When Captain Teixeira raised his head and let out a loud breath, they all began to stir. Captain Teixeira said to Tory, "You got to pull that handle kind of hard. The other way. The door slides back." After Tory got out, he turned. "You go ahead, Sylvia; I got to take my time." As Rose slid past he said, "Rose, I know you're feeling bad about Charlie. I think he's going to be okay. But there's another thing. This is your first funeral, right? I got to tell you the priest is going to say something when we throw the first bit of dirt on the coffin. I'm telling you now so you know. He says, 'The earth and the sea shall give up their dead and the corruptible bodies shall be changed . . . ' It always gets to me. It makes me see too much. Okay, here we go. Give me a little tug, would you? I stiffened up some."

Elsie looked at Rose's face as she took Captain Teixeira's hand. Since Captain Teixeira had bossed Rose around, Elsie expected Rose to have put on her mask of sullen compliance. Elsie's second guess, now that she saw Rose smile, was that Rose had been seduced by his calling her a beautiful girl. Wrong again. Rose was someone strange. Her smile was serene, confident, and womanly. She took Captain Teixeira's other hand and guided him out of the van. She ran her hand down his back as if straightening him. She turned and said, "Mom? You coming? You two should be together for this."

Rose's sudden grace was as mysterious to Elsie as Rose's music but more unnerving. More than their quarrels, this unforeseen full green leaf made Elsie foresee Rose's growing up and away from her.

chapter forty-two

The doctor, the neurologist whom May trusted right away, said she was sure that Charlie would make a complete recovery, but she couldn't say how long it would take. "He's very healthy; he's very strong physically and mentally. I think he'd get better on his own—the subdural hematoma has already shrunk by itself—but therapy will help with any lingering symptoms. I think that little speech impediment will clear up a bit faster, and he'll get his motor skills back faster, too. Some people think physical therapy is good for the brain. In any case, therapy will give him something to do. I can tell he's not used to just sitting around. That would drive him up the wall. Probably drive you up the wall, too."

Deirdre O'Malley, who was standing behind May, Dick, and Tom, said, "I believe in the mind-body link; it did a whole lot for me when I was hurt. But mainly I want to say you were great, really great. The neurosurgeon would've started cutting, but you—"

"Thank you," the neurologist said. "We actually worked it out together." She turned to May and Dick. "I'm sorry we couldn't keep you posted every minute, but we were both pretty involved. I'm glad it's looking good now."

May thought that Deirdre might be feeling rebuked, so she said, "This is the woman who dove in and pulled Charlie out of the water. She's an EMT."

"Yes, so I heard." She took a breath and added, "Good job."

When an orderly rolled Charlie out the front door, Dick was there with his pickup, Phoebe with her Saab, and Tom on a motorcycle. May said to Charlie, "You'll be more comfortable in Phoebe's car." She looked at Dick. Dick had said he was sorry for taking off by himself, but he'd added, "I just had to do something." May hadn't said anything.

Dick said to Tom, "Something wrong with that car of yours?"

"Still in the shop."

Deirdre said, "That's Walt Wormsley's motorcycle." They all looked at her. She said, "He used to do some work for me. But, hey, this'll work out. Tom, you can ride with your family, and I'll drive Walt's motorcycle. That way I can swing by and pick up some things from a friend's house and it wouldn't slow anyone down. It's okay—I've driven it before."

Tom shook his head. "I can't do that without Walt's say-so. Look, I'll take you, and everyone else can go on ahead."

May had been thinking of Deirdre as Charlie's shipmate and rescuer. She was taken aback when Deirdre bent over Charlie, whispered in his ear, and then kissed him on the mouth.

Tom cranked the motorcycle, Deirdre got on, and they were gone. Then Dick got in his pickup. He'd come up alone, let him go back alone.

May and Phoebe settled Charlie in the front seat. As they walked around the front of the car Phoebe said to May, "So it looks as if everything's going to be fine." May shook her head. No sense in tempting fate like that. She was also trying not to think of how mad she was at Dick. Maybe *mad* wasn't the right word—*broken* was more like it. Something was broken.

Phoebe said, "I'm just sorry you and Dick couldn't go to Miss Perry's funeral. And of course you're exhausted. Was that room they got you all right? They should have done that the first night. I mean, they could see we were just curled up on those awful chairs." May looked through the windshield at Charlie, who'd tipped his seat back and closed his eyes. Phoebe said, "Yes, we should get going." She got as far as the driver's door and said, "I've got tons to tell you. When I went to my friend's house, I drove Deirdre to *her* friend's house, so we talked, or I should say she talked. But I guess that'll have to wait. Let's just say I don't think we've seen the last of her. You'll be okay in the backseat? I'll scoot my seat up some."

May didn't want to talk or think; she didn't want any part of her to come loose. As she and Phoebe each took hold of their door handles, Phoebe said, "It's funny—she reminds me of someone."

May said, "Charlie's just falling asleep," but Phoebe had already jarred the idea loose: Deirdre looked a lot like Elsie. Maybe a dozen years younger but the same animal alertness, the compactness, the tomboy edge. The way Deirdre was ready to ride a motorcycle. But fair's fair, also ready to dive into the sea and pull Charlie out.

May got in. Charlie's seat was tipped back so far she could put her hand on his forehead. Charlie said, "I'm f-fine, Ma, I'm going to be fi-fine. Damn!"

"Don't worry. The doctor said that'll clear up."

Charlie touched his nose with his right forefinger, then with his left. "There. Could be worse. But what am I going to call you, Ph-Ph-Phoebe?"

Phoebe laughed the way she did around men. "Oh, we'll think of something." Phoebe touched Charlie's arm. "I'm sorry. I wasn't laughing because . . . It was hearing my own name."

"It's okay."

"You know, a little bit of a stammer has a certain charm. You'll have to watch yourself."

May willed Phoebe's hand off Charlie's arm.

chapter forty-three

E xecutrix. Jack enjoyed saying it as often as possible. "The first thing you should do as executrix is to go identify the assets. Real property, personal property, choses in action—"

"I know."

"Johnny won't be able to help this time around, since the state may have an interest."

"I know."

"But he could be helpful in informal ways. You may want more leave from Natural Resources, since your duties as executrix—"

"Jack, I know what to do."

But when Elsie stepped into Miss Perry's house she was surprisingly undone. Not by grief—she knew her grief—but by the house itself, which she suddenly didn't know. It was as if the house and everything in it were springing to life. She saw the door, the rack with Miss Perry's father's canes, the staircase, the bull's-eye window in the library—as if she'd once heard of them and was only now seeing them. At first she shrank back as if all these things radiated an energy that was opposed to her. Then she began to touch things: the desk, the mantelpiece, the corner of the glass-front bookcase. She said, "I am the executrix." It could be her word—to hell with Jack—a magic word. She didn't say it to diminish the house but to receive it. She'd meant to sit down at the desk, but the air was too charged for that, the light too heavy. She filled a pail of water, added a cup of vinegar, and cleaned the tall windows to the west. She used the bookshelf ladder to reach the bull's-eye window. She found a jar of leather preservative in a pigeonhole in the desk. The label read "Everett Hazard Book Shop." She dipped her fingers in it and anointed the leather bindings of all eight volumes of Gibbon's *Roman Empire*. And then the whole shelf of leather-bound histories. Parkman, Prescott, Mottley. This was the sort of executrix she would be, letting in light and applying balm. A curator. Or rather curatrix.

She would have charge of this house until the Perryville School took over. The library was to remain a library, the second and third floors to be a dormitory for the senior girls. And surely a faculty member to supervise them. The headmaster had spoken to her about the possibility.

She applied the last of the jar to Henry Adams's complete works. She smelled her hands—where could she find another jar?—and wondered what she could teach, how anyone could teach anything, since everything depended on everything else.

chapter forty-four

Rose screeched. She screeched with her mouth closed so it was half screech, half whinny. She took a breath and said, "It's not enough that I have to go to this . . . this finishing school. What do you think that'll be like with you—"

"It's not a finishing school. It's a perfectly good progressive school. I don't know where you got the idea that—"

"Whatever. Just when a few people have stopped thinking I'm a total loser, you're butting in and the whole thing'll start all over again."

"I won't be teaching *you*. And I'll be part-time administration, mostly at Miss Perry's house."

"Why can't you just go on guarding the Great Swamp?"

"Because they've replaced me with someone." This was half true. "I can stay on, but it would be at a desk job in Providence."

"So?"

"So I don't want to."

"So get your old boyfriend to fix it."

"How I decide to earn money is up to me. Besides—"

"And that makes my life up to you, too."

"Besides, he's done enough. And besides, you don't go around fixing things that way."

Rose cocked her head. "You're saying he's done enough *and* you don't go around fixing things that way? I hope you're not going to teach logic."

Elsie stared at her. Rose said, "What's the use?" and went into her room and closed the door.

Beside Rose's door there was a thermostat that controlled the heat in her bedroom. Elsie turned it down to fifty. She put another log in the woodstove. With the door closed Rose would be freezing in twenty minutes. After five minutes Elsie turned it back up. Part of what made her so mad at Rose was her own uncertainty—was she leaping boldly or curling up?

Elsie rode her Exercycle. Rose called through the door, "Mom! I'm trying to study!"

Elsie started to carry the Exercycle up the inside stairs to Mary Scanlon's empty room. It wouldn't fit. She used the outdoor stairs—the separate entrance that they'd thought discreet but that Mary, as far as Elsie knew, never used.

Elsie had been puzzled and hurt. She missed Mary and knew she'd go on missing her, but she recognized what Mary was talking about when Mary said she wanted to get out of the Rose-Elsie crossfire.

As Elsie pedaled it occurred to her that Rose could be a boarder at school. If Elsie worked full-time she'd get a free pass on tuition—maybe room and board were covered, too. What was she thinking? That Mary would come back then? That Rose would miss her and be nice? Or did she want her house to herself? For peace and quiet? That would be nice for a change. And of course she could come and go as she pleased. She hadn't had a sexual fantasy since she'd gone on leave to care for Miss Perry. Maybe she'd forgotten how. She'd certainly been hollowed, her senses had become simpler, her attention lifted out of herself. Some days she'd felt as young as Li Tran, or as if she were once again Miss Perry's pet student. Other days she'd felt ageless, gliding up and down the stairs, the swing of her skirt barely stirring the still air. How long had it gone on? A month? Forty days? She'd liked the feeling of her body being hollowed—she hadn't exercised, she'd eaten little. Now she was re-finding her body, and it was diminished, not up to hard exercise. Not even responding to fantasy. Had something else happened? Could it be that what she'd thought was a time of ascetic selflessness (for which Captain Teixeira had so sweetly praised her) was also when the first tendril of menopause was taking hold? Were her breasts smaller? Was there a bloom of down on her upper lip? Was that why she was snappish with Rose? And now unable even to conjure an imaginary lover?

She looked at the maple leaves outside the window, half of them still green, half tipped with red. Miss Perry always loved fall, would stop at the first sight of scarlet, lean on her walking stick, and recite, "Season of mists and mellow fruitfulness . . ." One time Elsie had been in the woods with Dick and, feeling a bubble of rebellion against Miss Perry's bookishness, she'd said to Dick, "That first bit of red gives me a pang."

"What? You don't like fall? I like fall."

"Fall's okay. It's just the first bit of red on the green. It reminds me of how I feel when I'm just starting to come and I don't want to stop fucking just yet." She'd laughed because she thought his frown was his first reaction and that in a second or two he'd see that she was being high-spirited, that she was flirting, she was joking . . .

But as she replayed it now—and she couldn't keep from hearing herself several times over—it sounded like coarse swaggering. She saw the mixture of puzzlement and distaste in his eyes. And only now it dawned on her that he hadn't just been shocked that she was mixing up natural beauty with private frenzies, he must also have thought that she was blithely waving a hand at a whole forest of her old gaspings and moanings.

She formed a sentence—"I meant *us*"—but it didn't get into her mouth. She was pedaling faster, as if she could outrace the banshee of embarrassment swooping after her. It caught the back of her neck and threaded down her spine.

Rose called up the stairs. "Are we going to eat? I mean, anytime in the foreseeable future?"

chapter forty-five

May tried to be fair. She reminded herself that Deirdre had pulled Charlie out of the water. That had to count more than everything else. So May was at a loss to say why it bothered her to see Deirdre putting Charlie through their exercise routine. The doctor said the exercises were probably helpful, certainly couldn't do any harm. So there Charlie and Deirdre were out in front of the house, sort of running in place in slow motion, lifting the right knee and touching it with the left elbow, left knee to right elbow. Deirdre said it activated the right brain–left brain flow.

It was worse now that Dick was out to sea again. It had bothered May some that Deirdre could get Dick talking, could ask him just the sort of questions to get him going. But Deirdre pulled Charlie into it, too. It turned out Charlie had done some research on red-crab habitat. Deirdre didn't come right out and suggest it, but she'd got Charlie thinking about going out with Dick to take a look. At least, Charlie asked a lot of questions about what sort of electronics were on board. It was a blessing May had waited for.

When Dick was in the house Deirdre slept in Tom's old room. She still started out sleeping in Tom's room, appeared to wake up in Tom's room, but May had heard her going down the hall to the bathroom and not going back to Tom's room.

May couldn't bring herself to ask the doctor about that sort of thing.

Rose came to visit. She came with Tom—May saw that Rose and Tom were thick as thieves, and that pleased her.

Everyone piled into the kitchen. May set out biscuits and jelly and watched, trying to keep herself away from her little dark wish that Rose wouldn't like Deirdre. But Deirdre held back, let Rose get all the attention from Tom and Charlie. When Charlie stuttered, Rose opened her eyes wide and then put her hand on Charlie's arm. Charlie smiled a little tugged-down smile. He said, "I'm working on it, Rose."

Rose said, "I'm in a play at school, and the hero stutters a little and the heroine likes it."

May felt one of her pangs of love for Rose. The thought of Rose at that school made her fearful, but she loved the way Rose touched Charlie, the way Rose was at home here.

May asked Rose if she could stay for supper. Rose said it was a school night, she had a ton of homework. Tom said he had to be off, too, and May got ready for another supper with just Charlie and Deirdre and her at the kitchen table.

It was Deirdre who said, "So can we come see your play? Or is it just for the school?"

May tried not to mind Deirdre saying "we."

"Yeah, sure," Rose said. "I mean, yes, they want people to come."

"You got a big part?" Tom said.

"Yes, but only because I can sing. It's a musical version of *She Stoops to Conquer.* Some guy in Boston wrote the music. It's not bad."

"Jeez, Rose. Right out of the gate and you're a star." Tom laughed. "Some of the other girls must be pissed off."

May said, "Tom . . ."

Rose said, "Yeah. Some." Rose's face tightened—Tom always did say one thing too many. Then Rose lifted her head and May saw how Rose would look when she was full-grown. Rose said, "A lot of the teachers went to Miss Perry's funeral, and one of them's the music teacher. It's not like I said, 'Me, me, oh, pick me!'" Rose said this last part in a squeaky voice that made Tom laugh. Rose added, "So let 'em be"—she looked sideways at May—"peeved."

Tom laughed, and Charlie and Deirdre joined in. May flushed. Tom said, "Well, there you go, Ma. At least you raised one of us right."

May turned to Tom to hush him before he got going the way he sometimes did, barking out joke after joke. Then, as if she'd struck a match that sputtered for a second and then burst into flame, she heard what Tom just said. It made her eyes sting. It wasn't really true, it couldn't ever be but a little bit true. It certainly wasn't meant to be said out loud like that. She took a step back, away from Tom, away from where he'd just plucked it out of her, Tom the magician taking a penny out of her ear in front of everyone.

She put her apron on, got busy fixing supper. She heard a chair scrape. She turned and saw they were all getting up. They weren't laughing. Tom put his hand on Charlie's shoulder; Charlie touched Tom's arm. May thought that was what she ought to have been worrying about. But here was Rose coming to her; Rose, who'd shot up over the last year, but not just that—her face was more definite. Girls grow up quicker than boys—May could say things like that now.

Rose said, "Can you come to the play? It's not till spring, but they're already getting parents to buy tickets. I know the songs; all I have to do now is get a kind of accent for the dialogue parts. Mary Scanlon said I should think of the way Miss Perry talked, but I didn't see her all that much, not when I was old enough to pay attention to people's accents. It's an old English play, but we're doing it as if it's nowadays. The joke is the girl is sort of upper-class, but she pretends to be the maid because the boy she likes doesn't stutter when he's flirting with the maid." Rose laughed. "It sounds silly, but we're getting it to be funny. So say you'll come."

From across the room Tom said, "You want to sound funny, talk like Phoebe Fitzgerald."

May said, "Yes, Rose," although she felt uneasy already; she'd never been up to that school, and the notion of going up there to see those private-school kids—a lot of them from

Sawtooth Point—put on a play making fun of the way people talk . . . And there she and Dick would be, talking the way they talked . . ."Yes, Rose," she said again. And then to Tom, "And don't you pick on Phoebe Fitzgerald."

"Have you ever noticed, Ma, that you spend a lot of time saying 'yes' to Rose and 'don't' to me?"

"Well, who wouldn't?" Deirdre said. "I just got here and that sounds about right to me."

Tom laughed. "Hey—I got to watch out for you. Come on, Rose, before she zings me again."

Rose leaned closer to May and whispered in her ear, "I'm glad Charlie's all right. That's so great."

Charlie and Tom were laughing together; Rose was whispering in her ear. She said, "Yes, Rose," again, as close to telling her she loved her as she dared.

chapter forty-six

Elsie was sitting outside Jack's new office on the top floor of the Wedding Cake, having second thoughts. She said out loud, "The truth is . . ." and couldn't finish her sentence. She'd thought that saying it out loud to herself would make her untangle her thoughts. The look of relief on her boss's face when she'd handed him her letter of resignation still hurt. And she hoped Jack wouldn't ever let slip to Rose how Johnny Bienvenue had helped with her severance pay and pension, or how Jack had handled the board of governors at the school. Jack ushered her in, and she interrupted his waving his arm at the view of Block Island Sound. She said, "I haven't really thanked you. I think I sort of took my own breath away."

"Not necessary. A good move all around." He came from behind his desk and sat beside her in the other visitor's chair. "Of course, you've got to settle Miss Perry's estate before you can officially start. As executrix you'll be in charge of whatever has to be done to the house before title passes. The will stipulates that the estate will pay for that. It's some extra work for you, but you're the only one who can make sure it gets done the way Miss Perry would have done it."

Elsie let Jack roll on, didn't even raise an eyebrow when he said, "Six months. Johnny did a good job. Usually takes a year. In addition, I happen to know there's a good feeling about all this—a charitable donation from a person above reproach. Not a lot of scrutiny." She only spoke up when he said, "Usually someone who's done the sort of caregiving you've done . . ."

"Jack. Don't."

"It's just that it strikes me . . . Why the Pierce boys and why not Rose?"

"Jack."

"Of course, as executrix you certainly can't award yourself compensation for prior caregiving, but there may be—"

"Jack, listen to me." He tucked his chin in, then gave a little start when she touched his arm. She said, "I know you mean well, and I'm grateful you're ready to go over all the ins and outs. But there's one part of all this I really want to leave . . . undisturbed." She was surprised, too—she could see her usual sharpness far away, like the rare appearance of the aurora borealis this far south, a pale green flickering just above the northern horizon. "So we won't talk about the time I spent with Miss Perry." She leaned back in her chair. "It's in its own—" She held her fingers around an imaginary ball.

"All right," Jack said. "A closed book."

"Sphere."

"Sphere," Jack said, and nodded. He leaned toward her and took her hand. "I understand, and I think it's admirable." Was he being nice or an old goat? Elsie thought she'd better free her hand before he started saying things like "I've always admired you."

She said, "Sally," and sat up straight. Her hand came loose. "Sally had some ideas." She couldn't think of any ideas. "Or maybe it was Eddie Wormsley. Or about Eddie Wormsley. I mean, it makes sense to use Eddie to do the carpentry, but you know that there's a certain irony there."

Jack said, "What?" and then settled himself. "Eddie's first-rate. I use him all the time. It's good practice to deal locally. You weren't thinking of someone else, were you?"

"No, Eddie's fine. I was just thinking of how skittish he used to be about coming up Miss Perry's driveway."

"Well, it's between you and him now. You'll get a fair price from Eddie. That woman manager of his, she can be the one to push a little too hard. I'm sure she imagined that I'd pay extra for the indoor court just because she looks so damn cute in her tennis skirt."

"That won't be a problem for me."

Jack laughed. He said, "Elsie, Elsie, Elsie," and patted what would have been her knee if she hadn't put her hand on it. "That reminds me. We haven't seen you out on the court for quite a while. I know, I know . . . But it's time you unwound a little, a little tennis, maybe come for a sail. A little salt air does wonders. Not that you look . . . On the contrary, you look positively splendid. And that reminds me of another thing. I've renewed your membership." He got up and opened a desk drawer. "We have a new system. This key card opens all the doors—the gate to the tennis court, the spa."

"Jack."

"And of course that includes Rose. A certain number of the Perryville students come down here to play after school—now Rose can join in. This is a gift I want to give. And what's the point of all this"—he gave a backhand sweep toward the windows overlooking the tennis courts and putting green—"if I can't do what I want?"

A moment ago she'd touched his arm and spoken gently.

She knew—she'd even warned Mary Scanlon—that Jack's good side was more of a problem than his bad side. The bit of fumbling and fondling, perhaps only affectionate, that came as an undertow to his generosity was easy enough to deflect. Of course, another aspect of his generosity to Rose and her was snobbish—he could bear to have poor relatives so long as he could endow them with trace elements of his life. But what really bothered her was his pontifical assumption that without his cloak of protection her life would be a mess. That assumption bothered her because she *had* let him help. How often? Often enough. And those times she'd told Sally about a problem, told her not to tell Jack and of course Sally did . . . They counted, counted as much as if she'd wailed, "But what's a poor girl to do?"

He must have sensed her stiffening. He said, "Think of it this way—it's for Rose." He put the card in an envelope and wrote "Rose" with a flourish. In smaller letters: "from Uncle Jack."

Rose would take it, would take pleasure in being a Sawtooth member, and take pleasure in having another place where she could get away from Elsie. Rose could go be adored by May, or drop by the Sawtooth kitchen and sing a song or two with Mary, and here was Uncle Jack giving her more treats.

Then, as with one of those puzzle pictures where the corner of a box seems to stick out but in an eyeblink is seen to stick in, Elsie saw Rose as sought after rather than seeking, pulled this way and that.

Jack licked the envelope and sealed it with the bottom of his fist.

Things wouldn't be like this if she had a husband. That thought was an even more contemptible wail than "But what's a poor girl to do?"

She took the envelope and said, "Thank you." She took it because her anger at Rose for being spoiled, at Rose's retinue for spoiling Rose, now turned to accuse her. What had she done for Rose? She'd quarreled and quarreled with Rose and relied on Mary and May to praise her. Now Jack wanted to stake a claim on Rose. Who was she to say no? Things wouldn't be like this if she loved Rose enough.

chapter forty-seven

During the January thaw the creek ran clear, rose a bit from the melting snow. The air was so still that when May opened the back door she could hear the gurgling around the wharf pilings. Nobody home but her. She put on her boots and headed downstream to look at the salt marsh. There was ice around the edge of Sawtooth Pond and some chunks bobbing along in the current from her creek and the other salt creeks that fed the pond. The tide was dead low, about to turn. The air was soft on her face. It was a relief to look farther than the walls of her house, to take in the stillness of the marsh. The lines of sight seemed longer with no green to break them—gray sky with puffs of white, gray ice with cracklings of white, the withered spartina broken or bent by winter wind. May loved the plainness. She'd be glad enough for spring, but the January thaw suited her fine. She scarcely dared say more than that, though she knew that when she dreamed a pleasant dream it most often was set in the salt marsh during the January thaw. Sometimes she saw the lace of ice along the banks of the creek, sometimes the long view she saw now.

She caught sight of a small boat coming through the breachway into Sawtooth Pond. At first she mistook it for a slab of ice, but then she made it out. Somebody rowing. It was the skiff Dick gave to Rose. Rose? What on earth was she up to, coming from the open sea? Water cold enough to kill you in twenty minutes. Even in the pond you could hit a chunk of ice and flip over.

May ran along the edge of the creek all the way to the mouth. The edge of the pond curved back away, so she stopped, raised her arms. She didn't yell; she was afraid she'd startle Rose, make her turn suddenly, maybe catch a crab.

It wasn't Rose. May recognized Deirdre O'Malley's green wool watch cap. She felt a rush of blood to her face.

Deirdre turned to check her course into the creek. She tilted her head when she saw May, kept rowing until she came up to her. She rested on her oars and glided by. She said, "That was just great!" May didn't say anything. Deirdre said, "This is a nifty little boat, scoots right along. Of course, I got the last of the tide going out and now it's coming in. You want a lift back to the house?"

A small plate of ice hit the bow, spun away. May said, "I suppose you know a thing or two about boats."

"Oh, yeah. Canoes, kayaks, skiffs. All kinds of boats."

"One time one of those fellows who keeps his yacht over in Point Judith—he took a wooden skiff out. Had an outboard. There was some ice, just a bit of a film. He went up and down the pond, cutting through the ice and slush. Wore a hole at the waterline."

Deirdre laughed, held the oar handles in one hand, and waved the other at the pond. "Hardly any ice."

"Course, it was his skiff. So it didn't matter to anybody but him."

"Oh." Deirdre took a stroke to keep from drifting downstream. "I thought this was, you know, a family boat."

"That's right." May let that sit for a moment. "It is." Another pause. "Dick made her especially for Rose." She turned and started back to the house. She got to the dock just before Deirdre. She said, "I'll give you a hand lifting her. No sense in dragging her across the dock."

They put the skiff on the slings. May readjusted them, wiped off some silt, and lashed the tarp over her. They walked back to the house without a word. Deirdre got as far as the kitchen when May said, "You might take your boots off."

Deirdre took them off and put them outside the front door. She went upstairs. When she came down she was carrying her duffel bag and her backpack. After she loaded her jeep, she poked her head back in to say, "Tell Charlie I'll call."

May felt nothing but dark pleasure until she began to get supper ready. Then she thought about just exactly what she was going to say to Charlie. One thing she'd do was set a place for Deirdre as if it wasn't much of anything, just Deirdre O'Malley getting her Irish up.

And then she thought again. Getting her Irish up? She'd surprised herself with how angry she'd been. Cold angry, nothing Irish about it. Angry because Deirdre had made her afraid Rose was out in the skiff. And angry at Deirdre for paddling around at night. Angry at women. Angry at men and women. Sick and tired of them.

chapter forty-eight

Rose phoned Elsie to say she was staying late at school to rehearse and would spend the night in a dorm room. Elsie said, "Okay. I only made a pot of soup for supper. It'll keep."

Rose said, "Okay, bye"—breezily enough to annoy Elsie. The thought that Rose saved her good manners for May's house annoyed her more, and it annoyed her even more that she was having this thought.

The sound of a car, didn't matter whose, was a relief. She opened the door. She'd seen the jeep in Dick's driveway—the woman getting out must be the one staying there.

The woman stuck out her hand. "I'm Deirdre O'Malley. We don't know each other, but I'm pretty sure you can tell me what I need to know. You're in charge of Miss Perry's estate, and I was wondering if I could pitch a tent out by Child Crying Pond."

"I don't see why not. But there's no road into it, not even a trail."

"I looked at the topo map. It's not far."

"But there's still a lot of snow, and it's wet. It'd be a slog. Why don't you come in?"

Elsie made tea. She said, "So you're the one who pulled Charlie out of the water. My daughter, Rose, told me."

"Right. I met Rose. I've been staying at the Pierces'. I guess we already know a lot about each other." Elsie must have shown that she thought this was abrupt. Deirdre said, "You were the one who went to Miss Perry's rescue. So we're both good scouts. And we both have jobs in the woods. I used to run an outdoor survival program."

Elsie said, "So you want to pitch a tent for the fun of it?"

"Okay. I had a little run-in with May, and I thought I'd better camp out for a bit. Do you know when the town library opens? I've got some writing to do."

"Not till one, I'm afraid. Look—if you want to reconsider sleeping in the snow, I've got a spare room these days. And I've just made supper. Rose is staying over at the school, so there's plenty. Not very elaborate, but . . ."

"That'd be great."

Elsie took Deirdre up to Mary's old room, noticed that Deirdre's clothes were wet, and asked if she'd like a hot bath. It didn't take long for Deirdre to settle in. One trip to the car for her duffel bag and knapsack, another for an old and bulky word processor. She was in and out of the bath, up to Mary's room wrapped in a towel, and back down for supper in a sweatshirt and shorts. She went out to get another log for the woodstove in her bare feet. Elsie thought Deirdre was overdoing the ready-to-rough-it message. It turned out there was more. Deirdre said, "I hear you got shot by some guy while you were out patrolling on your cross-country skis. I'm into cross-country skiing, too. That and white-water canoeing." She pulled up one leg of her shorts to show a scar on her outer thigh. "I ran into a pine that was stuck in a chute and flipped. This stub of a branch went way into my leg. So I guess we both get purple hearts."

Elsie said, "So what were you doing on the *Trident*? Are you an oceanographer, too?"

"No. I'm writing an article. I do stuff and then I write it up. Have an adventure, write something to make enough money to get up to something else."

"What if nothing adventurous happens?"

"There's usually a story. If I don't have one of my own, I can almost always find someone who's got one. I like the one about you catching Eddie when he shot a swan with his crossbow."

"You've certainly picked up the local news pretty quick."

"I heard some before. I knew Eddie's son back in Maine. And of course now I'm with Charlie."

Elsie was of two minds. She suspected that Deirdre had come down in her cutoffs on purpose, that there was, in general, a good deal of purpose. But she also thought there was some innocent part to this flurry of friendliness. And she was pleased to be treated as the senior resident of the territory, to receive ritual gestures of deference, and to give food and shelter as hospitably as a bedouin sheik.

Deirdre tucked her legs up under her on the sofa and sipped her chamomile tea. Elsie sat back in her chair. She could see why Charlie was attracted to Deirdre. She was something like Sylvia Teixeira, short-waisted, compact, and giving off a whir of ready energy. Elsie tried to think of someone else Charlie had been attracted to. Herself. Ages ago, before Rose was born. No—he'd had a faithful little crush even when she was plump and nursing Rose. Though he'd been quick enough to take up with Sylvia Teixeira when she sashayed up to him.

Elsie laughed at her spark of vanity—then twisted away from the thought of Charlie's pain when he found out about his father and her. She looked at Deirdre again. Deirdre seemed intent on linking herself to Elsie—all that shared nature and adventure lore wasn't just for fun. What else did Deirdre have in mind? What had Charlie told her? What else had Deirdre picked up about Elsie during her stay at the Pierces'?

Her curiosity about herself glittered for an instant, like the sparkle of sand just after a wave recedes. Then she thought of May and Charlie, of May and Dick and Charlie and Tom. She thought of May making what she could of all of them. She thought of how May came to love Rose, how May had kept a house that held three such different men and welcomed Rose.

There was no new fact in all this; no new resolve would come of it. She doubted that she could ever tell it to May without May tightening her mouth, feeling a distaste for Elsie's tainted attachment to them.

Deirdre stood and stretched, dangling her empty mug, the handle a ring on one finger. She said, "I'm all in." She washed the mug and said, "You're good to take me in like this."

A companionable note on a winter's night.

chapter forty-nine

Rose came home for supper the next day. She dropped her book bag in the middle of the room. She said to Elsie, "That's her car, isn't it? That's Deirdre O'Malley's jeep."

Elsie pointed toward the upstairs room. Rose said, "Come into my room."

Elsie said, "Pick up your bag and take your boots off."

When Rose got Elsie into her room and shut the door, she

have noticed that she'd be alone in the house. He said, "Did you think Charlie was going to move back home for good? There's no cause for you to go on blaming your fussing at Deirdre. It's natural he wants his own place. He'll come to visit soon enough." Dick was being reasonable, and May tried to be grateful. Dick said, "You can like or not like Deirdre O'Malley, but she got Charlie back here, and his being here turned out better than I could guess. He's coming out on *Spartina*." Still reasonable but with less of an eye on May. He tucked his logbook under one arm and picked up his sea bag.

May said, "Charlie didn't want to go on being mad at you. He just didn't see how to come back halfway." Dick dropped his chin. She let him think for a bit. She hoped he might think of what was wrong with his going off by himself to Boston, but most likely he was already feeling *Spartina* under his feet.

He surprised her. He said, "I shouldn't ever have been uneasy about you taking such a liking to Rose. I don't think I said anything—"

"You did."

"Then I shouldn't have. It's good how Tom and Rose get along. And Rose coming round to see Charlie as often as she did . . . Without you being the way you are with her, she wouldn't be the boys' sister."

She heard the thump of his bag in the bed of the pickup, the cab door slam, the engine catch, the crunch of gravel. He was off to sea, and she was standing on a patch of land. It might as well be an island, a dot on his chart he could put his finger on by tracing the latitude and longitude, coordinates he'd noted in his logbook.

She should be glad. She should be glad he'd said what he said, but she felt more alone than ever.

chapter fifty-one

Elsie liked her days at Miss Perry's house—the walk down the driveway surrounded by sunlight and the first pale green shimmer of budding trees, her second cup of coffee in Miss Perry's kitchen, the smell of wood as Eddie and Walt set to work turning a new banister, or planing a piece of window frame. The lathe was outside under a tent that fitted off the back of a van, but the smell blew in the front door. Elsie made sketches of the new floor plans for the upper rooms, lists of the pieces of furniture that would stay or go, happy to be interrupted by Eddie. Yes, the stone garden house needed a new door. The coping of the garden wall— Walt could take care of that.

In the afternoon Elsie put in an hour or so on the garden, uprooting the brambles and maple saplings crowding the rhododendron, boxwood, and old flower beds. Then she'd go round the house, leave her dirty boots by the front door, and pad into the kitchen in her stocking feet for an end-of-the-day talk with Eddie and Walt. Part of her pleasure was that she liked the way the work was going. Another part of her pleasure was spending the day with two men. Nothing electric, just a low-grade amiability. She wore work clothes, jeans and a denim shirt or her old uniform, but each morning, after Rose left for school, she took a look in the mirror.

Jack showed up once, but it didn't spoil her day. He came down from the third floor and said to Eddie that he didn't see why it was necessary to put a dormer window in the attic room that was being made into a single. Why not put in a skylight and save some time and money?

"You could bring that up with Elsie." Eddie tipped his head toward her. "All I know is the boss lady's on budget."

"Fire code," Elsie said. "All the upper rooms have to have a working window and some kind of ladder."

"We got hold of some chain-link ladders," Walt said. "They fold up in a wooden box, makes a nice window seat. Bolt the top rung to a floor joist through the bottom."

"So," Elsie said, "we don't even reach the aesthetic."

"Good," Jack said. "Sensible."

Walt said, "Otherwise we'd have to put up a big, ugly fire escape."

"I think he's got it," Elsie said.

"You're doing good work, Eddie," Jack said. "As always."

Phoebe also showed up once. Eddie beamed. Walt scowled. Elsie took Walt by the elbow and led him into the garden. She said, "I know. But take a deep breath and—"

"Yes ma'am, boss lady."

"You can drop the 'boss lady.' It wasn't all that funny the first time."

"Yes, ma'am."

"That, too." Elsie looked back through the door to make sure Phoebe wasn't coming out. "Just let her float in and float out. Come on. The three of us are doing fine, so don't piss your father off."

Walt sighed and sat down on a stone bench. Even sitting down he was almost as tall as Elsie. She said, "Does she always set you off like this? I mean, it's been years."

"No. Just sometimes. It's when she gets this extra-high note in her twitter. People think I'm worried about money. I don't give a shit about the money. I wouldn't mind if she married him. I'd like her better if she married him. It's her having everything just how she wants it and giving off her twitters like she's all wide-eyed and helpless. Hell, I don't know. Sometimes I feel sorry for her. When I said she has everything how she wants it, that's not right. She has Dad all lined up, she's making plenty of money, but she wants to be a duchess of South County. Like your sister, like Miss Perry. Ain't going to happen. Phoebe can play tennis at Sawtooth, she can get on committees to save the bay, she can do needlepoint for the Episcopal church. But she's stuck with Dad. She can't let him go 'cause he's the bread and butter, but then she can't let go hoping she'll get asked to the ball. Can't be much fun."

Elsie didn't say anything. Walt looked at his hand and ran his thumb over the calluses. She wondered if it was up to her to end the session, but Walt got up and said, "What do you think? Should we get the ivy off the wall? There's a couple of places it's pulling stones loose."

"Yeah. I'll put it on my list. You ready to go back in?"

"Yeah. You got me thinking, and that always slows me down."

Elsie laughed, then wasn't sure he'd made a joke. He didn't appear to mind. He said, "When Deirdre was staying with you, did you get to read any of that science fiction she's writing?" Elsie shook her head. "Maybe Phoebe's like a slave of the glass city."

Before Elsie could ask anything, she saw Eddie and Phoebe in the window of the kitchen door. Eddie held the door open and Phoebe stepped out, saying, "So there you two are! I won't stay a minute, I just had to check with Eddie—nothing to do with this, this is all gorgeous—though, of course, that's for you to say, Elsie. More to the point, I just saw your brother-in-law, I was taking a peek at the new dock Tom's putting in—Jack's completely happy about that—I mean, he tried to be grumpy, but that's just Jack. More to the point is that he's thinking of backing another production of Rose's operetta. For when the summer people show up at Sawtooth. Keep Rose but otherwise a professional cast. It's part of his plan to give Sawtooth a cultural dimension. I think it's a splendid idea, and I told him I'd help him any way I can."

Walt tried to catch Elsie's eye, but she wasn't amused by Phoebe; she was feeling the weight of another Jack incursion.

She was already worried about Rose being spoiled by starring in her little play at school. She'd had in mind that Rose get a summer job—pick crabmeat at the processing plant, bag groceries, bus tables. Get her hands dirty. Let her see what her mother's life had been for twenty years. And what was Jack thinking, anyway? Throwing a barely sixteen-year-old girl in with a troupe of actors . . .

Elsie sat down on the stone bench. It wasn't Jack. She could take Jack on any day of the week. It was the thought of herself at fifteen and sixteen—not so much what she'd got up to but how desperately sure she'd been that everyone was wrong about everything—that made her dizzily uncertain about taking on Rose. Rose was like her, Rose wasn't like her; she knew Rose, she didn't know Rose; Rose was a little girl, Rose was as fully armed as a grown-up; Rose was part of her, Rose was already out the door.

chapter fifty-two

Elsie turned down offers to drive her to the school auditorium for the opening. Sally and Jack, Mary Scanlon. Walt Wormsley offered her a ride on his motorcycle. She walked, taking a slight detour through Miss Perry's walled garden. The daffodils were over, but the peonies were in full bloom. She hoped that the sight of these extravagant flowers swooning on their absurdly long stems would put her in the mood for a play. She didn't like plays, especially plays with music. She'd read the original *She Stoops to Conquer* without cracking a smile. Mary Scanlon had told her there was a knack to reading a play and that Elsie didn't have it. But then Mary told her that the playwright was Irish, so she discounted Mary's enthusiasm. Mary said, "But don't worry, it'll come to life when you see it. And Rose'll be fine—she's putting her sassiness to good use for once."

"You've heard her?"

"She's come over to Sawtooth once or twice."

Of course she had.

Elsie got a smudge of rust on her hand tugging at the back gate. The gate popped open and hit her hip. She went back into the garden and kicked the head off a peony.

The auditorium was packed. Mary Scanlon waved to her and pointed to the seat she'd saved. Elsie saw Dick and May and Tom. A few rows back, Charlie and Deidre O'Malley. Eddie and Phoebe and Walt. All of them in their Sunday best, some of them doubtless a bit uncomfortable to be packed into a room with at least one other person who'd caused them pain or shame.

The house lights dimmed. Mary said, "You cut it pretty fine. Never mind, here you are."

The overture began. There was something like old-fashioned jazz, then something like a Charleston. Elsie couldn't see the musicians, but she thought she heard a banjo. Then there was a slower part with just a piano and either a clarinet or a soprano saxophone—Elsie couldn't tell them apart. Rose had played a recording of Sidney Bechet's "Shine" over and over until Elsie said, "Turn that damn clarinet off!" Rose had corrected her. Later Rose had asked her how she'd ever managed to learn birdcalls with her tin ear.

Elsie told herself she would have one more grumpy thought and then she'd be a good sport.

The curtain went up on a bright room with white wicker furniture. A genuinely middle-aged man with a full head of white hair—a faculty member?—and a girl made up to be his middle-aged wife were quarreling. It was nothing like what Elsie had read. No "prithee," "fie," or "I protest, sir." All right—it was 1923, not 1773.

A boy in plus fours breezed through to say he was off to a

roadhouse. His mother held on to his jacket and was dragged to her knees. The audience laughed. Elsie was reminded of another thing she didn't like about theater. Not just what if they forgot their lines, but what if they hurt themselves taking a pratfall? It was an annoying anxiety.

Elsie's mood changed when the father said, "And here comes my darling daughter." As Rose made her entrance, Elsie went cold with fear. Rose wasn't tucked away out of sight at the back of a church, she was under a giant eye. And then the audience was laughing at her. Rose trotted onstage with tiny steps. She came to a stop with a little hop and a shimmy that made her short beaded dress sparkle under the lights.

Elsie recovered when she saw that Rose wasn't undone. She thought, She's *meant* to be a dizzy flapper—headache band, her mouth lipsticked into a Betty Boop cupid's bow. And the father was getting a laugh—his eyes goggled, he put his hands to his head and sank into his chair.

"Oh, Daddy," Rose said. "It's what all the girls are wearing." She twirled her yard-long strand of pearls and caught it neatly.

The father sang a bit about girls these days. Rose knelt at his knee, looking sweetly submissive to this fictitious father.

At first Elsie didn't know what this new sound was. Rose joined in the father's song so softly it sounded like a single voice. As they went on singing, Elsie heard Rose's voice more clearly. She seemed to be singing more notes than the man, but they ended together. The audience clapped, and there were a few cheers. Elsie looked at Mary. She was sitting completely still. Mary closed her eyes for a second, then made a note on her program.

Then came the setup: the gentleman caller and his pal were sent to the father's house but were told that it's an inn, and then a female cousin told Rose about the gentleman caller—he was so bashful that he stuttered. "With girls like you and me," the cousin said. "With other girls, it's a different story."

"You mean . . . floozies?" Rose said.

"I mean anything in skirts to whom he has *not* been properly introduced."

And indeed when the cousin introduced him—properly—to Rose, the boy stuttered and stared at his feet. They sang a duet, the boy doing scales with his "Wha-wha-wha what was I trying to say?" while Rose trilled a tune. The boy left, and Rose did one of the other things that Elsie found unbelievable about theater—she made a speech to herself, the upshot of which was that she thought the boy handsome and she'd find some way to get him to behave like the roguish charmer he was said to be.

After another scene of folderol among the father, the mother, the cousin, and her beau, there was a blackout. The lights came up on a bedroom and the gentleman caller complaining about the inn's service—his bed wasn't even made. Rose came in carrying a load of bedclothes. She set about making the bed, more tidily and quickly than at home. But Elsie was struck by how good she looked in her maid's uniform—black dress and white bib apron belted tight around her small waist. She sang another duet with the boy. Elsie cocked her head, pleased that she recognized that it was the same song as before, but this time the boy tenor sang the melody and Rose chirped the in-between bits: "Oh, no, no, no, you stay on your side." Elsie wondered just where and how Rose had come by this nimble coyness, the not knowing that their hands touched as they tucked in the sheet, the exact length of time to let his hand linger on her shoulder before it became a yes but not slipping away so quickly that it was a cold no. Rose's hair was tucked up into a maid's cap. Two broad ribbons hung down her back, bobbing and swirling as she flitted around the bed, apparently breathless but still singing.

They stopped singing. There was applause, which unsettled the boy in the middle of a spoken line. He stood openmouthed, looking panic-stricken. Rose curtsied to him and said, "I'm sorry, I didn't hear you. Something about my palm."

"Oh, yeah," he said. Rose held up her hand. The boy

clutched it and said, "I'm a palm reader. Your left hand shows what gifts you're born with. Any fool can see you're beautiful and charming, but the right hand shows how generous you'll be with your gifts in the future."

Rose tucked her hands behind her back and said, "I'm *smaht* enough to know the *fu-cha* you have in mind." The audience laughed. Elsie jerked back in her seat. It was broad swamp-Yankee. It was May's accent. It was May's hitched vowels, May's deliberate rhythm. How could she do that to May? And to Dick. To her whole other family. Elsie burned. She was afraid of what May must be thinking. She was ashamed. And then she was angry again.

She had to sit through the rest of the damn play, her anger congealing during the subplots, reheating when Rose did it again: "An inn? Whatevah gave you that idea? It's Mr. Hahdcastle's house." The audience brayed their laughs. Elsie wanted to slap them silly.

And then all was revealed. Rose was really the daughter of the house, the boy tenor was cured of his stutter, the cousin got her beau, everyone onstage for the finale, all singing how happy they were. The audience applauded, the curtains closed, more applause. The curtain opened, the singers took a bow all in a row, then two by two, then the white-haired father led Rose forward and stepped back to let her curtsy by herself. He took her hand again, and together they leaned forward and pointed, palms open, to the little orchestra. The curtains closed.

Over at last. Elsie wasn't furious anymore. She was pressed into a cold gloom so thick she couldn't move.

chapter fifty-three

Mary took one look at Elsie and knew there was no talking to her. Mary had no idea what was wrong. She considered the possibility that Elsie was so pleased that she was overcome, but dismissed it after a second look.

Mary herself was so bursting with things to say that she got up and bumped across people's knees to get to the aisle away from Elsie. Of course, there were one or two little moments Rose could work on, but those could wait. What couldn't wait was seeing Rose, Rose still flushed and anxious, believing and not believing with every breath, wanting to hear that she was good from someone she could trust.

Jack was holding court in the hallway outside the greenroom. Mary would have slid by, but she saw Sally—she always made a point of being nice to Sally in front of Jack, the easiest way of reminding him to keep his hands to himself. When she held out her hand to Sally, Sally hugged her and kissed her on the cheek and said, "Wasn't Rose terrific! And I know how much she owes to you."

Mary's face grew hot with the pleasure of it. She took a breath and said, "Oh, she was born with that voice, it's a gift from God. But surely some of it must be from you, somewhere on your side of the family, though your sister has a tin ear. It's not from Dick, God knows." Mary heard herself taking off, as full-voiced as her father at a Christmas dinner after a drink or two—even the hint of a brogue he had retrieved from his boyhood. "Now, when it comes to the acting," Mary went on, "that's where you get a glimpse of Elsie, whether she's setting her cap for a man or pinning his ears back." And poor Sally had just wanted to say something nice in passing, not get reminded of the graft in Rose's family tree. "And that's just what the part needed—that clear soprano voice plus a bit of mischief." If only Sally would say something, Mary would be on her way, but Sally stood there, a pretty portrait against the wall, not nodding, not even blinking. If this was what the poor dear was like when Jack climbed into bed, no wonder Jack had a roving eye. "So she's in there, is she?" Mary said, pointing to the greenroom door. "I'll just poke my head in. She gets so . . . After she sang the 'Ave Maria' . . . Were you there at Sylvia Teixeira's wedding? She was more undone afterward than she was before. I mean Rose, not Sylvia. So she needs someone calm." Mary laughed at herself and rolled her eyes. She unplanted her feet and tipped herself through the door, saying, "Well, musically reassuring," to no one in particular.

There was hardly room to move, but everyone was moving. Mary backed away from a boy carrying a tray of pizza slices. The boy tenor. She said, "Great job."

He held the tray out to her. "Have some. You somebody's mom?" She shook her head, and he spun away. She fended off the cousin soprano who was avoiding the pizza tray. Mary said, "Good job."

The girl threw off a "Thanks," then took another look at Mary. "Sawtooth? I've seen you . . . You're not Rose's mother, are you?"

"Just a friend."

"Sweet. She's over there." The girl slanted her eyes toward the far corner. "Our wunderkind."

Rose was sitting on a folding chair surrounded by all the Pierces. She'd already changed; she had her maid's uniform draped over her arm, the cap in one hand. A shame she hadn't something prettier than a sweatshirt and jeans. May took the costume and said, "You don't want this smashed around in some big machine, somebody giving it a lick and a promise with a heavy iron. All those pleats in the skirt. I'll put a little starch in the apron and the hat. No starch in the ribbons. Starch'll make them too heavy to fly out."

A large man moved past Mary and planted himself in front of Rose. The white-haired baritone father. "What did I tell you? Old but true—a shaky dress rehearsal makes for a good opening night. And you were absolutely alive." He took in Dick and May. "And these must be your proud parents . . ."

Mary saw the man's elbows flap once—he was in the same state of prattle she'd been in with Sally. Rose said, "This is Mr. Callahan." Mary suspected he knew he'd got something wrong—he looked a little flummoxed. She was about to join in to distract everyone, but they were all dazzled by a camera flash. It was the cousin soprano. She snapped another picture and whirled away without a word. Rose stood up. "And this is my father, Dick Pierce. His wife, May. And these are my brothers, Charlie and Tom." Rose saw Mary and said, "And behind you is Mary Scanlon. She and I sang at Miss Perry's funeral together."

Mr. Callahan swung around eagerly. "I've heard it was glorious. Of course, a sad occasion. I didn't mean . . . I didn't know Miss Perry, I know *of* her."

Mary got a grip on his shoulder to settle him. She said, "As soon as I heard your voice tonight I knew we were in good hands." She turned him round, gave him a good, sensible pat, and looked at May to see how she was taking all this backstage blather. Mary said, "Reminds me of Saturday night at my old place." But May was staring at Rose with the same look as when she'd got down on the floor to give baby Rose a teddy bear.

And Rose? Although it had pleased Mary to see Rose handle a small awkwardness so smoothly, it also pained her to see Rose so perfectly self-possessed. She should be running around the room with the other kids, enjoying the last bit of buzz. The only one of the cast who had a word for her was this middle-aged baritone. Though, fair's fair, he knew what he was up to onstage, and he had the right word for Rose.

Charlie excused himself, saying he had to get up early. Tom cocked his head, about to make one of his remarks. Charlie shook his head once to shut him up. Rose followed Charlie for a few steps. Mary heard her say softly, "Thanks for coming. And thank Deirdre." Another trip wire Rose stepped over neatly. On her way back to her chair Rose said to Mary, "Where's Mom?"

Mary said, "She probably got stuck in the hall with Jack. Let's go see." She took Rose by the shoulders. Rose was stiff as a board, her eyes heavy. Mary said, "Come with me for a minute. Is there another door out of this madhouse? We'll just step outside for a breath of air."

They walked single file behind the stage along a narrow corridor made narrower by a cluster of ropes and pulleys, and down a staircase and out onto a loading dock. Mary said, "Aw, Rose, you should feel like a bottle of champagne."

"Yeah, right. Are you blind? Are you so dumb you can't see how fucked up it all is? Everything. There's not one normal person in my whole life. Not one. Mom should have given me up for adoption."

Mary said, "Aw, Rose," and held her arms out.

Rose batted them aside. "Why didn't you tell her? You were her big pal back then. Never mind—you wanted a baby, too. Except when you finally saw how fucked up it is, you moved out."

"And not a minute too soon." As quick as the words were out of her mouth, Mary wished them back. She closed her eyes. She'd been stung so fast in so many ways—her forearm still hurt where Rose had swatted it, and yes, she'd come to want Rose to be hers but not the way Rose said it, and yes, she'd moved out, she'd moved out for all their sakes, but try explaining that to Rose when she was spitting out every drop of poison in her. At the same time she saw Rose in the corner of the greenroom in the middle of the Pierces, as if posing for a family portrait—Rose putting on as stiff a face as she could—and all the while she must have been wondering what sort of a picture the other kids were seeing, what sort of curious or clever remarks she'd hear or overhear the next day. Mary had seen enough of this smart set as they lolled about on the porch at Sawtooth, making comments about someone's pathetic tennis game or someone's too-cute name for a boat. Maybe the whole school wasn't like the Sawtooth bunch, but from the sound of them they were the ones who were good at games, who could shrivel the son of the owner of the Dodge dealership in Wakefield or mock the dutiful straight A's of the Tran girls. And here came Rose, the new girl in the tenth grade—or whatever they called it here—and who was she? She was Jack Aldrich's niece; she was the music teacher's pet, and so she got a starring role—did she think that made her hot stuff? But there was the rest of the story. And now Mary saw what the cousin soprano was up to, taking a picture of the Pierce family and the bastard daughter.

The light from the building reached as far as the edge of the woods, where it blurred into the night mist. Mary said, "I don't mean that, Rose. I miss you something terrible. I miss being in our house together. It was just that I thought I was only making things worse between you and your mother— the pair of you as fierce as you are."

"You know what Mom's doing now? She's going to work here. You could have talked her out of that. If Uncle Jack wanted to help he should have helped some other way. And he is so full of shit. He thinks this place is like happy valley. In his dreams."

Mary said, "I'm not sure it would be different anywhere else, you coming in as a new girl and all. I went to parochial school, and the top girls there got after me. It's the girls, isn't it? But it can change as fast as the weather. It's just a shame you had your cast party spoiled. But that white-haired baritone got it right, you know. I knew you could sing, but you played the part as if you were her. And that little tenor—not a big voice but a sweet voice. You did right by him in your duets, you sang it *piano* so he could keep in the game but a *piano* that has some sauce in it. And your quartet! You were flying there, Rose, just opened up and soared. It's a nice piece of music, that, and the timing's tricky. All of you, your sweet boy tenor, and the baritone . . ." Mary touched her shoulder. "So, Rose, darling, you've had your say out here, and now it's time to go back in—never mind the jealous ones, but have a word with the ones who helped. There's the musicians in the band. They're not schoolboys, so you thank them. I'll be right with you."

Rose had listened with her head down but at the last looked up. "Okay. But you won't talk too much, right? I mean, it's nice what you just said, but let them—"

"Don't worry, I'll be—"

"—finish a sentence."

The greenroom was still a swirl. The actors had taken off their costumes and makeup but weren't letting go of a party. May and Dick got up when they saw Rose. May said, "Time for us to get home. I'll have this costume done by the afternoon. I can drop it by your house."

Rose said she'd walk them out to the parking lot. Mary was about to hold her back but then thought that since the band wasn't in the greenroom, they might be putting their instruments in their cars.

Just as they got to Dick's pickup Elsie swooped down and took Rose's arm. She said, "I have something to say to you." She led Rose off, three cars away. Mary didn't like Elsie's look and went after them.

Elsie, still holding Rose's arm, hissed at her, "How could you? How could you do that to her? And to Dick?"

"Mom! What are you talking about? What?"

"That accent you put on. That swamp-Yankee accent. You made fun of them. It's an insult."

Rose was silent. Mary said, "Oh, for God's sake, Elsie. It's a comedy. She could have done Irish. And I wouldn't—"

Elsie said, "You stay out of this."

"Is that all you have to say?" Rose said. "That's it?"

"Yes," Elsie said. "Except maybe this playacting, maybe this whole school, is a big mistake."

"Come with me," Rose said. "Come right now. We'll see if you've gone crazy." She pulled on Elsie's arm. Elsie pulled it free. Rose marched to Dick's truck, went up to the passenger window. May rolled it down. Elsie came up behind Rose. Rose said, "May, tell me honestly—what did you think?"

"Of your play? It's good. I told you it's good, and I think you were the best one. You sing even better than you did at Sylvia Teixeira's wedding. Of course, this time I could understand the words."

"So when I changed into the maid's costume—that was okay?"

"When that boy chased you around the bed? You were funny. Reminded me of Tom. I told him so just before he left. Tom up to his pranks. I liked when you were being the nice young lady, but I liked it when you cut loose on that boy and didn't let him get too fresh. And not a bad word in the whole play, not like some movies."

Mary couldn't keep out of it. She said, "Dick? What about you? Rose remind you of anybody?"

"It was Rose on her own up there singing, but I suppose I got to give you some credit, and not just for the singing. She reminded me of you when you were behind the bar in your old place. What do you say, Rose? You see Mary over in the Sawtooth kitchen. She still take the paint off anyone gets out of line?"

Rose laughed. Mary hadn't ever heard Dick and May so talkative. They'd looked grim in the greenroom, but now that they were out in the fresh air on their way home, the play was bubbling up in them. Dick started the motor. May said, "I'll bring the dress and hat over tomorrow lunchtime, if that's all right with you, Elsie."

Whatever Elsie said was lost as the truck moved and a bait barrel rattled against the side of the bed. Mary, Rose, and

Elsie watched the truck find a place in the line of cars headed out of the parking lot.

Mary said, "Rose, I think that's the clarinetist over there. In that station wagon. And the guy next to him—he's putting his bass fiddle in the back."

Rose wasn't through with Elsie. "I didn't expect you to like the play. I mean, you're practically tone-deaf. But you're out to get me. You're as much out to get me as the nastiest girl in school. At least she's going to graduate."

Mary said, "Rose—"

"You stay out of this," Elsie said.

"Oh, right," Rose said. "Pick on Mary just because you're wrong."

"I'm not so sure I am wrong. Maybe Dick and May were just being nice. They let you get away with anything over there, and it's gone to your head—along with this playacting."

"My head? You're the one who took Deirdre O'Malley in, and how dumb was that? You're the one who said you didn't want Uncle Jack to pull strings—you think you'd get a job here if it wasn't for him? And now you try to think of some way to fuck up the one thing I can do—not that you'd know anything about it—and guess what? You're wrong again. You think they're ashamed of how they talk? Why should they be? They live on a creek that's named for their family. They used to own Sawtooth Point. You think Johnny Bienvenue is ashamed of how he talks? Or Eddie Wormsley? You're the only one who cares. Well, you and Uncle Jack."

"Then how come you talked like them when you were being the maid? The one who makes the beds and cleans the toilets."

"That was aeons ago. I know you didn't get the music, but you might have noticed the costumes. Like 1920."

"And don't try to lump me in with Jack."

"What toilets? No toilets. Who went and got Jack to fork over a membership card to Sawtooth?"

"That's yours."

"Then how come it says 'Family membership'? You're the fancy tennis player. You and Phoebe Fitzgerald. I only go there to see Mary."

"That's enough," Mary said.

Elsie said again, "I told you to stay out of it."

"I'm not talking to you," Mary said. "I'm telling Rose she's screeching her voice. But the pair of you ought to shut the hell up." They both turned toward Mary. She said, "I've got half a mind to bang your heads together." They both opened their mouths. "By Christ, you say another word and I'll do it." As fast as she'd got angry, she felt a great sob coming on. She took a breath, and it came out a growl that scratched her throat. "Now, go home. The two of you. Just go on home."

Rose took two steps away and said, "I'm staying here. If I can't find a spare bed, I'll sleep on the floor."

Elsie set her jaw and marched off toward the woods.

Mary got in her pickup. She put the key in the ignition but didn't turn it. She laid her forehead on the top of the steering wheel, drained.

chapter fifty-four

Elsie woke up late after a bad night's sleep. She felt too tired to go work on Miss Perry's garden, too hungover with spent anger to pass a Saturday morning alone. She certainly wasn't going to call Mary. She got out of bed, pulled the comforter up sloppily, felt one of her lurches for Dick in her bed—funny how she could see him and feel neutral, edgy but neutral, but when she was alone be stung by wanting him. That bit of wondering swerved her back to bleakness. She put the teakettle on and said, "Fuck, fuck, fuck."

She got Charlie's new listing from information, hoped she'd get Deirdre, almost hung up at the thought of Deirdre and Charlie in bed together, one of them reaching across the other to get the phone.

She got Deirdre, who said she was about to go for a bike ride, but if Elsie didn't mind waiting an hour she'd love to stop by. "So Rose must be feeling pretty great. Tell her from me she was terrific."

Did that mean Charlie hadn't been bothered by Rose's accent? Or had he just not said anything about it to Deirdre?

Elsie put on a Rolling Stones tape. And to hell with Rose telling her she was tone-deaf. She could dance to it, she could sing along.

She stopped in mid-song. She'd forgotten that May was bringing Rose's maid costume. Elsie didn't want May bumping into Deirdre. She called May and said she'd come pick it up. May said it was no trouble to bring it over. Elsie said, "Well, if it's no bother, could you drop it off at the school? That's where Rose is. If you don't see her, just go by the auditorium. Someone's bound to be there."

"That'll be fine. I know the way now."

Elsie hesitated. Did May have a misgiving after all? She took a breath and said, "You really liked the play? Parts of it seemed odd to me. Maybe I was nervous."

"We were all nervous for Rose. But then it seemed she was born to do that sort of thing. Tom and I are going again tonight."

"But not Dick?"

"Dick and Charlie wanted to, but they took *Spartina* out this morning. Dick got one of his feelings. Or could be he heard something from Captain Teixeira. He didn't say, but then he never does. Took his harpoon, so he has swordfish in mind."

Elsie managed to thank her for taking care of Rose's costume. She thought of Dick on *Spartina*, all his thoughts at sea. She thought of Dick in this house with her. She wouldn't kiss him by surprise this time, not like the time he was holding baby Rose. This time would have nothing to do with Rose, nothing to do with May. He'd be here and she wouldn't go near him at first, she'd move around the room, bring him a cup of coffee and put it down without touching him. When he looked at her, she'd look back and smooth her skirt, smooth her skirt over her hip bones and wait for him to stand up.

She washed her face, went down to the pond, pulled off her knee-length T-shirt, and waded into the cold water up to her shoulders.

She was back inside and dressed when she heard Deirdre outside the door. Deirdre was flushed, her curly hair matted from her bike helmet. She was wearing a red uni-suit very like the one Elsie had in her closet.

"I should get a mountain bike," Deirdre said. "Get off the main road. Route One is all traffic and guys slowing down and beeping."

"Some of the back roads are smooth enough for your road bike."

"You ride, right? Maybe you could show me. And maybe we could go canoeing. I hear you have an old canvas canoe. Or is that Rose's? I don't want to touch anything of hers or May'll have another fit. Of course, what she's really mad about is me and Charlie."

"You look like you could use some water."

"Oh, yeah," Deirdre said. She unzipped her uni-suit six inches and fanned herself. They went in and Deirdre drank and drank.

Elsie said, "But Charlie knows that you and Walt . . . I mean . . ."

"But if Walt tells things to Tom, Tom can't help repeating what he hears, especially if he thinks it's funny. May and Charlie don't think anything like that is funny. And they're not exactly at ease with the idea of a liberated woman. Charlie only had one girlfriend before me. And he still feels guilty, like he marked her somehow. I told him I wasn't ever in love with Walt, it was just a thing. Boy, was that a bad idea. Of course, I was probably in a catch-22. Bad if I was in love with Walt, just as bad if I wasn't. Maybe worse. I don't know. All I know is I have to be careful, and I don't like having to be careful. Charlie read a little bit of this sci-fi thing I've written, and some of it's pretty sexy, and he brooded. It didn't take a mind reader. Had I done all that stuff? I was going to say it's all made up, but that would have left him uneasy in another way, so I said it was stuff the women talked about around the campfire when I was running Women in the Wilderness trips. Which is a tiny bit true. And he said he found it hard to believe that women go into detail, and I said some women do, more than you know. And he said, 'So you're going to tell some woman about us?' I said, 'I just listen.' Which made him laugh for the first time in a long while."

Deirdre lay on her back on the floor and pulled her knees to her chin. She said, "No, thanks. But do you have a banana? Or some cranberry juice? Something with potassium." She sat up, spread her legs, and lowered her chest between them. In a muffled voice she said, "You probably had some of the same problems with Dick."

Elsie waited until Deirdre sat up. She said, "I'll get you some cranberry juice."

Deirdre said, "Oh, shit. I'm sorry. None of my business. I wasn't fishing, I just thought you could maybe reassure me, like tell me that things just settle down by themselves." Deirdre lay on her back and put her hands over her eyes. "I should remember I get high after I exercise. And you're probably coming down after last night. That must have been something, your daughter up there . . . The thing is, I'm worried about Charlie out on that boat. After Charlie took off this morning I needed a good hard ride and someone to talk to."

Elsie put the cranberry juice on the table by the window. Had she ever been like Deirdre? So at a boil about herself?

She sat at the table and looked at Deirdre, who was doing some sort of breathing exercise. Had she ever told adventure stories about herself like Deirdre's white-water story? With some nature mysticism thrown in? Yes. Had she ever told stories about her sex life? Yes—not part of her repertoire lately, but yes, she'd told Mary Scanlon about Johnny Bienvenue, and yes, in her red-dress days she'd said some things that counted as sexual swaggering.

Deirdre got up and sat across from her. She said, "Oh, thanks," when she saw the cranberry juice, put one hand on her chest, and took a swallow. She leaned forward and looked Elsie in the face. "It's not just that we look alike."

"Oh?" Elsie leaned back in her chair. "I hadn't really . . . And I'm a good bit older than you."

"Maybe chronologically. Your biological age is what counts. We both keep in shape. But the reason we look sort of alike is we're both free women. We're not slaves of the glass city."

"Walt said something about . . . He said Phoebe's a slave of the glass city."

"Yes. Good. So you know the story."

"No, just what Walt mentioned."

Deirdre nodded. "I'll bring you the book. Are you into science fiction?"

"No," Elsie said. "Unless you count Ovid's *Metamorphoses*." She wasn't sure why she threw that in. She said, "That was years ago, when I was doing Latin with Miss Perry." She didn't like the eager claim Deirdre was making, but she didn't like herself as a snob.

Deirdre was unrebuffed. "I don't know about Ovid. But sure. All that Greek stuff—sort of science fiction."

"Ovid was a Roman."

"I really want you to read it. It'll make our getting to know each other go faster. You'll see what I mean. It's not just that we're both outdoors people. We make our own rules. We're like sisters."

Penance, Elsie thought. It's part of my penance to come

face-to-face with this doppelgänger, this would-be doppelgänger.

Deirdre said, "And I know I could learn stuff from you that
would help. I mean, it's eerie that you hooked up with Dick,
and here I am with Charlie. What I don't get is how come
May hates me and she seems sort of okay with you. You slept
with her husband. I'm just sleeping with her son."

Elsie sat up so fast her chair creaked.

Deirdre stood. She said, "I should put some water in this
cranberry juice. I should be rehydrating."

Elsie laughed. The woman was like a kid's paddleball
game. She smacked out a thought that got as far as somebody
else, but then her attention reached the end of its elastic cord
and bounced back to herself.

"What?" Deirdre said. "Is it because I'm so intense about
nutrition? No, wait, I get it. I'm wired. I used to get like this
when I'd been alone in my cabin, and I'd bike into the general
store and I'd be way too on. It made some of the old codgers
laugh, too." When she got to the kitchen sink, she put her
glass down. Her shoulders fell. She turned and said, "After a
while they got to like me."

"Oh, Deirdre," Elsie said.

"No, they really did. I wasn't flirting with them, either. It
was winter, and I was wearing so many clothes I looked like
the Michelin tire man."

"No, it's not that."

"It's that I'm annoying you. I should get on home. It's still
a ride to Narragansett."

"I'll give you a lift—I have a bike rack. Drink your juice
and relax a little."

That was enough. Deirdre walked around silently, looking at Elsie's bookshelf. After a while Deirdre said, "Thoreau.
You've got a lot of Thoreau. Have you ever wondered what
he sounded like? I've tried to imagine his voice. It's kind of
sad that voices disappear. I love the Maine accent. When I
was alone in my cabin for a long while I'd start hearing one

of the old guys from the general store, the one I liked the most. It was like he was there. You know how you get when you're living by yourself. One time I was splitting wood for kindling, I was holding the log with one hand round it and swinging the ax with the other. His voice said, 'Not so fast, they-ah, young lady. You might just want that thumb late-ah on.'" Deirdre laughed. Elsie was struck dumb. Deirdre said, "I thought what he said was pretty funny. Right, too. Next time I saw him, I told him what he'd said. He laughed at my version of a down east accent; he said it would take me a few years to get it right. It's just right for setting someone straight. I hope it doesn't die out. Children don't talk the way their parents do. Maybe it's TV. But Charlie didn't watch TV, and he has less of a Yankee accent than Dick and May."

"Wait," Elsie said. "Did Charlie say anything about the play? About the way Rose talked when she was pretending to be the maid? When she said, 'I'm *smaht* enough to know the *fu-cha* you have in mind.'"

"Oh." Deirdre squinted. "No. Not about that. Of course, I didn't go backstage with him, so they might have talked about it then. I don't think so, though, because he told me pretty much everything. Someone said Mary Scanlon taught Rose how to sing, and Tom said that he'd taught her how to be funny. Charlie thought that was a laugh. Charlie hadn't ever heard Rose sing. He missed Miss Perry's funeral, and he didn't go to Sylvia Teixeira's wedding—which he should have, it might have helped him see that people can just move on."

"That's it?"

"About the play. But one thing Charlie really liked was when the old guy, the actor with white hair . . . when he came over he said, 'These are your proud parents,' and Rose said, 'And this is my father, Dick Pierce. His wife, May. And these are my brothers, Charlie and Tom.' It wasn't just that she handled it. All the other kids from the play were just running around, making a fuss over themselves, and there Rose

was . . . Charlie really liked her saying, 'These are my brothers, Charlie and Tom.'"

Elsie resisted imagining the sound of Rose's voice, resisted
imagining Rose's state of mind when she'd grabbed her in
the parking lot. She dug in harder—her argument might
have been wrong, but she was right to worry. She thought
of Rose's saying, "If I can't find a spare bed, I'll sleep on the
floor"—pathetic teenage self-pity. Then Elsie gave way. Rose
had said, "This is my father . . . These are my brothers," when
Rose was the center of attention.

She'd been horrible to Rose.

chapter fifty-five

May was just finishing ironing when the phone rang.
She said, "Hello?" There was a pause. A women's
voice said, "Mrs. Pierce? Please hold, I have Mr.
Aldrich on the line for you." Another pause and she heard a
booming voice. "Hello, May! Sorry about that. I've got people
running in and out. This is Jack Aldrich."

"Hello, Mr. Aldrich."

"Jack, please. I saw you were at Rose's play—wasn't she
great? I knew she had a voice, but what stage presence. We
couldn't have guessed, could we? It seems like yesterday she
was a little girl. Look, I'm sure you've got lots to do. So I'll get
to what's on my mind. I want to apologize. I've been remiss
about being a good neighbor. I've been thinking about how
many ties we already have. I guess you must have heard from
Rose that I'm going to put her play on over here." May wondered how Mr. Aldrich knew about her and Rose. It could be
Phoebe'd been a chatterbox. She hoped Mr. Aldrich wouldn't

go on about that. "And your boy Tom," he said. "I can't say enough about him. Great job building the new dock. More than building—he's got good ideas about our whole water-front. I could see a future for him here at Sawtooth. I know he works for Eddie Wormsley, but one of these days he may want to be part of something bigger. I like the cut of his jib." May supposed she ought to say something, but she was still nervous and bothered by Mr. Aldrich's trying to sound like an old salt. Mr. Aldrich kept right on; she didn't have time to say thank you. "There are all sorts of ways we can get together. One thing just occurred to me. What if I bought a little easement from you, just to put a footbridge across Pierce Creek so a few of our Sawtooth nature lovers could get across to the nature sanctuary? Way down at the tail end of your three acres. I don't think you'd even see it. If Dick is changing over from the red-crab fishery and getting back to lobstering, there might be a readjustment period, and a healthy payment for an easement might bridge the gap. More than bridge the gap."

"Dick's at sea."

"Yes, I understand that. I'm looking forward to talking to him, too. I just want to give you time to give it some thought on your own. You could talk to Eddie Wormsley—he'd be the one to build the bridge—and Eddie could tell you he and I work things out fair and square, like old shipmates."

There he went again. But what bothered her more was his saying he and Eddie work things out fair and square, and not a minute before he'd been talking about hiring Tom away from Eddie. She said, "Eddie is Dick's oldest friend. He put us up after our house got knocked in."

"Yes, indeed. Eddie is the salt of the earth. I loved my cousin Lydia, but I'm afraid one of her few faults was that she was unfair to Eddie." It took May a second to realize he was talking about Miss Perry. Another second to realize he'd heard what she said about Eddie but that he didn't under-stand it. He swept on. "Of course, to her credit Lydia held Dick in high regard, and Charlie and Tom were great favor-

ites of hers, too. She was a model of how fortunate people
help out . . ."

May heard the unspoken "those less fortunate." That bothered her. But there always seemed to be two things to be
bothered about in every breath this man took in and let out.
The second thing this time was that in his hearty speechify-
ing voice he was talking about the biggest things in her life. It
was like being hugged by someone you didn't know.

"I'm sure you've got things to do, so I won't keep you. I'm glad
we had this talk. Oh. I'll be sending over a couple of guest passes
to Sawtooth. They're good for everything, including Rose's play.
I know you saw it at the school, but this promises to be even
better, something all of us South County folks will be proud of.
Best to Dick when he comes in. I'm glad we had this little chat."

What on earth?

The call had made her so nervous she had a shaky time
getting Rose's uniform onto the hanger. She'd said hello
to Sally now and then, but she didn't believe she and Jack
Aldrich had said ten words to each other in as many years.

She drank a glass of water and was able to iron the maid's
cap with its two long ribbons. She called Phoebe, got the
answering machine at the office. Mary Scanlon was likely
over in the Sawtooth kitchen, not a good time to bother her.

She put the cap in a paper bag, punched a hole in the
bottom so the ribbons hung free, and taped the bag to the
hanger. She'd just talked to Elsie on the phone about Rose's
costume, and that made it almost natural to call her.

Elsie's voice was a little odd, but there was no going back.
"I've just had a phone call from your brother-in-law. I don't
want to be unfriendly to him—"

"What's Jack up to now?"

"He was pleasant enough, but I have to say it was out of the
blue. It made me a little nervous. He said how we were neighbors and how he was doing things for Rose and for Tom—"

"And then he wanted something."

"Yes. He said just a little easement."

"Look, May. You don't have to do anything; you certainly don't have to do anything just because Jack wants it. You remember those *Just So Stories*? Miss Perry read them to Charlie and Tom. There's one about a camel who asks if he can just put his nose in the tent—it's a cold desert night—and the guy in the tent finally says, 'Okay, just your nose,' but before you know it the camel's inside, the whole hump and hooves, and the guy's out. So you're right to be nervous, especially if Jack's sounding extra-nice and jolly. I don't want to alarm you, but I know Jack. He's got his eye on Tory Hazard's house; he's got his eye on your house. It might start with an easement. You're on the only piece of land between Sawtooth and the wildlife sanctuary, and he'd dearly love to have a nature trail right through to it, so be careful if he starts talking about letting people from Sawtooth make a little path. It'll get bigger. Jack'll talk about community, he'll talk about nature, but he's really only for Sawtooth. He's Sawtooth, and Sawtooth is him."

May was alarmed. She'd thought of Jack Aldrich as a phantom neighbor, a ghost that made itself known by producing cottages, tennis courts, and docks. Now he condensed into a sharper picture, a real man in a suit who talked to her as if he knew her better than she knew him.

Elsie said, "I've warned him off once about your place. If it comes to anything, I think Sally would be upset, and he's reached that age when he doesn't want trouble at home. And now that I think of it, Rose has come into his worldview—well, this little piece of the world—and she can be fierce these days. And I don't mind taking him on, either. I'll certainly keep an eye on him. Anyway, I'm glad you called. And thanks again for taking care of Rose's costume."

May couldn't remember if she'd thanked Elsie. She found herself out the back door halfway to the wharf, staring at the creek. That didn't surprise her. She occasionally thought she was still in the kitchen and found herself in a different room, having forgotten what she was looking for. What surprised her was that in the same way that her notion of Jack Aldrich had suddenly condensed into a person, her notion of Elsie was changing. She'd called Elsie almost by accident, but now that she had, now that she'd called purely for herself, she saw Elsie all of a sudden and awful clear. It was like the time when she went wading for quahogs with Charlie. They were waist-deep near the mouth of the creek, feeling with their toes. Charlie gave her a face mask. The bottom jumped up at her, but in the squeezed-up space there was a bit of wrack fluttering in the current, specks of silt streaming past it so clear you saw each one and how one was deeper than another even though they were just a hairsbreadth apart. It was a world of life down there. She didn't want to see all that each time she went feeling for quahogs with her toes, but there it was. And there was Elsie talking on the phone, talking fast that way she had, going off one way and back another, right there in front of you with all that energy running through her.

May saw how Dick would have wanted to touch her. She saw this without pain.

chapter fifty-six

Mary woke up, closed her eyes again. She pulled the sheet up over her face, decided she didn't have a headache, just a terrible thirst. She said, "I wonder if you'd get me a glass of water," which meant she knew she was in bed with the white-haired baritone. Nothing wrong with that. And when he brought her a glass of water and said, "Now, where can we get a really good breakfast?" she thought that was just the right thing to say. It only bothered her that it took her a moment to remember his name. Ah, there it was—he went by his initials—JB, JB Callahan.

The other thing that bothered her (once she'd drunk some water and made her way to the bathroom wrapped in the top sheet) was that the two of them were in the guest room of the Perryville School. JB didn't seem anything but happy, and told her she looked like a Roman goddess. She pulled back the blinds and saw, just outside the door, her pickup covered with dewdrops. The dew was a good sign in that it meant it was still early enough to have that really good breakfast. It was a bad sign in that it would be clear to anyone at all that the truck had been there for the night without giving itself so much as a shake. Who knew how many of the kids were Sawtooth brats who would have seen her truck coming or going round the back of the Wedding Cake with a load of groceries? She didn't want to make a fuss, so she was thinking of the least fussy way to bring up the problem as they got dressed. He was humming the tune to "Down by the Salley Gardens," another good omen. She pulled back the blinds again. A bunch of kids sauntered across a patch of lawn, too far away for her to see their faces. Oh, dear God, and what if Rose was wandering around? Hadn't her last words been "I'll sleep on the floor"?

Apparently her peeking past the blinds made enough of a fuss. He said, "Okay. You got your keys? Let me know when the coast is clear."

"It's just that Rose spent the night in the dorm. But let's just go—she'd recognize my truck, anyway."

"What kind of a school is this? Don't they have morning prayers? We could go back to bed until they're all in the chapel. Or until they're all in class."

"It's Saturday. I don't know what they do on Saturday."

When she started the engine she realized she had no idea how she'd got through the maze of buildings the night before. She came round a corner and had to stop for a line of students—a line stretching across the narrow road onto a porch and then into what must be the dining hall. The students made way for her to roll through. She was concentrating on the road but caught the motion of JB waving his hand.

There were still a lot of dewdrops clinging to the hood. They'd slid a few inches, leaving what looked like the traces of a herd of snails.

"Is Rose your niece? Some sort of relative?"

"Was she there?"

"I'm afraid so. You came by just now to show me around. That's our story, and we'll stick to it. *Honi soit qui mal y pense.*"

"And what might all that French mean?"

"Fuck 'em if they can't take a joke."

"You're pretty bouncy for this early in the morning."

"Well, I had a pretty good night."

"Is that all?"

"A sweet, splendid night. You have lovely shoulders. Skin like gardenia petals. What are you doing tonight?"

"Hard at work."

"Then what about tomorrow morning?"

"The famous Sawtooth Sunday brunch."

"Then Sunday afternoon?"

"We'll see. But right now do you really want a good breakfast? Would you rather have an omelet or pancakes and sausage? Do you like your omelet a bit runny?"

"I hope this means we're going to your house."

"It does." He made a pleased noise in his throat. She said, "Not a house, just a small apartment."

He leaned over, slid the hem of her dress an inch higher, and kissed her knee. "There's my big knee," she said. "I've often wished my knees weren't so big."

"No. Just right for your long legs. I like walking beside your long legs. I can't wait till we go swimming so I can see your long legs waving in the water."

All right. Let him keep talking himself into it. He said, "How small an apartment?"

"One bedroom." That would be the reason he was asking— the possibility of a roommate. "I haven't been there all that

long. I used to share a house with Rose's mother and Rose.
Since Rose was a baby, in fact. For one reason and another,
I'm on my own for a bit."

There was a pause while he absorbed this. It was a pause
during which she could have said, "And yourself?" She put
off any questions that might tip a weight onto the rest of the
morning.

chapter fifty-seven

After Elsie dropped Deirdre off in Narragansett she
drove back to the Perryville School. In the parking
lot she had second thoughts. If she went tramping
around the grounds looking for Rose, Rose would be embarrassed. "Oh my God—there's my mom." Find a student and
send her? A teacher? "Your mother's out in the parking lot.
She wants to see you." Just as bad.

Elsie thought she'd write a note and leave it in Rose's
mailbox. Or did only boarders have mailboxes? She dimly
remembered day students having separate message boxes.
And the stigma. "Yes, he's cute, but he's a day student." When
Elsie had been mad at Rose she'd thought other kids' giving
her a hard time was just what Rose needed. Now that Elsie's
remorse peeled her to the quick, she felt the sting of every
embarrassment she might inflict, had inflicted.

She saw kids walking past Main to the dining room. She
slid down in her seat. Easy to imagine their talk: "Who's that
woman sitting in her car, that really old Volvo? I think it's
Rose's mom." "No, Rose's mom and dad drive a pickup. He's
like some kind of fisherman; you can smell fish in the truck."
"Don't you know about Rose?"

Elsie said out loud, "I'm sorry, Rose." She peered over the dashboard. Everyone at lunch. She found a ballpoint, tore off the blank corner of a map, and started writing. The pen went dry. She found a pencil in the glove compartment, its point broken. She had a knife; she always had a knife. "Hey, did you know Rose's mom carries a knife? A humungous knife." "That's nothing, she used to carry a pistol." "She should've had a shotgun—you know, to get Rose's dad to marry her." Teenage girls: every oddity a deformity, every deformity an anguish to Rose.

Okay. Enough. Just write the note. She'd give it to a secretary in Main before lunch was out.

Her first draft on the piece of map was a mess. She rummaged through the debris under her feet and found an old electric-bill envelope. When she put it up on the dashboard to write she saw the white-haired baritone walking into the parking lot from the road. She tried to remember his name from the program. She got out and waved, said, "Excuse me, you're in the play, you're Rose's father in the play." She sounded like an idiot, but then the man looked odd himself, looked like he'd slept in his suit and hadn't noticed it yet.

He said, "Yes," as if he had to think about it.

"Yes," Elsie said. "You could do me a big favor. I'm Rose's mother. You'll see Rose before the play, right?"

"You're Rose's mother . . ."

"Yes."

"Well, then, I practically know you. You're Mary Scanlon's friend." He looked a little less dazed. "What's the favor?"

"To start with, you could get in the car."

As he slid onto the passenger seat, he eyed her bare hunting knife. She said, "I was sharpening a pencil," and sheathed it.

He laughed. He eyed the mess in the back, poked at her pruning shears. "And these are for cutting your nails?"

She didn't have time for a joke. "I garden. Can you give this note to Rose? You're sure you'll see her?"

"Yes. The music teacher's giving a supper party for the cast before." Now he looked at his suit. "You don't happen to have an iron tucked away back there? I've got another shirt but just the one suit. I was going to go back to Boston after the show, but now I'm staying through Sunday. Or Monday."

"Here's one of Heloise's Helpful Household Hints—hang your suit in the bathroom while you take a shower. The steam takes the wrinkles out."

"Is that right? Are all you Rhode Island women so good around the house?"

Elsie looked at him. She said, "Did you know Mary Scanlon before?"

He blushed. "We just met, but she was kind enough to give me a tour of the countryside. She just dropped me off on her way to work."

Elsie thought, And up on the road out of sight. She said, "I'm glad. We had a fight last night, so I'm glad she had someone to take her mind off it. She used to live with Rose and me."

"So she said."

"It was sort of a three-way fight. I was wrong. The note is for Rose."

"Okay."

"Did Mary think Rose was good?"

"My God, yes. And she's right. You and I might have a talk about Rose. There's a gift there."

"I'm not all that musical. Mary's the one who taught her."

"Yes. Mary has a fine voice. But Rose . . . The music teacher here is good, but Rose might want a voice coach as she comes along. Someone serious but not pushy. I could ask around; you're not that far from Providence."

"Is that how you learned? Your own voice coach?"

"God, no. I'm an amateur like Mary. I'm just doing this because I know the part—I wrote the lyrics. The music teacher's a friend, and he's a friend of the composer. That's why we're doing it here, while we're waiting for—"

"I'll tell you what," Elsie said. "I'll take you to my house and you can iron your shirt."

"That's very nice of you."

"If you're staying through Monday, we should iron your suit, too."

He laughed. He had a nice laugh, something Mary had noticed about Johnny Bienvenue. He said, "I've never been so well looked after."

Was he flirting? Was she? It had been a while since she had the full attention of a man. Well, Jack.

Elsie said, "You've never been so well looked after? I guess Mary cooked you breakfast."

He blushed easily with his fair skin, up to the roots of his hair. She said, "Hey—it's okay, I'm her best friend."

As she started the engine, May's car went by and pulled up next to Main. May got out with Rose's maid's uniform over one arm and a bag in the other. Two white ribbons hung out, fluttering as May walked briskly toward the auditorium. Everyone was taking care of someone else's wrinkles.

He said, "You know how Mary gets her omelets so light? She beats the egg whites separately. It's something to see, the way she twirls the whisk and her hair hanging down her back, bobbing in its own rhythm. And she knows all the old songs." He hummed a tune. "You must have heard that one. 'The Rose of Tralee.'" He sang, "'The pale moon was rising . . .'" and broke off with a faraway look.

Good for Mary, then. The man was smitten.

chapter fifty-eight

The first thing Tom said when he came in was "Walt's put his foot in it this time."

May said, "I thought he was finally settling down."

"He was," Tom said. "But he picked another fight with Phoebe. She told him for the umpteenth time that it made a bad impression—his driving over to the job at Sawtooth on his motorcycle. He leans back in his chair and asks her what she's doing all those times she's going up to see Mr. Salviatti. He says it right there in front of Eddie and me. Then nobody said anything, and Walt must have figured he'd hit a nerve. He said, 'I don't mind what anybody gets up to, it's just that you're the one talking about bad impressions.' Phoebe did that thing she does—she goes all soft and puzzled. She says, 'Why, Walt, I'm not sure exactly what you mean.' And then Eddie says—and you know Eddie, he never gets riled but this time he says, 'I know what you mean, and you got about one minute to apologize. Phoebe is the model for an angel.' It did sound like he just meant something soppy, and Walt laughs. That made Eddie go another shade of red. Phoebe says, 'It's the statue, the one that's going to go down by the town docks.' Walt is squinting like he's ready to hear more and maybe mumble his way out of it, but it's too late. Eddie starts barking, 'Stand up! Take your hands out of your pockets!' and he pulls Walt out of the chair by his shirtfront. Walt whacks Eddie's hands down. They're chest to chest, real close to it; I mean, that close. Phoebe gives a little shriek and starts batting me on the arm, like I'm supposed to do something. So I get my shoulder in there and I'm face-to-face with Walt. Not exactly face-to-face, since he's bigger than me. I feel his breath on my forehead."

Tom paused. May said, "Go on. I was afraid of this; I've been afraid of this for a long time."

"Eddie was still shoving, and I couldn't help leaning into Walt, so he got pushed into sitting down again. And then it just popped into my head to do something funny. So I sat in Walt's lap and I said, 'Walt, honey, maybe we should tell them *our* secret.' None of them has much of a sense of humor. Walt just stood up, and I landed on the floor. Walt left. Eddie stood there. Phoebe sat down. She didn't cry, but she kind of mewed. I said, 'Blessed are the peacemakers, for they shall end up on their ass.'"

May said "Tom" reflexively, though "ass" wasn't all that bad. She was mainly thinking of how they all felt. Phoebe and Eddie, of course, but she imagined Walt wishing he'd kept his mouth shut, but once he'd said what he said and with Eddie coming at him, it had to boil over.

Then she replayed Tom's mimicking the three voices; she heard Phoebe saying, "Why, Walt, I'm not sure exactly what you mean," and she saw Phoebe going all wide-eyed and tilting her head. But it was Walt's saying "I don't mind what anybody gets up to" that was the bigger spark. The truth was that it was Eddie who didn't mind. He hadn't minded Phoebe's going off for her ski weekends, or her going off to Sawtooth in her short tennis dress or going up through Mr. Salviatti's electric gate—all that dancing around in places Eddie didn't go, to get the kind of attention Eddie figured was brighter than his. As long as it was between Phoebe and Eddie, Eddie could maybe go glum or mopey when Phoebe left, keep extra-busy while she was away, and be happy when she came back.

But there was Walt, who by all reports had been getting along fine with Eddie while they were working on Miss Perry's house—there was Walt, Eddie's own flesh and blood, putting words to Eddie's unthought thoughts. There was Walt Wormsley looking like Eddie and sounding like Eddie but bigger and louder.

And by all accounts Walt had been around a lot of women. That would give his remark about Phoebe a sly knowingness. May could see how Eddie wanted to knock Walt down.

Tom said, "Okay. Let's pretend I said 'butt.' Or maybe 'rear end.' I'm just glad Walt didn't knee me in the . . . below the belt."

"Oh, stop joking around. This is . . ." May saw Tom shake his head at her. "I'm sorry. You did the right thing there. I mean, getting in between them. I'm not so sure about your trying to get a laugh out of it. Though I suppose that's what got Walt out the door. Lord, I don't know what they can do now. Two men. And father and son is even worse."

"I don't know why you say that. There's mother and daughter. Rose is staying over at the school on account of something Elsie said. It's kind of an inconvenience for me. Rose used to run my work clothes through the washing machine. She said I could throw in some of Dad's, too."

"You shouldn't ask her to do that. Rose has her schoolwork and her play on top of that."

"I give her rides, and while the wash is getting done, I help her with her homework. Don't look so surprised, Ma. I'm good at math. I'm the one who figured out where to put the new moorings in Sawtooth Pond. Got to set them so the boats don't bump into each other. Had to use the Pythagorean theorem. See, the hypotenuse is from the mushroom anchor to the buoy—"

"Not now, Tom. I'm worried about Eddie, and you're all over the place with washing machines and moorings."

"Well, Jack was impressed. He's got room for more sailboats, and that's cash in his pocket."

"Since when do you call Mr. Aldrich 'Jack'?"

"Since he told me to."

"I'm not so sure I want you mixed up with Mr. Aldrich."

"Eddie does a lot of work for him."

"And you work for Eddie. Has Mr. Aldrich been after you to work for him?"

"Jack's not crazy about Phoebe. He likes Eddie, good old steady Eddie—but he thinks I'm good with boat owners. Jack doesn't see me spending my life banging nails alongside Walt. Come on, Ma. Don't be a stick-in-the-mud."

That was one way of saying it, May thought. Another was that she didn't like things getting beyond what they were supposed to be. Or people. She could put up with a few bits of disorder—Dick on land was one. She supposed she could get used to one disorder or another if the disorder stayed in the place it started. But here was Mr. Aldrich getting after her, getting after Tom, and Eddie and Walt and Phoebe . . . and she was worried about Charlie with Deirdre. It was like storms joining up, and then everything was chaos. She took a deep breath and closed her eyes. She let her breath out, opened her eyes. She said, "I suppose it doesn't hurt to talk. Just don't count on something that's just talk. And remember, Eddie's our friend." She needed to settle down some more. She added, "You had your lunch yet? You go pick some peas and I'll heat up the meatloaf."

"You're going to think I just came by for a free meal."

"I got more peas than I can eat, what with your father staying out so long. Meatloaf, too."

Tom took the basket but stopped at the doorway. "You know, it's not necessarily all a bad thing, Eddie losing his temper. I suspect Phoebe might like the change. She's been trying to gussy Eddie up; she thinks that's how she'd like him better. But she'll get a tingle off of his growling at Walt. Maybe another tingle when she thinks, Oh, what if he growls at me?"

"I wish you wouldn't talk like that. You shouldn't think things like that about other people. Go pick some peas. See if you can keep your mind on that."

Tom sighed. "Oh, Ma. That wasn't . . . You know, it's not just peas you got too much of. It's disapproval. I hope it's just me stirs it up."

May didn't have time to answer. Quick as that, Tom thought of something else. He twirled the basket. "When I get back, I'll tell you some other news. Nope—I can't wait. Mary Scanlon's got a boyfriend." Then he was out the back door.

She wasn't going to bring it up to defend herself against Tom, but she'd made her own kind of peace with Elsie. Maybe Tom meant Deirdre. May had pounced on her for taking Rose's skiff. True enough that Deirdre didn't know how Dick made Rose cry, how Rose's crying was in the grain of that boat like her first coat of paint. All right, then—there was Deirdre flying in out of nowhere, not linked to anything or anybody around here, and then there she was padding down the upstairs hall at night. Yes, she dove in to save Charlie. May tried to keep that in mind. It didn't hold. Maybe Tom was right. Maybe she should be weeding out some disapproval. She might let Tom take Dick's dirty clothes up to Elsie's washing machine, but she was no closer to allowing Deirdre a quiet place in her thoughts when Tom came back in with the peas.

chapter fifty-nine

D eirdre said, "I don't think Charlie's going to marry me."

"Why do you think that?"

"May's been nicer to me. She'd only do that if she was relieved. Charlie must have said something to her."

That struck Elsie as shrewd. She was surprised until she thought that it was the sort of shrewdness the self-absorbed could be good at. Elsie said, "Could be. Or it could be that May's got other things on her mind." Elsie stopped wheeling her bicycle up her driveway to let Deirdre get ahead, out of talking range. She'd been happy enough to have Deirdre as an exercise partner, to get pushed harder than she could push herself. She'd also considered Deirdre as offering a retrospective of her own vanities and vices, a harsher scouring than her unaided memory. But Deirdre offered this unconsciously, and Elsie missed Mary Scanlon and Miss Perry, and now that Rose was busy, she missed Rose. All of them had set her straight, or at least straighter.

By the time Elsie got inside, Deirdre had poured herself cranberry juice and recited her litany of carbohydrates, glycogen, electrolytes, even though they'd cut the ride short when it began to rain. Deirdre drank and then lay down on the floor to stretch. She said, "It could be that Tom told Charlie some stuff Tom heard from Walt."

"I thought Charlie knew about you and Walt."

"I was off and on with Walt, so there was stuff in between. Walt didn't mind hearing about it. In fact, it turned him on. A lot of guys are that way. With Charlie I've got to be careful. What is it with Charlie? He probably gets it from May—her way of seeing everything in black-and-white."

Elsie sighed. Lying on her back, Deirdre pulled her legs over her face. She kept on talking. Elsie caught muffled bits and pieces, enough to recognize that this was another litany, this time of Deirdre's sexual adventures, some of which Elsie had heard but not in a single recitation. Something about being jounced in the bed of a pickup. How Deirdre had come on a couple skinny-dipping in a stream and waded in—first time she let a girl kiss her, first time she gave a guy a blow job underwater. How Deirdre had been on a canoe trip—a bunch of guys, two women. She'd borrowed the other woman's blue wet suit, hung it to dry on the guy-rope of her pup tent. After dark one of the men crawled into her tent.

Deirdre sat up, raised one knee, and twisted herself around it. "He wasn't, like, her boyfriend, just a thing he thought of. He whispered, 'Linda. Okay?' I went, 'Uh-huh.' Weird rush."

Elsie said, "I can imagine your telling these things to a guy in a bar. I can't imagine telling them to someone you want to like you."

Deirdre twisted herself around her other knee. "I don't really go to bars. I'm more an outdoor person." It took Deirdre a few seconds to frown. She said, "Hey. It's just us here. When did you get to be all judgmental?"

"I'm not judging what you get up to. It's just the way you're—"

"What? Adventurous?"

"Endlessly fascinated with your adventures."

"It's not like you haven't done stuff."

"It's just not something I go on about."

"I don't mean recently. When I said you and I are alike, I didn't mean now you're older. But then, maybe I am more adventurous."

"'Adventurous' is one way of putting it."

Deirdre stood up. She said, "Where do you get off with that tone? Like you get to look down on what I've done and judge."

"I'm not judging what you've done. You said 'tone.' Okay. Tone. Your tone."

"Well, screw you. I'm going."

"It's raining. I'll give you a ride."

"Don't bother." Deirdre put her bicycle helmet on. With her hand on the door she said, "You are on May's side. Everything black-and-white."

"May is more complicated than that."

"I guess screwing her husband makes you an expert? Screwing her husband makes you part of the family."

Elsie said, "It's going to rain harder." She pointed out the window. "The wind's picking up." Deirdre went out the door.

Elsie sat by the window and watched the rain dot the pond. She'd let Deirdre think they were friends. Better not to lead her on. She'd been harsh. It was about time. There was a lull. She thought, Deirdre's not good enough for our Charlie.

chapter sixty

Mary took JB to see her old restaurant. They ate breakfast on the terrace overlooking the salt marsh. The breakfast wasn't as good as the ones she used to make here, but the view was better than she remembered, a maze of hummocks and creeks all the way to the back of the dunes. The sun was still low, the light soft as it came through the trees on the higher ground between Sawtooth Creek and Pierce Creek. At the time—fifteen, sixteen years ago—she'd been relieved to sell to Jack. Now she wondered.

She was just as glad JB was leaving her to her own thoughts, shielding his eyes with one hand as he peered this way and that. When he said, "Ah!" it was so loud and sudden it made her jump. He pointed.

"Yes," she said. "A heron. There's a lot more birds over here than at Sawtooth Point. All those boats and people."

He said, "Above the salt creek's gloss of light—" so conversationally that she almost said something back. He went on—

> *"The great blue heron's pillowed flight*
> *Belies his eager appetite.*
> *Alighting on the bank he cocks*
> *His head. With freeze-frame steps he stalks*
> *The unsuspecting mummichogs."*

She laughed. "Do you know what a mummichog is?"

"Yes. A little fish. One of those Indian names Rhode Island keeps in use. Like 'tautog' for blackfish, 'squeteague' for sea trout. In Massachusetts, except for the name itself, we papered over the Indian names with British ones. Gloucester, Worcester. Here you've got Quonochontaug, Watchaug, Usquepaug."

"Did you look up that little ditty because I told you we were going to look at a salt marsh?"

"I didn't look it up. I wrote it. This morning, before you got up."

Mary had laughed at herself in the past for wishing for poetry from a lover. Now here it was and she was wishing he'd go back to being quiet. What was wrong with her? They'd made love Friday night and Saturday afternoon, and then on Sunday night when she was all done in from work they'd fallen asleep curled up like kittens in a box. And here he still was on Monday. As her father used to say, "What do you want? Egg in your beer?"

She said, "Well, it's not every visitor from Boston has such enthusiasm for Rhode Island names. And not many could dash off a rhyme with mummichog."

"I was working on a poem about you—"

"I'll bet you say that to all the girls." Dear God, where did that twitter come from?

"But I thought I'd warm up with something lighter."

A different part of her brain fizzed, and she said, "There was an old maid from Nantucket . . . No end of rhymes there."

His white eyebrows gave two wing beats. Puzzled, hurt. She looked away, then looked at him again, at his new expression of amiable concern. If she didn't get off by herself, she was going to bite his head off.

chapter sixty-one

Elsie didn't quite get the name of her opponent in the Sawtooth tennis tournament. Patty something. They were both a little late. She hadn't seen the woman before, but then she'd been playing either at night with the assistant pro on the indoor court or with the Perryville girls up at the school. She'd signed up for the tournament because Jack had told Sally not to. "Wouldn't look good if the owner's family did well."

The warm-up took Elsie by surprise. Patty had a heavy topspin forehand that kept Elsie deep behind the baseline. It wasn't until well into the first set that Elsie got the rhythm. Patty liked banging the ball, moved Elsie from side to side but without trying for the very edges of the corners. It was the great big bounce that made Elsie take the ball so high her shoulder was up to her ear.

Patty covered her own baseline with a couple of long-legged straddle steps as she took her looping backswing. Patty was enjoying herself, Elsie thought, not just because she was winning but because she was in love with her strokes. When Elsie started chipping back short balls, Patty stopped having fun. Her knees seemed to get in her way as she galloped forward. If she got her racket on the ball, all she could do was scoop it up, usually high enough for Elsie to have time to come to net and put it away. Elsie took pleasure in making this pretty player turn awkward, sometimes punching the ball at Patty's feet, once in a while floating a lob over her before she got her balance.

During the changeovers Patty began to take more time, carefully toweling off her face and hands, fiddling with her wristbands.

Elsie came back from 2–4 to win the first set 6–4. Patty sat on a bench. She smiled up at Elsie and said, "You're certainly making me scramble." Her red hair was getting a pretty curl, her face was flushed, the veins in her throat were sky blue. Elsie felt like a vampire, ready to drain this succulent girl.

Elsie said, "I haven't seen you around—not that I'm exactly a regular."

"I just moved up here from Washington. My fiancé used to belong; he's a friend of Jack Aldrich's. He gave us a summer membership. Is there a water fountain?"

Elsie pointed to the bubbler. Patty kept her knees straight as she leaned over. The back of her skirt tilted up—a wren dipping at the birdbath, tail feathers twitching. Patty's sheathed bottom was full and dainty. If I were a man, Elsie thought, I'd have her just like this. A flurry of feathers—peep, peep, peep—and into the underdown.

Patty wiped her mouth and said, "And—small world—my aunt works here." Elsie's eyes tightened and fixed on Patty's face. She should have seen the family likeness. "Is your aunt

Mary Scanlon?" If she hadn't quarreled with Mary, Mary
would have told her. So it served her right.

"Yes. My father's sister. I haven't seen her for ages. My
father was in the navy, so we were all over the world while I
was growing up, and then I worked in Washington. But now
it looks like Rhode Island is home. At least until the election.
I'm working on a congressional campaign."

"You're working for Johnny Bienvenue?"

"Right again," Patty said. "I keep forgetting what a tiny
state this is. Oops—I've got to watch that. I was actually born
here—my father was stationed at Quonset—but I've got to
stop saying 'tiny state.'"

Elsie heard herself say, "Don't worry, we know it's small,"
even as she felt the details gathering into a wave. She looked
at Patty's left hand. "So you're engaged."

"Yes. After what I've seen in Washington, I swore I'd never
be a political wife, but here I am—working just as hard and
not even on the payroll anymore. After you finish me off
I've got a meeting with a Mr. Salviatti. We're going to Westerly to talk with some Italian stoneworkers. When my father
was stationed in Naples, I learned some Italian. I suppose you
know Mr. Salviatti, too."

"Yes." Elsie was dizzy with being taken by surprise, dizzy
at having foreseen—how long ago?—the perfect wife for
Johnny.

Patty got up. She was as tall as Mary. She said, "You know,
I wasn't paying all that much attention, they just told me 'Go
to court number two.'" She stuck out her hand. "I'm Patty
Scanlon."

"Elsie Buttrick."

Elsie felt Patty's hand. Not a quiver. She watched Patty's
eyes. Not a flicker. Could it be he hadn't told her?

"Oh my God, you're Aunt Mary's housemate! She's absolutely crazy about your daughter; her old Christmas letters
were all about Rose. Rose this, Rose that. Rose, Rose, Rose.
And, of course, Johnny was crazy about you."

So that was it—a little pat on the head.

Patty said, "Wait—I'm just getting my bearings here. Sally Aldrich is your sister. That means your brother-in-law's the rock-ribbed Republican going against the grain to back Johnny. Sometime I'd love to hear you explain him. But look—we'd better start playing again if I'm going to get to Mr. Salviatti. Any last-minute notes on him? Johnny just said, 'Speak some Italian, get the names of all those cousins of his in Westerly.' Is he short? I could wear flats."

"Not too short. Old, but he likes pretty women. Traditional Catholic—he sent his daughter to Catholic school, Monsignor Prout. Rich, but he was snubbed by a lot of the old Yankees. He likes that Jack took him on as a partner in all this"—Elsie pointed at the Wedding Cake—"but he rolls his eyes when Jack's being an asshole. Oh—you could admire the road to Westerly. His company repaved it."

Patty tipped her head a notch at the end of each sentence, clicking it into the file. Elsie wondered at herself—here she was being a good little helper, showing off that she, too, could have been the good political wife.

And then she was rolled by the bigger wave tumbling through the water. She'd mocked Johnny when he showed up on the *ProJo*'s list of Rhode Island's eligible bachelors— ex–altar boy in search of a wife—mocked him, thinking she didn't care. And then she'd erupted. At herself for being impossible? At him? Whatever Elsie had wanted and not wanted, however on-again/off-again she and Johnny had been, whatever muddle of mockery and fury she'd felt, she'd perfectly conjured this vote-getting, child-bearing, Italian-speaking, red-haired Irish-American beauty. And there was Patty Scanlon walking to her side of the court, scooping up a ball with her racket and giving it a bounce, carelessly floating into Rhode Island, not knowing her fortune had been told in the *Providence Journal* Sunday supplement.

It was true for a moment, and then not true. Elsie could no

more reduce Patty's life than Patty could reduce hers by saying, "And, of course, Johnny was crazy about you."

Patty said, "I forget—did you serve last?"

"Yes." Elsie reached over the net and flicked a ball toward
Patty. Elsie felt the first breath of the noon sea breeze. Johnny
had been an awkward tennis player but a graceful skater,
speeding around thick-frozen Hothouse Pond, somehow
making his solid body fluid. She could let that go. Another
thought came to her with a slower, deeper breath than physical yearning. She thought, He was the nicest man I ever slept
with.

Elsie won. She played well, but the more decisive factor
may have been that Patty wanted to be on time for Mr. Salviatti.

chapter sixty-two

Tom brought Mr. Aldrich to the house. Mr. Aldrich
asked about their putting up one of the Sawtooth per-
formers. Dick said, "That's up to May."

May couldn't fault him but wished he'd just said no. She
said, "I'm afraid things are just too unsettled, Mr. Aldrich."

"Jack, please. I understand completely. Don't give it
another thought. What I'm really here for is something a bit
different." He turned to Dick. "I'm trying to give that son of
mine a sense of what Sawtooth really is. My thought is that it
shouldn't just go to him on a platter. I'm more old-fashioned
than that. I'm going to have Jack Junior spend a week in the
kitchen with Mary Scanlon. He's already spent more than a
week with Tom here, getting the waterfront in shape. I have
to say Tom's got just the right touch—knows when to kid

with the boy, knows when to get tough. But what I was wondering is if you've got a spare berth on board *Spartina*. Just for one trip. Because when you come right down to it, the sea is what's giving us all a living. I don't know if you've read *Captains Courageous* by Rudyard Kipling, but the lesson that boy learned on that fishing vessel is just what I have in mind."

Tom said, "The way that boy ended up on that schooner is that he fell off a yacht and the fishermen pulled him out of the drink. I hope you're not planning to make Jack Junior do it the hard way."

Mr. Aldrich said, "Well, that's sort of amusing, Tom."

May closed her eyes. Tom didn't try again.

"Jack Junior has sailing experience. He can steer a compass course," Mr. Aldrich said. "I'm not saying he could replace one of your regular hands, but as an extra hand, someone to take the wheel now and then. Just the odd moment. And, of course, he wouldn't get a share."

Dick didn't say anything.

Mr. Aldrich sat comfortably in the silence, staring straight ahead, as if he was thinking it over himself. After a while he said, "There's another thing. Tom asked me about it and I gave him the best answer I could, but he—you and he— should ask an experienced banker. This is a valuable property. I know you know the assessed value, but the appraised value might surprise you. I know you had some trouble getting a bank loan years ago when you were building *Spartina*. I think you'd find things are a lot different now. You could mortgage this property, have enough to take care of problems, get ahead of the game. I'd be glad to take you in to meet the manager of the bank. Very sound man." Mr. Aldrich tilted his head toward Tom. "I should add, I wouldn't have thought of this on my own. Tom and I have had some talks. He's got a good business mind."

"See, Ma. I can be all business when it's time for business."

May said, "What about your job with Eddie?"

"There's plenty of guys who can bang nails. I've learned a

thing or two, but the future there belongs to either Phoebe or Walt."

Mr. Aldrich said, "Sawtooth Enterprises has more room for growth." He got up. "Well, I've got to get back to my desk. Perhaps in a few days we can have another chat. Entirely up to you. At your convenience. Tom knows how to reach me on my private line."

May was relieved to see Dick get up and shake hands, even if he hadn't said more than four words. After Mr. Aldrich left, Tom looked at Dick. Dick said, "If you stay to supper, we can talk. I've got a couple of things to do at the boatyard. Bang a few nails."

"Is that a joke, Dad?"

"Whole damn thing might be a joke."

"Nothing funny about making some money."

"While I'm at the yard, you might take a look at the books. Charlie's been telling me some things about the projected red-crab population. If I have to retrofit for another fishery, I might need that bank. Captain Teixeira's already converting one of his boats; he gave me a copy of the work order. It's in the file." But Dick didn't set right off, stood with his hand on the doorknob. He said, "God, that man tires me out."

"He's being nice to Rose these days," May said. "Putting on her play and all." Tom laughed for no reason May could fathom. May said, "Even seems to see something in you."

But after Dick left and Tom went to Dick's worktable, May thought she'd better call Elsie again. Not just yet, maybe next time Mr. Aldrich showed up. She'd said he was being nice, and she hadn't said it just to contradict Dick. Mr. Aldrich appeared to be asking a favor and offering favors in return—nothing mysterious about that, as far as it went. What was mysterious to her was what it must feel like to be him—going up and down in South County, taking it all in, thinking about what he might get up to with whatever struck his fancy. The only power to choose she had was whether to make a fuss or let things be. May wondered if she could just let everything be. Let Deirdre settle down with Charlie. Let Dick get into debt so he could keep going out to sea. And when he came back with a bag of clothes soaked in salt and old bait, let him take them up to Elsie's washing machine. Would letting things go their own way make her easier, or would things pile up so high she couldn't bear it?

In the next room Tom groaned and said out loud, "Oh boy. Oh boy, oh boy."

She said, "What is it?"

"Nothing much. Nothing that Dad's marrying a rich widow wouldn't fix."

"Well, don't go making jokes like that when your father gets back."

"Don't worry, Ma." Tom stuck his head round the edge of the door. "Dad's got a great sense of humor."

Now that made her laugh.

chapter sixty-three

Elsie was restless. When she got back to her house she tried to settle down to read. No use. She went for a bike ride, all the way to URI and back the long way around the Great Swamp. Faster than she and Deirdre had done it, fast enough so Deirdre would have been breathing hard. When she got off her bike at the end of the paved part of the driveway her legs were trembling. But she didn't want to go sit in her house. She got the key to Miss Perry's front door from under the rock where she'd left it. She locked the door behind her, wanting to seal herself inside the dark house. She trailed through the library, fingering the books. The smell was all that appealed to her. On the mantelpiece she found the card that Everett Hazard had sent Miss Perry. He'd drawn an Egyptian hieroglyph. Under it was his handwritten translation: "Paradise is a man's own good nature." Not today. That sort of thought was like pot—cheered you up only if you were in a good mood . . .

Elsie had framed it, meant to give it to Tory Hazard after Miss Perry's funeral but had decided to wait. Tory had stopped Captain Teixeira from reminiscing about her father. Now Elsie felt less patient with her, Miss Perry's proto-pet, the nicer one. Captain Teixeira probably thought Tory was more like Miss Perry. Johnny should have married her for her good nature and her old Rhode Island name, get out the old-Yankee vote. Too bad, Tory—he picked the red-haired Irish navy brat. Who was off singing "O Sole Mio" to Mr. Salviatti, not wearing high heels because she was so tall. Let her be tall. When she chased a tennis ball, she ran like a giraffe.

She opened her fist to look at the key—a large, old-fashioned key with a trefoil handle, the sort of key she'd seen in a painting hanging from the belt of the châtelaine. Châtelaine, my ass—she was the housekeeper. She should be wearing Rose's maid's uniform—that cap with the long ribbons.

She trotted up the stairs all the way to the tower room, hoping one more puff of exercise would make her mindless.

In the old days it had been a maid's room, some poor waif from County Clare saying her beads in her neck-to-ankle nightgown. Or was she waiting for the young chauffeur to sneak up the stairs? Soon it would be a Perryville girl sleeping here, one of the good students—this was a prize room, the window high enough to look out to sea through the top of the copper beech after the leaves fell. Now it was shaded except for one ray that flickered through an upper corner of the window, dotting the floor beside the armoire, just missing the mirror set in its door. Eddie and Walt had moved it all the way up from the basement after Elsie pointed out there was no closet. Lots of manly grunting, Walt on the heavy bottom end, dripping sweat from his forehead onto his face reflected in the mirror. Eddie four steps up, navigating the turns. Elsie trailing behind, keeping her mouth shut even when they just missed gouging the wall, but on the last narrow flight of stairs, apologizing—"Jeez, guys, I didn't think it'd be this hard."

When they'd finally set it down in the middle of the room they both started laughing. Eddie stopped and said, "I don't suppose we could've used a block and tackle and brought her through the window."

Even Elsie had seen it was a preposterous idea but so Eddie-like that she'd started laughing, too.

And there it stood now, looking as if it had always been there, unmarked by the effort, not even a streak on the mirror, since Walt had wiped it with the hem of his T-shirt, a surprising delicacy after all the heave-ho.

Elsie began to feel better, as if reliving the men's heavy lifting was the exercise that she'd needed. She unfolded the doubled-up bare mattress on the cot and stretched out. The women she'd been snarling at were dwindling, as remote as the waif from County Clare, as the grade-grubbing prize girl, and soon they were no more than dust motes passing through the bar of light.

She woke up. The sunbeam had moved just enough to be bouncing off the mirror, dit-dit-dah-dit. But the blinking seemed to be making a puttering noise. She rubbed her eyes. It was a motorcycle idling. She got up, combed her hair with her fingers, and looked at herself in the mirror. She raised the window. Walt waved and yelled, "I figured it was you." He killed the engine and said, "I saw you riding your bike. Thought you were Deirdre. Lucky it's you. I can't find the key. I left some beer and lunch meat in the fridge. I thought the lunch meat might go bad."

"I've got the key. Shall I toss it down?"

"No, don't do that. It'll get lost in the ivy or you'll ding my bike."

"Okay, I'll come down."

"Or you could let down your hair."

She was at a loss for an instant. She knelt on the window seat and raised the screen, as if the screen made it harder to hear. "What?"

"Let down your hair. Like in that fairy tale."

It wasn't that she hadn't heard him. "Yes," she said. "Rapunzel." She leaned out and lifted one of her short curls with her fingertips. "I think you've got the wrong girl." He went back to his motorcycle. She called out, "For all you know I might be the wicked witch." He didn't say anything—had she been too obviously fishing for a compliment? He hung his helmet on the handlebar. All right, he was going to stay around.

"Tell you what," he said. "You could open up that window seat, and we could test that escape ladder."

"You want me to climb down?"

"Or I could climb up."

She opened the lid of the window seat. She began to lower the chain-link ladder over the stone sill, letting the links slide through her hands. When it was halfway down she grabbed a rung and held it. She felt the ladder sway. She let the rung slide from her palm to her fingertips, then let it fall. She stepped back and watched. The chains grew taut as they took Walt's full weight. As he climbed, the top links scratched the stone sill, scribbling white marks, lines and arcs of a hieroglyph easy enough to decipher.

chapter sixty-four

Mary missed JB terribly as soon as he went back to Boston. She regretted whatever bad moods she'd let him see. She feared he'd come to his senses as soon as he got to the big city. He said he'd be back as soon as he could. God knows she'd heard that before, though not lately. A part of her was loopy as a teenager, but another part administered a slow drip of wryness. So her fingers trembled when she got a letter from him care of Sawtooth, but she wasn't undone when it wasn't a love letter.

Dear Mary, you never answer your damn phone. You're the only person I know who doesn't have an answering machine. So call me. Best time would be next Sunday after you get through with the Sawtooth brunch.

He didn't pick up the phone right away—in fact the message on his answering service was well under way when his real voice cut in. He said, "Wait a second, we'll have to wait," while his recorded voice was saying, ". . . to send a fax, or leave your name and number after the beep." "Okay. Mary, are you there? It'll record for a bit, then click off. Sorry, I've been right by the phone, you just caught me the one minute I was in the can. Wait. I'll turn the TV off."

Not sweeping her off her feet.

"Okay. Here we are. Look, something's come up. Don't know where to begin. Do you know Tory Hazard?"

"I know who she is. So how have you been?"

"Yes, you're right. How are you? You sound great. I can't wait to see you. What day is today? Oh yeah, of course it's Sunday. Are you still at Sawtooth? At your place?"

"I just got home. Is something wrong?"

"No, no, could be good. I can be there in two hours. Would that be okay? Sunday traffic's all the other way, could be an hour and a half."

Mary thought this might well be what she wanted but that he needed a few pointers on presentation.

He said, "What time is it? Not three yet. So it'll still be light."

Their first three days had been a tumble of energy, and

then, after she got over her Monday-morning snit of wanting to be alone and he'd gone for a swim and come out with his teeth chattering, she'd taken him home, put a warm quilt over the two of them, and they lay there, good-humoredly chatting and dozing. A bit more poetry out of him, not his own, Yeats—"'And I shall have some peace there, for peace comes dropping slow . . .'"—and he'd trailed off. Now here he was tumbling again.

"So when were you doing all this calling?" she said. "Maybe that's my fault—I shut the ringer off if I've worked late."

"Oh, all the time. Doesn't matter, here we are. So where were we? I'm all set. How are you?"

"Wait—what's this got to do with Tory Hazard? And why does it have to be daylight?"

"Will it drive you nuts if I hold off till I'm there? I'm listening to myself and I'm not doing it right."

He was at the door before she finished the Sunday paper—she'd read more thoroughly than usual. She'd brushed her hair and put on a dress as soon as she'd hung up the phone.

When they headed south on Route 1 she said, "We're not going to Sawtooth, are we? That's the last place—"

"Not quite."

He pulled into the driveway of the old Hazard place; the name was still on the RFD mailbox. He stopped between the barn and the small house. Years ago she'd been to Mr. Hazard's bookshop in Wakefield, never here, though the stone wall on the far side of the house marked the beginning of the Sawtooth property. He walked around the outside of the house, nodding to himself, turning to look at her with an expression on his face that left her even more puzzled. Eagerness and confusion?

He had the key. He let her go in first but then went into a trance in front of the full bookshelf in the main room.

He said, "She's pretty sure he'd just bulldoze this."

"Okay," Mary said. "Time's up."

He ran his hand through his hair. "I've known Tory for a while, not from way back, not from when her father was still alive. So I never met him, so I can't tell what she means when she says I remind her of her father."

Mary had seen Tory at Miss Perry's funeral. Haggard, attractive. Mary wondered for a moment, then was sure that he'd had an affair with her. An instinct and then an additional reason: women who have doted on their difficult fathers don't bring them up lightly. "Let's clear up the bulldozing," she said. "Just to start with something easy. You mean Jack Aldrich."

"Right."

"And he's made your Miss Hazard an offer."

"Right."

"But she'd rather sell to a rumpled old guy who loves books and reminds her of dear old da."

"Okay, close enough."

"But here, my dear Watson, is where the trail becomes more difficult to follow. One possibility is that you just want my expert advice as a former owner of South County real estate. That's too simple for all the fuss you're making. Another is that your old pal Tory Hazard wants to install you here with an eye to the pair of you starting up again. That would mean you're hopelessly obtuse in more ways than one."

"Jesus, Mary. I knew this wasn't going to be easy."

"And I'm ruling out your dropping to one knee and proposing to me. I'm certainly taken by your full head of lovely white hair and your spouting poetry, but neither of us is that headlong. At least I'm not."

"I'm glad you—"

"So what are we doing here?"

"What do you think of the place so far?"

"You should buy it. For all your talk about being immune to extraneous impulses, you're being smitten by an impulse. What does she want for it?"

"Two-thirds of what Jack Aldrich is offering. And my

guess is he hasn't completely untied his purse strings. I would do it; I'd do it tomorrow."

Mary began to laugh. She said, "If I'll go in on it. Do I just guarantee your mortgage, or do I get to move in?"

"Move in."

"With you."

"With me."

"So we'll have a candlelit dinner tonight, throw ourselves into bed, and first thing Monday morning we'll seal our vows in front of a mortgage-loan officer at the Wakefield Trust."

"Are you making fun of the idea as a way of saying no, or are you making fun of the idea as a way of getting used to it?"

"Have all your affairs with women been on such firm financial grounds?"

"Not when I was younger. I was married for eleven years."

"Any children? Wait—don't tell me. We may need something to talk about during the long winter nights."

She was enjoying herself. She thought she should have been horrified, but she liked that he'd come unraveled. She also liked that there was no one she would ever tell this story to, however it turned out.

The sun had sunk low enough to be pouring though the west windows, raising the temperature and a stuffy smell. She went out to the back porch, where there was a light breeze, just enough to make the porch swing sway on its chains. She sat on it and began to push herself back and forth with one foot.

He came out and said, "Well, how would you have done it?" She laughed and shook her head. He sat down on the porch step and stared at the ground. He said, "I know what it is. It's money. I can't even talk about it. It makes me shy. And then that makes me go nuts."

"You're not broke, are you?"

"No. I have a brother who takes care of my money, the family money, such as it is. He's younger than I am, but he's a lawyer. I asked him if I could buy a house, and when I told him how much, he said I shouldn't aim so high."

"So you thought of me."

"No. I thought of you before. If he'd have said, 'Go ahead, you're rolling in dough,' I'd have laid it at your feet."

"Your brother—you get along with him?"

"Oh, yeah. There's no arguing with him, but he's the right man for the job. My sisters and I would have pissed it all away. I would have invested in plays, none of which made a dime. I suppose I could have pressed a little, but aside from the fact that talking about money seems to puree my brain cells, I'd have felt bad poking at him after all he's done. He arranged college loans for my two daughters, for my sisters' kids, too. He does our taxes, does something smart about everyone's old age. Of course, he has a lawyer's mind—always thinking about what could go wrong."

"So how do you live? Do you teach? You sometimes sound like a teacher."

"Used to. I gave that up once I was through supporting a wife and two girls. Now I just scribble away; some of it makes lunch money. When things get tight something turns up—a book review, a theater review, someone wanting help with a script. I used to do advertising jingles, but I was walking down the hall at the end of a day and I passed this guy's office. He was talking on the phone; he said, 'Hey, if you're stuck you can always call Callahan. He'll give it some fizz.' Then he laughed and said, 'And he works for peanuts.' Pissed me off. Pissed me off enough I jumped right over my neurosis about money. I sent in a bill for a thousand bucks. They paid it. That pissed me off even more—made me think of all the times I'd got peanuts. Pissed me off so much I never went back. I thought, Well at least I'm over that neurotic tic about money. But it was just on vacation. When it occurred to me to send the check back, I couldn't find it. Turned out I'd cashed it. After a while it came back to me. I'd paid cash to get my car fixed. Okay, but what about the rest of the dough? Then the weather turned cold and I went to get my overcoat, and next to it was this other overcoat, this great big Irish tweed thing the size of a tent. The label said, 'As woven for the sporting princes in the days of Irish kings.' I mean, you don't fall for that sort of blather without remembering it. It was as if someone had slipped me a Mickey. It's worse when I have to deal with money *and* people I don't like. It's not as bad when I'm with guys I get along with. Like this musical with Rose—if that gets picked up, I'll make a few bucks out of it and I won't go haywire."

"You mean you didn't get paid anything up front?"

JB, who'd been perking up a little—though still looking at the backyard rather than at her—slumped. "That's just what my brother said."

Mary laughed. She tried to stop. She tried to stop because she doubted she could explain to him that she was laughing at herself, at how she'd been thinking of him as a font of knowledge, a master of the world and good fortune, and herself as girlish and unsteady. And here she was old enough to know a good thing was never as grand as it seemed at first.

"Anyway," he said. "That's why I mixed up everything and it came out . . . half-baked? Raw? Would you say raw?"

"Underdone and overdone. But never mind all that now. We'll catch our breath and see where we are in the morning."

Wasn't this the way she'd been with men in the old days— feeling excitement, feeling herself the lesser, and then having to be Wendy for some oversized Peter Pan? She gave that game up in her mid-thirties. She'd thought she was old then. She felt younger now. Was that in spite of or because of her years with Rose and Elsie? Perhaps she wasn't feeling young at all, just weightless. The last thing she'd said to them, God help her, was that she'd bang their heads together. The words had flown out of her crazily, more in anguish than in anger—an explosion as inevitable as the bursting of a milkweed pod, each of them blown out and up in separate arcs. Only weeks ago, but it seemed it was on the other side of a break in time. But the cruelest trick of time was how it rushed you by the good parts. As soon as Rose had got so much of what Mary wished for her, became so like the girl Mary hoped she would be, all those wishes and hopes, having spent years in the future, gave off one spark in the present and passed into memory. A minute ago she'd been laughing. It served her right. Yes, he'd been gruff and brusque, then bumbling, and finally ending up flailing like a beetle on its back trying to get right side up. She'd poked him and laughed, fairly tortured him with her cross-examining.

She said, "Come on, then. Come sit on the swing with me. You'll be better off here than sitting down there staring at your shoes."

One thing he did nicely—he didn't push off too hard, just a brush of his foot in time with hers.

The sun sank low enough to take on its first stripe of red. The shadows of the stone wall and the scrub cedars grew longer.

This slowness was an unlooked-for relief. The time with Rose that had stung her near to grief was inside her—out there, time was moving more peacefully, a slow slip of the land through its veil of changing light.

Her first thought when she came to was that he had the sense to let her be.

chapter sixty-five

When she was reduced to one word it was *thorough*. He came through the window headfirst and pulled his body into the room, walking his hands along the floor. He ended up full-length at her feet. So far, it was her idea. She could laugh it all off. She could help him get up and see what happened when they put their hands on each other. She was pleased for the moment to turn the idea in her mind, register the flush of her skin against her second thoughts. But during the time he lay there without moving—perhaps only seconds—the room seemed to tilt toward him. He got to his feet and pulled the ladder up, carefully folding it into the window seat. He closed the lid, looked out the window. He said, "There's our bikes out front." He pulled the window down and said, "I guess that's okay."

So she was next. He held her shoulders, kissed the side of her neck, lifted her hair—all the preliminary attentions. When he kissed her, her mouth felt faraway. She was impressed by the way he unzipped the front of her bicycle suit and slid it down both her arms at once. When he moved his hands down her bare back and inside the suit, she clenched her buttocks. That reflex of vanity was the only bit of response her mind provided. When she'd been the girl in the red dress her thoughts had woven through her, little strands of commentary that made her shiver as much as skin on skin. Now her mind was blank. She certainly felt this and that—she felt his unpeeling the suit down her legs. She may have lifted one foot and then the other. Another set of attentions and she felt herself divided into more zones—his hands on her rear keeping her upright, his mouth ranging up and down her front, and her own breath brushing the roof of her mouth. Nothing on the screen of her mind, although she could tell that her hips were moving. And soon enough her breath was stuttering out of her, and then she was being tipped onto the bed. She felt her hand touch the bare mattress. For an instant the hand was distinctly hers. Then it disappeared from her mind as abruptly as it had appeared.

After he made her yelp he propped himself up on his hands and knees. She felt the air on her skin as one more touch urging her on. It was then that the word *thorough* occurred to her. He rolled to one side and lay still.

When he began to touch her again, her head felt heavy, but her skin tightened. She closed her eyes. Her brain felt stoned, but her body began to jitter again, a circuit of nerves humming in the dark.

This time, when she thought *thorough*, the word seemed coarser.

The sun was almost down. She lay on her side along the edge of the narrow cot. She looked for her bicycle suit. In the dimness the red looked black. She stretched her arm out. She couldn't reach it. She didn't feel like moving. She let her hand rest on the floor. Her stomach growled. She put her hand on it and realized she had to pee. She went down the hall, feeling her way to the bathroom in the windowless dark. When she came back she put on her bicycle suit. She thought, Well that's that. It was a surprise to hear herself in her own mind. She thought that she'd never noticed the noises she made. She tried to remember the noises she used to make. She must have made noises, because one time someone had put his hand over her mouth. But now, as if there were an echo in this strange little room, she heard herself yip.

The late light from the sky filtered through the leaves of the copper beech. There were no shadows, just a steady half-darkness.

She used to do this sort of thing and then fly away. Now she felt like a ghost of herself—there was her body, and she couldn't get back into it.

She used to do this sort of thing and go home laughing, laughing at how she'd made a man lurch out of his well-tailored life, at how the hand that knotted his tie and signed the letters on his desk had trembled to touch her.

Now she was the one lurched out of her life. The body down there was enjoying the aftereffects.

He sat up and ran his hands through his hair. Had he been asleep? Or had he watched her tugging her bicycle suit back on? He got up and went down the hall. Of course, he knew where the bathroom was, he'd worked on it, he'd carried the armoire up the stairs. She'd been his boss.

That should have done it.

She heard the toilet flush, the faucet run, his hands splashing water. What a ridiculous set of sounds to pay attention to. But apparently not for her nerve ends. When she heard his footsteps in the hall, her breath caught in her chest and she couldn't stop the whir of what would happen next.

Part Three

chapter sixty-six

Here it was well into spring, pretty near official summer, and it didn't feel like it to her. She felt as tight-packed as unturned earth. She'd been busy enough—got the house in order; put the woolens away; repainted Rose's boat and revarnished the oars, since Dick kept putting that off; got the tomato vines staked.

It was more than just being by herself, doing and making lists to do more. What she was doing didn't jibe with what the rest of them were up to. She wanted them all back in the house, and at the same time she couldn't pull back from being at odds with them. Tom with his get-rich-quick ideas, Charlie sticking with Deirdre. Dick going off to the bank, buzzing with the same desperate energy as when he was building the boat but more dangerous now that he had more to put at risk.

They'd been pulled together in the house when Charlie was here and Tom brought Rose to visit. It made her wish for winter again.

Dick had come back from the bank, sat down at the kitchen table, and said, "They wouldn't make a loan on *Spartina*. Just on the house. I should've kept my mouth shut, but I told them that the last time a hurricane came by, *Spartina* just needed some paint, it was the house needed fixing. I told them I built both, I'm the one ought to know. They think the house and lot are worth something. They're worth something because of what Jack Aldrich has done at Sawtooth. And it's not so much the house, it's the lot. Funny damn world where it's not my work—it's someone else's work next door that makes them hand over their money."

May had said, "Well, a boat is more like a car. It goes down as soon as you drive it off the lot." She added, "I mean, that's how they think," but it was too late. Of course, she saw how Dick was insulted, how what he'd put his mind to and what he'd made with his hands and put to use for sixteen years got weighed on a scale in a bank office and barely made it tip. It wasn't until now, with Dick five days out, that what she herself felt rose up in her. She felt slighted. She didn't expect anyone up at the bank to know anything much about her house, but as offhand as you please, Dick weighed the house as less than his boat. Just another thing he'd made out of wood when he had time to spare. Put the shingles on and go out to sea again. She was the one who felt every inch of it in her fingertips.

If there was a balance between the two of them, her house had to weigh as much as his boat.

She wished she wasn't alone now, now that she was finally delving into herself, turning over what she'd kept buried. She'd been reproaching herself for having driven Charlie away, for being cranky with Tom . . . She'd been worrying that that was why she felt like a stony field. What she turned up now was that she didn't forgive Dick for driving to Boston without her. And clinging to that—she wasn't sure just how—was that Dick got Charlie to go out on *Spartina* with him. They didn't make peace here in this house, not here where she lived, where she'd got over her pain, where she'd let them see that she'd come to love Rose. Dick had taken Charlie where Dick was in command, where Dick could forget everything but the sea and hope that Charlie would melt into that forgetfulness with him.

And now Dick had gone and put her house at risk. He'd got Tom looking at the accounts, gone off to Mr. Aldrich's bank—got himself mixed up with all that machinery of invisible money. And then put out to sea without another word. At least he knew what he was doing out there. Though this time, as if to show how tangled up he'd got, he'd taken Mr. Aldrich's son along—not that that would make a difference if he couldn't make a bank payment.

She stayed angry, fiercely angry, until midday. She took a mattock and dug a slit trench just outside the wire fence around the garden. She buried a band of chicken wire in it. Something, likely a groundhog, had been getting under the fence. She took some pleasure in thinking of his frustration. He might end up cutting his paw or getting a claw stuck.

Then she was alone again, sliding off the crest of her anger into the trough. She thought of calling Phoebe, but Phoebe was in a tizzy over Eddie and Walt's going at each other. And even if Phoebe was smart about real estate, Mr. Aldrich cast a spell on her. Mary Scanlon was more down-to-earth about Mr. Aldrich, but even if it was her day off, she'd be up to something with her new boyfriend.

Spring was getting into everyone's bones but hers.

She wished that Deirdre O'Malley didn't set her teeth on edge. If Deirdre wasn't so impossible, she could've helped with all this; nobody said she didn't have brains. Maybe Deirdre would grow out of being stuck on herself.

May called Elsie. She said, "I was just wondering if you talked to your brother-in-law. He came by—"

"No, but I just talked to Sally. She's worried sick. How long has *Spartina* been out?"

"Five days."

"Jack Junior was supposed to send a radio message; Sally made him promise."

"Well, Dick doesn't like to get on the radio till he's homeward bound. Doesn't want the other boats knowing just where he's working."

"I suppose I could tell her that. She just asked Jack to call the Coast Guard station, but he said to wait. What did he say when he came by?"

"That wasn't today, it was a while back. About mortgages and the like."

"Oh." Elsie paused. "So you're not calling about . . . Okay, I see. And you're right, that's probably something to worry about, but just now Jack and Sally are on the subject of Jack

Junior. And you're right, I did say I'd do something, and I will. I suppose I could tell Sally you're not worried. And about Dick not using his radio. You don't know if there could be a storm out there that we don't know about here? I mean, they're out, what, two hundred, three hundred miles?"

"That's where the shelf drops off, but Dick gets out there and follows the edge. Or he could take a detour if he thinks he might spot a swordfish. If Sally needs to keep busy, she could call Captain Teixeira. He's at home, but *Bom Sonho* is out, so he'd know what the weather's doing." May immediately regretted saying "If Sally needs to keep busy." She remembered standing right where she was now with this same phone in her hand when she heard about Charlie. She said, "I'm sorry. I shouldn't have said—"

"No, I understand. And you're right. Sally would be better off talking to Captain Teixeira. All she's doing now is getting furious at Jack. I mean, Jack pretty much ordered Jack Junior to do this. Jack's got a thick hide, but she might say something sharp enough . . . And then if it turns out nothing's wrong, he'll be insufferable. God, family life."

May liked Elsie's voice, liked that last sigh. She wondered what it would be like to have Elsie as a friend, worrying about her the way she worried about her sister. And they could talk about Rose. May thought she'd always be grateful to Phoebe for driving her to Boston, but when Phoebe zigged and zagged she wasn't as good at it as Elsie. And Elsie didn't need as much help about how things worked. Phoebe came back to herself more often, all that talk about some old beau. And then posing for Mr. Salviatti's statue. May felt guilty. She'd call Phoebe right after this, see how Phoebe was doing with Eddie and Walt.

"Look," Elsie said. "I'd better get back to Sally. I haven't forgotten about Jack and what he might be up to. I'll give you a call. And maybe we'll see each other at Rose's play. You're awfully good to go three times. I'm afraid I had a little fit after the first night. Did Rose say anything?"

"No. It seemed to me she was fine. You'd have thought it might go to her head, but she was just as steady as if she'd been doing it all her life. The second night was just as good. She was, I don't know, bouncier. You know how she acted the maid's part—kind of sharp-tongued and sassy? The second night was more like sweet and sassy. She sounded like Mary Scanlon when she sings those Irish songs and puts on her brogue."

"You mean when Rose was talking? She did it in an Irish accent?"

"Just when she was pretending to be the maid. When she was being herself—I mean, herself in the play—she sounded even swankier. Like Mr. Aldrich if he were a girl."

Elsie laughed. She said, "Now, there's a picture."

May hadn't meant to be funny, but she was pleased she got Elsie to laugh.

After that phone call May went out to the garden again. She pulled weeds until she filled a bushel basket; she made a hole in the compost pile and buried the weeds deep enough so their roots would be too hot to do anything but rot into black earth. She didn't know the science of it, not exactly how the microbes made the old leaves and the green weeds and garbage so hot, but she knew how to manage it, get it working so it dissolved not just her vegetable peels but eggshells and fish bones—and even some of Dick's bait when it got too rotten—into crumbly soil that smelled sweet.

When Tom showed up May was still out in the garden. He said, "I've been trying to call." Then he just stood there, sliding his hands on the top of his pant legs. He finally said, "Charlie's coming over; I called him and he's coming over."

May said, "What for?" There was a dazzle of light in her eyes when she jerked her head.

Tom said, "It's probably going to be all right. *Bom Sonho*'s on her way, and it's still light. The Coast Guard got a fix on the distress signal. *Bom Sonho*'s closest; she'll get there faster than the Coast Guard. They're pretty far out. Captain Teixeira's on the radio with *Bom Sonho*. They were hauling pots when the Coast Guard radioed to see if anyone was close. They just cut the line and put a buoy on it. They're on their way."

"What happened?"

"They don't know. That's the thing, *Spartina* got on the mayday frequency—but when *Bom Sonho* switched to their working frequency, nothing. Charlie told me there's an EPRB on the dory—he said what it stands for, emergency position something. Maybe RB is radio beacon. Charlie knows."

"How cold is it out there? The water?"

"Yeah, I asked Charlie that. He says it depends where the Gulf Stream is today. But they've got the dory. They've got survival suits. And look—it could just be they've lost power or fouled their rudder. Charlie said they can set off the EPRB and it doesn't mean they abandoned ship."

"Let's go inside." May knew Dick wouldn't send a distress signal if the engine quit. He'd be below working on it for a long time before he sent a distress signal.

When they got to the kitchen, Tom said, "Captain Teixeira says I can bring you over, be right there while he's on his radio."

"I should get Rose," May said. "Do you know where Rose is? I just talked to Elsie on the phone. It didn't sound like Rose was there."

"Elsie's with her sister," Tom said. "They just got to the dock; that's where I talked to Captain Teixeira. I don't know how they know—Captain Teixeira, maybe. He and Elsie are pretty tight. They went into Captain Teixeira's radio shack."

May thought it would be like a circus over there. Dick would hate it if he found out.

Charlie's car pulled in. May went onto the front porch. She said, "Tom told me. You better go listen in with Captain Teixeira. Call me as soon as you know something. Tom, you can go with him or you can stay here. I'd just as soon be here, where I can keep busy."

She'd said those very words not two hours ago, and now they were a judgment on her.

Tom looked uncertain. May said, "Or here's what you could do. You go on up to Rose's school. I think they're using the auditorium to get the Sawtooth show ready. Rose'd like it if you're with her."

The boys left. May went into the kitchen and sat by the phone. She pictured *Spartina*, then felt rather than saw the cold, gray distance. She thought of Captain Teixeira bowed over his radio. He'd be speaking Portuguese. She'd been unkind about how Catholics carried on, about Mr. Salviatti's angels, about Captain Teixeira's big Catholic family, but now she saw Captain Teixeira's hand holding the microphone like the priest holding that little wand he shook water out of when he blessed the fleet, and in her mind she went down on her knees before Captain Teixeira and confessed her sins, the spite and anger she'd let loose against Dick and his boat.

chapter sixty-seven

Sally was at Elsie's door, knocking and calling; she was inside saying, "Can you come? Can you come right now? Something's happened. I called your Captain Teixeira. They said he was at the dock because something's happened. Can you come?"

On the ride over, Elsie tried to reassure Sally, but when they squeezed in behind the people in the radio shack, Elsie became alarmed at the silence. After a while the radio crackled, and there was a rush of Portuguese. Captain Teixeira turned to Charlie and said, "*Bom Sonho*'s close. She got her own fix and the Coast Guard fix. She's close, and she's looking."

Sally said, "What's happening?"

Charlie turned. He saw Elsie, slid his eyes to Sally. "*Spartina* sent a distress signal. The Coast Guard sent out a call. *Bom Son-ho*'s the closest boat. She had a fix of her own when Dad called her, but she lost contact. It could just be . . . it could be a couple of things. Maybe *Spartina* lost power." He turned back toward Captain Teixeira. He said, "I sh-should have been on board." Without looking away from the radio Captain Teixeira held Charlie's forearm and gave it a shake. Elsie understood it wasn't *Spartina* losing power. She hoped Sally hadn't understood.

Another silence. It seemed to Elsie to grow denser, as if compressed by everyone's thoughts. Captain Teixeira's shaking Charlie's arm was in it; Charlie's self-reproach was in it. What else was pressing through the silence? Was there reproach in Charlie's look sliding away from her? Was he thinking, Why is *she* here and not May? Elsie felt the silence urging her to self-reproach so she would be more cleanly prepared for bad news.

She tried to stop. She couldn't stop by herself. She leaned against Sally. No help. She imagined Sally reproaching herself for not having protected her son from Jack's notion of how to make a man of Jack Junior.

She knew hers was a superstitious muddle. Her dumb pleasure in the tower room had nothing to do with what was happening at sea. What was happening at sea was physics, it had its own physics. But what was happening to her in this small room had its own physics, too, a rush of shame into the vacuum of not knowing.

Another crackle, a short sentence in Portuguese. Then four words that she could tell were counting—one, two, three, four. Captain Teixeira said to Charlie, "He sees them; they're all there. He's working her around to pick them up."

In the next silence they all moved a step closer to Captain Teixeira's broad back. At last another longer set of Portuguese sentences. Captain Teixeira answered, seemed to be giving orders. He didn't translate. Charlie said, "Did you say 'helicopter'?"

Captain Teixeira said, "Yes. They're all on board. Your father didn't have his survival suit on. The dory was stove in. They were lying across a piece of her. It was awash. Wait. I'll see if they can ask Tony." After another back-and-forth he said, "Tony's not so good, either. He unzipped his survival suit and tried to hold your father against his chest. Tony's below. They called a helicopter for your father."

Elsie heard the words. They hung suspended for a moment. Then she saw Dick, Tony clutching Dick; she felt the waves rocking them, washing over them. She felt Dick getting colder.

She heard herself cry out. She grabbed Sally's sweater, but it slipped through her hands.

When she came to, Charlie had his hand under the side of her head. He said, "Don't move yet."

Sally said, "Elsie, are you all right? Did you hit your head?"

"No," Charlie said. "It came down on my sh-shoe. The top of my shoe."

Like something to be scraped off, a bird dropping.

Captain Teixeira translated, "They're waiting for the helicopter. Okay, he's come to. He's groggy, but they got a good pulse. Tony's okay to stay on board. Okay. After they get Dick on the helicopter, *Bom Sonho*'s going to haul that one line of pots, then come in."

"What?" Sally said. "Why don't they just come in?"

Captain Teixeira turned. He said, "Elsie, what happened? Lift her feet, Charlie. Put your jacket under her head and lift her feet."

Sally said, "Why don't they come in as fast as they can?"

Captain Teixeira, who'd been leaning toward Elsie, sat up straight. "Mrs. Aldrich, I thank God your son is safe. They got him in a bunk all wrapped up. He's doing good. Him and Tran and Tony. They had suits on. They got cold, but they stayed dry. I thank God *Bom Sonho* was close. I thank God she's a fast boat. And the men on her did the right thing. So now I think it's okay we let them earn what they got in those pots."

Charlie said, "Excuse me, Mrs. Aldrich. Can you lift her feet? I've got to call my mother."

"I'm fine," Elsie said. "I'm going to sit up."

Captain Teixeira said, "You help her, Charlie. Hold her shoulders. Is your mother alone? If she's alone, you should go to her. Not a phone call. You see how Elsie keeled over."

Elsie shut her eyes. Jesus, what else? Charlie put his hands under her shoulders and pushed her as she sat up. She leaned forward and grabbed her legs so he wouldn't have to go on touching her. She said, "I'm sorry, Charlie. Sally needed me to come."

He stood up. She heard him shake his jacket. He said, "Mom sent Tom to find Rose. If he finds her, he'll bring her back to the house. So Rose might be there. Is it okay with you if I tell her along with Mom?"

"Yes."

Sally said, "May I at least speak with my son?" Elsie was glad someone else was a problem.

"He's in a bunk, Mrs. Aldrich. The radio's in the wheelhouse. When he's on his feet, and when they're not busy, maybe there's a good time. Right now I can have someone tell him you're glad he's safe. You can say that right now into this microphone."

"Who will I be speaking to?"

"My grandson. He's Ruy Teixeira like me. And he speaks English like me."

Charlie was gone. Elsie was glad that the first words Sally said into the microphone were "thank you."

At least Sally was redeeming herself.

Elsie tried to concentrate on the hopeful news. She thought of Dick's blood warming his body, reaching his brain. She tried to think of what could comfort him for the loss of *Spartina*. She kept being interrupted by Charlie's scorn for her. She could have defended herself against that, she could have been unashamed of her crying out, unashamed of her graceless sprawl—if she didn't feel weakened by the echo of her crying out and sprawling in the tower room.

She got to her knees. She said to Captain Teixeira, "*Spartina* went down?"

"Yes."

"But Dick's going to be all right?"

"Yes. They got him warmed up. You go home. Don't drive yourself. Mrs. Aldrich, you got a car? Maybe you can drive your sister, make her take it easy. Your son's okay. Come back after a while. When *Bom Sonho*'s steaming home, you can talk to your son."

chapter sixty-eight

May called Elsie early the next morning. May said, "They're keeping Dick in bed over at the hospital, but he's all right. I expect Rose told you."

"Yes. But thank you."

"There is one other thing. Your brother-in-law called me. He was perfectly polite and said he was glad everyone's safe. But then he said it's better if we don't talk about it. He said he'd prefer that we get together after Dick gets home. That way—I wrote down what he said—we can make a dignified joint statement."

Elsie said, "That's Jack, all right."

"When I told Dick, he laughed. Then he swore at him. He said Jack Junior's a poor fool, but Jack's something worse. You know Dick gave the boy his survival suit. Dick wasn't going to say anything, but now that Jack's horning in, Dick's in a state. I don't blame him—I just don't think it'll do any good for him to go round talking the way he's doing now. Maybe if he gets to talk more while he's still in the hospital, he'll get talked out. I put you on the list for this noon. I hope you'll go."

"Yes," Elsie said. She pulled her bathrobe tighter around her. "I'm sorry Jack called you. On top of everything. You must have had a terrible day."

"It went by pretty quick. From the time Tom told me until Charlie came, it wasn't but an hour or so. Charlie came in and first thing he said was 'It's good news.' Before then I had Rose and Tom with me. I should have asked you before—you're all right, are you? Charlie said you took a turn."

Elsie's face twisted. When she opened her mouth there was a whoosh of breath.

May said, "What?"

"It was that little room," Elsie said. "The air got thick."

"Charlie said Captain Teixeira didn't let up in the details, so that must've been hard, Dick being fished out, nobody knowing if he was drowned or frozen."

Elsie had no idea what she said. She might not have said anything.

"Anyways," May said, "he's over there now, on the top floor. I'll tell him you're coming. Eddie's going after supper. I had a time putting Phoebe off. I didn't like hurting her feelings, but when she gets hold of a story . . ." May sighed. "You'd think we could just be thankful and have done with it."

"Yes," Elsie said. "I'm sure Phoebe will understand. You can say how you were in a daze."

"I wasn't."

"I just meant—"

"I know what you meant. I'll get it straight with Phoebe. Right now I've got to call Tony. There he was holding Dick on that piece of dory, so I want to thank him. At the same time I got to ask him to stop going round saying Jack Junior's a Jonah."

"I'm not sure what that means," Elsie said. "He was the one who was swallowed by a whale."

"A Jonah's someone who brings bad luck to a ship. That's why they chucked Jonah overboard."

When May hung up, it took Elsie a moment to get her balance. What was odd was that May sounded so sure of herself, and yet she was submitting to Jack's pompous edict. But one thing was clear—May told her to go see Dick.

* * *

It was Rose who saw it first. She said, "Mom, you've got a skunk stripe."

"What are you talking about?" Elsie was still in her bathrobe, poking through her clothes to pick out a dress. She went into the bathroom to look in the mirror. Just to the side of the crown of her head there was a streak of white. She covered it with her hand.

Rose was standing behind her. "It's okay, Mom. It's cool. Really."

Elsie took her hand away. She ran a brush through her hair, thinking the white might be mixed with the dark, that she could pluck the white like the occasional gray. The white was thick and pure all the way to the roots. Had she cut herself? Scraped her head when she fell over? No—her head had landed on Charlie's shoe. Her body did this, as involuntarily as it had sprawled her across the floor in a faint.

"I told you, Mom. It looks good. Stop standing there staring—you'll be late for Dad."

The white streak was involuntary, but she would decide what it marked.

Rose held up a dress. "You look good in this."

All right, then—everyone was urging her to go see Dick.

chapter sixty-nine

I was terrible," JB said.

"I'm getting over it," Mary said. "Can I trust you to make the coffee? I'm up to my wrist in cod. I hope you like codfish cakes. I season them myself, so don't put ketchup on them."

"This is how dumb I was. 'Come live with me and be my love' / And you will be half owner of / Two acres and a bungalow. / A sound investment for your dough. / And by the way, I'll be your beau."

JB came up next to her and stuck the piece of paper in the flame under the frying pan.

She said, "Oh, for God's sake, don't get any of that mess in my food."

"I'm repenting in dust and ashes."

"Fine, as long as it doesn't slow you down making the coffee. And when you've put the coffee on, you could squeeze those oranges over there."

While she'd been lying in bed she'd watched him scribbling at the kitchen table and muttering to himself. She'd woken up in a good mood, drowsily thinking of breakfast, remembering what she had in the fridge, finally settling on codfish cakes mixed with parsley, scallions, and minced green and red peppers. They'd fry up gold, dotted with red and green. She'd woken up with a sense of what breakfast would look like, but she'd also been seeing the colors of the field at sunset. She said, "It's more than two acres. I'd say closer to three."

"You're right. It's two-point-seven. I'll write you a poem with two-point-seven."

"Never mind your poems." She flipped a codfish cake. She was enjoying bossing him around, and he seemed to understand it was breezy enough to be a good sign. "I'd like to have another look at the place. Just walk around at midday by myself. I'm not promising anything. But let's say I think it's a good proposition . . ." She flipped another. "If Jack Aldrich finds out I'm buying land he wants, he might just get mad enough to fire me. I don't know enough about hiding things in corporations and holding companies and the like." She flipped the third and fourth. "And since that sort of talk might send you off the deep end, I think I should meet your brother. I don't mind being a fool about sharing a bed with you, but when it comes to money, I'd rather talk to your brother. Mind you, it's all still *if.* Of course, since he's your brother, I'd have to find a lawyer of my own for the final deal. That enough romance for you? Have I swept you off your feet?" JB laughed.

He didn't say a word while they ate. She finally said, "You're showing off. You're showing off being silent."

"When I'm happy I talk a lot. When I'm really, really happy I don't talk as much."

"I didn't say yes, I said maybe."

"I know. I'm just enjoying the way your mind works. And I'm thinking how my brother will approve. He won't say anything, but he'll breathe a sigh of relief."

"I hope you're not thinking I'm going to take over from him. A little incapacity in a man can be charming. Like not being able to tie a bow tie. Complete helplessness is another matter altogether."

JB said, "What I meant was—" but then the phone rang.

It was Rose. She started so fast that Mary only heard a few words—*Spartina,* Dad, hospital. Mary said, "Rose, Rose, wait. Is he all right?"

"Yes. He's in the hospital, but they're just making sure. Here's the thing. The reason he didn't have his survival suit on is that he gave it to Jack Junior. You'd think Uncle Jack would be falling all over himself with gratitude, but he's being a shithead. Now he's saying it was Dad's job to have survival suits on board. Mom's furious at him. Aunt Sally is mad at Uncle Jack *and* Mom. Anyway, don't be surprised when you get to Sawtooth and run into Uncle Jack. I just thought I'd warn you. Oh, May's put you on the list so you can go see Dad."

"How are *you*, Rose?"

"I'm okay. I mean, there was a little while when Tom got me and we didn't know. He kept telling me it was probably okay, but he didn't know. Oh—Mom was listening to

Captain Teixeira's radio just when they pulled Dad out and she fainted. Now she's got a white streak in her hair. She's embarrassed about it, so when you see her be sure to tell her it looks good."

Mary said, "Oh, Rose . . ."

Rose said, "Look—I've got to go. I'm at May's house, and they're all just coming in the driveway."

After Mary hung up, she sat down at the kitchen table and began to cry. She was taken by surprise—on one side relief that Dick was all right, on another distress for Dick's losing *Spartina*. But what undid her was Rose—whether Rose was being bad or blurting out a kindness for Elsie, Mary ached for her.

After she wiped her eyes, she patted JB's hand. She was glad enough he was there, but she didn't feel at all like explaining everything to someone new in town—fresh off the boat, as her father used to say.

"So that was Rose," he said. "Is everyone all right?"

At least he knew Rose, and, come to think of it, he knew Elsie. He knew a thing or two about Jack Aldrich. And mightn't he have heard South County stories as he lay in bed with his old flame Tory Hazard? That thought put her in a drier mood. She said, "Yes. Rose's father's boat sank, but everyone's safe. Captain Teixeira had one of his boats close by, thank God." She turned and said, "You've heard of Captain Teixeira?"

"Yes. He and Tory's father were friends. Tory thought it was a model friendship. Captain Teixeira must be ancient by now."

"He is. I don't know what keeps him going. I guess being the patriarch. I'd always hoped Dick would end up like Captain Teixeira—he could keep on being crusty but in the middle of family who know when to let him be in charge and when to let him *think* he's in charge. Now that Dick's on the beach, he'll get fierce all over again. He'll get restless and hard and foolish just when he should be getting older and wiser. He'll be sixty soon enough, and he'll tear himself apart trying to be young again. He was a terror when he was building *Spartina;* he'd get up to anything. And even after, he took her out in a hurricane when he had a wife and two sons and Elsie pregnant with Rose. What is it with men and this big rush to be a hero? And he went and did it again—giving his survival suit to that little twerp Jack Junior. Oh, I know it's honorable and noble and God knows what else, but I'm as certain as I'm standing here that Dick felt that flash inside him that said, 'Here it is—a moment of manly glory.' And that's it, it's a flash. And there's Elsie taking care of Rose for years. And Miss Perry as well. And here Dick is, the hero of the hurricane and now the hero of the shipwreck. A day then, a day now, and all the men cheer. Christ, I don't know why we put up with you."

JB had tilted his head agreeably when she'd got to Elsie and Rose and Miss Perry, but at her last outcry his eyebrows shot up.

"I shouldn't have gone off like that," she said. "The man's in the hospital."

"But he's all right?"

"Yes. But that boat was everything. Going to sea in your own boat—if you're not rich enough to buy land, that's the last place you can go be on your own, and to hell with what they're doing onshore." She sighed. "So I love him for his free spirit *and* I think he's a selfish old bastard. It just occurs to me. I may have got it wrong when I said he gave up his survival suit in a flash. It may have been part manly code: this is what you do if you're captain. But I wonder if it didn't cross his mind that he was teaching a lesson to Jack Aldrich—this is how a man does things, you desk-hugging landlubber in your yacht-club blazer. I wonder if Jack didn't get a whiff of that, and that's why he . . . I'll tell you what. Call up your pal Tory and tell her we're buying. If Jack fires me, I'll start a restaurant right on his front doorstep."

"I was thinking of a used-book store."

"Fine. Both. But I'm in a mood to stick someone in the eye, and it might as well be his nibs."

chapter seventy

D ick said, "May said she was sending you over. You here to take care of me like you did Miss Perry? Last night they were fussing like I'm on my last legs, so don't you join in. Either make me laugh or get me out of here."

Elsie stood still. She'd been imaging something sweeter, but this was better. She said, "You're awfully bossy this morning. You have any other complaints?"

"The food's no good."

"You haven't even been here a whole day."

"All I got last night was some kind of broth, and breakfast was instant oatmeal. What'd you do to your hair?"

"I'll tell you when you're not being rude about it." She walked to the edge of the bed. She thought, This doesn't count. She bent over and kissed his mouth. She touched his cheek and kissed him again. She turned around and pulled up a folding chair and sat down. She was going to hold his hand, but it was bandaged so thickly it was as big as a boxing glove.

He said, "Jesus, Elsie. I said 'make me laugh.'" He closed his eyes. After a bit he said, "Could you crank the bed up?"

She raised the bed and plumped his pillow. She put her hand on his cheek again, looked at his face, felt the air between their faces. All this was more deliberate than a kiss.

She sat down again, and after a while she said, "I'm sorry about *Spartina*."

"I'll tell you—it's not tearing me up like I thought it would. It's hard to say how come. It's like I've been inside myself, and inside there was this big dark space. It wasn't something to be afraid of, not like being stuck underwater. I don't mean that thing they say, that you see your whole life. It wasn't like a newsreel. All I can say is I feel like I got taken apart and put back together."

She wasn't sure what that meant, but it made a space in her.

He said, "Not that that takes care of any real problems. The insurance company's going to take their own sweet time. Say they need to 'investigate the cause of the accident.' I don't know how they figure to do that. The Coast Guard helicopter spotted a lifeboat floating just under the surface not so far from where *Spartina* went down. The pilot got a look when the lifeboat rolled up on a wave. He guessed maybe eighteen or twenty feet. Spotty red paint over what looked like metal. We sure as hell ran into something, and a derelict steel lifeboat fits the bill. The Coast Guard sent a cutter to recover her, but she must have sunk before the cutter got there. *Spartina* likely banged the last bit of buoyancy out of her. It was likely her bow punched into us. Likely. Likely is all anyone's going to know." Dick folded his arms, curled over them. "Tony says the hole was big as a door. Below the waterline. Water coming in knocked Tran off his feet. Tony came up and took the wheelhouse door off its hinges, see if that'd work. I went below. I couldn't see the hole, just the surge pushing Tran around. No way we were going to . . ." Dick sat up and waved his bandaged hand. "So I told them to get the hell out of there."

Elsie said, "Dick, I'm . . ." She held her jaw but cried anyway.

"Yeah. I know. But come on, Elsie. We're all in one piece."

"Yes." Dick reached across with his good hand and touched her arm. She took a breath and said, "What happened to your hand?"

"That's another thing got a hole in it. Only reason I'm still in here is a specialist has to take a look, see if there's nerve damage. We were banging around some getting into what was left of the dory, hit my hand on the sharp end of a busted strake. Jack Junior—you got to feel sorry for a kid gets called Jack Junior. The reason the dory busted up was Jack Junior launched her on the weather side. We'd lost steerage way by then, so I couldn't swing *Spartina* around. You know how high a dory rides before she's loaded, bobs around like a cork. She would've held the four of us and settled down. But empty as she was, she bounced up against the rail and cracked her gunwale and another couple of strakes. Tony and Tran were below, seeing if they could get a pump working. I was in the wheelhouse, on the radio. I saw Junior; I was banging the window and yelling, but he couldn't hear me. The poor bastard had been seasick the second and third day out, but he was strong enough to get the dory over the side. We were wallowing, and I guess he just shoved her whichever way was downhill at the time. We were sinking by the bow, so that made it easier, too."

"Why did you decide to give him your survival suit?"

Dick tilted his head back against the pillow. "I didn't decide."

"What do you mean?"

"I just did it."

"You didn't think about, I don't know, your family? And Rose?"

"No."

"'No'? Just 'no'?"

"You mean right then and there? *Spartina* going down, the dory on the wrong side, making sure Tony and Tran come up from below, wondering how far away *Bom Sonho* is. Not exactly a moment for wistfulness."

She'd pushed and he'd pushed back, not angry, just hard and neat. She knew him, oh, God, she knew him—she'd kept on knowing him, she knew him when she watched him splicing a cable by the dock, weaving the wires and pulling them taut. She'd seen him; he hadn't seen her. He had no idea.

He was talking again. She heard him say, ". . . zipped him up and got him the hell out of the way."

She rocked forward. She hugged herself, her fingers digging into her arms. She said, "You dumb bastard, you almost killed yourself. You're the love of my life, and you damn near died."

chapter seventy-one

When Mary came in with a basket of food slung on one arm, Dick said, "You look like Little Red Riding Hood on her way to her grandmother's house."

"There's a codfish cake that's still warm and a beer that's still cold, so no more wisecracks."

She'd started to unwrap the tinfoil when she heard Jack's voice winding down the hall from the nurses' station. It was Jack's hearty tone. "Quite right. I'm not on the list, but I am on the board. Would you be good enough to call the administrator's office? I'm Jack Aldrich. No need for him to come up. I'll see him on my way out."

A minute later Jack swung into view. "So there you are, Captain Pierce. Glad to see you safe and sound. Awfully sorry about your boat." He turned to Mary. "Glad to see you're cheering our patient up with a bit of Sawtooth cooking." Mary opened her mouth, but Jack sailed on. "Just stopped by to make sure we're taking good care of you."

"No complaints."

"Glad to hear it. I won't stay a minute, just to mention that if you have any trouble with the insurance company, let me know. The director's a Sawtooth member. Cut through any red tape." Jack patted his suit coat pockets. "Good. Oh. There is one other small thing. That deckhand of yours, the one who's related to Captain Teixeira. Word got back to me that he's telling an unpleasant story about Jack Junior. At the moment Jack Junior's in Boston with his mother, so I haven't heard his account, but in a situation like this the less said the better. I wonder if you—as his captain—could tell him to pipe down. He's not doing anybody any good."

"Not much I can do," Dick said. "Right now I'm not captain of anything. What Tony does is his concern."

"Let me suggest that it may be your concern. One thing I gathered is that the life raft was broken and that there weren't enough life jackets to go around."

"Survival suits."

"Yes. Life jackets, survival suits, that sort of thing."

"There's a difference."

"I'm sure there is—"

"A survival suit is personal gear. Tony and Tran bring their own, same as they bring boots and foul-weather gear."

"I see. Your regular crew. You may be beyond reproach as regards your regular crew members, but it could well be that the owner's duty is more onerous as regards an invitee."

"Jack Junior came on board to work. I wasn't running a cruise ship."

"Not a cruise ship, of course, not a cruise ship. I was making a finer distinction." Jack held his hands up. "But forgive me. This isn't the time for . . . that sort of thing. Occupational hazard of mine. A subspecialty of mine used to be admiralty law. Much better to keep this a matter of fellow feeling. I put myself in your shoes, and I imagine the shock. Is this really happening? Is she really sinking?" Jack looked down and wagged his head. Mary almost laughed. Jack lifted his head and said, "A trying moment for a young man who's suddenly caught in a maelstrom of people rushing to take measures, some of which were to ensure their own safety. Perhaps it's the first time the boy has ever heard the words 'survival suit.' I'm asking you to imagine how he felt at that moment."

"No need to imagine," Dick said. "He felt underdressed for the occasion."

Mary laughed, bit her lip to keep from laughing again. Jack glared at her. He said to Dick, "I didn't know you could be so amusing." He smoothed his suit coat and said, "I wish you a speedy recovery." He left.

Mary said, "I shouldn't have laughed. I'm afraid that pissed him off even more. Maybe he'll get over it when he finds out. But why didn't you tell him?"

"Not my place to. And this way he'll run into his own hot air. His kid screwed up, but I feel a little sorry for the kid. I might even ask Tony to lay off. But I don't mind that I pissed off Jack Aldrich. He set my teeth on edge from the beginning—the way he talked to the nurse out there."

"There's that," Mary said. "And all the while he was talking you to death he gave no thought that your beer's getting warm and your codfish cake cold."

chapter seventy-two

When May got home from grocery shopping there was a minivan in the driveway and two men in her backyard. They were measuring the distance from the septic tank to the well. Then they measured from the septic tank to the creek. She said hello and asked them what they were doing. One of them started to answer, but the other stepped in and said, "You'd be better off asking over at the township office. I wouldn't want to misspeak."

May put the groceries away, came back outside. The man who didn't want to misspeak said, "That's a big garden. You use manure? Cow? Sheep? Pig? Chicken? Anything like that?"

She pointed to her compost pile. "It's vegetables and leaves," she said. "I don't use anything else." If he didn't want to misspeak, he shouldn't go trying to blame something on her garden. She said, "I'm May Pierce. I'm married to Dick Pierce. And that there"—she pointed—"is Pierce Creek. I take quahogs out downstream. Flounder, too. If you're looking to find some runoff, you're looking in the wrong place." She took a breath. "You going to inspect those Sawtooth Point cottages? Those yachts moored in Sawtooth Pond? You think they all pump their waste at the boatyard the way they're supposed to?"

The man tilted his head, not a yes or a no. As he left he said, "Sorry for any inconvenience," but that didn't mean anything, either.

She went flat. Then she was embarrassed at how she'd bristled and got on her high horse. But what were they after? She called Phoebe.

Phoebe was reassuring. "When we repaired your house—that was, what, fifteen years ago?—we got a building permit and a new certificate of occupancy. But I'm going to the township office anyway; I have to get some permits. I'll chat somebody up about your place."

Phoebe called back after lunch. "It's just Jack. Apparently he wanted to make sure he could say to prospective buyers how clean the water is. And he owns Mary Scanlon's old restaurant, and that's up that other creek that comes into Sawtooth Pond, so he came in and waved his hand over the map in a vague way that included you. They pretty much snap to when Jack wants something. So that's what that was all about."

May went back out to the garden. Dick hadn't said when he'd be back, just that he was looking around for another boat here and there, maybe Wickford, maybe as far as New Bedford. May pulled weeds and buried them in the compost pile. The wind had backed to the southeast, likely to blow in a fog, good for the garden. It also carried the usually unheard

sounds from Sawtooth—a blurred voice—someone shout-
ing at the tennis court? The distinct sound of a car door, the
whine of an outboard motor. All those people who could go
anywhere. Jack, who could wave his hand across a map.

chapter seventy-three

The first news of trouble Mary had was from Rose.
Mary hadn't made peace with Elsie yet, but Rose still
came to Mary's apartment to get some more help with
her songs. The second time Rose came, she said, "I'm not sure
I want to sing at Sawtooth."

"Why on earth not?"

"Uncle Jack is doing something, and Mom is furious. She
tried to explain it to me, but I don't get it. Uncle Jack wants
to buy Dad and May's house. I thought Dad and May should
just say no, but Mom says there's a way he can make them.
It's some tricky legal thing. Anyway, she wants me to quit the
show. She said that when you find out what Uncle Jack is up
to, you won't want to work for him, either."

"Ah, well. That's always a question. But you—I'd hate to
see you miss this chance—you'll learn a lot singing with
trained singers. JB says that rehearsals are going well and
that they're crazy about you. You're not nervous about it, are
you?"

"No. I mean, I was, but it's fine now."

"Your mother gets furious at Jack all the time. Why don't
we wait a bit and see what Dick and May have to say? This
could just be Jack's hot air."

That afternoon Jack showed up in the Sawtooth kitchen,
all smiles.

"Mary, Mary, Mary—it always cheers me up to get a whiff of whatever you're cooking. Could you come up to my office for a minute? I'd like to discuss what we're going to serve the dinner-theater crowd. Do we have enough waitresses? Oh, and things in general. Take your time. I'll be up there the rest of the afternoon."

When she went in he was pacing back and forth in front of the seaside window. He gestured toward a chair for her but kept on pacing, his hands clasped behind his back, his chin to his chest. He said, "All those years ago, when I bought your restaurant, I gave you a fair price."

"More than fair."

"And I'm paying you a fair wage."

"Yes."

"And you absolutely deserve it. You're one of the pillars of Sawtooth. And I hope that over the years we've had a friendly relationship."

"You've stepped on my toes now and then, but we get along."

"Well, good, because I'd like some help. I know you and Elsie are close, and you and Rose." He stopped pacing and faced her. "Elsie has just told me Rose isn't going to sing in our show."

"Elsie told you," Mary said. "But what has Rose said?"

"Elsie wouldn't let me talk to her. I tried to explain to Elsie that I'm doing this in large part for Rose's benefit."

"You may have suggested Rose, but the director auditioned her."

"Of course, of course. Rose is splendid. I didn't mean to imply anything to the contrary. And I certainly don't want you to get touchy. Everyone's become so damned touchy, I can't say a word without someone taking it wrong. If people could just keep from mixing up things . . . The show is one thing." Jack chopped at the side of his desktop with his left hand. "And the rest of it is another thing." He chopped the other side.

"And just what is the rest of it?"

"I'm surprised Elsie hasn't told you. She's boiling over in public. We've quarreled about one thing or another over the years—she even tried to keep me from buying Sawtooth, some nonsense about natural habitat. She never did understand the facts of life."

"I think Elsie knows the facts of life."

"All Elsie knows is flora and fauna. Back then Sawtooth was bound to be sold, and in any hands but mine it would have become an eyesore. I've preserved its natural beauty, and I've made a limited number of members happy. Elsie forgets that they need a natural habitat, too. But that's not the issue now. Now she's saying that I'm after the Pierce property in some vindictive way. There is nothing personal involved. I'll admit I spoke a little prematurely about those damned survival suits, but I was acting out of a father's reflex. All that talk hit a nerve, and I jumped. I'm happy to let Captain Teixeira have the last word about survival suits. I'd be happy to shake Dick Pierce's hand. No ill will, despite his clever remarks. But that's not the issue, either. Not relevant. I've had my eye on that land for years, part of a master plan. It would be a godsend for the Pierces if everyone would just calm down. I could help Dick Pierce out of financial difficulties on a businesslike basis. Dick could buy another boat, buy a nice little house. There's a fixer-upper in Snug Harbor I happen to own that I'd sell him below market. If Elsie would keep her nose out of it, the Pierces would see reason, but Elsie is acting as if she's some sort of authority on what happens around here. Authority is something you earn. You earn it by taking positive steps that build something of value, something that benefits the community. You don't become an authority by being a maverick complainer. The fact is that Sawtooth is an economic engine; it's a public benefit, and that fact is recognized by the people who actually run things, people with whom I have a long-standing relationship. The Sawtooth master plan is bound to go forward no matter how much noise people make. What it boils down to is 'The dogs bark, but the caravan passes.'"

Mary said, "Well, then, I don't see how you need any help from me at all." Over the years she'd seen Jack as laughably pompous, bumptious, and occasionally offensive but occasionally robust and even attractive in his billows of enthusiasm for everyone—everyone at Sawtooth—to have a splendid time. Now she saw him becoming denser and heavier.

But then, as if guided by some counselor lodged inside him, he beamed at her pleasantly. "You're quite right. All that's a matter for another day. The more immediate issue—and for this I do need your help—is Rose. I don't believe I told you how grateful I am for all you've done for Rose. What would Rose and Elsie have done without you? I've done a thing or two myself, behind the scenes, as it were, but I think now is a good time for you and me to put our heads together. Next year Rose will be thinking about college. In my day a solid B average at a good school and a note from the headmaster and you were in. I'm not saying that was fair. I'm sure a lot of perfectly good people got left out. But then it got to be testing, testing, testing, and the good colleges got filled with a lot of overachieving test takers. Everyone got bored. What the admissions people are looking for now is an application that says, 'I've been to the moon.' I've raised money for Brown, I've given money to Brown, and I couldn't get my own son in. I could write a letter for Rose and it wouldn't weigh more than a feather. Well, perhaps a little more. But this show is Rose's trip to the moon. Among other things, I have good reason to believe that it'll be reviewed not just by the *Providence Journal* but the *Boston Globe,* the *Hartford Courant,* and possibly some sort of notice in the *New York Times.* I've had some press kits printed up, and we've sent them out everywhere, from Boston to New York."

"I understand," Mary said. "I'd love to see Rose in the part, but—"

"She'd be cutting off her nose to spite her face."

"But your master plan is—"

"Apples and oranges."

"You can say 'apples and oranges,' but you're asking Rose to go against her own family."

"If Elsie would stop yelling at me, I could say to her what I've said to you. I'm Rose's uncle; I'm doing this for our family."

"I was thinking of Dick and May."

Jack leaned back in his chair, waved a hand, and let it fall in a way that made Mary wonder if he filed Rose and Dick in his mind as separately as apples and oranges. "There is no particular reason you should know this," she said. "But as much as Rose grew up in Elsie's house, she grew up in Dick and May's house, too. I brought Rose over there when she was just learning to crawl. She's close to May and Dick, and her two brothers."

"I'm glad to hear that, glad to hear they're all being so modern. And I must say for a girl born with what used to be something of a stigma, our Rose seems to be everyone's darling. I think that says something about the community we have here."

Mary twisted against the arms of her chair. She thought she'd made a straight statement, but Jack was impenetrable in his—what? Oblivion? In his sense that his approval or disapproval was what everyone needed to go on living?

Jack said, "And I'm trying to do what's best for the community in general. Highest and best use of the Pierce property, and for that matter the old Hazard property. I'm not insensible to the needs of the Pierce family. I'll see they're made right. Among other things, I'm bringing Tom Pierce along in an enterprise of ours. That's on the one hand. On the other hand, there's Rose. I made sure she got a scholarship at the Perryville School. I've done one or two things for Elsie's financial security, and now I'm trying to chart the best course for Rose."

"The Hazard property?" Mary said. "You mean that old barn where Mr. Hazard stored his books?"

"A bit more to it than that. That's in the offing. I'm keeping in touch with the daughter. As it is now, it's landlocked, but as part of Sawtooth it'll have access to Sawtooth Pond and our bit of beach. And presto—it's vastly more valuable. The same thing applies to the Pierce property. That's on a creek, but it hardly counts as waterfront—you can't take anything bigger than a skiff up it. The new Sawtooth members will be able to moor their sailboats here. We have a ketch in here now, forty-two feet length overall, seven-foot draft." He swiveled his chair to look over Sawtooth Pond.

Mary was glad he'd appended his boat footnote. It gave her time to recover from the news that Jack considered himself still in the hunt for the old Hazard place. It also let her begin to consider her own wishes without Jack's exhalations fogging up the room.

She said, "It's time I got back to the kitchen. I'll be having another talk with Rose in any case, and I'll tell her about your college notions, but I won't be your agent. I've already told her what I think."

"And what do you think?"

"I love her singing."

"And I hope you have some feeling of obligation to Sawtooth."

Mary kept herself from saying, "That's apples and oranges." She said, "As soon as we get this evening's meal on the table, I'll be thinking of ways to make things come out right."

Halfway down the stairs she thought, Dear God, at the very end there I might as well have bobbed and curtsied. It was that sliver of shame that pricked her into examining her conscience. She hadn't lied, but she'd prevaricated. "That old barn . . ." Odd—she'd started out no more than going along with JB, but now she'd become the hungrier one. And what difference was there between Jack's land hunger and her own? She could say to herself that she wasn't in it for money, but the priest lecturing her old confirmation class on the seven deadly sins would have made short work of that.

Avarice wasn't just about money. It was desire for the things of the world.

When she reached the swinging door from the dining room to the kitchen, she looked through the porthole and stepped out of the way of a waitress with a tray of napkins and silverware. And what if she went to Jack and said she'd give up her contract to buy the Hazard place if he'd let Dick and May stay where they were? She hadn't examined her conscience this relentlessly for ages, but the sisters and priests had taught her well enough how to do it as painfully as possible. Now she pictured Rose in front of her asking her to save May and Dick's house.

chapter seventy-four

After Phoebe found out that the township was considering—or possibly already planning—to take May and Dick's house and three acres by eminent domain, May and Dick went to see Phoebe and Eddie's lawyer.

Dick asked right off what it would cost.

"Hard to tell," the lawyer said. "It's an interesting case. That's not good news for a client. Now, if you were suing for damages, I could work on a contingency-fee basis. But you'll be defending against a taking. If you win, you'll end up with what you started with."

"And your bill," Dick said.

"Yes."

"Can't we sue Jack Aldrich? He's the one behind all this. He's the one aiming to end up with our land."

"He hasn't done anything. I mean, nothing actionable."

"He's pushing the township."

"I know. It's not right. But this is a troubling area of the law. Here's what's happened to the law concerning eminent domain—"

"This going to take a while?" Dick said. May put a hand on his arm.

"This is a preliminary consultation. No fee. Then we'll see what you want to do. Okay, then—eminent domain used to be for things like public roads or parks. In 1954 the Supreme Court said that a project 'need not actually be open to the public to constitute public use.'"

"Sounds like mumbo jumbo to me."

"Yes. On its face it does sound self-contradictory. Anyway, that opened the door to what they said last year—eminent domain can be used so long as the project is 'rationally related to a conceivable public purpose.' It looks as though that means simply increasing a township's tax base."

"So any son of a bitch rich enough to build something fancier than what's there can just grab it? That's the god-damnedest thing I ever heard of."

"I know, I know. I can see how you'd like to punch Jack Aldrich in the nose. If I thought that was the only satisfaction you could get, hell, I'd hold your coat."

Dick gave a grunt. May turned and saw the side of his mouth twitch, as close to a laugh as she'd seen anyone get out of him since he lost *Spartina*.

The lawyer said, "I understand Jack Aldrich made you an offer—"

"I told him our place isn't for sale."

"If it looks to him as if this eminent-domain taking is going to drag on, he's likely to get impatient. You ever hear that old song 'I want what I want when I want it'? He's that kind of guy. If you make it look like you're going to fight—"

"He knows we can't afford it."

"I'm saying if it *looks* like a fight. As it happens I've asked around, tried to find some help. Unfortunately the groups that are fighting this sort of thing are stretched thin. But Jack

Aldrich doesn't have to know that. If we can make enough of a show, he's likely to make you a better offer. You could end up with an equivalent house and something more toward a new boat."

May was glad this lawyer was talking to Dick in a way that seemed to settle him down. Easier on her if Dick was mulling things over instead of stomping around. This lawyer said "new boat" and got Dick looking out to sea. She said, "Mr. Aldrich said something about a little house in Snug Harbor. It doesn't have but a scrap of a yard, let alone a place for a garden."

"Okay. Phoebe told me about your garden. I can see you'd miss that. What else would you miss?"

May squeezed her hands together and looked away from the men. The lawyer said, "Just give me some idea. It'll help me if I have some sense of the place."

"It's where everything is. It's where Charlie came to get better after he got hurt. It's where I cook. I'm pretty much either in the kitchen or in the garden. It's where someone like Phoebe comes to visit. It's where Mary Scanlon used to bring Rose when she was little. It's where Rose and Tom came to visit Charlie. And we were all there together when Charlie came to tell us *Bom Sonho* picked up Dick and his crew." She stopped when Dick shifted in his chair and scraped his feet back. She said, "It's where Dick keeps his logbooks and his accounts. And there's his gear, some of his bait barrels and pots and harpoons. So it's a workplace, too. I expect that has more to do with what you're asking."

"No, it's good. It helps to have the family story. Jack Aldrich tells a story about public benefit. We've got a story about a family place. Where your son came home after his accident, where your family gathered to wait for news of a ship lost at sea. It has some weight. Jack Aldrich has to have some concern about how this'll play out in the court of public opinion." He got up. "Let me know if you'd like me to represent you. I can't promise to rectify the situation, but I think I can improve where you come out."

Dick didn't say anything on the ride home. When they got there Dick didn't get out, just stared straight ahead with his hands on the wheel.

May said, "What did you make of that?" Dick bobbed his head a couple of times but didn't answer. May said, "I'm not so sure I like that it's all going to be a story. I thought I was just talking to him. He said 'court of public opinion.' That makes it sound like he's going to put us on a float in the Fourth of July parade."

Dick said, "I was there. I was thinking what it would all cost, where the money would come from. And I heard your story. Charlie, Tom, Rose. Kitchen, garden. Charlie, Tom, Rose. And, oh, yeah—it's where Dick keeps his gear."

May closed her eyes, couldn't think straight. That wasn't what she'd said, was it? She certainly hadn't said it like that.

"You can get out here—I've got to get going," Dick said. "A guy saw Rose out in that boat I built for her. He wants one just like it, willing to pay pretty good money. I've still got the plans over at Eddie's. Might as well be doing something to earn a dollar."

May said, "Will Rose mind?" The words just popped out.

"I talked to Rose. I guess you think I don't talk to Rose. She said it's okay as long as I paint her a different color. I got to get going."

chapter seventy-five

Phoebe started talking before she was through the front door. "I'm getting the old heave-ho, too, so I can totally relate. Of course, I knew the school was going to get my house sooner or later, but still . . . . Anyway, now I'm going to roll up my sleeves for you. I don't care if Jack Aldrich never speaks to me again. Oh, I know I dreamed of buying a Sawtooth cottage, but there we are—some things matter more than others."

May said, "Let's go into the kitchen. I've got to keep an eye on a pot that's boiling."

Phoebe followed her, sat down at the kitchen table, and pulled out a notepad. "I've made a list of people who'll be on your side, and we'll get a committee together and then we'll plan a bigger meeting. I thought it might be a little awkward for you, so I've already talked to Elsie. She told me that Rose is going to drop out of her show, so that's a start."

"I don't want that," May said. "I want Rose to sing."

"Oh, May. I really think . . . I mean, we need every bit of pressure we can think of."

"Not that."

"Honestly, May, I'm as big a fan of Rose as anybody, but—"

"No."

Phoebe frowned and shifted her notepad on the table. "Well, we can revisit that. I've talked to Mary Scanlon—"

"I'm sure she'll want Rose to sing."

"This was on another subject. Mary wouldn't say exactly, but she has something in mind. Maybe it's about Mr. Bienvenue—he *is* her nephew-in-law, and he is running for Congress. But the main thing is to get out and beat the drums. I know that's not your cup of tea, so I'll do as much of it as I can, but you've got to get in a fiercer mood."

"I don't know what good a mood's going to do. Dick and I talked to your lawyer, and he as much as said the whole thing'd cost more than we'll ever have."

"That's if it goes on and on. If you just show you're ready to fight . . . Eddie and I can lend you enough for the first round."

"That's generous of you, but I can't borrow money I don't see a way of repaying."

"Well, then, we could start a defense fund, get some donations."

"I can't see going begging, either."

"Really, May—there are perfectly good people out there who just don't want to see something unfair. If you let your scruples tie you in a knot, you won't have a chance against Jack Aldrich. He's already out there claiming he's a public benefactor. We have to be proactive; we have to get our story out there, too."

Phoebe was being as emphatic as ever, but she'd slowed down. May got up and stirred the pot of rose hips and apple slices. She fitted her jelly bag in a sieve over another pot and poured the fruit in. For a moment she listened to the juice trickling through. She said, "What kind of a story do you have in mind?"

"This is your house. This is where you raised your two boys. Not to mention Rose."

"That's the part I don't want getting out all over."

"What part?"

"Rose."

"But as far as you and Rose go, it's all to your credit."

"Credit or not, I don't want people saying things about Rose. Not unless it's about how she sings."

Phoebe sighed. "I guess we can work around that. At any rate let's have a little gathering, just a few people you know well. Of course, I'd like to invite Piero, too. He's still a shareholder in Sawtooth—a minority shareholder, but he's someone to be reckoned with. He's a great admirer of yours, he knows you and I are friends, and he and I are very simpatico these days."

"I thought that statue of yours was all done."

"It is, but he's teaching me Italian. I've always wanted to pick up a little Italian." Phoebe knitted her brow. She said, "I think I may have made a mistake." May was afraid she was about to learn more than she wanted. Phoebe said, "Piero and I are plural, so I should have said *simpatici*." Phoebe laughed. "Oh, May. You looked stricken. I hope you're not . . . He's a dear, dear man, and that's really all there is to say. Of course, his daughters are grown up and his wife spends most of her time in a convent up in Worcester—Piero has been very generous to it—so he's rattling around by himself in that big house. Oh, he has his garden and his business interests—he's still very vital. But the essential point is that he can help us, and I'm in a position to ask him."

May lifted the sieve off the pot. The juice looked about right for a half-dozen jars. She turned the burner on. Warm as the juice was, it wouldn't take long to come to a boil. She looked at Phoebe, who seemed to have plumped up. May didn't want any more of Phoebe's darting this way and that. She didn't want to be curious, let alone suspicious. What was Phoebe up to, telling her these things—"he's rattling around in that big house," wife and daughters gone?

Did Phoebe want her to get wide-eyed at how she made men go weak at the knees? Did Phoebe want her to admire what a friend she was to go up there and trade on her charm? May said, "If Mr. Salviatti wants to talk to Mr. Aldrich, seeing as how they're partners, I guess that'd be all right. But just as a matter of what's fair and what's not. I'd as soon you didn't talk about anything private."

Phoebe wrinkled her forehead. "Oh, for heaven's sakes, May. It's not as if Piero isn't involved—Jack has already called him to have a talk about all this. Maps and financing and who'll make a fuss and what Jack means to do about it. We're just lucky that I happen to be on such good terms with Piero." Phoebe took a breath. "And I may as well come right out and say that of course Piero and I talked about Rose. One of the reasons he admires you so much is that I told him how good you've been with Rose."

The juice came to a boil. May set the timer and wiped her hands on her apron. May found herself nodding, not because she agreed but because she should have figured that Phoebe couldn't help herself.

"How good you *are*," Phoebe said. "And I never would've dreamed . . . I mean, think of all the people who know you and . . . For example, I'm sure Mary Scanlon talks about Rose to her new boyfriend."

"Mary Scanlon has a right to."

Phoebe put her palm to her cheek as though she'd been slapped. She sat up very straight and said, "Oh dear."

That was Phoebe, too—she might run on and on or she might just give a little peep. To put a patch on Phoebe's hurt feelings, May said, "Mary's as close to Rose as I am." She felt herself going blank. She wasn't tired, she'd just had enough of going round and round. She said, "What's done is done." Her voice sounded far off. "I know you mean to help."

"Of course I do. And I understand how much stress . . . I mean, it's been one thing after another—Charlie's accident, Dick's boat, and now your house. I'm not surprised you're on edge."

There Phoebe went again. But this time Phoebe wasn't really present to May. What Phoebe said was sharp for a half second, then blurred, then gone—like the trail left by a fish swimming through phosphorescent plankton.

May said, "I guess it'll be all right so long as the next time you see Mr. Salviatti you make sure to tell him what I told you. I don't want Rose talked about, not in the argument about this house."

Phoebe floated to her feet. "Yes, of course. I'm on my way there now. And don't worry, Piero is very understanding. I'd trust him with any of my problems."

Phoebe went to the downstairs bathroom and came back with her hair brushed to a shine. After she went out the door there was a trace of perfume. May closed her eyes and saw her things—no, more like ghosts of her things—the canning jars, the kitchen table, the cedar chest, Rose's skiff. There they went trailing in Phoebe's wake, up the hill and drifting through the bars of Mr. Salviatti's gate, then disappearing into the swing of Phoebe's skirt as she climbed the front steps.

The timer buzzed. May turned off the burner. At first she

thought her little daydream was about whatever tomfoolery
Phoebe got up to. But then she felt peaceful, as if whatever
was to happen with people wanting this or that didn't matter all that much, as if she'd been waiting for something to
shake her loose from her fretting and her disapproving. She'd
been right and she'd been wrong, and either way was just
more trouble for somebody. It'd be nice if she could figure
out just how she got to this quiet. Now she was content to sit
and wait for the juice to cool off enough to pour into the jars.
She might tighten up again, but for now she was unfolding,
easy as that.

chapter seventy-six

Yes, I'd like to," Elsie said, "but look, there's a sort of
crisis going on and I'm pretty much . . . I'll give you a
call when things settle down."

She'd never heard Walt's voice on the phone. He sounded
like his father.

"Yeah. I heard Phoebe talking to Dad. So you're into all
that, too. Wait. Dumb of me. I guess you're right in the middle. I'm used to thinking of you off in the woods on your
own."

"In the woods—don't I wish. But right now I really do
have to get going."

When she hung up she kept on pressing the phone down
as though that would seal him off. The afternoon in the tower
room could have been years ago, should have been years ago,
shouldn't be a piece of the puzzle in her mind. She'd been trying to think about who could have some influence on Jack.
Sally was still away with Jack Junior. Johnny Bienvenue had

returned her phone call. He'd said, "It sounds ugly, but I can't jump in without some homework. I'll send someone down to the township office to see what they say. At least that'll let them know I'm taking an interest." A dime when she'd asked for a dollar. Johnny might not have sold his soul to Jack, but he might worry about crossing him. It could also be that Patty Scanlon was rationing his help to an old lover.

Could Captain Teixeira do anything? Not with Jack but maybe with Johnny—promise him every vote in his extended family, speak up for him in the Portuguese community.

Rose had fired her one shot, but Mary Scanlon had convinced Rose—and May agreed—that Rose should go ahead and sing.

May had told Elsie that Phoebe Fitzgerald was persuading Mr. Salviatti to work on Jack. Elsie felt a pinch of competitive envy. Elsie felt bad about this envy, then felt an even more alarming envy that Phoebe, whom she'd dismissed as a giddy flirt showing her pretty legs to the boys, had turned out to be the hardheaded one, while she herself had nothing to offer but outrage and a day of fruitless phone calls. And now that she'd just got off the phone with Walt, she might as well cut a switch and lash her own bare legs.

Out of the house. Not down the hill to Miss Perry's. Straight into the woods. Plenty of daylight left. A good hard hike until she owned her own body, until she was her own motion. Nothing splendid about this neck of the woods, close-packed second growth fighting it out for a hold in the rocky soil, a few pines pushing up fast and spindly to get to the light. She had to circle a patch of barberry, damn foreign barberry, even more bristly and thorny than the native. On the other side was a bit of surviving meadow—all these hills were cleared of old growth by the colonists so sheep could graze. In the twentieth century it had gone back to scrub. The beautiful trees were pets of the big houses.

She felt better being sour about the woods than sour about herself.

She felt even better in the middle of the small meadow, seeing the blue summer sky. There were a few black locusts that had managed to grow tall on the edge of the clearing. She saw a bird flit out of a hole in the trunk. Female bluebird, just the tail blue. It swooped down and around the tree, then fluttered back up to its hole. It did it again, and this time Elsie saw what it was up to. A blacksnake was climbing the locust, taking advantage of the deeply ridged bark. How did the bird know? Did it hear something? Did it smell something? Had it just come out of its nest by chance? For that matter, how did the snake know there was a nest up there? Did the snake actually calculate that a hole was likely to have a nest in it? It was a long way to climb just to see. Or did the snake keep an eye out for birds bringing food back?

The snake was moving slowly, inching up. Hard to tell its length, since it was curving and recurving. Now only a few feet from the hole. The bluebird was fluttering, peeping near the snake's head. The snake kept climbing.

Elsie threw a stick at it. Way short. She found a rock. It hit the tree above the hole. It frightened the bluebird more than the snake.

When she watched a mayfly struggle out of its case in a streambed and swim to the surface, she didn't root for the mayfly more than the trout coming after it. What was the difference? Pretty bluebird, ugly-ass snake? What was in the hole, anyway? Eggs or nestlings?

Too late, anyway. The snake was in the hole, only six inches of tail hanging out. The bluebird fluttered up and down. Why didn't it start pecking at the snake's tail? If it wasn't going to do anything but chirp and flutter, to hell with it. Elsie looked around the sky, hoping a hawk might show up and spy the snake's tail. But even to a hawk's eye the tail might look like another ridge of the soot-gray bark.

Elsie sat down. After a while the snake pulled in its tail. The bluebird perched on a twig, certainly tired out after all that frantic swooping and hovering. Elsie wondered what it felt. Was grief a word that translated? Resignation? Did the bird picture what was going on inside? Elsie herself wasn't altogether sure. Did the snake bite the three or four nestlings to death and then unhinge its jaw to swallow them at leisure? Or did it eat one while the others squirmed? Did the live ones know what was going on?

The snake was successfully doing two things at once—finding a meal that it would take days to digest *and* a place safe from hawks, owls, or feral cats. Did it feel clever? Or was it no more reflective than a clam worm that gnawed its way down a quahog's siphon, ate the meat, and then curled up inside the shell to take an armor-plated nap? Predation and refuge in one move. She remembered going through a bucket of quahogs she'd forked up (okay, she was a predator, too) and finding a loose-shelled one. She'd opened it up with her thumbnail and seen the perfectly coiled clam worm. She'd had an instant of revulsion and then a longer moment in which she recognized the elegance—the elegance of what she saw and the elegance of the clam worm's endgame.

She was pleased to have put the snake and the clam worm together in a single sentence in the language of mute creatures. She had a tick of longing to know the whole language, but she was happy to see what she saw, and if what she saw linked to something else she'd seen, she was a little bit happier. A vanity but an okay vanity that in this part of her life she was modest and severe.

The male bluebird showed up. The two bluebirds perched on a branch. After a while they flew off together. Had the female somehow told him? Given a warning? Given a twitch of courtship that reset the nest-building and mating cycle?

Although it was not official Natural Resources policy, a number of officers took to breaking the eggs of mute swans. The mute swans, unlike the whistling swans, were introduced and had thrived, taking over feeding and nesting territory from the native swans and from Canada geese. Smashing the eggs didn't work. The mute swans laid another clutch. The officers then sprayed the mute-swan eggs with silicone. The mute-swan mother kept sitting on them—in vain, since no oxygen got to the embryos. If the blacksnake had eaten eggs, would it be as easy for the bluebirds to produce another clutch as for the mute swans? All that swooping, all that mother frenzy, erased? But if there were nestlings?

The bluebirds were gone. A minute or two of fluffing and bobbing and off they went.

Elsie let that part go. She jogged back to her house, found a hammer and a flashlight. She filled both pockets with ten penny nails. Back to the locust. She gathered some thick sticks, nailed one onto the tree, stood on it, and nailed another. She climbed up and down until she had the last rung nailed just below the hole. She banged a single nail in, above and to one side of the hole. She dropped the hammer, held on to the nail with her left hand, and worked the flashlight out of her back pocket.

She held still for a moment before she moved her face in front of the hole. All that banging and clambering might have pissed the snake off. She turned the flashlight on, used its flat face to block most of the hole. She peered in. Hard to see at first—the snake's coils were piled on top of one another, its head turned toward the back of the hole. It didn't move at first, then raised its head. She saw two tiny claws sticking out of its mouth. The snake rippled, and the claws moved an inch farther into the gape.

She saw a bulge in the snake—was it two or three baby birds? At the back of the hole was another motion. One featherless nestling still alive.

The snake swung its head, and Elsie dropped the flashlight. It clattered down, hitting the rungs of her makeshift ladder. She lost her grip on the nail but grabbed the topmost stick. It tilted and she slid, hugging the tree with her arms, hitting one rung after another with her feet. She bumped her way down, burning her hands on the bark. She scratched her cheek on something. Her feet hit the ground, and she tipped over backward, a jounce on her ass and a slow roll onto her back. She lay still for a bit, knocked silly. When she stood up a nail slid down her leg. She reached into her pocket and sent another nail through the hole in it.

She closed her eyes. She made a high humming noise that popped her eyes back open. Silly-ass woman. She picked up the two pieces of her flashlight. She screwed the head back on. Didn't work. Must have busted the bulb. She swished through the grass with her feet until she uncovered the hammer. She stuck it in her belt, shoved the flashlight in her good pocket. She felt her cheek. A fair amount of blood on her fingertips. Some had dripped onto her shirt. She pulled her shirttails loose to wipe her cheek. All the buttons but one were torn off. One knee was scraped and was beginning to stiffen. It loosened up as she started home. She turned around at the edge of the meadow. She spied the hole by following the nailed-on sticks, the top two of them dangling askew. A lot of clumsy fussing to see what she could see. She wondered how the snake would get down. Its stomach was ruffled like the fish-scale bottom of her cross-country skis—slid forward smoothly, gave a little traction to keep from sliding back. Maybe the snake would come down in loops, curving and recurving so that parts of its length pointed up to get a grip. That would be something else to see, but there was no telling when it would come down. A vulnerable time, that zigzag descent—a hawk by day, an owl by night.

She felt a pang at what she wouldn't see. But what she *had* seen—the slow swallowing of flesh and bones, the peristalsis she'd only read about and imagined in pale abstraction—now it was hers.

She tucked her shirt back in and went into the woods. Long shadows for the first bit, then diffuse light, dim but not dark.

She'd seen what others would call horrible or even frightening, and yes, she'd felt horror and she'd had a moment of fright, but these were pushed aside by the sight, the intense sight, that made the alien intimate.

By the time she got to her house it was almost dark. When she opened the door Rose called from her room, "Mom! Where have you *been*?" Rose came through the door saying, "May's been trying to find you. Everyone's . . ." She stopped and said, "What happened? Oh my God, are you all right? What did you do?"

"I'm fine."

"You're all bloody; there's blood all over—"

"I scratched my cheek. It looks worse than it is." Elsie went to the bathroom mirror. She cleaned her cheek. It was a little worse than she'd thought—an L-shaped cut, a dangling triangle of skin the size of her thumbnail. She washed it and taped a gauze pad over it. She took off her shirt and cleaned her face and chest with a washcloth. Wiped off her knee. Rose was standing behind her. Rose said, "How did you do all that?"

"I was climbing down from a tree and I slipped. Nothing much."

"Climbing a tree? What for? Never mind—Mary and Dick and May and some other people are at May's house. I said you'd be back by suppertime. That's what you said. Can you go now? It's like a meeting, and I said we'd come. And can you do me a favor? Don't tell them you've been wandering around climbing trees. Just put on some clothes and make something up. And put on long pants; your knee is gross. They've all been busy about May's house. They're waiting to hear what you've been doing."

chapter seventy-seven

P hoebe had arranged it all, but now she was looking as if May was supposed to say something. They were all sitting at the kitchen table—her family, Mary Scanlon, and Eddie and Phoebe. And Mr. Salviatti. Phoebe had come early, and then Mr. Salviatti, who arrived in a big black car with a chauffeur. She'd only seen such a thing in movies. The driver just sat in the car. May had said to Mr. Salviatti, "There's plenty to eat and drink if your driver would like to come in."

He said, "Ah, how kind you are, but he likes to smoke and listen to the radio." Phoebe had laughed in a nervous way, and May worried she'd said something out of place. Mr. Salviatti had asked to see her garden. She thought he might be doing it to get her over her mistake, but he'd asked a lot of questions and even picked up a handful of soil and smelled it.

Phoebe had called them in, bustled around to get everyone to sit down, cleared her throat, and said, "Whatever's on the stove smells scrumptious, but let's just start in with a few words about what's going on." And that was when she stopped right there and looked at May.

May felt a little updraft of nervousness through her arms and chest. She took a breath and froze. She'd been all of one piece just the other day, right here in her kitchen. She looked at Dick. He was frowning and staring at the table. She looked at Mr. Salviatti, who lifted his chin and tilted his head, which reminded her of the way he'd said, "Ah, how kind you are." She said, "Kind. You're kind to come." And then what? Now the problem was she didn't feel right crying her troubles out loud. She closed her eyes and smoothed her apron. She was startled that she still had it on, ought to have taken it off before they came. That distracted her enough so that she said, "What is going on is pretty much a mystery to me. Phoebe explained some of it, the law about taking land, but I can't say that I can recite chapter and verse. And it's a mystery to me how all of a sudden Mr. Aldrich's changed. He was perfectly polite and friendly the one time he came by. So I just don't know."

Phoebe patted her arm. What was Phoebe thinking she needed to be patted for? She'd made a fool of herself there at the beginning, that car and chauffeur set her on edge was all, she didn't need patting in front of everyone—that just made it worse.

Phoebe said, "Well, that's the question in a general way, but before we get to the more technical side—I have a little outline I went over with my lawyer—I'd like to color in the human side. Even my lawyerlike lawyer—" She gave a little trill of laughter. "Even my lawyer got emotional. So where we start is that May and Dick have lived here on Pierce Creek for years—the name tells you something right there. And Dick and Eddie built this house, May raised her two sons, and Dick and Eddie rebuilt the house after the hurricane. I mean, talk about sweat equity. And May has cultivated the—"

May stood up when she heard a car pull in the driveway. Thank goodness for something to put a stop to Phoebe making them into a charity case.

Rose and Elsie.

Rose said, "I'm sorry, May. Mom had a little accident. We'll just sit down over there."

May saw the gauze pad on Elsie's cheek, a blotch of red showing through. She said, "Looks like it's still bleeding. Come over to the sink." She got the first-aid kit. When she peeled the gauze pad off she said, "Oh, my. Dick, you ought to take a look."

Dick rolled up his sleeves, washed his hands, and held them up. He nodded to May to pull a fresh paper towel. Elsie laughed and said, "I'm not a doctor, but I play one on TV."

"He's handy at this," May said. "He's always patching up his crew."

Elsie said to Dick, "I'm glad your hand is better. No nerve damage?"

"Nope. Hold still." He held Elsie's chin. "Might need a couple of stitches; you don't want a scar. I'm going to put a butterfly on, just to hold that flap. What was it did that? Looks like it tore more than sliced."

"A stick."

"You wash it out with anything?"

"Soap and water."

"Wood's dirtier than a knife. Not as bad as a fish spine, but still . . . I'm going to pour something in. Might sting." He turned his head and said, "You go on with your talk. We can hear."

May sat back down. She said to Phoebe, "Maybe you could get to the lawyer part."

Phoebe clapped her hands and said, "I know, I know. But this is the crux of the matter, and it takes some concentration. I've made copies. The law part is page one; page two is some ideas about what I call 'political pressure points.' Take two sheets and pass them on."

The fuss of passing the papers around got everyone to turn their attention back to the table. May folded her hands in her lap and looked at each face in turn. They all knew the story. She'd asked Dick to tend to Elsie. They all heard that. They could all see that she let things be.

Phoebe was lecturing briskly, not interrupting herself. May was glad to see Charlie and Tom paying attention.

May stole a glance at Dick. He was touching Elsie's cheek, the tip of his thumb under the cut, his fingers above it. He put the butterfly bandage across it, fastened a gauze pad over the cut. May touched her own cheek. Dick gave Elsie his seat at the table. He got a small bench from the back porch, and he and Rose sat side by side, as if May had arranged that, too. Let them all see Rose was at home here. Phoebe told everyone to turn to page two. May looked at them all turning their pages and thought of them all at once, all of them cross-stitched to one another. May was grateful, after all, for Phoebe and her notes . . . And wasn't it just like Elsie to come tumbling in like that? Time to get back to the business of the house. May was content that people showed up to help. She'd been shy about speaking up but quick enough about getting Dick to bandage Elsie's face. If May's feelings had been completely pleasurable she would have mistrusted them.

chapter seventy-eight

When Phoebe was done, she turned to May and said, "Let's have that lovely chowder and then we'll see where we are."

Dick said to Elsie, "You better not chew till you get that sewed up."

Tom offered to drive her to the hospital. Mr. Salviatti said, "Tom, you should stay. My driver's here." He held Elsie's elbow and led her out. He held the car door open but didn't close it. He said to the driver, "This lady is going to the hospital. Wait and bring her back, please." He said to Elsie, "Everyone will still be talking. I'll listen to everyone, but you and I know Jack. When he wants something he won't stop. If he's blocked one way, he'll find another and another and another. Even if all the people in there get a hundred names, two hundred names, on a petition, he can find more. He lines up piece after piece. He's holding a fund-raiser at Sawtooth for Mr. Bienvenue. He can fire Mary Scanlon. He can find someone other than Eddie to work on Sawtooth. Even you—your contract with the school is for only one year. When the bank learned that Dick lost his boat, they were worried that he couldn't make his payments on his mortgage. Since the bank was worried in that way that banks worry, Jack was there. He has a company that bought the mortgage for eighty cents on the dollar. So that is Jack the octopus. But he has from time to time another side—a desire to be the prince, to be seen as just and generous. So after he has shown that he can squeeze everyone, perhaps he will let go for a moment. Do you remember when he bought Mary Scanlon's restaurant? He felt no pain at paying a little too much. But he also offered her a job. I doubt that she would have sold unless she could keep doing what she loves and does well."

"How do you know all this? About Dick's mortgage?"

"Because Jack has a notion that I am a clever man, he wanted me to see how clever he is. If this were a game of chess, one would say that he controls the board."

"So what are you saying? We should give up?"

"No." Mr. Salviatti gestured toward the house. "All this resistance will make him angry at first but then perhaps stimulate his imagination. A basic principle of negotiation is to imagine things that the other side wants that are not so dear to oneself. His offer of a little house in Snug Harbor is an overture of that kind. Phoebe has told me about Mrs. Pierce's garden, and I have just seen it. The Sawtooth corporation owns some pieces of land not so far away. There may be a possibility there for something that will make Mrs. Pierce happier. Believe me, if I were an equal partner I would put a stop to this. As it is, I can only suggest ways to discourage the octopus and encourage the king's largesse. Jack has very little regard for the people in there. But he esteems me." Mr. Salviatti cocked his head and lifted a hand as if to say, "Who knows why, but there it is. And, of course, you. It is possible that in front of you and me, and perhaps Mr. Bienvenue, Jack will not wish to . . . There is an Italian phrase, *fare una brutta figura,* to make an ugly face—but it means much more." Mr. Salviatti abruptly leaned back and put his palm on his chest. "But I am keeping you from caring for your wound."

And with that Elsie was whisked away. When the chauffeur leapt to open the car door and then the door to the hospital lobby, she felt ushered out rather than ushered in.

What did she expect? All those citizens were members in good standing. She'd been nothing but a disruption in May's house. She'd thought herself the maverick spirit of woods and streams, but her merit badges were out-of-date. She was no longer a forest ranger; she was no longer being as good as a daughter to Miss Perry. She'd come to the meeting with nothing. May told Dick to tend to her, showing the gathering that she was no more than a scar on an oak branch where a vine had been pulled off.

Courtly old Mr. Salviatti had seen her out.

Her knee hurt. Her cheek hurt. The hospital smell was making her sick to her stomach. She went up to the desk and said, "I think I need someone to sew me up."

chapter seventy-nine

There she was in Jack's office again, Jack beaming again and saying, "Mary, Mary, Mary!" When he got through beaming and squeezing both her hands, he sat at his desk. "So Rose is going to sing," he said, "and I'm very grateful for your help. I think it's a good thing for everybody . . ." He sat down, spun his chair to look out over the yacht basin, spun back to face her. "I love this view, the boats, the pond and the sea. Do you ever miss the view you had from your old restaurant? The creek and the salt marsh and the dunes. And if you stand on tiptoe you can even see a bit of Block Island, can't you?"

"Yes."

"You know, there's a technical name for that line of light where the sky and the sea meet."

"The horizon."

"Ah. In fact, it's what makes the horizon hard to determine. That indeterminate zone is called the *glimmer*. A lovely word, and nice to know it has a sliver of specialized meaning. You could see the glimmer then. From your old restaurant."

"Yes."

"It's going to be vacant again. My people there are giving up the food business. I'm not sure what I'm going to do with the building. It has two big rooms and a kitchen—all one floor. Is that right?"

"Yes."

"An acre or so."

"Yes."

"On a quiet side road. I suppose it would be a nice place to live. Make the old barroom into a bedroom, the dining room into . . . what? A dining room. So that would be easy."

"I imagine so. But you'll want an architect's opinion. I'm the cook."

"Oh, Mary, there's much more to you than that. It's not many people can steal a march on me. There I was about to buy Tory Hazard's house and barn, and what do I find? A corporation is the new owner. But it wasn't more than a day's work to—as we lawyers say—pierce that corporate veil. A nice Irish lawyer in Boston, who has a nice Irish brother who wrote the libretto for . . . You see where we end up. So my hat's off to you. Oh, I was irritated for a moment, but now I'm . . . interested. So there you are, one of the holdouts in the way of Sawtooth. So I'm interested in finding out if you'd like your old restaurant back—not qua restaurant, of course. You wouldn't want to be competing against yourself."

"The barn on the Hazard property has to be a bookshop. The reason Tory Hazard sold to JB and me is so it wouldn't be bulldozed. So I don't see—"

"So she told me. I was a great admirer of her father, and

I wouldn't dream of anything that wouldn't honor him. She seemed surprised, by the way, to learn that you and Mr. Callahan are more than business associates. *'Agnosco veteris vestigia flammae,'* as Dido famously says—'I sense the traces of an old flame.' My plan for the barn is to make it the Everett Hazard Memorial Library. We have the Robert Beverly Hale Library down the road, but it's very small, and now that I've brought so many more readers to the area, another library would be a public benefit. I don't need to underline the public-benefit part—everyone seems to be learning a little law these days. But I'm sure that you and I and your Mr. J. B. Callahan have no desire to enrich a battery of lawyers. If we can reach an agreement on the real property, I can see a place for Mr. Callahan in our Sawtooth cultural program. A stipendiary position. You see? I'm looking for ways to make everybody happy."

Mary closed her eyes for an instant. She'd been fearing it would come to this—not Jack's iron hand in a velvet glove but facing her own wishes. She said, "I see you're a marvel at mixing the carrot and the stick to get us donkeys to move along. Of course, you haven't mentioned a price at all. But before you do that, I should say that there is one thing that could get me to consider your plan. If we agree to sell you our house, will you leave Dick and May alone in theirs?"

Jack sat back in his chair, spun away for a moment. She hoped that he might be satisfied with half of what he wanted, that he might be willing to imagine that there were other wishes as urgent as his own.

He spun back and leaned forward. "Mary, Mary, Mary— I'm glad to hear you say that." She lifted her head. "It shows me that you're thinking creatively about our problem." She sighed. She wasn't surprised when he said, "It shows me you're halfway to seeing the whole picture." And there he was doing his old soft-shoe, nimble for all his pomposity. "Sawtooth Point is a discrete piece of land with natural borders that will be on a sound financial footing and will support our traditional values of nature and culture."

Had she sighed again? Had she raised an eyebrow? As if she'd dissented from a sacred text, he leaned even farther forward and snarled. "I'm serious, God damn it. I'm no Johnny-come-lately. I've been putting Sawtooth together for years—make that decades. It's the core of my life. Piece by piece and year after year, while most people were fiddling away their lives, just one day after another. Eat, sleep, work, eat, sleep, work. So when the cat comes into the kitchen, the mice scurry around and squeal. And then dive back into their little holes."

Mary was surprised to find herself staring at him with pity. His last speech was how he really felt—no more hoo-ha about the benefit to South County—but it was more saddening than horrifying. How alone he was . . . If he'd been a poor crazy out on the street with no company but the voices in his head, you'd want to find him some help, but with a fortune in the bank he could keep himself propped up in his well-staffed isolation. In that isolation, after his hours calculating the dimensions and costs of his maneuverings, he couldn't help but think of the people involved as obstructions in front of his bulldozer, as objects of more or less tensile strength—some were pliable, some were stiff and breakable. She imagined his mind grinding and grinding, perhaps with pleasure, during the morning, with a duller satisfaction during the afternoon, but by evening and into the night, the unstoppable grinding would begin to wear the coating off his nerves. He would list his kindnesses to Elsie and Rose, and wonder at their ingratitude. And hadn't he been good to Mary herself? And Eddie Wormsley and Phoebe—where would they be without his giving them work? But there they all were, gathering around Dick Pierce. And in the middle of the night it was cold comfort that he had his "long-standing relationships with the people who actually keep things going"—they weren't the ones murmuring in the corners of his empty room, nothing he could make out, just a rustling of ill will. And come to think of it, the poor man would be missing his wife—whether he'd sent her away to mind Jack Junior or if she'd swept off in anger.

Jack cleared his throat, and Mary realized that her silence was making him uneasy. He said, "Where were we? Ah—I may have sounded . . . I didn't mean *you* when I said 'mice.' You're sensible enough to come up here and have a sensible discussion. Of course, you'll want to talk it over with Mr. Callahan."

"I was only thinking all this must be hard on you."

For an instant he appeared touched—the set of his face softened. Then grew tight again. He shut his mouth so hard his lips disappeared. He took a breath and said, "Not in the slightest. This is my meat and drink. Which reminds me—don't you have to be getting back to the kitchen?"

Mary laughed in his face.

Unaccountably, Jack laughed, too. Did he think he'd been funny with his little skip from "meat and drink" to "back to the kitchen for you, my girl?" Hadn't he heard himself being an asshole? Dear God, they were every one of them being got the better of by a man who was tone-deaf.

chapter eighty

With every day that passed it looked as though Jack was going to get his way. Elsie thought she'd been the screwup, but it turned out nobody else was getting anywhere, either. She recognized that she wasn't purely out for justice—Dick would admire her, May would tolerate her, Jack would howl. And Rose? Every time Rose set foot in May's house, Rose would have to think, Mom was the one . . .

Elsie shook it off. Too much dithering. Try again.

She phoned Mary Scanlon. Elsie was moved when Mary told her she'd offered up her new property if Jack would leave the Pierces in peace but not moved enough to offset her anger when Mary said that she talked to JB and that they couldn't outspend Jack on lawyers. "Besides," Mary said, "JB is sure he wouldn't think of anything else, and he has to get back to his own work." She added, "I'm remembering how I love it there at my old place."

"Well, May and Dick love where they are, too." Elsie hung up.

She tried Johnny Bienvenue again. He said he'd done what he could—he pointed out that he was the ex–attorney general and not yet a congressman, not in a position to horse-trade.

"And Jack's holding a fund-raiser for you at Sawtooth."

"Yes, he is. That was arranged a long time ago. Look. I sent someone to talk to the township. They say nothing's definite; they're waiting to see if things work out privately."

"The threat of eminent domain is part of the—"

"And I talked to Jack. His position is he's making a generous offer, more than generous, and when he gets the property, a slice of it's going to be for a public footpath to the nature sanctuary. And it's going to be hard to make the case that he's throwing the Pierces out on their ear. He's offering another house plus some cash. The demographics have changed. If South County were still farmers and lobstermen it'd be different. Now there are more people around who look at land as fungible. That means—"

"I know what *fungible* means."

"—one acre of farmland is worth another acre of farmland, one acre of waterfront is worth another, et cetera. Now, if Jack was robbing them blind . . ."

Elsie said, "So it's money, money, money. I thought you were better than that."

He sighed. "I'm reporting the common opinion, not espousing it."

"Have fun at your fund-raiser." She hung up.

She walked down to the mailbox. She opened a letter from the Perryville School. It was a bill for one hundred eighty-five dollars. What the hell was this? Rose was on a full scholarship. She didn't go back to her house; she cut through Miss Perry's garden and marched into the school office. She plunked the bill down on the secretary's desk. "What is this about? 'Incidental fees'? What is that?"

"I'm not sure. There's supposed to be a code number. But there's no code number; I don't know why. I'll get someone to go into the file after lunch."

"I'll do it myself." The secretary opened her mouth and blinked. Elsie said, "I'm faculty, I'm administration." She pulled Rose's file. The charge was for incidental room and board. Elsie said out loud, "I thought she slept on the floor. Well, maybe not. But it was all for that damn play."

In the file she saw the tax return she'd had to submit for Rose's scholarship. An Aldrich scholarship—that egomaniac put his name on everything. And there was Dick's tax return. Of course—both parents. She couldn't resist looking. Dick's gross income was a lot bigger than hers, but his net was much lower. Interest on debts, fuel, maintenance . . . Ah. Child support. She'd noted it in her monthly bank statement, but now she saw it as . . . what? More than a tenth of his net, closer to an eighth.

It was then that it occurred to her that this was how Jack was so well informed about Dick's finances. She said to the secretary, "Who goes over these files? The scholarship committee?"

"Yes."

"And who's on that?"

"The headmaster, the dean, three board members—"

"Mr. Aldrich?"

"Yes. He's chairman of the board. They meet in his office over at Sawtooth."

"And they take the scholarship files over there?"

"Yes—I mean, I make copies for them."

"And what happens to the copies? Do you go get them?"

"No. Mr. Aldrich takes care of that. They're confidential. I think he has his secretary shred them."

Elsie jogged back to her house, got in her car, and drove to Sawtooth. Bold. Time for her to be bold. March in and tell him . . . what? That he'd abused his position as chairman of the board of the Perryville School, used a confidential file for his private scheme, that unless he gave it up, she'd go to the board and make a big enough stink so he'd lose his chairmanship. He loved his chairmanship, part of being the laird of South County. And there'd be a taint on his good name. They'd have to take his name off the Aldrich scholarship.

Halfway up the stairs to the top floor, she stopped. She was sure he'd cheated, but what proof did she have? All right, all right—go in softly. She was here to ask a favor. What? About the one hundred eighty-five dollars. As head of the scholarship committee, he could clear that up. Penny ante for him, not for her. Hat in hand, poor Elsie. But somewhere in his files . . . Get him out of his office. How? Yell fire? All right, all right, something more sensible. She'd think of something.

No secretary in the anteroom. Lunch hour. She knocked on the office door. No answer. Tried the knob, not locked. Easier than she thought. And if he came back? She'd be writing him a note. On the memo pad on his desk she wrote, "Dear Jack, A problem I need a little help with." All right, enough there. Files? No steel filing cabinets for Jack, solid oak. Under what? *S* for Sawtooth? *L* for land? *P* for Pierce? No, no, and no. Start from the beginning. And there it was—Adjacent Properties. There was Hazard, and there was Pierce Creek property. Indeed. Erase the people. And there was Dick's tax return. She pulled it out. There it was in her hand. But now what? If she'd thought to bring a camera . . . All right, all right. A witness. Go down to the kitchen and get Mary. Ah. She'd been mean to Mary on the phone—got in an angry jab and hung up on her. But still, Mary wasn't for Jack.

She took a step toward the door. Idiot—there was the phone on Jack's desk. Mary wouldn't have to come up; all she would have to do was listen. And better yet—fortune favors the brave—there was a list of in-house extensions. One for the front desk, two for the kitchen. She imagined Mary under oath—"Yes, Elsie called me from Jack's office. I could tell it was in-house . . ."

Mary answered, "Sawtooth kitchen."

"It's Elsie. I'm in Jack's office and I found Dick's tax return. Jack shouldn't have it; it's part of the scholarship file."

"Elsie, I don't—"

"Just remember. Dick's tax return. In the Pierce Creek file."

Jack's secretary called through the open door—"Mr. Aldrich? I'm back from lunch."

Elsie hung up.

The secretary said again, "Mr. Aldrich?"

Elsie thought of saying something in a gruff voice, maybe "Close the door, please, Miss Swift." No. Grade B. She called out, "I'm waiting for him. It's me, Elsie."

Miss Swift poked her head in. "Does he know you're here? He didn't say . . . I thought he was going to play tennis." She looked out the front window. "Yes. There he is." She looked at the open file drawer. "I'll go get him."

"Thank you."

Miss Swift hesitated. Thought better of whatever she was going to say. Left.

Elsie took a breath. Leave the file drawer open? Yes. And she had the tax return in her hand. Let him come in and figure it out. Better yet, lay the tax return on his desk. She'd stand up and stab it with her finger.

Jack came in wearing his tennis whites, his face and knees pink.

"I've just got a minute. Or I might say that you've just got a minute. Miss Swift tells me . . . Never mind. What are you here for?"

She braced herself to feel as if she was in uniform again.

"That paper on your desk." She took a step toward it to stab it with her accusatory finger, but he beat her to it. He picked it up. "Is this from in there?" He pointed his own accusatory finger at the file drawer.

"Yes. And it shouldn't be. The scholarship files . . . That's supposed to be for the scholarship, the confidential scholarship meeting. You're using it illegally."

Jack sat down. He said, "'Illegally.'" He wasn't indignant, just musing. He said, "Miss Swift, could you come in here for a second?"

Miss Swift practically stood at attention.

"Could you find the Sawtooth S and L file? And then go down and tell them I'll be along in just another minute."

He riffled through the file and pulled out a copy of Dick's tax return. He held it out to her. "As the mortgage holder in due course, we acquire all the information Dick submitted to the bank: the appraisal, outstanding debts, and, of course, tax returns. So it's in the S and L file and cross-filed under Pierce Creek. And there we are. Anything else? Well, yes. We should remember nursery rules. I won't go into your room and play with the toys in your toybox if you won't play with mine." He got up. "I'll see you out."

chapter eighty-one

I should have said, I should have said, I should have said . . . Nothing. Just as well she'd said nothing.

By the time she drove out the Sawtooth gate the heat in her face was gone. Cold. Cold to her core.

She got home. Too incompetent to do anything but slump onto the sofa and curl up. Everything that came into her head was in miniature. Tiny scenes on a one-inch screen. Jack laughing, saying to someone outside the frame, "I caught Elsie snooping through my files." He laughed, and everyone joined in. He said, "No, no. Just sent her home."

In all the years she'd known him she hadn't ever lost an argument to Jack. Oh, he'd got his way, there was Sawtooth Point turned into his gated domain. But she'd been right, and now she was wrong—wrong and nakedly foolish.

It wasn't fair that this one time, this one technicality, should undo her.

It wasn't fair that men got the verbs and she ended up with adjectives. Jack plotted and squeezed and bulldozed. She was caught *snooping*—pathetic participle, half verb, half adjective.

It wasn't fair that she knew South County, had hiked and waded and paddled all through it, knew the animals, the insects, the trees, the rocks, and the ponds, and Jack shuffled papers and owned it. He put on his wizard lawyer's hat, pulled out his magic papers and wrote his magic words, and—presto change-o—they cast a spell. Okay, Jack was bad, but maybe she wasn't good enough. She'd served her time in the woods and marshes, and used up that goodness in taking Dick to bed. No sudden accident—she'd wanted him, wanted to have their child. And then? She'd been good again, good with Miss Perry, as good as a dutiful daughter—Captain Teixeira said so. And she'd absorbed the stinging side of Rose and let May and Mary have their share of Rose's affection. Of course, there was another way of weighing that—what single mother wouldn't be grateful for help? All right, all right—but here she was now, fighting to save May's house . . . so May would say to Dick, "Go do your laundry in Elsie's washing machine"? She knew what that meant—she was sure she knew what that meant. But twenty minutes ago, she'd been just as sure she had Jack dead to rights. Could it be that May only meant for Dick to visit her the way Tom visited Rose? Elsie had sifted Dick's report of that do-your-laundry remark and his dumb male puzzlement, stuck in the literal. She herself had sifted it into finer and finer grains. She'd imagined May's coming to a grim indifference—he could go do his laundry the same way he went to sea. Over the horizon. She'd imagined May settling on the phrase "Do your laundry" as willed blindness. Elsie had also imagined a barb of disdain— "Go do your *dirty* laundry." Take it up there—all that smell of rotten bait, of diesel fuel, of overspiced food your Vietnamese and Portuguese crew cook up for you, and your captain's swagger. Then go get cleaned up and come back home and make yourself useful.

This wasn't some silky French arrangement, two sets of books for the business, two sets of books for *la vie conjugale*. This was Yankee stoicism. Less said the better.

It sounded right. The problem was that she couldn't be certain. She couldn't march up to May and say, "I've been meaning to ask you—do you *not* want to know?" She vaguely remembered from college physics something about uncertainty, about indeterminacy. The very observation is an intrusion by the observer that ruins the experiment . . . Was that Heisenberg, or was it Schrödinger and his cat?

Since when did she worry about certainty? She used to thrive on taking chances. She used to be good at keeping her balance. Now she was sprawling again. She'd been wrong about Dick's files, fallen out of a tree, got poked in the face with a stick. Fainted dead away in Captain Teixeira's radio room. Losing her footing right and left. And no skipping over that she'd opened the window to Walt, lost her grip. Falling was when she stood still as he unpeeled her bicycle suit; falling was when she was nothing but breath, so weightless that he hoisted her up and swung her onto the bed, nothing to it.

A trickle of heat in her. Immediately chilled. If anyone found out. Him and his "This is like a dream come true." Ripe for telling. A Deirdre O'Malley story.

She shook it away, back into the pile of her other mistakes—all in a clump all since . . . when? Since Rose's play. Her headlong charge at Rose. Her tin ear. No, worse than a tin ear. Something was wrong with her inner sense, whatever part of the brain it was that gave her a moment of insulation between her first impulse and rushing ahead. But how could she have known about the Sawtooth S&L's holding Dick's mortgage? Stupid girl! Mr. Salviatti told her.

Never mind if she wasn't good enough—what if she didn't know what was really going on? She used to be pleased by how alert she was. But now, if she was sleepwalking, how would she find her way?

chapter eighty-two

J ack sent Elsie a copy of the plans for his new property. The attached handwritten note read: "To save you another trip to my office." The first page showed a bridge across Pierce Creek and a raised boardwalk leading to a gazebo in the nature sanctuary. The architect's drawing included a woman in a wheelchair on the boardwalk. Jack included a copy of a letter from Elsie's old boss at Natural Resources, approving the plan and praising Jack for "encouraging public access in a way that minimizes impact on the environment."

Elsie leafed through the plans in a rush of anger. The second time through she made a more careful and bitter assessment. The wheelchair was a shrewd touch. Natural Resources was always on the defensive about access to nature for the disabled.

Page two was a map that showed a small parking lot in place of Dick's front yard, another smaller footbridge across the creek, and a path and a ramp to the boardwalk. All in all, Jack would lose only a narrow strip of the three acres to the general public. The royal road was from Sawtooth, across the downstream edge of Dick's three acres. There was plenty of room for the three new cottages, daintily sketched in. The contractor for the boardwalk, bridges, gazebo, and cottages was to be Wormsley and Fitzgerald. So Eddie and Phoebe had rolled over. And, Elsie noticed, the company was no longer Wormsley and Son. Had Phoebe finally edged Walt out? Or did Walt just get an urge to ride off on his motorcycle into the north woods? A small bubble of relief there.

Page three was another map. Everett Hazard's old barn was to be the Hazard Memorial Library. The house was still there, labeled "private dwelling," and in the field two more cottages. So—six house sales and six new Sawtooth memberships—Jack would rake in almost two million dollars. Of course, he'd have to pay Eddie's company to build the five cottages. Those would cost Jack—what?—a half million. And Jack would have to pay something to Mary and JB, but just the difference between the Hazard property and Mary's old restaurant. For Dick and May, Jack was throwing in a small rickety house in Snug Harbor and an unplowed field that didn't even border a paved road—getting those items off his books. She was pretty sure he had a tax dodge in there somehow. By her rough calculation Jack would come out with a net profit of a million and change. Jack's making money wasn't painful in itself; he'd always been annoyingly rich. It was his triumph that was hateful. Half by bullying, half by finagling, he'd rearranged people's lives and won. What's more, she counted it as his fault that she was angry with most of the people she cared about.

She was about to shriek when Rose emerged from her bedroom. Half asleep, she shuffled to the bathroom. Midday. Rose's diva schedule.

Elsie had given in to the show at Sawtooth. Rose had sat across from Elsie at the dining table and listed the arguments for her singing and not singing, laying out the fingers of her right hand and her left hand.

"I owe it to the rest of the cast." (Elsie recognized a Mary

Scanlon note). "Of course, Uncle Jack deserves to be hurt. But May told me that she can't bear it if I don't sing. She says she'd feel worse about that than having to move. And she says they're going to have to move anyway. But you think . . . you think I'd be a selfish little shit."

Rose let her head fall on her hands and began to cry.

"No," Elsie said. "I never said that." She saw Rose as a child again. She saw Rose being pulled back and forth across the splinters of the grown-up fight with Jack. She said, "It's okay, it's okay. We did what we could. You did as much as any-body."

Rose had kept on crying. "It's okay," Elsie said. "Mary wants you to sing. May wants you to sing."

Rose lifted her head. Elsie waited for Rose to look at her, to look to her for the final word.

Rose sniffed and wiped her nose with the back of her hand. She went to the kitchen sink and splashed her face. "I guess," Rose said. She patted herself dry with a dish towel. "I guess they know I'm only really happy when I'm—"

"Onstage." Elsie didn't mean it to sound as sharp as it came out.

"No," Rose said. She turned around. She wasn't angry. She sighed and said, "It's not like that. It's more like when I'm singing, I'm more music than I'm me." She shrugged. "It's hard to explain."

Elsie was irritated by Rose's "I'm more music than I'm me," dismissed by Rose's "It's hard to explain." She'd been trying to comfort Rose, she'd invoked Mary and May. She'd hoped, of course, that Rose would come back to her. All right, then. It wasn't enough to be moved by Rose's tears and to coo a few soothing words. And she hadn't even done that all that well. "Only really happy . . . onstage." That toad of a remark had hopped out of her mouth before she could stop it—a reflex of all her old quarrels with a difficult child.

Lucky for Rose, then, that she had Mary and May to swad-dle her. Elsie didn't let that thought hop out of her mouth.

With some effort, she said, "Rose. Rose, I know that sometimes I'm a difficult mother."

"It could be worse."

Elsie had laughed.

And now here was Rose at midday in her nightgown and bathrobe. Elsie erased the word *diva* from her thoughts. She said, "How'd it go?"

"Fine."

"You want some breakfast?"

"Maybe later."

"You know, if you don't eat at least a little breakfast the first hour you're up, your body thinks that—"

"I know, I know. I know what my body thinks, thank you."

Rose stopped her slow shuffle and shook her head. She turned toward Elsie. "Mom, I almost forgot. Tomorrow's the day everyone's going to help May with her new field. Well, not everyone. Mary's got to work at Sawtooth, but JB's going, and Deirdre and—"

"I know. Deidre's picking me up in her jeep."

"I'm going but not till later. May said I should sleep in. So I hope you can get there early."

"I'll be early."

"This means a lot to May after everything that's happened."

"I know."

"You were late when we all went to May's house."

Elsie waited until Rose was brushing her teeth, her knuckles stopping her mouth while she worked on her back molars. Elsie said, "Let's try to change the rhythm. I may have a tin ear, but I've got a sense of rhythm. So I won't nag you, you won't nag me. I've been angry at Jack and in a bad mood because I screwed up. You're working hard, you're doing a grown-up job, and you should get to be a little temperamental." Rose pulled the toothbrush out and leaned over to rinse her mouth from the spigot. Elsie said, "But I think we could both—"

"Mom, I get it."

chapter eighty-three

When Elsie got to the field she recognized the place. At first she just took in Eddie on his tractor and the little crowd of volunteers, but then she saw the row of black locusts. Her sticks were still there, the two top ones dangling askew.

It took them a while to get organized, since Eddie kept deferring to May and May kept deferring to Eddie. Phoebe said, "You've got a plan, Eddie. Don't keep it a secret. I've got to get back to Sawtooth."

Everyone got a crowbar or a spade and lined up. Eddie said, "Okay—put the rocks here in my front scoop. When I've got a load, I'll dump them over there. If you've got a crowbar, stick it in a ways. If you hit a rock, find an end and pry her up. Get someone with a spade to dig around and loosen her up."

The grass was still wet with dew, but the sun was high enough to make it hot. Before long their boots and pant cuffs were soaked and their shirts were getting wet with sweat. Eddie's tractor engine chugging along behind them was noisy enough, but it was the rocks clattering into the front scoop that made conversation impossible.

Eddie yelled, "Whoa!" and drove off to dump a load. Deirdre said to JB, "You'll ruin your back if you don't bend your knees. Watch how Tran does it."

JB said, "Don't teach your grandmother to suck eggs," and May laughed. JB, encouraged by this, said, "This kind of work is in my blood. Listen, O'Malley, I'll bet you don't know who's the second-most-important man in Irish history."

"I'll bite," Tom said. "Who?"

"The man who invented the wheelbarrow and got the Irish up on their hind legs."

"Oh, God," Deirdre said. "Not that old wheezer."

Eddie came back, shut off the engine, and rearranged them in pairs. May with Tom, Deirdre with JB, Elsie with Tran.

It was satisfying, more satisfying than weeding Miss Perry's garden. Deeply satisfying to probe with the crowbar and find the edges of a big rock. Dig under it and then have at it with the bar. If it didn't budge, Tran would get another crowbar and the two of them would pry at it until it tore loose from the earth. All shapes and sizes. Some the size of a loaf of bread, some as big as a car tire. Elsie probed around one that turned out to be long and narrow, a piece of granite shaped like a mummy sleeping bag, the foot end angling up. Eddie dumped a load and came back. He lowered a corner of the front scoop under the lip of rock that Elsie had dug free. He drove forward a half foot, gave a delicate pull on the hydraulic control. The rock tipped up a few inches. Eddie yelled, "Oh, boy! You found the granddaddy!" Another grunt of the engine, another twitch on the hydraulic, and another and then another, until the rock reared up as tall as a man. They all stood admiring it, admiring Eddie, admiring themselves—looking back and admiring their wake of trampled grass and empty pockets of dark earth.

Eddie shut off the engine. "I thought for sure she'd break in two. Let's eat lunch and think what to do with her. Won't fit in the bucket. Maybe put a chain on her and drag her. Make a hell of a tombstone."

They sat in the shade and ate their sandwiches and drank from their thermoses. Elsie was savagely hungry and thirsty. She should've brought two sandwiches.

May said, "Is Rose going to come?"

"She said she would," Elsie said. "She's sleeping in. She had a show last night. Deirdre left her a map."

"That's good," May said. "Thank you, Deirdre."

Eddie came back from walking around and shaking his

legs out. He said to Deirdre, "I see you got a ball on the back of your jeep. I should've thought of that. You think you could go back to my place and hitch up a wagon? We could put the little rocks in it. Save me going back and forth with the tractor every ten minutes."

"Sure. I'll pick up Rose on the way."

"You might see if Dick's at a stopping point with that skiff he's building," May said. "He's over there in Eddie's shed, the big one with the tin roof."

Elsie lay on her back and pulled her knees to her chest. Three hours of digging, tugging, and lifting had knotted her up some, but as she let her back relax, she felt light and hollow. She heard JB say, "I'll come along. I'd like to see what a boat looks like half done." Out of nowhere, out of the sky, out of the ground she lay on, a ferocious desire filled her. It was as unasked for and as real as a dream. She hugged her knees closer to her, she saw Dick working, she smelled wood shavings, she felt herself coming into the shed, not a word, just the air between them growing so dense they could sense each other through it.

She rolled onto her side, pressed her cheek into the ground to stop her trembling.

Deirdre said to JB, "You're just trying to get out of work. Never mind. Hop on in."

Elsie listened to the jeep jounce and rattle away.

"I doubt Dick's going to come," May said. "If he's got to wait on something for his skiff, he'll go over to Wickford, look at a lobster boat might be for sale. He say anything to you about that?"

Tran said, "Maybe Wickford. Maybe New Bedford. He's looking all over. Lot of things on his mind, but finding a boat is number one."

Eddie walked around the upright slab of rock, came back, and asked Tran to help him put a chain around it. "I'll keep her propped up, you get the chain on snug, then you back off and I'll tip her over. Then you come back and fasten the chain to the cable from the winch. Then I'll go over there and snake her in."

Elsie propped her head up on her elbow. She hoped what they were going to do would be brutal enough to distract her. She said, "How come you just don't drag it with the tractor?"

"That winch there could move a house. The tractor'd either rear up or spin. You'll see. In fact, come on—I'll let you run it."

Eddie had Tran twist the chain around so the hook would end up on top. He gave the rock a little shove, and over it went. Elsie had expected more of a seismic thud. Eddie moved the tractor; Tran unreeled the cable and fixed its hook through a link on the tail end of the chain. Eddie climbed down beside Elsie. He pointed to a red plastic knob on an upright lever. "Okay. Give that a pull. Just don't run that rock up onto your toes." Nothing much at first, just taking up the slack. Then the cable went taut and the chain scratched into the rock. Elsie left her hand on the knob, a light buzz in her palm. The reel turned steadily. There was a visible but surprisingly noiseless tension on the cable, no thicker than her little finger. The enormous rock began to move. It wagged a little at first, as if trying not to come, then gave in and swam straight toward her, thick end first, like a whale.

This was wizardry; this was hands-on witchcraft. She'd used a walkie-talkie, seen radar and sonar screens, wondered a little at invisible waves, but now it was her hand pulling a ton of rock across the ground she stood on.

Eddie said, "Whoa, there. Close enough. Now you want to push that lever the other way, just a touch. Give us a little slack so we can unhook her."

She thought she ought to feel her own physical strength dwarfed, she ought to feel put in her place. In a whole morning of poking, prying, and lifting, she hadn't moved as much weight as this winch had in the last minute. So what a puny little thing she was . . . Didn't feel that way. The morning's work had got her blood up—she'd flushed every muscle in her body with blood and oxygen, and that rush reached every capillary and nerve in her skin. She'd moved rocks; she'd moved a boulder; she could drink a pond dry; she could run all the way through the woods, kick open the door to Eddie's shed, and make Dick hold on to her furious body.

The hook on the chain was wedged tight in the link. Eddie tapped the next link over with the ball of his ball-peen hammer, and everything popped open. The chain slid down either side of the rock into two puddled heaps. Eddie turned the tractor around, eased the lip of the front scoop under the rock, and lifted it a few inches. Elsie pulled the chain free. Even through her gloves, she could feel the heat in the links.

Eddie said, "Let's see if we can get another couple of hours out of this crew. This isn't work you can do all day. If we push too long someone'll end up dropping a rock on their foot. I'm kind of worried about that old fellow. Maybe you can get him to talking every so often; that'll give him a rest. Least if that girlfriend of Charlie's doesn't get after him. When they get back, you might let her know to go easy."

Sweet, mild Eddie. A universal donor. Another kind of man might have sensed the state she was in.

They heard the jeep before they saw it. The rattling was louder with the empty cart in tow. Just the three of them. May said, "I didn't expect you'd get him. Was he there?"

"Yes," Rose said, "but he was just leaving. He said to tell you not to wait supper. He'll get something to eat on his way back, and then he's going to work some more on the skiff. Might be late."

Elsie wished it wasn't Rose letting her know where he'd be.

chapter eighty-four

The sea breeze came up while they ate lunch, not so salty as down by the marsh. A bit of pine in the air, a bit of forest mast, but mostly crushed grass and turned earth. May breathed deep. They'd got the better part of an acre cleared of rocks, and she was grateful for how hard everyone was working. That was part of why she felt so good. Another part was that what with sticking their crowbars and spades in and prying the stones up, they were loosening the soil, letting it breathe. She liked having a commonsense reason for feeling good.

She'd caught herself humming as she'd shoveled. If she went on like this, pretty soon she'd be like Mary Scanlon, bursting into song whenever she felt like it. But then May thought, If that's how Mary feels, let her.

Mary had told her how Mr. Salviatti had gone in to see Mr. Aldrich, taking Mary in tow. "I don't know why. He talked about fresh peas and then he said, 'Ask Mary,' and I nodded, and he said, 'Fresh corn, a half hour from stalk to kettle. Ask Mary.' I couldn't get a word in, but neither could Jack. Finally Mr. Salviatti leans in and says, 'Look, Jack. We don't want that land for more houses. I'm in the road business, I know what it would cost to put a road in there. And water and sewage. No ocean view from that lot. We might not make our money back. What makes money for Sawtooth? It's our oceanfront, it's our tennis club and yachts. And it's our good food. So this way we have vertical integration. Mrs. Pierce knows how to grow good vegetables; Mary knows how to cook them. And I know how to make sure nobody has problems.'" Mary had laughed. "People have been wondering for years. He was joking. You know how I know? Going down the stairs from Jack's office, I said, 'So how come you had me along?' And he says, 'You're the muscle.' And we both cracked up. You know what I think? Jack got his way with legal shenanigans and throwing his weight around, but he's cut himself off. He's up in his office with nothing but his maps and files. You've got a gang of friends. It's them—them and your way with your old garden—that got Mr. Salviatti on your side. And he figures he'll have more fun with us raggle-taggle gypsies. I've got to cook at Sawtooth on Saturday, but I'm bringing Mr. Salviatti over Sunday afternoon. His car can't make it over that jeep trail, so we'll use my pickup. It's late in the season but time enough for some root vegetables. Turnips, parsnips, celeriac. You could use some of those rocks you pull up to line a root cellar. Eddie could help you make one. In the fall you could have a barn raising, a little red-cedar barn. It'd be grand."

May had said, "Plenty to do before that. If we get a second acre cleared, I got to plant some winter rye." It was just like Mary to run ahead like that, but now May thought she herself needn't have got so tight-lipped.

Eddie started up the tractor. Elsie was the first one on her feet. She said, "Come on, Rose. Get your hands dirty. JB can drive the jeep."

May said, "Rose has got her show tonight. She can drive the jeep. Is that all right with you, Deirdre? Tom's been teaching her to drive."

"Sure," Deirdre said.

"I'm sorry, Elsie," May said. "I just thought . . ."

Elsie waved and picked up her crowbar. "Come on, JB, get your shovel. You're stuck with me." Off she went, jab, jab, jabbing until she clinked on a rock, a small, sharp note that cut through the rumble and mutter of the tractor as it inched forward. That note got the rest of them going. May watched Elsie wave to JB to come shovel away some earth so she could stick her crowbar in under the lip of the rock. And there she was heaving on the crook end of the bar, putting her legs and back into it, all coiled up so her work pants pulled tight on her rear end. JB touched her back. Of course he would. All that hum of energy. He pointed the tip of his shovel at the other side of the rock. Elsie nodded, and JB dug out the edge. Elsie jabbed a couple of times, got the bar in deep enough to pry. The rock tilted up, a flat rock, not so big after all, about the size of a boat cushion. Elsie and JB crouched down to lift it, wiggled it a bit, and heaved it into Eddie's front-end scoop.

May poked here and there, dug up a pretty melon-shaped rock with a white stripe around its middle. She walked back to show it to Rose before she dropped it in the cart. Right there between the tractor and the jeep it was too loud to talk, but when she got to digging again the noise wasn't so bad, even a comfort. It put her in mind of a beehive.

She hit a fair-sized rock, waved to Tom to bring his crow-bar. When he threw the rock in the scoop, Eddie turned off the motor. Eddie did this from time to time so he could tell a joke, give everyone a couple of minutes to stretch. May looked back down the field. The lay of the land was on her side. It tilted up a bit from the south, just about right to catch the fog when it blew in. A good overnight fog was as good as watering—it came up from the sea but left the salt behind, settled a freshwater dew.

Eddie started the tractor again. May pried up another rock, flipped a bit of sod in the hole, grass side down, so it'd rot. Another good thing that went on in the dark. She'd be like Dick when he got to lobstering again, setting his pots so the lobsters would creep in—all that went on in the dark, too. She'd go to bed tired and likely a bit sore tonight, and plenty of nights after, but she'd go to bed satisfied. She knew well enough that whatever got done by way of clearing and tilling and sowing was the least of it. Most of it was what came out of the earth, what came from the fog and rain, from the sun hitting the slight southerly tilt of the field. The work was to put her field in the way of these providences.

That was enough about that. Who'd be set for work tomorrow? She looked around. Elsie was doing more than her share but had something else to do Sunday. Eddie and Tom were on. And Deirdre—when all was said and done, Deirdre would do. Tran was on the payroll—Dick was paying him some so as not to lose him when Dick got a boat. She suspected that JB would be aching, but he could drive the jeep. Rose had her Sunday matinee. No Eddie on Monday, but he would leave the tractor for her. They'd use the jeep and wagon to move the compost from her old place, spread it on the little patch where they'd scalped the sod. Plant that patch next week, another patch the week after. Sow the second acre in winter rye, plow it under for next year. Plenty to think about, plenty to do. She wanted nothing better than to set herself to it.

chapter eighty-five

At the end of the workday Elsie turned down a ride in Deirdre's jeep. She walked past the barberry thicket and through the woods, the trees now heavier with green, the patches of late-afternoon light wavering on the mat of old leaves and roots. It was then she thought, Am I going to? Am I really going to? Before she reached the house she'd decided, and by the time she got there she was floating, drifting in the current.

Rose was there, walking around the living room bent over at the waist and chanting over and over in a low voice, "How now, brown cow." Then Rose lay on her back and closed her eyes.

Elsie said, "Be sure to drink some water. You've been—"

"I did. I will. Right now I'm concentrating, okay?"

When Rose was in the bathtub, Elsie said, "Do you want something to eat?"

"I eat after. And yes, I have a ride back, and no, I won't make any noise coming in."

Once Rose was out the door, Elsie got rid of the people in her mind. By the time the sun was behind the treetops they were gone. It wasn't just a matter of knowing Rose would be onstage, Mary Scanlon in the Sawtooth kitchen, Charlie at sea, everybody else in bed by ten. Elsie sealed off their presences, shuttered them. She let the house grow dim. She moved through the light from the sky coming in the south window and the softer light coming up from the dark mirror of the pond. She brushed her hair in front of the bathroom mirror, watching her hands in the half-darkness. She would be a shadow on her way to find Dick.

The sky was still bright in the west. Under the trees it was dusk. She noticed nothing but her white sneakers finding their way down the hill, through Miss Perry's garden, up and around the school, onto Ministerial Road. She stopped short of Eddie's driveway, picked her way through the scrub pine, angled toward the back of the yard. The tractor shed was dark. Beyond it there was a glow in the back window of the work shed. She went around to the front, stood outside the spill of light through the open double doors. She combed her hair with her fingers, smoothed her skirt over her hips, surprised by her own touch. She called his name. His shadow moved across the square of light. She said his name again.

He said, "Jesus, Elsie."

She laughed. "That's what you always say."

She moved backward into the dark. She tapped her hand on the top plank of a pile of lumber to give him a bearing. He took a few steps. She saw his white T-shirt moving in starts, like frames of an old silent movie. She took a step forward, and he stumbled into her. She held on, pressing her mouth into his shoulder. She shuddered, hard enough to loosen his grip. He let his hands fall to his sides.

She was too much for him, she was a sudden squall, he didn't know what to do. She'd fallen out of the sky. She'd been falling from noon to dusk, imagining herself, not him, not him standing there, night-blind.

Now they were both standing stupidly. She was stupid. She would feel even stupider stumbling back through the woods. She said, "You can give me a ride home." She walked toward him, into him. She said, "A ride home," into his face.

He put his hands on her shoulders. She pushed one hand away with the back of her forearm. She grabbed his other hand by the wrist, tugged it off her shoulder. It slid across her collarbone onto her breast.

She stood still while he touched her through her dress. She let herself lean a little. When she thought he couldn't stop, she began to move. When she knew he couldn't stop, she did what had taken his breath away years ago—she stood on tiptoe and hooked her knee around his thigh, her bare skin climbing the rough bark of his jeans.

Afterward she was glad it was dark enough not to see his jeans and jockey shorts around his knees, his work shoes still on, her dress pulled up to her armpits, her white sneakers back on the ground after waggling in the air.

The evening star was over the top of the trees on the other side of Ministerial Road.

She didn't want either of them to start worrying yet. She moved her hip closer to his and said, "I haven't seen so many stars in a long time. Too many trees at my place."

"Even more stars, you get out to sea."

"You find another boat?"

"I got my eye on one."

"Good."

"Needs work."

She laughed. He lifted his head to look at her. She said, "We're going all clipped Yankee. Next thing you say better be a long sentence." He laughed. He settled on his side, made himself comfortable against her, as if they lay like this in ordinary life. Now that she'd fallen out of the sky, she saw that this was what she really wanted.

She pulled herself closer to him. "I had to come see you. I was thinking about you all day. I think about you a lot; this time I couldn't stop." She touched his back. "Lie down again. Just for a bit." He lay on his back, looked straight up. She said, "Don't worry, everything's all right."

"Funny you say that. I have this dream every so often. Last thing in it is somebody saying that. A woman's voice."

"Maybe it's me."

Dick laughed. Elsie hit him on the shoulder. He said, "You can't be everything. Anyway, this was a voice I don't know. Maybe just a thought. The idea of the place, some place I've never been. Looked like pictures I've seen of fjords. I was in a skiff. I wasn't rowing, I was standing in the stern looking forward, but she was somehow moving up the fjord. The water was calm. The hills were steep, covered with trees, came right down to the water. There was this breath of wind; maybe that moved the boat. Maybe the voice was mixed up with the wind." He let out a long breath. "Mostly when I dream, something's wrong and I got to fix it. But every so often I get this calm dream."

"Oh, I don't know about that. You want me to tell you what *I* think this dream's about?"

"I guess you're going to."

"It doesn't exactly defy interpretation. Your boat sticking out in front of you, sliding into this lush fjord."

Dick held his hand up, thumb and forefinger apart, maybe measuring the distance between two stars. He said, "So you figure you get to be the fjord. I was figuring it was just me finally getting to take a vacation."

"No reason it can't be both."

Dick let his hand fall. "Trouble is, you're not some far-off place I've never been to. You're here. You're part of here; we're part of here."

"Yes, I am," she said. "We are." She held his shoulder and kissed him. She let herself roll onto her back. "I've thought that all along. The way we know things. The way you know the sea, the way I know the woods, the way we both know the salt marsh. The way we live in the natural world. Our sense of—"

"That's not what I was getting at. Okay, we both get out in what you call the natural world, but we live in South County. It isn't some big city, everyone coming and going, everything up in the air." Dick blew out a breath. "Forget the big city. What the hell do I know about that? I know the people here; we both know the people here. We're in Eddie's backyard."

"Eddie. I wouldn't worry—"

"No. It's not just Eddie."

Elsie said, "All right, then. May."

"I won't say anything about May. But it's something else. I haven't got to it yet." He closed his eyes, took a breath. "It's Rose. I'm kind of an awkward father, anyway. May and Rose get along great, Mary Scanlon and Rose get along great, you and Rose . . . I hear you scrap some, doesn't mean you don't love each other." Dick touched her head, slid his fingers through her hair so gently she was surprised when he said, "But I don't think any of you women spend a minute thinking about Rose and me."

"Of course we do," Elsie said. "At least I do."

Dick said, "You don't need to jump. Far as I'm concerned, it's just as well. Suits Rose and me fine. After I made that miscue, told her she'd get thin if she took up rowing . . . Rose came around. Not right away. Said she wanted me to go out in her skiff with her, teach her stuff. We went out a lot, still do often enough. We don't make a secret of it. Just that nobody notices."

"Well, I'm glad. I want things to be good between you and Rose."

"Now you show up and it's like I'm being tumbled by a wave. I'm not saying I haven't thought about it. I have. I do.

And okay, right now we're drifting in that fjord, and you're saying, 'Everything's all right.' But in just a bit we're going to get in my truck and I'm going to drop you at the bottom of your driveway because Rose might be waiting up for you."

"Rose is doing her play. And afterward she's staying to eat something. She won't be back for quite a while."

Dick shook his head. "I'm not just talking about where Rose is right now. I'm trying to say—"

"Well, yes, of course. This isn't something Rose should have to think about. No one should have to. Just you and me."

"I'm talking about me. When I see Rose it goes fine, but it's not that often, so I feel kind of fragile."

"And you think I'll make you more fragile?" A bubble ran up her spine. Elsie found herself sitting up. "I see. I'm one thing, then I'm another. I show up looking amazingly like the girl of your dreams but it's just a spell and there's a flash, and presto change-o, I'm a terrible hag, I'm turning into the worst witch of all—Rose's mother."

"You can joke if you want—"

"No. That's not what I want." She turned toward him, leaning over him. "Where do you think Rose came from?" And then she said, "I want to be the one you feel fragile about. I want you to feel so fragile you're in awe. You should be in awe. You should be in awe of the white streak in my hair; you should be in awe of how I fell out of the sky, of how I was falling all day today." She lay back down.

Dick didn't say anything. She said, "We were peaceful. Just now, just before."

"I know," he said. "I know."

Elsie was dizzy and tired. She looked up. The stars seemed to be receding in a slow eddy.

He drove her the whole way. When he turned into the driveway he said, "I guess it'll be all right." The house was dark. He saw her to the door but left the motor running. He said her name, but it was too dark to see his expression. He got back in his truck.

She'd made her headlong desire come true, but having seduced Dick, she'd seduced herself. She'd seduced herself into wanting more, so much more that she'd blurted out a terrible selfishness—"I want to be the one you feel fragile about."

The taillights flickered as the overhanging brush popped back in place behind the truck. She leaned against the front door. So Dick thought Rose was an impediment. Of course, it wasn't as if she didn't know what he was talking about. Up in May's field she herself had wished it wasn't Rose who said out loud where Dick would be. Elsie felt dizzy again, more than with the simple tiredness that made the stars appear to swim away and up.

chapter eighty-six

Jack buzzed the kitchen on the intercom and asked Mary to come up to his office.

He was sitting at his desk, his head propped on one hand. He got halfway to his feet and then plopped back down. He looked a mess. His shirt was wrinkled, his hair sticking out, a bit of white stubble on his face, one cheek dark red. He leaned it on his hand so heavily it squeezed one eye shut.

He said, "She called me a shit."

Mary sat down.

"She's never said anything like that. I don't mean . . ." He waved his hand back and forth in front of his face. "Of course, in a trivial way. But she said it deliberately. With due deliberation."

Mary had thought it might be Elsie; now she realized it must be Sally.

"She never said anything like that before. When she was angry at me about Jack Junior, she yelled and cried, and that was understandable, that was a mother's fear. But this is all about something she doesn't understand. I thought she was listening; she sat there as if she was listening—I grant you, it's complex—but without any regard for what I was saying, she said, 'You are a shit.'"

It crossed Mary's mind that "due deliberation" didn't fit with "without any regard for what I was saying," but the man was at a loss. She shook her head and sighed. She also wondered how she came to be Jack's confidante. If he had only her, God help him. She said, "Had she been traveling all day or anything like that?"

"No," Jack said. "She just drove from Boston. She was perfectly calm when I showed her the drawing of the boardwalk to the nature sanctuary. She even said she was glad Eddie Wormsley got the job. It was when I turned the page and was explaining the new map .... I was pointing to it and I heard her suck in her breath, and I turned and she said it. I said, 'What?' and she said it again."

"And you?" Mary said. "What did you do?"

"I just stood there. She turned on her heel and went into the bedroom. I waited a suitable time, then I knocked on the door. There was no answer, so I said I thought she should come out when she was ready to . . . I can't remember my exact words."

"*Apologize*?"

"No, it was more in the manner of . . . I may have included the word *apologize*, but it was primarily a request that she hear me out."

"So it's about your getting Dick and May's house?"

"The Pierce Creek property, yes."

"And what did Sally say?"

"Nothing at first. And then something about how I'd finally cut her off from Elsie. That this was the one thing Elsie really cared about, and I'd done it when Elsie couldn't reach her, I'd done it behind her back, I'd arranged to have her leave.

Of course, that's utter nonsense. She left of her own volition. And God knows I've done a great deal for Elsie."

"You said that?"

"I may have, very briefly. But I wasn't going to argue my case through a closed door. I said I'd be back when she wasn't hysterical. I said she could reach me here. That was yesterday. I spent the night." He nodded at the far side of the room. There were chair cushions on the floor.

"You must be exhausted. Have you had something to eat, then?"

"No."

"I can bring something up in no time at all."

"No, thank you."

He got up and began to put the cushions back on the chairs. He held the last one against his face. He wheezed three times, his body jerking a bit after each one. She thought he was smothering a sneezing fit but then thought he was crying. He gave a groan and dropped the cushion. She got up and patted his back. She said, "She's still feeling the shock of Jack Junior. Him being pulled out of the sea. Sally was there by the radio, her and Elsie. And didn't it turn Elsie's hair white, and didn't she faint dead away? And Sally was surely clutching herself just as hard at the thought of her son. It took her that way, and it took you another, and there you went making yourself feel better the only way you could think of. But you've tried to make amends; at least there's May with her five acres." Mary wondered at herself. Why was she granting this man absolution? Was she a sucker for a few moans from a great hulk of a man? She said, "Of course you shouldn't have called her hysterical."

She gave him another pat. He clung to her, saying, "Oh, God, Mary, you've got a good heart." And there he went squeezing the breath out of her, and sure enough, there went his hand onto her bottom.

"None of that now." She gave a good shove to his shoulder with the heel of her hand, and another for good measure.

He dropped his hands and said, "No, no, no, I didn't mean . . . I'm sorry. You're so tall, your waist is higher. Completely inadvertent. Your goodwill. I'm grateful for your goodwill." He pulled the cuffs of his blazer down and went back to his desk. "You're right, we should call down for something to eat. Don't you go; one of the girls can bring it up. What would you like? I think just a sandwich and some coffee for me. Same for you?"

"I should be getting back to the kitchen."

"Not just yet if you don't mind. There's something I thought of. Won't take long."

He ordered his club sandwich and coffee. When he was done he said, "What I was thinking—and you can help me with this—is that my explaining everything to Sally won't be enough. But if Sally could hear how pleased May is with her garden project, it would demonstrate that I haven't laid waste to the community. So I thought that I'd invite all the parties involved for dinner here. Everyone who may have felt a little bit nicked but for whom in the long run I've done something. The whole Pierce family, Eddie Wormsley and his partner—she's a friend of Mrs. Pierce's. And Elsie and Rose. The show will be closed by then, so Rose is free. And Johnny Bienvenue and his new bride—I'm looking forward to getting to know her, particularly if she takes after you. And, of course, you—not just in your capacity as aunt but because you're close to everyone involved—a matrix, as it were. And we'll invite your friend Mr. Callahan. We'll have a big table out on the screened porch; it'll be like those big family celebrations Captain Teixeira has down on the town dock for his tribe. When you think of it, almost everyone is related to everyone else—there you are Elsie's old friend and housemate and the new Mrs. Bienvenue's aunt and practically a second mother to Rose." He cocked his head. "Indeed, Rose. Rose is actually part of everybody's family. Who can say no to a party for Rose? So I thought we might do it on V-J Day—we're going to have fireworks, launch skyrockets from the beach. I've always liked that about Rhode Island—I believe we're the only state that officially celebrates V-J Day. Of course, that's not until August. The Fourth of July would do. So—fireworks, perhaps a poem from your friend, a song from you and Rose, and a general feeling of reconciliation. What do you think?"

Mary laughed.

"I see I've taken you by surprise," Jack said. "But I've been mulling over a gesture of goodwill for some time. The effect that it will have on Sally is a fortunate addition. The sign of a good plan is that it has coincidental benefits."

What was taking her by surprise was how quickly he reinflated himself. He was at it again, certain that what suited him would suit everyone.

"So we should think about the menu," he said. "Of course, you're one of the honored guests, so whatever we plan should be something you can prepare the day before. Maybe a bouillabaisse? Doesn't that just simmer all day?"

"Speaking as the cook," she said, "that's easier said than done. You have to add different fish at different times. I'll think of something."

"I'm sure you will. Shall we plan it for the Fourth of July or V-J Day?"

"The Fourth," she said. "If you pick V-J Day someone might think you're celebrating dropping the atomic bomb."

He squinted at her but opened his eyes wide at the knock on the door. He boomed, "Come in!" And then, "Ah, splendid!" as the waitress set the salver before him and lifted the lid.

chapter eighty-seven

Dick told May no. But then Phoebe called May and said, "Oh, let's go! Among other things, it's to honor Rose." Dick heard May out, looked away, and said, "Up to you."

Sally called Elsie. "I don't know, I don't know," Sally said. "I think he's trying. We had a terrible fight. I honestly thought it was the end. But then I let him come back and talk, and it's more complicated than I thought, and he seemed truly miserable. I think he really cares about you, and he cares about you and me. And I said everything's flying apart, and he said all he was asking was that I just please, please, let him try. So I don't know, but I couldn't stand it if you're mad at me."

Elsie waited a second too long, and Sally cried. Elsie said, "No, I'm not mad at you." And then, "Yes, I'll come."

Mary said to JB, "You don't have to come. You could say you have a business appointment."

"On the Fourth of July?"

"Some sort of writing deadline, then."

"You don't want me to come?"

Mary sighed. "I have to be there. You don't. That's all I'm saying."

"I think you're still worried I'll put my foot in my mouth. You forget I've been up there clearing rocks with half the people coming to the party." He shot his white eyebrows up and cocked his head.

She knew him well enough by now to see he was filling up

with a compliment to himself. She said, "I'm sure they were all amazed at how you made the day pass so brightly."

"You're very close. What they actually said—what they actually said at the end of the day as they hoisted me on their shoulders—was 'Lucky Mary Scanlon—no wonder she's never looked happier.' And then we all sang 'Bringing in the Sheaves.'"

"Never mind, then. There's no pricking your balloon."

"Oh, for God's sake. I just said that because you said . . . Look. I live here now. I'm living here with you. I'm getting along with your friends. We had a fine time up there in May's field. It was *two* days, by the way. Now that there's this stranger occasion, you're worried. You've been worried before—you worried that I'd talk too much and May wouldn't like it. It turns out May and I get along just fine. You can't keep on poking me at every turn—watch out for this, watch out for that. You've told me the stories. I can take it from here."

"All right, all right. I'm glad you're finding your way. That's not what I was talking about at all. I was only offering you a way out of an evening of Jack's telling us he means nothing but the good of all his subjects."

"It's a party," JB said. "You like everyone else who'll be there. The food will be splendid, the fireworks spectacular. Listening to a bit of his hypocrisy is a small price—"

"He's not a hypocrite. A hypocrite knows he's pulling the wool over our eyes. Jack is devious enough, but he truly believes that everything he does is for an almighty good—if fools like us could only see. There's days I feel sorry for him, him living in the middle of a little ball of his own notions. There's not a glimmer of anything else. Oh, he knows there are other creatures who have to be dealt with one way or another. And he's good at that—I mean, skillful at keeping on in his own direction. It only occurred to me the other day—he never really apologizes. He says, 'I'm sorry, but sometimes a good storm clears the air.' Or he says, 'I'm sorry you were offended.' He's like one of those little Coast Guard boats—all sealed up and self-righting."

"So why is he throwing this party? I mean, if he's that oblivious . . ."

"Ah, well. That's me going on about him as a loonie. He's not altogether oblivious. There's him wanting his way no matter what, but then there's him feeling an ache he doesn't know much about except it's an ache. Of course he's upset that his wife's upset, and he means to show her that he's taken with one hand but given with the other. He knows how to keep a wife, at least a wife who's got no other way to live. It's people like Elsie and Dick who puzzle him. He looks down on their messy lives, and at the same time he has a suspicion that they have something, some wild nerve, that makes them ready for anything. Each time some tail end of their doings floats in, he wonders if they're getting more out of the world they live in than he gets out of his." Mary sighed. "If he knew them better, he'd see the long stretches of their ordinary days, he wouldn't envy their giving off the odd spark. It's as though he thinks Elsie had Rose or Dick had a shipwreck to make him feel dull. But he keeps that ache of envy buried. He thinks to himself he's bringing pieces of land into a proper order. He doesn't see he's got another motive. He's trying to make everyone in his life subordinate to him— to owe him money, to be on his payroll, to be bound to him. That's one thing this dinner is about—here you all are at my table, there's Eddie working on the gazebo and May in her garden, and I've put in a word for Dick with the insurance company, and Mary's cooking, and there's Elsie with a job at our school, and Johnny Bienvenue is looking forward to our fund-raiser, and let's not forget Rose's success in our show, and she certainly deserves every penny of the Aldrich scholarship. Of course, he won't say that out loud, but he'll have a moment of seeing himself as the great heart that's pumping the blood through the system, and it's only decent to hope that that moment will do for him and that he won't look around the table and see something else. And it's not resentment that would do him in—that would mean he's still part of the mix—it's that he might see that whatever he's taken and given is taken and given. Now we've all had ourselves a shake and we're back to living our lives with each other and he's just something that happened."

Mary sat down. When she caught her breath, she looked at JB. "What?" she said. "And all you wanted to know is if you should wear a coat and tie. You poor man, you didn't know what you were getting into."

"I didn't know I was taking up with a Greek chorus."

"And what's that supposed to mean?"

"It means you have uncanny sympathy for everyone."

"That's just the inside out of 'Everyone loves Mary Scanlon.' I'm not sure that that says much for my brain."

"Then you missed what I just said about your brain. I love your brain. Forget what I just said about your poking me. I'm glad you're telling me things. I'm glad I'm here with you. I've never been gladder about anything."

It took Mary a moment to let go of the rhythm of their back-and-forth—and, deeper than that, her worry that everyone else was bobbing up and down . . . They could wait this once while she sat still for this breath of pleasure.

chapter eighty-eight

All by herself in her house, Elsie argued with Dick. She let Dick argue back. When she said, "Maybe Rose is more like Tom. Tom's happy to live and let live," she imagined Dick's saying, "Yup. Tom's a happy-go-lucky guy. Nothing against Tom, but just as well he makes his living on land, don't need to be so strict. Rose is Charlie's sister, too."

Elsie argued that she knew Dick in a way that no one else

did, that she needed him as much as anyone, that she only wanted a part of him, that she was part of his life, that they were bound together in their own way . . . And Dick said, "I won't argue about that. It's just that arguing doesn't get as deep as how I ought to get along with Rose."

"We'll see," she said out loud. The sound of her voice startled her, then made her laugh at herself, then made her worry that she was getting too crazy.

She needed to get outside. Not through the woods to May's field. Down to the salt marsh? No—someplace she hadn't been with Dick.

She went for a slow jog on the beach, swerving away from the spill of waves, swooping back onto the hard, wet sand as they slid away. Just enough of a dumb game to keep her half alert, half lulled, her eyes half closed against the westering sun. Sandpipers skittered away from the reach of a wave, skittered back to peck at sand-flea holes. Gulls lofted themselves, hovering until she jogged by. Familiar rhythms, familiar colors, even the inch of shadow cast by half a quahog shell and then another and another. Everything was as repetitive as the stir of small waves breaking, the hiss of their receding. She saw a small boat coming toward her alongshore, sixty yards or so out. It was dark against the glare off the water. Someone was rowing. As it came closer to being abreast of her she saw it was two people rowing, the oars in the air together, dipping together. She stopped, raised a hand to shield her eyes. Looked like they knew what they were doing. When the boat was straight out from her she saw that it was white. She watched the port-side oars swing toward the bow, pull harder toward the stern. As the boat moved past her the sun lit up the colors of the rowers' shirts and then their faces. Dick and Rose.

When they got farther away the sunlight struck the water behind the boat and she lost their faces in the brightness that trailed them. And then all she could make out clearly was the blinking of light on the narrow transom as it rose and settled in the easy swell.

A wave she didn't hear foamed over her running shoes. Her feet sank into the sand. She stood so still that sandpipers ran close by her.

She didn't understand her astonishment. It was like and not like seeing the indigo bunting, drab in the shade, electric blue as it flew into the light. It was like and not like the time she watched Dick weave the strands of a cable splice, his blunt fingers intricate in a way she didn't know. Like and not like Rose making her entrance onstage, the laughter from the audience alarming until it was clear that Rose knew what she was doing.

The litany of what she'd seen and what she made of it blurred. Good. Let Dick and Rose alone. She knew, without argument, that she wouldn't mention seeing them to either of them. She knew in spite of what she'd wished for, what she would not stop wishing for, that she could also wish not to cast a shadow on her daughter, on her daughter's awkward father, on that graceful man.

chapter eighty-nine

Elsie had misgivings. What good could come of all those people crammed into one room?

Rose was full of beans. Her show was over; it was as good as being let out of school.

There would be people Elsie didn't want to see. There would be people Elsie wanted to see but not with each other.

"I hope we get to dance," Rose said. "I want to see Uncle Jack shake that thing." She laughed and looked at Elsie, then rolled her eyes and sighed. She said, "Maybe you'll think the hat's funny." She put on a tiny white yachting cap with a plastic anchor on the front. "Come on, Mom. It's a goof."

When they got to Sawtooth, Rose tugged Elsie along to the kitchen. Mary Scanlon looked up and said, "Dear God—it can't be time already." She set a timer and handed it to one of her staff. "That's for the roast vegetables." She set another timer. "And that's for the pig." Rose peered through the glass door of the oven. "Roast suckling pig," Mary said. "Thank God there's a bit of a breeze or it'd be too hot for a heavy meal." She turned to a waitress. "Before you bring it in, there's a holly wreath goes on the head."

Rose said, "Or you could put my hat on it. It'd look like Uncle Jack."

May came in with a basket of tomatoes. She said to Mary, "Last ones out of my old garden." She set it down and hugged Rose.

Mary caught the eye of another of her staff. "These'll go right into the salad. They're grand, May. Don't think of them as the last—we'll put them down as the first in your new account."

"No," May said. "They're not that much, but they're what I'm bringing to the meal. So we're not just eating crumbs from the rich man's table.'

Elsie thought, Trust May to cast a pall. But there were Mary and Rose laughing, and May turning to Rose with a smile. Rose said, "And Mary and I are singing for our supper."

There was Rose standing in the middle of the women who'd raised her. When Rose flew away, what then?

May said, "Come say hello to your father. He's out there on the side porch with your uncle Jack."

Mary laughed. "I can hear the silence all the way in here."

May and Rose left. Elsie watched Mary whirl around the kitchen, a peek at the ovens, a word in everyone's ear. Mary came back to Elsie and said, "I've just got time to change. His nibs gave me a key card to the spa. Good for one day." She laughed. "If it hasn't expired by midnight, I'll treat myself to a whirlpool bath." She took Elsie's hands. "You're not still mad, are you? You seem . . ."

"No." Elsie sighed. "I don't know. I'm not in the mood for a party. Not this party."

"Ah, well. Think of it as our party more than Jack's." And Mary was gone.

There'd been a time when she could tell Mary everything.

The sunlight was slanting into the screened porch. As Elsie walked in she narrowed her eyes against the glint from the forks and knives, the light refracted through the wineglasses. In the bright haze the people were faceless shadows.

On a sideboard there was a row of framed photographs. Rose said, "Oh no. I hate that one. I look like someone just—"

"Grabbed your ass," Tom said, and laughed.

"That's enough of that," May said. She turned to Rose. "I think you look pretty. And look at how the ribbons are flying out."

"Well at least I'm not the only one on display," Rose said. "There's one of that statue of Phoebe."

Mr. Salviatti cleared his throat. "I hope you won't find fault with that one. My cousin made it."

"It's a wonder," May said. "And you're generous to give it to the town."

"What I'm wondering," Tom said, "is how all that wind got there. Your cousin set up a big fan or something? Get that robe all blown up against her . . . I mean, it looks great, no two ways about that. I was just wondering."

"There is the model, and there is also the imagination of the artist. *La sua fantasia.*"

Everyone was getting jostled. Eddie and Dick were looking at a photograph of Miss Perry. Dick said, "That's a nice picture. So don't say anything about how she chased you off her land."

"Wasn't going to. I know how good she was to you and your boys."

Dick said, "No need to bring that up, either." He half turned and said, "Hello, Elsie." He cleared his throat. "Just keeping Eddie here in line." He turned back to Eddie.

Here was Dick in this life. Not a flicker of anything else.

Dick and Eddie moved apart, and Elsie looked at Miss Perry's picture. It was an old picture, Miss Perry behind her desk at school. Thirty, thirty-five, years ago. If she hadn't made Elsie her pet, coaxed her into Latin and botany, into believing that these woods and marshes needed her and that the genius of the place would reward her, she might have flown away. It had been an arranged marriage. Miss Perry gave her a piece of land, and Elsie built a house. But it was prepared by the teacher-student courtship, the long walks in the woods that had been a mixture of myth and science. One time the two of them had come into a pine grove in spring, the air a haze of yellow pollen shot through with sunlight. "It was perhaps observing this sort of fertile occasion," Miss Perry had said, "that the Greeks hit on the idea that Zeus came to Danaë in a shower of gold."

Nature into myth, myth into nature. Had Miss Perry known that she was binding Elsie to her? To this place? Had Miss Perry been a wily spinster weaving spells? Or was she unaware, for all her eccentric knowledge, of how her generosity and loneliness spun around each other to make a magnetic field? Was that what had drawn Elsie into Miss Perry's long old age?

Elsie stepped back, found her way out the door to the lawn between the Wedding Cake and the docks. The grass was a perfectly even green. The sailboats bobbed at their moorings, all facing the last of the sea breeze blowing just hard enough to ruffle the water and make the halyards chime against the hollow metal masts. Near the mouth of Pierce Creek Eddie's crew had already put up the new footbridge and the first bit of the boardwalk into the nature sanctuary. Neat work, but nature was meant to be a tangle.

JB came up beside her. "Pretty damn gorgeous."

"If you're a member."

"Ah." He turned to her. "Try thinking of them as a tribe with their own peculiar rituals . . . No, wait. I'm sorry. There

I go again. Annoying good cheer. Gets me into all sorts of . . . At Logan one time I was in a long shuffling line, only one ticket agent for the whole mob of us, so I was humming a tune. Maybe I sang a word or two. All of a sudden the little old lady in front of me lifts her head and says—you could hear her the whole length of the line—'What a little song-bird we have here! What a puffed-up little rooster going cock-a-doodle-doo!'"

JB tipped his head of white hair to one side, and his face wrinkled. She wasn't sure if it was from amusement or renewed embarrassment. His eyebrows crept down and then up. She thought, If those eyebrows were caterpillars, we'd be in for a long, cold winter. That tripped her into laughing.

"Oh, fine," JB said. "Take her side." But he was laughing, too.

"I wish we could just stay out here," Elsie said. "I either want to pull myself into my shell or bite everyone." His eyebrows went up again. "Oh, I don't mean you. In fact, I want you to sit next to me at dinner and tell me another story."

"Nothing I'd like better, but I'm afraid there are place cards."

Phoebe opened the door and called out, "So there you are, you two. We're about to sit down."

Walt stuck his head out over Phoebe's and said, "Yeah, soup's on. Hey, Elsie, I brought something for you."

"Not now, Walt," Phoebe said. "We're trying to get everyone to sit down. Elsie, you have Mr. Bienvenue and Piero, you lucky girl."

Elsie thought, I should grow older, have peaceable friendships with people like JB.

Phoebe said, "And Mr. Callahan, you have Sally and me."

"Then I'm a lucky boy."

"Oh my," Phoebe said. "You do turn a girl's head." She batted her eyelashes. Elsie couldn't tell if Phoebe was already tipsy or just trying too hard. At least she was keeping Walt in check.

The four tables were set in a square, all the chairs on the outside. In the pit in the middle there were potted flowers and ferns, all below eye level. Phoebe apparently thought that the seating arrangement meant that conversation was supposed to be general. She asked May what she was planting in her garden. May murmured her list; Phoebe gave a cry of delight and sang a bar or two of "Oats, Peas, Beans, and Barley Grow."

Elsie thought of saying, "What a little songbird we have here!"

Phoebe kept on around the table. She asked Johnny Bienvenue how his campaign was going. Johnny said Patty was a great help—she'd given a speech in Italian. Phoebe gave a little trill. "Me, too. *Anch'io parlo un poco italiano.*" She turned to JB. "Oh, you're going to just love it here in Rhode Island. It's tiny, but it's really very cosmopolitan. I mean, think of Dick's boat!"

Half the people here didn't want to think of Dick's boat. Elsie winced on her own and then again at the hard silence.

"I mean the crew," Phoebe said. "There were Captain Teixeira's nephew, who's Portuguese, and that nice little Vietnamese man."

There was a low chorus of the older men clearing their throats. Elsie saw Jack drawing himself up, but it was Dick who spoke to Phoebe. "You mean Tran. When I first met him he said his name was Tran. I got used to calling him Tran. Turns out that's his last name. His first name's Khang."

Elsie wondered why Dick was getting Phoebe out of trouble. He didn't like Phoebe. To be nice to May, then? Penance?

Phoebe murmured, "Khang Tran, Khang Tran. Thank you."

Everyone turned to a neighbor. Mr. Salviatti said to Elsie, "I have seen a mysterious bird. I believe you know birds, yes? I saw a flock of pigeons over my garden. As they all turned I saw a flash of green. I thought it was perhaps a trick of the light. But they turned again and I saw an entirely green bird— an emerald in that gray setting. Are there green pigeons?"

Elsie savored the pleasure of knowing, the pleasure of another white-haired old man attending to her. "I'll bet it was a monk parakeet. It's a kind of parrot. People imported them as pets, and some got loose. There've been a lot of sightings. They're doing okay in the wild."

"But why is it flying with the pigeons?"

"Monk parakeets like company. They even build nests for three couples."

"Ah. How satisfying to find someone who knows such things. And I have meant to ask: Phoebe—that is the name of a bird?"

"Yes. A little gray bird, so it's hard to tell apart from the other little gray birds, but its call really does go, 'Phoebe, Phoebe,' and it wags its tail a lot."

"And sometimes its tongue. Poor Phoebe. She meant no harm, but there is an old saying—'One does not speak of rope in the house of a hanged man.'"

For an instant Elsie warmed herself to the idea that Mr. Salviatti preferred her to Phoebe. Knowing things, getting credit for knowing things, murmuring complicitly with a nice old man—in fact, her second nice old man of the evening—these were minor pleasures, but pleasures.

Jack looked at Mary, who nodded to the waitress, who set about clearing the soup plates.

Elsie added a Miss Perry footnote. "Phoebe is also the name of Diana when she's the moon goddess, the same way Phoebus is the name of Apollo when he's the sun."

How long before she turned into Miss Perry? Mixing nature and myth, teaching at the Perryville School, bird-watching and botanizing with a pet student, surrounding herself with nice old men? Elsie felt the bark forming on her skin.

"Diana," Mr. Salviatti said. "She is the goddess of the hunt, isn't she?"

"Yes, that, too. Although she did something terrible to a hunter. He saw her skinny-dipping, so she turned him into a stag, and his hounds tore him to pieces."

Mr. Salviatti said, "A drastic fairy tale. I wonder what is the point—to make men fear the sight of a naked woman?"

"Well, he was a Peeping Tom. Of course, you're right, she was drastic. But all the gods had their bad days. Think of Zeus and all the women he raped. Even Apollo was going to jump on Daphne—she had to turn herself into a tree." Elsie couldn't stop; footnotes were sprouting from her like leafy twigs.

Mr. Salviatti said, "I envy you your knowledge of these gods. They are human, at least. As a boy I was instructed in the lives of saints and martyrs. Saint Francis throwing himself in a thornbush to rid himself of desires of the flesh. How sad and inhuman . . ."

Two waitresses carried in the suckling pig and started around the tables. Rose jumped up and put the yachting cap on top of the holly wreath.

"Right, right," Jack said. "We'll make him a member, and then we'll eat him."

He made room for the waitresses to put the pig in front of him, but Mary waved them on. She said, "They'll carve it in the kitchen. Just time enough for Rose and me to sing. Come on, Rose. We'll stand over in your corner so everyone can look out at the boats. The barcarole from *The Tales of Hoffmann*."

Mr. Salviatti said to Elsie, "A *barcarola* is a boat song." So he was leafing out, too.

Rose started singing. Mary leaned toward her, put an arm around Rose's waist, and joined in, "Oh, how lovely is the evening, is the evening . . ."

How Mary loved Rose; how Rose loved Mary. Elsie looked around at all the faces tipping with attention and pleasure. How everyone loved Rose and Mary. Elsie watched them sing, watched them sway together, watched them breathe. She could hear their voices go up and down, she could hear the rhythm and see them swaying in time, but it was as if everyone else glided with them like fish while she wallowed.

Applause, applause. Walt whistled. Phoebe said, "Walt. Really."

He said, "Come on, Phoebe. Let the good times roll." He cocked his head and yelped.

Rose patted him on the head and said, "Down, boy." Tom and Deirdre laughed.

Elsie felt left behind by rowdiness, too. It wasn't that she disapproved. She wasn't Phoebe, for God's sake. She used to be the one to start trouble. She'd said she wasn't in the mood for a party—that was turning out to be an understatement. It wasn't that she was sour on these people—she was sour on herself.

Patty said, "Aunt Mary, how about one of your Irish songs?"

"Maybe later.'

Jack said, "Quite right. There's an order to this . . . to these festivities."

Walt got up and began working a book out of the side pocket of his jacket. His cuffs rose halfway up his forearms. Elsie guessed he was wearing a suit of Eddie's, a size too small. It made Walt appear even larger.

"What?" Jack said.

"I've got a little present for Elsie."

"Walt," Phoebe said, "not in the middle of—"

"There are a number of presentations," Jack said. "I'll be sure to call on you when the time comes."

Years ago Elsie had been at a dinner table at which there were three men she'd slept with. She'd had several reactions almost simultaneously—a thrill, a sadness that whatever desires she'd had were gone, and a fear that somehow everyone would know. Her reactions had been to all three men as one group. This was different. Walt was an embarrassment. Johnny was a sigh. Dick was part of her life. This time there was no thrill, no wonder at the transience of desire. There was only the fear that Walt would blurt out some galumphing remark that would strip her naked.

Walt said, "It's your party, chief."

Rose and Tom laughed. Encouragement from that corner of the room. Jack and Phoebe trying to shut him up. Stirring Walt up both ways.

Dick had said, "We live in South County." All right—she got that part. She could see almost all of the people she knew in South County sitting in this room. Why wouldn't Dick see that they could sit in a roomful of South County without anyone knowing anything—without knowing anything worse than what everyone already knew? There wasn't a soul here who didn't know that Dick was Rose's father. But that brought her hard against Dick's notion that his sleeping with her was violating a taboo because she was Rose's mother. God knows fishing-boat captains had their superstitions—they had their logbooks and their charts, but as often as not they'd decide where to fish using some sense they couldn't explain. All right, then—she wouldn't reason with him. She'd find a way to drift into his mind as another sign, as gently irresistible as the wind in his dream.

Mr. Salviatti raised his glass to Mary, seated across the pots of ferns and hollyhocks. "Exquisite! The singing and the pig."

The waitresses cleared the plates. Jack stood up. "And now we'll hear something from our new neighbor, who has written a poet . . . a poem. A poet who has written a poem. Mr. Kelly."

Mary said, "It's Callahan."

"Yes," Jack said. "Mr. Callahan."

"'Wading in Sawtooth Pond,'" JB said, and went on in a conversational tone. "The pond is like an oculus . . ."

Elsie hoped for more from JB. In the few up-to-date nature poems Elsie had read, the poet saw something and right off the bat it reminded him of something else, usually about himself. At least JB was committing his offenses against nature on paper. Jack was actually fucking it up.

> *"Marsh-elder leaves sift sun and shade,*
> *And on the shallow maze of rocks*
> *A leopard changes spots."*

Elsie looked at JB. Hearing this prettiness from this large man was like watching a bear crochet. People shouldn't write about nature until they'd been bitten by something larger than a tick. Now she sounded like Deirdre O'Malley showing her scars.

JB continued his processional wading around Sawtooth Pond.

> *"Pierce Creek brings in a haze of silt.*
> *The light sinks in—goes flat—until*
> *It gilds a sunken stone with shafts—*
> *Child's drawing of the sun."*

It was hard to tell when it was over, since JB hadn't been standing up. Phoebe peeked at him and then patted her hands together, setting off a polite clapping. Phoebe raised her glass and said, "I love it. It's so . . . It's so relatable to." She emptied her glass.

Walt got up again, holding his book. Jack waved at him to sit down. Walt said, "I'll just slip in here in the middle of the order, and then you get to bat cleanup." Walt put a finger on the cover. "Can you see? This woman warrior here . . . I'll pass it around." Even ten feet away Elsie saw the picture. A woman in a fur skirt and halter was pointing a spear at a man cowering beside a swan with an arrow in its breast. Walt said, "This really happened. Elsie caught my dad when he killed a swan with his crossbow. And what'd she do? She let him go. So here's to Elsie, for knowing what's what and for letting Dad bring home Christmas dinner."

Eddie said, "I wasn't the only one going after some free-range meat. One time Elsie was onto Dick for poaching clams right over there in the nature sanctuary."

Johnny Bienvenue laughed. "I guess that gives us all something in common. Elsie was hiding in the bushes when I poached a trout."

"Oh, Elsie," Phoebe said. "What an adventurous life you lead! Is it all in Deirdre's book?"

"It's fiction," Deirdre said.

"Well, that's right," Walt said. "But it's sort of based on Elsie."

"It's set in the future," Deirdre said. "It's science fiction. The heroine has superpowers."

"Right," Walt said. "But there's a picture of Phoebe posing as an angel—"

Eddie said, "Knock it off, Walt."

"Hey, all I'm saying is that Elsie's picture ought to go up there alongside the others."

"It's not Elsie," Deirdre said. "Look at the picture. She's way taller. And the free women are at war with the men. They only use their seed to repopulate the tribe."

Elsie went rigid. She couldn't look at anyone.

Jack tapped his fork on his glass. "This is not the order of business."

Sally said, "Jack, I think it's time for the fireworks. People are coming out onto the lawn."

"Are they meadows? I mean members. They can wait. I have remarks." Jack stood up and stared at a sheet of paper. "Who do we have here? I can't quite read . . ."

Sally said, "It really is time for the fireworks. Why don't you just say how glad you are that everybody's here?"

"Because people talked." Jack took a breath and said, "Now, then." He furrowed his brow. "Odd. To say 'now' and then say 'then.'" He sat down. "My wife is right. Can't go wrong saying my wife is right."

Elsie looked up in time to see Jack's head sink into Mary's shoulder. His mouth was open, so it looked as if he was biting her.

Somebody laughed. Sally said, "Jack, stop that!"

Dick got up behind Jack. He straightened him, one arm under Jack's sagging side, the other cradling his head. Dick looked at Elsie, said her name. She rose from her chair. Something terrible might be going on, but she drifted toward Dick's voice.

Dick said, "He ever take a turn like this? He look anything like Miss Perry did?"

She felt Jack's cheek. It was cool and clammy. She couldn't find a pulse in his neck, but he was slumped so his collar was almost up to his chin. She said, "Yes."

Deirdre came up behind them and said, "I'm an EMT," but the rest of what she was saying was drowned out by an explosion. Then a series of smaller bangs. Elsie saw all the faces turn red and then white and then blue. Shadows crept up the walls, then faded.

Dick said to Elsie, "Let's get him out of here. There's some kind of sofa in the front hall. Grab my hands under his butt."

There was another explosion, followed by a shower of green stars whistling and shimmering. The people on the porch and lawn oohed and aahed. Elsie's head brushed Dick's shoulder as they joined their hands. Dick's grip was matter-of-fact. He said, "Deirdre, pull the chair out of the way."

Sally was standing in the doorway. Her face was pale and dazed. Elsie's pleasure at Dick's choosing her, at their touching each other, was doused. She'd thought shame was what she'd felt when Walt put her on display. That was embarrassment. Thinking of her own pleasure while her sister was feeling terrible was shame.

Sally followed them as they moved through the empty dining room. Deirdre shoved chairs out of their way, then came back to the open porch and yelled, "Is there a doctor here? We need a doctor in the front hall."

They lowered Jack onto a sofa. Sally said, "Shall I call the hospital?"

"I think you'll want to stay with him, Mrs. Aldrich," Dick said. "We'll see to calling."

Deirdre was just getting back, made a quick turn to the phone at the front desk. She raised her voice over a ripple of rockets. "Sawtooth Point! The big white building. You can't miss it, it's lit up like the Fourth of July."

Sally said, "It *is* the Fourth of July." She said to Elsie, "Ask someone to call the gatehouse. Tell them to keep the gate open."

A man in a seersucker suit appeared. He said, "I'm a doctor."

"Of course you are, Henry," Sally said. "I'm afraid something's the matter with Jack."

Elsie went to the front desk, then came back beside Dick. She said, "We should go out . . . No, you should go out front to flag the ambulance. I think I should stay with Sally."

"Good. And think of something else for Deirdre to do. She's about to get on your sister's nerves."

"I'll tell her to keep people away. She'll like that."

Dick said, "That'll do it."

It was all right to think of him remembering the two of them doing this together. Just for one more second. All right for her to think of him seeing her as quick and good. She nodded and turned away.

When she got back to Sally, Sally held her hand. Sally started to say something, but there was a boom that rattled the windows. And then the big finish, rocket after rocket, without rhythm, an idiocy of noise. Sally put her hands over Jack's ears. The EMTs were suddenly there. Sally held Elsie's arm, and the two of them followed the gurney. The EMT said, "Only room for one of you," but Sally wasn't letting go of Elsie. The EMT said, "Okay, hop in. It's just down the road."

chapter ninety

Elsie and Sally sat side by side in the South County Hospital waiting room.

"I feel terrible," Sally said. "I've been so mean to him. Do you think that had something to do with this?"

"No," Elsie said. "Absolutely not."

Sally nodded slowly but then said, "How do you know?"

"Back when Miss Perry had her stroke, I talked to her doctors about—"

"A stroke? You think he's had a stroke?"

"No. I don't know. I mean, it could be a lot of things. If the doctor doesn't come out soon, I'll go in."

"No," Sally said. "Stay here. Please."

After a while Sally said, "There seem to be a lot of people here in the middle of the night."

"It's the Fourth of July. That kid who just came in with his hand in the air. Probably a firecracker or a bottle rocket. Maybe a bonfire. Kids light bonfires on the beach. When they run out of fireworks, they pick up burning sticks and throw them into the ocean. I used to chase them away from the nature sanctuary.

"People are staring at us," Sally said. "I wish we weren't so dressed up."

"I don't think they're staring. They're just looking around."

"Maybe I should take off my pearls."

"I don't think it's the pearls. They're just curious, wondering if we're sisters."

"Well, we are," Sally said. "I couldn't bear this without you."

And then the doctor was there, inviting them to an office, gesturing "after you" with his clipboard.

"I see nothing immediately grave here," he said. "Nothing immediately grave. We'll keep him overnight. I'd like to run some more tests, talk it over with a colleague."

"But something's wrong," Sally said. "What is it? Does it have a name?"

"I'll be more certain later on, but it looks like a transient ischemic episode."

"'Transient,'" Sally said. "So whatever it is, it's come and gone."

"Well, yes and no. It's certainly a warning sign. Things will be clearer when his blood alcohol goes down. In any case, we'll talk about a different regimen. Get the blood pressure down. Is there a lot of stress in his life?"

"There have been some difficult moments in the last few months." The doctor, although junior enough to have drawn a Fourth of July shift, knew to wait. Sally added, "Well, yes. Our son was on a ship that sank. Jack was taking land from people whom he forced to sell, so he was quarreling with practically everyone. And I'm afraid his big reconciliation banquet didn't go smoothly." The doctor waited again. Sally said, "I don't know why he can't be happy with Sawtooth the way it is. I'm afraid he's one of those people who always wants more. I actually asked him once why he wanted more, and he said, 'What's wrong with wanting more?' Some time later I told him."

Elsie was surprised—she didn't think Sally let herself see things so plainly.

"More," the doctor said. "If he wants more years, he'll have to change."

Sally sighed. The doctor said, "I'm going to give you something to help you sleep."

"Not right now," Sally said. "I've got to get home."

"A pill," the doctor said. "After you get home."

Sally laughed. "Of course. All this is making me a little dull."

Elsie said, "Come home with me. They'll still be roistering around at Sawtooth."

"Oh, Elsie, how will we get there? We don't have a car."

"My car's at Sawtooth. It won't take me fifteen minutes to walk there."

"All alone? In the dark? Along Route One, with all those cars with men in them? You're not wearing your pistol anymore. I'll come, too."

"So you can lash them with your pearls." That got a tilt of a smile out of the doctor. Sally didn't think it was funny. Elsie said, "Never mind. We'll hardly be on Route One. Once we get across, we can cut through the old Hazard place."

When they got to the stone wall at the edge of the Sawtooth property, Sally stopped and said, "What's going to happen to all this? What will I have to do?"

Elsie said, "Mary Scanlon runs the restaurant, Eddie's doing all the outside stuff, Tom Pierce can run the waterfront." But before she was through saying this she saw that Sally wanted something else. Elsie said, "Don't worry. I'll help you. I can get you help. You heard the doctor, nothing grave. All Jack has to do is stay in the hospital and then live sensibly. All you have to do for a while is stay with me."

Sally began to cry. Elsie held her until what seemed like the last sob.

"Oh dear," Sally said. "I'm sorry. I'll be fine now. Except my shoes hurt."

"Take them off. It's all lawn from here on."

When they got in the car, Elsie started to tell Sally the story JB told her, but Sally was caving in. She was all thumbs trying to fasten the seat belt. Elsie did it for her, and Sally leaned back and closed her eyes. It was only as they reached the steep part of the driveway and the tips of the overhanging branches swept the sides of the car that she came to. "Honestly, Elsie. You live in a briar patch. People will think you're some kind of eccentric recluse."

"You sound like Miss Perry. She once called me a ragamuffin just because I had bark on my shirt. From carrying in her firewood, I might add."

"Oh! You forgot her picture. Jack meant for you to have it as a present. He meant to give all those pictures as presents. That's something I can do tomorrow. If Jack's all right. I don't think I could do it if . . . There's three of Rose. I know one's for you, another for the Pierces. Who else?"

"Probably Mary Scanlon."

"Of course."

Elsie thought it might be occurring to Sally that these were people Jack had bullied in his landgrab, but Sally said, "Rose. You all have Rose in common. It's wonderful, really. I worried at first things might be difficult for her, but look at her now."

Elsie pulled up by the front door. Going around to help Sally undo her seat belt saved her from having to say anything. Sally said, "I can manage. It's just that it buckles in the wrong place. And think of Jack Junior, who started out with everything and now he's ashamed to show his face in South County. I'm not saying that out of jealousy, just saying how strange . . . Oh, there's a note on your door."

Elsie switched on the outside light. The note was from May.

> *I'm taking Rose home with me. I don't want Rose to be alone, but I don't want you to worry about Rose not being there. She's fine, just kind of tired and upset, which is natural. I hope your brother-in-law is alright. In the morning Rose is going to help pack some things, so she'll either be at our old house or moving things to Eddie's. We won't call in case you had a long night at the hospital.*
>
> Sincerely, May Pierce

> *P.S. I meant to thank you for your day of work in my field.*

The P.S. made Elsie light-headed. Did May somehow have an intuition how that day had ended? Elsie put her hand on the wall. After a breath, she thought, No, otherwise not this breezy note . . .

Sally said, "Is something wrong?" She took the note and scanned it. "You're not worried, are you? It just seems a nice thing to do. So I'm going in and take that pill. Shall I sleep in Mary's old room?"

"The bed's not made up. Take Rose's bed, she's away for the night. Her pajamas are in the bottom drawer."

"Maybe I should call the hospital before I take that pill."

"I left my number. I'll stay up for a while, just in case. I may go jump in the pond for a second, but I'll be back before you're in bed."

Sally hugged her again and went inside. Elsie walked down to the pond, hung her dress on a branch, put a rock on her bra and underpants—a breeze was still skittering in the treetops. She was in up to her knees when she heard a motor. It slowed, seemed to be turning into Miss Perry's part of the driveway. She thought it might be Dick—Rose was at his house, after all. She was fumbling with her dress in the dark when she heard the motor more clearly, a more urgent buzzing than Dick's truck. She got the dress on, pulled the zipper so hard it tore loose. She made it up the slope in time to see a single light bouncing over the last bump.

She waved her arms and said, "Turn that thing off."

Walt killed the engine, pulled his motorcycle onto the kickstand. He said, "Sorry. I forgot Rose might be asleep. I figured you'd still be up, what with taking Jack to the hospital."

He'd changed into a T-shirt and jeans. He was, as Mary Scanlon would say, a fine *figger* of a man. He was an embarrassment. He was someone she'd leaned out the tower window and flirted with, and he'd come up the ladder and fucked her brains out.

Walt said, "You forgot your book."

"Oh God, that idiot cartoon."

"I got it right here."

Were men ever embarrassed by their mindless incidental

coupling? What was embarrassing her even more than the fact that Walt had had her, had pulled orgasms out of her like fish on a trotline—what embarrassed her more was that he kept mixing her up with Deirdre O'Malley, that fun-house mirror reflection of herself.

"It wouldn't fit in my pocket, so I stuck it under my belt. Just a sec. It slipped down some." He put his hand in. "Damn, it's in there tight." He undid his belt buckle and tried again. "Wait. It's gone down the leg." He stood on one foot and raised the other. "It's way in there." He dropped his pants below his knees. "Okay, there she is." He held it out with one hand, clutched his pants with another. She didn't want to take it; it would be accepting that version of herself. But he wasn't going to be able to pull his pants up unless she took it. On the other hand, she got some satisfaction from seeing him hobbled.

Walt waggled the book. The glossy cover—the caricature of her as an Amazon rippling with sexual muscle and witchery—blurred in the pale available light. She could take it and be done with it.

Walt was looking over her shoulder. He said, "Hey, Rose. Didn't mean to wake you up."

"I'm not Rose," Sally said. "Who are you? Oh, Walt. What are you doing here? And pull up your pants."

"I'm just bringing Elsie her book. It got stuck—"

"That book," Sally said. "You've caused quite enough trouble with that book. In the middle of Jack's speech. It's been a very trying evening, and I have to say part of it has been your fault. All those lewd jokes."

"That was Phoebe," Walt said.

"Don't quibble. It's very late. Just take your book and your motorcycle and leave."

Walt's head was down. Elsie was about to feel sorry for him, but he was just tucking the book under his chin while he buckled his belt. "Relax, I'm not hanging around. But it's Elsie's book." He handed it to her. He wheeled his motorcycle to the steep part of the driveway, jumped on, and rolled away silently.

"I never liked him," Sally said. "I never liked him, and I never trusted him. My God, Elsie! What happened to your dress? He didn't try anything, did he?"

"No. That was me. I yanked the zipper off. Down by the pond."

Somewhere near the bottom of the hill Walt's motorcycle coughed twice and then revved.

Sally said, "I'm getting foggy. Must be that pill."

The motorcycle faded away.

Elsie went in with Sally and sat by the bed. Sally said, "You'll listen for the phone?"

"Yes. You can go to sleep. I can hear the phone out here. It'll be all right."

She went down to the pond to get her shoes and the rest of her clothes. A relief to be alone. She'd been holding on to herself all night.

She slipped her dress off. The air on her body was cool. She stuck out her right leg. It looked good, but everything looked good in this soft night glow. How long would she look good?

A cooler puff of air. The wind was backing to the southeast. Fog before long.

Sally was three years older and looked good. Of course, Sally was the pretty one. Pretty dresser, too. But even in Rose's pajamas and getting on her high horse with Walt, she looked good.

A first wisp of fog in the treetops.

In two years Rose would go away to college. May dreaded it.

She waded in up to her knees. A frog, then another and another, plopped into the water. She pushed in, gave a little frog kick, and glided, steering herself with her trailing hands. Just another frog in the pond. Did a frog take pleasure in the slip of water along its skin? She turned onto her back and floated. May dreaded Rose's leaving, but unless Rose went far away, easy enough for a mother to show up. They had days for that sort of thing. And here with the house to herself, on a day when Dick came back to port, she could offer this fresh-water pond as a comfort, let him wash away the salt.

Unnatural mother to wish her child gone.

Now that she was floating quietly, the frogs were back on the bank or on their lily pads, croaking in chorus from one side of the pond to the other. The noise used to annoy Mary Scanlon. She said she got over it by imagining one side was saying, "Frog's legs! Frog's legs!" and the other answering "Supper! Supper!" A cook's-eye view of nature.

The fog was coming on, shrouding the oval of sky over the pond.

And then Mary had made her claim on Rose, luring her into their duets. Did Mary know how they closed her off? That her own singing was no better than the two-note croaking all around her. Now that it was getting darker, it seemed louder.

Be fair, be fair. Mary's singing lessons had been the making of Rose. And if Mary laid claim to part of Rose, she'd earned it. Perhaps there was no such thing as purely unselfish giving. Here she was herself in the pond, in the land that Miss Perry had given her. And it was Miss Perry's making a pet of her that started her own immersion in nature . . . She remembered Miss Perry's coming to a halt on one of their walks in the woods. Miss Perry had turned to her and said, "Do we stand outside of nature, or do we stand inside it? Is nature everything *but* us? Or is it simply everything?" Miss Perry peered at her and added, "I don't expect an answer. It's an unanswerable question." But Miss Perry went on asking it. She'd given a little sideways hop with both feet. "Outside?" Hop. "Inside?" Hop.

It must have been years ago. Not many hops in Miss Perry after that. And finally Miss Perry had to cling to Elsie's arms to lower herself onto the toilet seat.

All right, then—whether calculated or not, there was an undertow to giving. She herself wasn't exempt. She had used her dutifulness to Miss Perry as a counterweight of goodness, not just in the balance of her own conscience but in hoping that Dick would weigh it in her favor.

The fog had settled, settled in so low and thick she couldn't see it as fog. She held up her hand to see if she could feel the drift of wind. Nothing. Too many trees. She had an instant of panic, then laughed at herself. She was in her own little pond. She was a stone's throw from her house. She dog-paddled toward shore, feeling for the bottom. She crawled onto the bank, stood up, and took small shuffling steps, hoping to run into her shoes or clothes. Maybe she'd left them farther from the bank. She took a sideways step and then inched forward. Turned and tried the other way. Nothing. All right—leave them till morning.

The frogs had stopped. Now she couldn't tell where the pond was. She closed her eyes, tried to imagine where she stood. It only made her dizzy. She was breathing too fast, little shallow breaths. She made herself breathe deeply. She managed to calm her panic but then imagined everyone was laughing at her—Warden of the Great Swamp, Free Woman of the Wilderness. Everyone could see her standing there, ridiculous and naked.

The frogs began to croak again. At first the noise was everywhere. Then she heard the last half of a croak, a frog who ended late. She stuck her arm out toward it, the other arm away from it. Think slowly. Follow that arm away from the pond. The house is up. Away and then up.

She turned herself carefully and took a step. She jumped when something touched her leg. It stung her shin. She jerked sideways and fell. Thorns. She was lying on thorns. She saw red dots in front of her eyes as if the pricks and scratches were sending signals into the dark. The pain was fresh for a moment. It eased a little when she lay still. She was on her side. She pushed herself up to her knees. The frogs began to croak again. Had she stopped them by crying out when she fell? Or had being pricked and scratched blotted her hearing?

Stupid, stupid girl. She was in the bullbriars on the wrong side of the pond. How had she got so turned around?

With her finger she found a tendril across her shoulder, plucked it off, and held it away from her as she stood up. Another tendril scratched the side of her thigh. She slowly turned toward the frog noise, groped with her free hand, hit another branch of thorns. She stood still, holding briar shoots in each hand. Was it Mr. Salviatti who'd called this down on her? Him and his Saint Francis, who threw himself into a thornbush to rid himself of lust. Unfair. Yes, she'd gone to Dick and taken him by surprise. Unfair to call that lust. It was years of loving him that carried her, not lust. And when she saw Dick and Rose in Rose's skiff she'd tipped her balance toward his wish, toward his grace with Rose.

She inched her fingers down the branch in front of her and bent it until it broke. She floated her hand ahead of her, touched another shoot. How many between her and the pond? She shivered, part panic, part cold fog.

Walt in the tower room. She'd let the ladder rungs rattle down before his motorcycle even stopped ticking with heat. Walt and his motorcycle, a prick on wheels. She'd fainted in Captain Teixeira's radio shack from shock but from shame as well. All right then, thorns for that. She took a step toward the pond, scratched her legs, her arms that she held crossed in front of her. She kicked her legs free, tripped and fell forward, her knees on the bank, her hands sliding into the water.

She caught her breath, pulled herself into the water. The scratches stung. To make sure she was going straight across she measured the depth—waist deep, shoulder deep—and dog-paddled until her hands touched bottom. She clambered out. She felt the comfort of grass on her palms and knees. She got to her feet, took two, three, four uncertain steps. She could tell she was going uphill only because her calf muscles stretched. She put her hands out. She touched the wall. She trailed her hand along it, around the southwest corner. A steeper bit up to the northwest corner. Slower now, one hand on the wall, moving her feet carefully until they found the doorstep. She sat down.

She couldn't go inside, not yet. Her panic had shrunk her. Inside she would stay pressed into herself. She realized she was rocking forward and backward. She filled her lungs several times until she could sit still.

She touched her legs. She couldn't tell if she was bleeding. Of course she couldn't. She was still wet from the pond, still a little stupid.

She lifted her head as if she saw or heard something. It was here, exactly here on this doorstep, where she'd been nursing baby Rose when Dick had got out of Eddie's truck, when he'd stood awkwardly in front of her and said, "Here we are," and waved his hand to take in South County from Narragansett to Westerly. Poor man, seeing her with baby Rose, Rose who'd fallen out of the sky. He hadn't known what to say. Even with Rose in her arms and her breasts full of milk, she should have made room to consider what she'd done to his life.

And then how slow she'd been when they were lying under the evening star in Eddie's backyard and he'd said, "We live in South County." She'd kept on trying to say, "We live in nature," while he was working his way to saying, "I'm sort of an awkward father."

She'd tried to think it might be no more than one of his moody turns, that she'd descended on him so fiercely that he had to push back to get his balance. She was wrong. It was too tightly woven and finished, as hard as one of his cable splices. She understood and she didn't understand. It was like the word *cleave*—to split, to hold together.

At least she was a desire he was forbidding himself, a desire strong enough to need forbidding.

Now she would forbid it, too, for him and Rose.

Would it be harder when Rose went off to college? For an instant she saw herself alone in her house, but she veered off to see Rose lugging a duffel bag into her dorm room, meeting a roommate. Oh, Rose, you'll have to go through your story all over again. You'll be on your own, no Mary Scanlon crooning songs into your ear, no May doting on you, no father to build you a skiff.

And when you come back, will you be changed?

Elsie imagined Rose in front of the house. A car door closed. Rose was standing next to someone from her new life. Rose said, "This is where I grew up."

What? Elsie sifted Rose's voice out of the fog again. How did Rose say it? Over her shoulder? And then tilt her head and point with her chin? What? That's it, Rose? That's your little nod to where you were everybody's darling?

No. She would be the Rose who smoothed the back of Captain Teixeira's black suit coat before they went into the graveyard to bury Miss Perry. She would be the Rose who said to Captain Teixeira and her, "You two should go in together." When Captain Teixeira told Rose what the priest would say— "The earth and the sea shall give up their dead"—Rose nodded once and touched his arm, another womanly gesture. Elsie herself had needed that warning; perhaps he'd had her in mind, too. What would women do without the comfort of old broad-backed men?

She hugged her knees. She felt the cold fog on her back, cold breath of the sea. She'd been conjuring little ghosts out of it, snippets of Rose and everyone around Rose; she'd been rattling Miss Perry's bones . . . as if the fog were taking part in her story. Too big for a story, it was part of the same thing over and over, the sun heating the surface of the ocean, vapor rising into clouds and fog, blowing over the land, turning back into water and running back into the sea, carrying bits of earth, the earth made of cracked and crumbled rock and the dead matter of everything once so busily alive.

She let go of her knees and stood up. She smacked the sides of her legs to warm them. She needed some of her old sassiness, too. Okay—here's an answer to Miss Perry's unanswerable question, "Do we stand inside nature or outside it?" In the end, inside it. But not yet.

She went back inside. She looked out the big south window. The fog was still thick, but in the east a faint gray light was pushing into it. All the people who'd come to her in her vigil were asleep, asleep in their houses along this bit of coast between the hills and the sea. Rose, Dick and May, Mary Scanlon and JB, the Tran family, old Mr. Salviatti, and even older Captain Teixeira.

Here we are. We live in South County.

ACKNOWLEDGMENTS

The chief acknowledgment is to Anthony Winner, who gave careful criticism and encouragement from the beginning of *Compass Rose* and for years before and after.

Christopher Tilghman, who read the next-to-last draft and helped define the large triangle of time.

My assistants over the years (and fellow writers and artists): Will Boast, Tara Yellen, Kimberley Stromberg, Hannah Holtzman, and Memory Blake Peebles (who discovered the cover and co-suggested the title).

My agent, Michael Carlisle, peacekeeper.

My editor, Carol Janeway, necessary challenger and longtime friend.

Stephen Jones, Lenny Chesney, and Wiliam Tongue for information about the sea.

Sam Droge and John Rowlett for information about birds.

Robin Fray Carey and Carolina Reid for information about social media.

The University of Virginia and the Sewanee Writers' Conference for employment and collegiality.

Peter Taylor, Kurt Vonnegut, Vance Bourjaily, William Maxwell, and Hubert Butler—mentors.

My wife, Rosamond Casey; my daughters Maud Casey, Nell Casey, Clare Casey, and Julia Casey—the basis of my life.